ALSO BY BECKY MANDELBAUM

Bad Kansas: Stories

The

BRIGHT SIDE
SANCTUARY
for ANIMALS

A Novel

Becky Mandelbaum

SIMON & SCHUSTER

New York   London   Toronto   Sydney   New Delhi

Simon & Schuster
1230 Avenue of the Americas
New York, NY 10020

First Simon & Schuster hardcover edition August 2020

SIMON & SCHUSTER and colophon are registered trademarks of Simon & Schuster, Inc.

For information about special discounts for bulk purchases,
please contact Simon & Schuster Special Sales at
1-866-506-1949 or business@simonandschuster.com.

The Simon & Schuster Speakers Bureau can bring authors to your live event.
For more information or to book an event, contact the
Simon & Schuster Speakers Bureau at 1-866-248-3049 or
visit our website at www.simonspeakers.com.

Interior design by Ruth Lee-Mui

Manufactured in the United States of America

1   3   5   7   9   10   8   6   4   2

Library of Congress Cataloging-in-Publication Data

Names: Mandelbaum, Becky, author.
Title: Bright side sanctuary for animals / Becky Mandelbaum.
Description: First Simon & Shuster hardcover edition. | New York : Simon &
Schuster, 2020. | Summary: "From the winner of the 2016 Flannery O'Connor Award
for Short Fiction comes a tender and funny debut novel set over one emotionally charged
weekend at an animal sanctuary in western Kansas, where maternal, romantic, and community
bonds are tested in the wake of an estranged daughter's homecoming"-- Provided by publisher.
Identifiers: LCCN 2020002282 | ISBN 9781982112981 (hardcover) |
ISBN 9781982113001 (ebook)
Classification: LCC PS3613.A52955 B75 2020 | DDC 813/.6--dc23
LC record available at https://lccn.loc.gov/2020002282

ISBN 978-1-9821-1298-1
ISBN 978-1-9821-1300-1 (ebook)

For my mother

Toto did not really care whether he was in Kansas or the Land of Oz so long as Dorothy was with him.
—Frank L. Baum, *The Wonderful Wizard of Oz*

I can, with one eye squinted, take it all as a blessing.
—Flannery O'Connor

The

BRIGHT SIDE
SANCTUARY
for ANIMALS

Mona

It was midnight in Kansas, and the bigots were awake. The brothers' house was like all the other houses in St. Clare: wind-torn and lonely with a roof that drooped as if tired. Light played against the windows, causing the interior to flicker and grin. Sitting in her '85 Chevy, Old Baby, Mona imagined the Fuller brothers inside, shirtless and drinking cheap beer, probably watching one of those mean reality shows about someone who's morbidly obese or has too many children. More likely, they were watching Fox News.

Go to sleep, little racists, she chanted in her head.

When the house finally blinked into darkness, Mona waited fifteen more minutes, just to be safe. It was strange to sit alone in her truck, without any animals. She kept expecting a wet nose to stamp her neck. To reach an arm back and touch fur. To hear the jingle of a collar. After all these years, she was used to feeling lonely, but she was not used to being alone.

When she was certain the brothers were asleep, she took a deep breath and stepped out into the star-heavy night. The air smelled sweet, of dried autumn grass, but also dirty, like cow pies. The night was so quiet Mona imagined all the birds and bugs holding their breath, trying to hear infinity. On nights like these, she imagined the sky as a blacktop road stretching all the way from St. Clare to Lawrence, where her daughter, Ariel, had run off to six years before. On nights like these, she wondered if Ariel was looking at the same sky.

Heart pounding, she made her way to the pasture's corner, where the reason for the night's adventure stood facing the road. In the dark, she could hardly make out the sign's letters, stamped with all the careless glory of a lower-back tattoo. MAKE AMERICA GREAT AGAIN.

She was not an immoral person and felt a flicker of guilt for stealing, that most basic of human rules, but then she remembered who the brothers were—the same men who'd reported one of their workers, a young man named Joss, to ICE; men who rode around with a bumper sticker on their truck that read, WELL-BEHAVED WOMEN MAKE SANDWICHES. Every time she saw their truck, she wanted to scratch the sticker with her pocketknife, but she had learned, over the years, not to make trouble, because trouble for her meant trouble for the animals, and trouble for the animals was not something she cared to risk. Until now.

This was October, the presidential election just around the corner, and she wanted to do something bold. With the animal sanctuary up for sale, she needed new ways to feel powerful, lest she drop dead the moment she signed over the Bright Side. She'd made a couple of calls to her representatives, but the whole thing felt silly. ("You're a mouse complaining to the humans about the glue traps," her ranch hand, Gideon, had put it.) This was Kansas, after all. So here she was. Maybe she was acting a touch crazy, but so was everyone else. At least her crazy felt right.

The sign had looked smaller from the road, like something you could pick up and toss so long as you had enough adrenaline going. Now, face-to-face with it, she realized the sign was not only taller than her but also longer across than her arms could reach.

Damn it, she thought. She would need help.

Hers had always been the kind of life in which she had only a couple of people to call. She was unlike the buttoned-up, mosquito-brained women of St. Clare, with their potlucks and Bible studies and cadres of children and grandchildren. Women who went to church and showered every day, whose husbands referred to them as "darling" or "doll." Even if she'd wanted to (which she did not), the women of St. Clare wouldn't have let her run in their circles anyway, not even if she showed up with her hair flat-ironed, nails painted pink. Not that she owned a flat iron. Or nail polish. She had a hair dryer, but that was for the dogs after their baths.

She knew her role. She was the crazy Jewish lady who kept hundreds of animals but not a single piece of china. *Does she even own a comb?* she'd once heard Millie Hunter ask Deb Canright at the swap meet, to which Deb had said: *I hear she doesn't even use toilet paper. She just goes on the lawn with the dogs.* She'd grown used to the looks people gave her in town, to the feeling of being watched and monitored like an active volcano. She knew she smelled like shit and looked wild with her unwashed hair and dirty clothes. But she didn't care. To her, the dirtier she looked, the harder it meant she was working.

It was true she had only a few friends, but they were good people. *Her* people. And so, she called the one person she knew would always answer, not only because he was steady as a clock but also because she wrote his paychecks. He picked up on the second ring.

"Mona?" Gideon asked, voice gravelly with sleep.

"Come on out to the Fuller place. I need your help."

"What are you doing out there?"

"I'll tell you when you get here."

"You're not tipping cows, are you?"

"Gideon, just hurry."

She blinked her headlamp three times, to signal her location. Eventually he found the stepladder and joined her on the other side of the

Fullers' fence. He was in his usual uniform: blue jeans and the red-and-green-checkered Pendleton Ariel had gifted him years before. It was the only relic of Ariel he refused to retire after she ran away, not for any sentimental reason, Mona knew, but because it was a good coat. What Gideon didn't know was that it had originally belonged to Mona's ex-husband, Daniel, and that whenever Gideon wore it, Mona was reminded both of the husband who had left her and the daughter who had run away.

"You didn't kill anyone, did you?" Gideon asked, the smile audible in his voice.

She clicked off her headlamp, the world dissolving into darkness. "Not this time."

When she told him the plan, he did not disapprove as she worried he might. He did not even seem surprised. "Let's be quick then," he said briskly. "If anyone drives by, it's game over."

They managed to get the sign from the ground, the stakes sliding out like candles from a birthday cake. It really was no problem, once you had enough hands on it. Now the trouble was getting it over the barbed wire. Gideon went first so Mona could pass the sign from the other side. He must have snagged himself on a barb because he jumped back, the sign hitting the fence post and ringing out like a gong from a mountaintop. From the distant barn, one of the Fullers' cows mooed, then another, until a game of cow telephone filled the night.

When a light in the brothers' house flashed on, Mona felt an anvil of terror fall through her body. "Shit," she said.

They waited, frozen, fingers aching from the cold. When the light finally went off again, Mona exhaled, felt the anvil begin to lift. "All right," she said, "let's hurry."

They moved in total silence. Soon they were over the fence and en route to the truck, where they set the sign into the bed. When it was done, they quietly high-fived and then took a moment to look around them, at the sky and the moon and the miles of dark prairie and twinkly star stuff holding them in place. Their home. Only then did Gideon ask, "So why did we just do that?"

"Because," Mona said. "We're resisting."

"You mean stealing?"

"I said resisting, and that's what I meant."

Back at the sanctuary, Mona poured two glasses of semi-flat Big K and opened a box of rock-hard Thin Mints circa who-knows-when. The house dogs danced around, confused but excited the humans were up late. For the first time in a long time, Mona felt hopeful. She wondered if this could be her new calling after the sanctuary sold, the cartoon-strip version of her life. She'd travel the country, pilfering signs. Eventually a masked Republican senator would punch her in the stomach—*POW!*—and throw her in the clinker.

"What happens if they find out it was us?" Gideon asked, donning his coat to head to bed. He lived in an old camper van on the other end of the property. The Man Van, Ariel had called it.

"They won't."

"But if they do?"

"There's no use worrying about what's not going to happen."

By the time Mona crawled into bed it was nearly two in the morning. And yet, when she woke three hours later to start her chores, she felt invigorated. Stealing the sign was the closest thing to fun she'd had in years.

The older brother, Big John, came roaring down Sanctuary Road at noon the next day, his truck kicking up dust as it pulled through the gate. Mona's first instinct was to duck into the barn. The next was to somehow cover up the sign, which was still in the back of her truck, visible to the world.

To keep him from pulling up to where her truck was parked, she jogged down the drive to meet him. She wished Gideon was around, but he'd gone to Middleton to buy kitty litter.

Big John rolled down his window.

"Can I help you?" Mona asked, trying to keep the fear out of her voice.

"Let me park, and I'll explain myself." He pulled off to the side of the driveway, taking care to avoid the dogs weaving around his truck. When he got out, Mona felt a little relieved; Big John was always smaller in person than she remembered. He wore a green plaid shirt tucked into jeans. The corner of a strawberry Nutri-Grain bar poked out from his pocket.

"Warm day for October, isn't it?"

"You can thank climate change for that," Mona said, knowing it would piss him off.

"Well," he said, chuckling, "I don't know about *that*."

"You here for a dog?" she asked, playing it cool. "I've got a real sweet heeler who could use a home."

"The reason I'm here is slightly more serious than that."

Mona felt the anvil again. Here it was. Would he hurt her? Would he hurt the animals? As if cued, two of the dogs who'd circled his truck came over and sniffed his feet. A cattle dog named Old Crow lifted his leg near Big John's shoe, his eyes flicking up toward Big John as if to ask: *What do you think about this, tough guy?*

"Cute," said Big John, side-stepping the urine.

"It means 'welcome' in dog."

"Look," he said, clearly bothered. "I'm here because I'm interested in your property. I can't meet your asking price, but if you're willing to wiggle, I can keep the equines, the pigs, the sheep. The dogs and cats would have to go, of course. And the birds and whatever other creepy crawlies you got, but all the farm animals can stay. I'd do that for you. As a neighbor. It's the offer I'm willing to make."

It took a moment for Mona to process what he was saying. That he was not here about the sign. That he had not come to accuse or confront her. "You want to buy the Bright Side?"

"Well, it wouldn't be the Bright Side under my name. It'd be a Fuller ranch. An extension of our grandma's property—our property. This way, Sydney and I can stay close but not under the same roof." He smiled. "I know how it looks to everyone in town, two grown brothers living together in our grammie's old house."

Mona was feeling too many things at once. She hated the Fuller brothers, but here was Big John, with his dirty sneakers and ugly haircut. He seemed sort of pathetic. Harmless, even. Then there was the matter of the sign. If he walked thirty steps toward the house, around the oxbow bend in the drive, it would come into view.

"I don't know," Mona said. "I honestly wasn't expecting any offers this soon. It just went up last week."

"I know how hard it must be, to let this place go. Which is why I'm hoping my offer will make it easier. I could give you time to transition, and you wouldn't have the worry of finding homes for the big animals. Nothing has to go fast. I'm also willing to take on your worker—the Mexican one. What's his name? Gary?"

"Gideon. And he's from Texas, actually."

Big John waved a dismissive hand. "Whatever. I'm willing to keep him on, to manage the animals. Whatever you're paying him, I'll match it plus some. So long as he's legal."

"I just said he was born in Texas."

"Well, all right then. God bless Texas."

"Why are you doing this?"

"Why not? I get the land at a discount, you get the peace of mind.

We're neighbors. That's what neighbors do." He smiled, revealing a piece of something green between his front teeth.

"The pigs and the chickens—you wouldn't slaughter them? Or sell them to someone who's going to slaughter them?"

"We'll keep them until they die, and then we'll use the land for something else. That's the deal I'm willing to make. I won't promise back rubs or bedtime stories or whatever else they're used to, but I can promise they won't become bacon."

She thought of the bumper sticker and then of Joss. Mona hadn't known Joss well, but he would come over once a month to play cribbage with Gideon, the two of them eating microwave popcorn and drinking Hamm's, Joss quizzing Gideon on his Spanish. Giggling like teenagers at jokes Mona didn't get. On one of these nights, Joss fell in love with a cat named Cat Stevens whom he ended up taking home. Who knew where Cat Stevens was now? Nobody had seen Joss since August.

This is a bad man, she reminded herself, looking at Big John. But here he was, in the flesh, trying to do something kind. The truth was that Mona hadn't spoken much to Big John or his little brother, Sydney, over the years. They'd moved to St. Clare when they were teenagers, to live with their grandmother Loretta after their parents died in a car wreck. Mona and Loretta hadn't exactly been friends, but they'd lived on the same road, and in a town as small as St. Clare, that counted for something. When Loretta passed the year before, it had disturbed her how quickly the brothers, now men, overhauled their grandma's estate. They wasted no time replacing her ceramic garden frogs with NO TRESPASSING signs, swapping her colorful lawn pinwheels for American flags, her bird baths for blank space, her floral curtains for white slatted blinds. With the money she left them, they expanded her herd of Jersey cows along with the small crew of workers who knew how to turn their milk into money. Their final bit of maintenance was to report Joss to ICE.

Since Loretta's death, Mona had only spoken with Big John in passing—at the post office, in the hardware store—mostly about the weather or the state of the animals. How he'd lost a cow to a breached birth or how Mona had lost a litter of puppies to Bordetella. They were neighbors, in that they lived miles apart on a road on which not many people lived. When it stormed, they saw the same lightning. When the sun shone, their animals felt the same heat. Really, it was the younger one, Sydney, who had always creeped her out—the skull tattoo on his neck, the bags beneath his eyes. He and Ariel had been friends when they were in middle school, after the brothers first moved to St. Clare. Mona never did figure out why they stopped spending time together, and although she'd felt disappointed at first, that her daughter had lost her only friend, she was eventually relieved. A few months before, Gideon had shown her Sydney's blog, a sloppily written eyesore filled with neon fonts and run-on sentences in all caps. She'd read a few paragraphs but had to stop after a line about the streets running red with the blood of homosexuals.

"I need to think," was what she told Big John. "Can you give me time to think?"

"Certainly. Nothing's set in stone. We're working with Play-Doh here. That's all."

"All right," Mona said, although she couldn't shake the feeling that somehow, the Bright Side was already his.

Big John pulled up his jeans and nodded toward the house. "Mind if I poke my head in?"

"Oh—you don't want to do that. It's a mess in there. Really. We can set up another time."

"Sydney and me, we're not too tidy ourselves. Two bachelors in a rancher. You can only imagine." He was already making his way up the driveway, which would have pissed Mona off even if the sign wasn't in her truck.

"Really, we'll do it another time." She held her hands out like stop signs. "Please."

"Just a glance," he said. "In and out."

"This is my property," she said, a new anger in her voice. An anger that felt good.

But by now he had already rounded the curve and spotted Mona's truck. "What in the name . . ." he said, eyes locked on the sign. When he looked back at her, he was smiling. "I figured it was teenagers from another town. Never would have suspected a grown woman."

This made Mona laugh. As if a *grown woman* wasn't capable of stealing a sign. A voice in her head said, *Well, you did need Gideon's help*, and she said to this voice, *Shut it.*

"You know, maybe if you and your brother quit underestimating *grown women* you'd find a couple to make you sandwiches."

"What sandwiches?"

"That asinine bumper sticker on your truck. About well-behaved women making sandwiches."

"I bought that truck on Craigslist—the sticker came with the rig."

"And you didn't bother to take it off?"

"I thought it was kind of funny."

"Well. My point exactly."

"And what point is that?"

"That you're an asshole." She could feel her heart racing—how long had it been since she'd called someone an asshole? "And a chauvinist."

He smiled, a mean smile. "Look at you, Miss Dictionary. Now if you'll excuse me. I have some phone calls to make." From his back pocket he removed his phone and took a series of pictures. "And to think I came out here to do a nice thing."

"You can have the sign back if you really want it," Mona said, feeling that although she was not in immediate danger, there was danger lurking for her ahead. It was stupid of her to call him an asshole. It was stupid of her to have stolen the sign. She thought of what it would mean, for Gideon to keep his job. For the farm animals to stay on the property. There wouldn't be a better deal coming.

Sensing something was awry, a pack of dogs, led by Old Crow, began to approach Big John. A German shepherd named Katydid leaned into Mona's side, as if to say: *I'm here if you need me.*

"I don't want the sign," said Big John. "What I want is for you to call off your fucking dogs, because if they run in front of my truck, I'm not stopping." He slammed his door. Engine growling, he made an aggressive U-turn, kicking up a cloud of dirt along the way. He was not joking about not stopping. Mona began frantically calling for the dogs, grabbing the ones closest to her by the scruffs of their necks.

Big John sped out the driveway, not bothering to close the gate.

All day, Mona waited for something to happen. When Sheriff Donner eventually showed up, she felt almost relieved. She'd introduced Donner to the love of his life, a golden retriever named Red Dog, and for this, she knew, she could get away with anything this side of murder. She still remembered the day Donner came around looking to adopt, how he'd halted in front of Red Dog's pen as if a physical force had stopped him. Red Dog was only a bag of bones, afflicted with ear mites, heartworms, and a big gray wart that sat on his lip like a tiny raw meatball. "That wart will fall clean off in a month and you'll never know it was there," Mona had told the sheriff. She was worried about Red Dog, who'd been at the Bright Side for nearly three months—unusual for golden retriever puppies. Donner had looked at her, a flare of hurt in his eyes. "Are you suggesting he isn't perfect the way he is?" Here was a grown man, kissing a dog on his warty black lips. From then on, whenever Mona ran into them, Red Dog would look at Donner, as if to remind him that even though he was about to happy-jump all over this lady he used to love, he still loved Donner first, best, and last. And so, when Donner stepped out of his car, sans Red Dog, Mona worried, for the first time, whether she might really be in trouble.

"You shouldn't have done it," Donner said. He'd parked his car in the gravel visitors' lot and walked the rest of the way to where Mona was sitting on the front porch, cutting dreadlocks from the fur of her wolfhound, Opal. The old dog had fallen asleep as soon as she heard the scissors—she'd always loved a good pampering.

"Done what?"

"Don't play with me, Mona."

"Well, who says I did it anyways? What happened to innocent until proven guilty?"

"I can see the sign right there." Donner pointed to the truck where the sign still lay. Why should she have moved it? Big John had already taken photos. What was done was done.

"Can't a woman have a sign?"

"We all know it's not yours, Mona."

"Can you prove it?"

"Can *you*?" asked Donner, his tired eyes meeting hers. "Look, I know you're going through a lot. I'm the last person who wants to see you sell this place—you do good work. Not everyone here under- stands that, but I do. But when it comes to the law, I have to draw a line. I have voters, and those voters have expectations. Especially now, with things the way they are."

"Just spit it out, Donner."

"I'm saying Fuller wants me to press charges, and there's enough evidence for me to do it, but between you, me, and the lamppost, I don't really want to. I'm saying this is a warning. I'm saying if he presses the subject, the next time I come here I'll be coming with a warrant."

"Oh, don't be dramatic," she said, cutting a carrot-sized dreadlock from Opal's underbelly.

He said, "Don't be dumb."

Ariel

Happy hour, a week after the election, and downtown Lawrence was buzzing with pissed-off liberals. As Ariel made her way down Massachusetts Street—Lawrence's central nerve, known as Mass Street or simply Mass, as if it were a holy place—she counted how many times she heard the new president's name (or, if not his name, then one of his thousand monikers: The Cheeto-Elect, The Orange One, He-Who-Must-Not-Be-Named). After three blocks, her tally was up to seven. The whole town had its hackles up.

Head down, she walked past a crowd of women holding signs that read, LOVE TRUMPS HATE!, RESIST!, and I'M NOT USUALLY A SIGN PERSON BUT WTF? She'd once heard on a podcast that when a plane is going down, there are two types of people: those who will help and those who will sit, paralyzed, unable to even speak. She'd always wanted to be the first kind of person, jumping into action with a calm but powerful resolve. She realized, now, that everyone *wanted* to be the first kind.

She'd left the clinic early to meet her best friend, Sunny, at the Taproom, a cavernous establishment with leather booths on the main level and a sticky dance floor in the red-lit basement. She and Sunny had spent many good nights on this dance floor—nights that, in retrospect, blurred into a single, sound-filled ball of light. A firework.

Sunny had texted her that morning. *Meet for drinks later? There's something I want to show you.*

Yes, Ariel had said. *I have news for you, too.*

There were many things Ariel liked about Sunny, but a big one was that Sunny understood what it was like to escape one life and slip into another. She'd grown up dirt-poor in Petersburg, Alaska, and understood down to the minute how hard she had to work to outrun the life her parents had lived. She had a ten-year plan that did not involve marriage or children but rather a PhD by twenty-eight, a job with benefits by thirty, and a starter home by thirty-five. In this way, she was living the kind of life Ariel had imagined for herself when she left home six years before. Sunny did not fool around with men or drugs but allowed herself, every Saturday night, to dance her brains out at the Replay. This is how she and Ariel had met: two women who were too shy to ask a waiter for more water but who elected to booty-grind for three hours straight, shouting explicit lyrics until their throats were raw.

Sunny was sitting in their usual corner booth, drinking a ginger smash and reading something on her phone. The left side of her head was shaved so that when she wore her hair up, like she did now, she took on a feral, Mad Max look Ariel found at once frightening and chic. Another thing Ariel admired about Sunny was that she always looked good. Tonight she wore nude lipstick, a brown peasant dress that flared out at the wrists, and silverware earrings—a tiny fork dangled from one ear, a spoon from the other. *When you wear sweatpants,* she'd once said to Ariel, *your thoughts wear sweatpants, too.* Ariel had thought then of her mother, who used to wear the same shit-caked Levi's for a month straight.

When she saw Ariel, Sunny set her phone on the table, screenside down. "Bring it in," she said, standing for a hug. She smelled like she always smelled, of the DIY shampoo she made from castile soap and coconut milk. "How are you holding up?"

"I'm okay," Ariel said. "Same as everyone else—confused. Shellshocked. Ready for a drink. You?"

Sunny returned to her ginger smash. "I'm pissed, but it's better than being numb. I was worried I'd be numb."

"Same," Ariel said, although she did feel numb.

They spent their first drink exchanging stories and complaints, citing different news articles they'd read and different theories they'd concocted. While Sunny thought it was cowardly to move to Canada, Ariel didn't see the problem—why not go where you wanted to go? Why was it anybody else's business? Plus, poutine. They were on their second drink when Ariel asked Sunny what she had wanted to tell her.

"You go first," Sunny said.

"Okay." The nervous knot in Ariel's stomach tightened. "Dex— he sort of proposed."

A dribble of ginger smash snaked down Sunny's chin. "He what? When? How? Why?"

"Last week. The morning after the election."

Just as Ariel had imagined, Sunny's eyes bugged out. "Is he insane?"

That had been Ariel's first thought when Dex slipped onto a knee that morning. Either he was insane or extremely hungover or both. The night before—election night—he'd gone to a bar where you could get a PBR and a shot of whiskey for five dollars: the Hillary special. He'd tried to convince Ariel to join.

"Don't you want to be out so you can celebrate?"

"You're assuming he's going to lose," Ariel had said.

"Of course he'll lose. All the numbers say he's going to lose."

"But what if the numbers are wrong?"

"They won't be," Dex had said. "You'll see."

In the end, he'd agreed to come home at ten, to be with her. But ten o'clock came and went. Then eleven. Then twelve. As the hours passed, her disbelief about the election transformed into rage at Dex. When she called, his phone went straight to voicemail. Too frazzled to sleep, she toggled between the news and a YouTube video of baby goats playing with a lemon.

Dex had stumbled in at three in the morning, humming a song from a car advertisement. He fell into bed and wrapped his arms around her. "It was fucking *crazy* out there. Everyone was so sad, and Buddy kept buying everyone tallboys—"

"Your phone was off," she said, removing his arm.

"Buddy took it from me."

"He won," she said, her body hot with anger. "You weren't here, and he won."

"I know. You were right."

"It's not about me being right."

"Then what's it about?"

"It's about you not being here."

"I'm sorry."

"You've said that already."

"I'm *sorry*, Ariel."

He put his arm around her again, and this time she let it stay there. Eventually they fell asleep.

Like all mornings-after, the sun had risen, bright and oblivious. The newspaper appeared on their porch, parents walked their children to school. It was a beautiful day: sunny, temperate. Beside her, Dex lay with his face smashed into his pillow. She examined the freckles on his shoulder and recalled how she used to trace them, running a finger from his ear to the top of his spine, down the side of his body, over his pancake butt and down the back of his thigh and over, where his legs came together. She used to love touching him, loved the way she could abandon herself with him, how he abandoned himself with her, both of them shedding whatever it is that separates humans from the rest of the animal world and reverting, temporarily, into their most basic selves: scent, hunger, pleasure.

Now, more than five years in, she wanted to wipe the freckles into her palm, toss them out, start over. She wanted to begin again in the place where she loved Dex absolutely, an inflating love that colored her life the way a sunset could cast an ordinary field into lambent silver. Their first year together, everything he talked about carried a certain magic: huevos rancheros, the Far Bar, PBR. She had spent many months believing these things were intrinsically superior because Dex liked them, and because they were unfamiliar to her, as exotic as the names of foreign cities. When she finally drank a PBR, she could hardly believe the taste; it was an awful, cheap beer, somewhere on the spectrum between urine and water. The first time she went to the Far Bar, she discovered a dead fly in her rum and a peephole in the women's bathroom. Like this, the years had cooled the fire in her belly. But it was the way love worked, wasn't it? Nobody could stay in puppy love forever—it would be madness. Nothing would get done. The whole world would slip away in a daydream of sex and brunch.

The morning after the election, Dex had kissed her on the nose, his face smelling like a headache. "Happy first day of the apocalypse," he said, rubbing his eyes—eyes so beautiful Ariel had once tried to search online for their exact color in Behr paint. Shallow Pond wasn't exactly right, but it was close.

She said, "Oh God, I thought it was a nightmare."

"Why don't we go out for breakfast? It might cheer us up."

"I don't want to be cheered up."

"So you just want to eat oatmeal and be miserable for the next four years?"

"He won't last four years—it's impossible."

"Okay, Ariel. But what if he does? You're just going to sulk the whole time?"

"You're not getting it."

"Let's go to the Roost. I'll buy you a Bloody Mary."

With this, she got out of bed. She felt responsible to her sadness, to the sadness of others. She knew she had it easy in the grand scheme of things, but there were others out there whose lives were in real jeopardy—undocumented immigrants who might get deported, sick people whose health care might disappear. She didn't understand how Dex could think about cocktails at a time like this. Then again, he always thought about cocktails.

She found herself thinking about the time her elementary school gym teacher, Coach Kell, punctured her lung in a horse-riding accident and the district put out a request for a sub. Perhaps as a result of some sudden desire to participate in the community, or maybe as a way to get out of the house and away from her mother, Ariel's father had volunteered. Three times a week, as she and her classmates filed into the rubber-scented gymnasium, she was disturbed anew to find her father standing under the basketball hoop in white gym shorts and tube socks, eager to call roll so when he came to her name he could break into a grin so embarrassing Ariel would wish she had been the one to puncture her lung. Her father knew nothing about sports or physical health—he was a poet, after all, for whom exercise generally consisted of walking quietly around the pasture, head bowed in contemplation. The other students immediately sensed his weakness and took advantage, convincing him that Coach Kell let them run wild in the fields around the school. The dread Ariel felt going into gym class was of the same variety she felt now, imagining the new president in the White House.

She sat on the living room couch, uncertain what to do. She felt compelled to clean—to vacuum or put away the water glasses and cereal bowls Dex had left out—but years from now, when she looked back on this day, she wanted to remember something powerful: writing letters to her representatives or marching in a rally (surely there was a rally somewhere nearby?). She'd taken the day off from the clinic for this very reason: to celebrate or protest. But now, the day stretching out ahead of her, all she really wanted to do was sleep. There was a packet of peanut M&M's in the freezer, and she was thinking about those, too.

She was still sitting there when Dex came downstairs and sat beside her. "I want to ask you something," he said, "but it's probably bad timing."

"You could wait until it's good timing."

"But what if I really, really want to ask now?" He was twitching his nose, a nervous tic.

"Dex, just ask."

"Okay," he said, taking a breath. He then slipped onto the floor, took a knee, and presented a small toy turtle—she hadn't even noticed he'd been hiding anything behind his back. The turtle had a green shell and yellow felt skin. Tiny black beads for eyes. "Will you marry me?"

She stared at the turtle, then at him, then back at the turtle. "What is that?"

His eyes fell on the turtle. "It's a ring box. I thought you'd think it was cute. Is it not cute?"

Her heart was galumphing so forcefully she worried it might shoot from her chest and knock the turtle clean from his hands. "I think you're supposed to open it," she said.

"Oh, right." He flicked the box open to reveal the ring. It was not a diamond or any recognizable stone. It was more of a rock, dark gray with chips of white.

"What is it?"

"It's a dinosaur bone."

"Really? From what kind of dinosaur?"

"Ariel, you're supposed to say something. Say yes."

"Yes," she said, feeling light-headed. Here was the man she loved—however complicated that love might be—on his knee, asking to be with her forever using a turtle and a piece of an animal so ancient she couldn't exactly comprehend it. They'd been dating for nearly six years, and she'd been waiting for this moment for at least the last two. Over the past few months, she'd convinced herself she didn't want to be proposed to, that the whole thing was fundamentally sexist. She'd even entertained the idea of proposing to him but realized she didn't feel strongly enough to buy a ring. But now here he was. Here she was. Here was the turtle.

He collapsed into her lap, pressed his cheek against her thigh. Then he raised his head and kissed her, pushing her back against the couch. "I love you," he said. "More than anything."

"I love you, too," she said, taking his hand and letting him lead her upstairs to bed.

She'd just taken her shirt off when the doorbell rang. "Fuck," Dex said.

"Fuck what? Don't answer it."

"I have to—it's Buddy."

"Then definitely don't answer it."

"He has my phone. He told me he'd bring it by this morning—I completely forgot."

Buddy was always stealing Dex's belongings or coming up with elaborate schemes that would require Dex to hang out with him. Once, while she and Dex were out to dinner at Cafe Beautiful for her birthday, he'd texted Dex that Scarlett Johansson was at the Jackpot, signing autographs. After listening to Dex whine and beg all through the main course, Ariel finally agreed that they could skip dessert to go see her. When they showed up to the Jackpot, it was just Buddy and a few other dudes, everyone drunk and cranky. Ariel pretended to be mad because Buddy had spoiled their date night; in reality, she, too, had wanted to see Scarlett.

"Don't do it," Ariel said. "Just say no."

"I have to—he drove all the way here."

"But you just asked me to marry you." They hadn't had sex in a while, and now she was hungry for it. To feel close to him in the way they knew best.

"It'll take two seconds. Lightning speed. Zip zap."

Knowing Dex would not be lightning speed or even dial-up internet speed, Ariel grabbed a book off her nightstand—she was re-reading *Annie John* by Jamaica Kincaid for the third time. Twenty pages later, she could still hear him talking to Buddy at the front door. When she listened, she could make out snippets like "teeny-tiny mermaid tails everywhere" and "in the back of her van, a live baby deer." Buddy had a deep, radio-announcer voice that carried no matter the volume. Once, at a mutual friend's wedding, he'd scream-whispered to Ariel, "Nipple slip, bridesmaid two," and the whole wedding party had turned to scowl at them.

In the end, Ariel had fallen back asleep, *Annie John* and the little felt turtle on the pillow beside her. When she woke, Buddy was gone and Dex had made pancakes, eggs, and grapefruit mimosas. She ate until she was full and drank until she was tipsy. For moments at a time, she forgot what was happening in the world and saw only her kitchen, where Dex had filled a skinny vase with aster and the air smelled of coffee and grapefruit. Dex was right—it had cheered her up, a cheer that ultimately made her feel guiltier than ever.

Now, in the bar, Sunny was stirring her drink, a tic that meant she was aggravated. "So tell me. Why, out of all the mornings, did he choose that one?"

"I don't know," Ariel said. "I think he was just trying to cheer me up."

Sunny rolled her eyes. She didn't totally dislike Dex, but often tried to sell Ariel on the benefits of single life. *How can you like men right now?* she'd asked after the "grab 'em by the pussy" tape came out. Ariel tried to explain that, in the grand scheme of the male species, Dex was a good example. He was the person she trusted most in the world, because every time she turned to him, he was there. If love was anything, she thought, it was the promise of unconditional attendance (what this said about her history of love, she didn't like to think). There was also the fact that he made her happy—and wasn't that the goal? Happiness? All these years later, she could still hear her mother clicking her tongue: *Happiness is a hot turd straight from the ass of capitalism. The pursuit shouldn't be happiness, it should be helpfulness. Goodness.*

"So, what did you say?" Sunny asked.

"I said yes—what else would I say?"

"Well, there's *no*, and *let's talk about this later*, and *I'm not sure yet*—"

Ariel knew there was no use discussing the matter. "Sunny, I just wanted you to know."

"Okay. Now I know."

"What is it you wanted to tell *me*?"

Sunny adjusted in her seat. "I don't want you to freak out. But I was bingeing on the news this morning, and I found this article."

Sunny slid her phone toward Ariel. The headline read: *Fire at Animal Sanctuary Ruled Arson*. The hair on Ariel's arms rose to attention. She scrolled down and immediately recognized her mother's barn. Her stomach fell a thousand feet, hit a precipice, and fell a thousand more. A million miles away, an Otis Redding song she loved was playing on the bar's stereo. *Fa-fa-fa-fa-fa*. Dex had once said of Otis Redding that he was his own emotion—*You can be sad, you can be happy, or you can be Otis Redding*.

"It's your mom's place, right?"

"Yes—that's our barn." A barn fire had always been her mother's biggest fear, the way other mothers feared car crashes and cancer.

Nobody was injured in the fire, the article continued, *although a mare and her foal died from smoke inhalation.*

"How the fuck is that nobody?" Ariel said out loud, causing the couple in the adjacent booth to turn and look. Sunny put a hand on her arm.

Another picture revealed a swastika painted on the door of the detached garage where her mother kept the rabbits and rodents. Ariel was staring at the swastika, her heart pounding with rage, when something caught her eye. There were words next to the swastika, the letters slanted and fuzzy, nearly illegible—*Dirty Jews*. She blinked a few times but the words remained. *Jews*, not *Jew*. She knew, then, that whoever wrote the message intended it not just for her mother but for her as well. The article didn't say who had done it, only that the suspect was in custody. Ariel couldn't imagine who would do such a thing. Her mother wasn't popular in town, but she certainly wasn't hated.

"Did you get to the end?" Sunny asked.

Ariel was having trouble seeing—there were tears in her eyes. She blinked them away, not wanting to cry in public. The last paragraph read, *The fire comes at a particularly difficult time for Ms. Siskin, who put her sanctuary up for sale last month.* Her stomach turned again, a wave of heat. How could her mother sell the sanctuary? Where would she go? Where would the animals go? It was impossible, like someone putting their own head up for sale. Her mother was the Bright Side, and the Bright Side was her mother.

She put down the phone. "What do I do?" she asked.

Sunny tapped the edge of her glass. "I don't know, but if something like this happened to my family, I'd go. No question."

"But it's been years—I can't just show up."

"There's this crazy new thing called the telephone."

"What if she won't talk to me?"

"And what if you don't call at all? What's the difference then?"

Like always, Sunny had a point.

Mona

It happened the morning after the election, during a time Mona considered holy—a workless hour when even the moths rested their wings and the stars nodded off. It was Opal the wolfhound who woke her, howling like a banshee at 2:30 a.m.

Mona had sat up in bed, head pounding. She'd drank three beers the night before—the first alcohol she'd had in years. While it was true she disliked alcohol for the effect it had on people—people like her father—she also considered it a useless expenditure, as impractical as throw pillows or perfume. The beers were Gideon's—he'd purchased an assortment of drinks, chips, and candies for the occasion. ("What is this, the Super Bowl?" Mona had asked, to which he'd responded, "Same idea, uglier cheerleaders.") He'd wanted to spend the evening with his girlfriend, Joy, who was at a watch party with her cousins in Wichita, but Mona asked him to stay. *There's too much work*, was her reasoning, but she knew Gideon saw through her. She didn't want to be alone.

The beers had made her light-headed and bloated, but she'd been grateful for the buzz when, state by state, the news anchors delivered the verdict, solemn as doctors reporting a fatal diagnosis. Out of curiosity, Gideon had changed the channel to Fox News, where everyone was celebrating, their faces flushed with smug cheer, as if they'd just gotten their first kiss and the whole world had been there to watch.

"How can the same thing look so different?" Mona had asked.

Gideon had shrugged. "That's people, I guess. I didn't drink Pepsi until I was nineteen because my dad was a Coke man."

Mona had gone upstairs then, eyes dry and head ringing, leaving Gideon in front of the television.

Part of her was relieved to hear Opal howling; the dog was in the late stages of bone cancer and had fallen into a monk-like silence, rarely leaving the couch and eating only what food Mona fed her by hand. Mona figured they had a week left together at most.

"Hush, girl," Mona whispered, turning onto her side. "Go back to sleep." Outside, the sanctuary stirred. It was not uncommon for the dogs to wake in a fit of barking that would cause the sheep to bleat, the donkeys to bray, the chickens to cluck. Tonight, she could hear someone—maybe her mare, Ginger—running around and whinnying. Perhaps there was a coyote. If so, the donkeys would run it off. The animals would settle down soon enough.

Opal howled again, and Mona was about to put a pillow over her head when she caught sight of a strange glow outside her window, where her barn stood. Inside the barn was Squid, a paint horse she'd rescued from a traveling rodeo the summer before. With Squid was her foal, a sweet, knob-kneed mare Gideon had named Aleira.

Mona sat up, watching dumbly as the sky outside her window turned gray. Opal licked her hand. *What's the matter with you?* Opal asked with her eyes. *Get up!*

Mona threw on pants and a jean jacket and hightailed it outside, Opal limping loyally behind her. By the time she reached the barn, she found Gideon already in motion. A pack of dogs had followed her from the house and were now running back and forth, barking at the fire as if it were a stranger who might be scared off. Beyond the barn, the sheep were bleating, thinking it was time for their morning hay.

"Where's Squid?" Mona shouted.

"She's in there," Gideon called back. "They're both still in there."

The other horses had disappeared into the pasture, but Ginger still paced the paddock, waiting for Squid and Aleira to come out. She reared up and then galloped in circles, the fire flashing in her eyes. She and Squid were friends.

Gideon sprinted toward the barn. He was too far away to hear Mona shout for him to be careful. Of course, he wouldn't be careful. This was Gideon. He loved the horses as much as a man could love anything. Mona had learned, only recently, that he sometimes woke in the middle of the night to walk with them in the pasture.

Perhaps Mona had left the little Coleman lantern burning or had failed to notice a chewed-up electrical cord. Unlikely, but not impossible. She would have suspected lightning, but there were no clouds, only a Kansas sky so certain and infinite it was the closest thing she'd ever known to God.

Now, down Sanctuary Road, blue and red lights disco-flashed against the horizon.

It was then her German shepherd Katydid spotted a figure moving behind the barn. Katydid went after the shadow, one streak of darkness chasing another.

"Fuck off!" came a man's voice from the shadow. Then, a cry of pain and the sound of Katydid growling.

When the figure emerged from behind the barn, Katydid's mouth locked on his wrist, Mona saw who it was. Sydney Fuller, Big John's little brother. He was wearing all black and had shaved his head clean down to the skin.

In the strobe of the police sedan's headlights, Sydney met her gaze. She remembered the little boy who'd played clarinet with Ariel—his round face, the painful-looking acne on his chin. How he'd once kicked dust into a dog's eyes and laughed as the dog ran away, sneezing. He was older now, his jaw lean and angular. It disturbed her, suddenly, the fact that children transform so completely. For a moment, she thought he was winking at her—a knowing, malicious wink—but suddenly both of his eyes were fluttering. He was not winking, but crying.

After the firefighters had doused the last flame, after Doc Powell had declared Squid and Aleira dead from smoke inhalation, after a deep, eerie silence settled over the sanctuary, Mona sat with Gideon in the living room, where they took turns looking out the window at the smoldering barn.

A saying had entered Mona's head and wouldn't leave. *My barn having burned to the ground, I can now see the moon.* It was an old samurai poem her ex-husband, Daniel, used to recite whenever he wanted to look on the bright side. At first, he'd used it in earnest—like when Mona's father died and left her the money she needed to buy the sanctuary. The poem had, in fact, been the inspiration for the sanctuary's name—but, over the years, he'd begun to use it ironically. His toast would fall on the ground, butter-side down, and he'd say, *My barn having burned to the ground, I can now see the moon.* Meaning *I'm going to eat a doughnut.*

Now there was no triumphant moon, just the milk-white glow of dawn. A charred roof. A black hole yawning above the stall where Squid and Aleira had taken their grain. Soon the barn would not even belong to her—none of it would belong to her. The night felt like a dream. Her entire life, sometimes, felt like a dream.

Gideon made strong coffee and opened a sleeve of Ritz crackers neither he nor Mona touched. *Like sitting shiva*, Mona thought. After her mom died, when she'd asked her father about sitting shiva, he'd told her, *With your mom gone, there's no sense doing all that Jewy stuff.* By this he meant Mona would no longer attend the synagogue in Wichita where she and her mother had gone every Saturday morning for as long as Mona could remember. In the sanctuary, she and her mother would listen as the rabbi filled the room with his booming voice. All the songs were in Hebrew, but still Mona understood, through the sheer tenor and urgency of the rabbi's voice, that he sang about the power, love, and rage of God, about how terrifying and lovely it was to be alive. What Mona liked best about these mornings was that it was just her mother and her—Mona's father, raised Catholic, never came along. Afterward, they would get lunch at a restaurant called Piccadilly, where Mona would order spaghetti and her mother would order a salad with tuna fish and cottage cheese. This was the Jewy stuff to which her father referred—those sacred mornings with her mother. To Mona, Judaism had little to do with God and everything to do with her mom.

As far as Mona knew, it was sacrilegious to sit shiva for a horse, but this was the least she and Gideon could do, these hours of quiet reflection. They had loved that foal, sweet as anything. And Squid. There wasn't a mom in the world as good as Squid.

She felt dizzy thinking about everything she needed to do—call Coreen about borrowing a backhoe to dig the graves, tarp the roof of the barn, contact her homeowner's insurance. All this, in addition to the regular chores. All this, in addition to the fear that now roiled in her gut and the sadness that gripped her each time she imagined what it must have been like for Squid and Aleira, trapped in the barn as smoke rushed in. Despite everything, she was grateful the barn's structure remained. The firefighters had worked quickly. How they'd come so fast, Mona couldn't figure, but she was not about to question this particular miracle. That she was nearly out of hay had been a great source of stress but now seemed like incredible fortune—if her hay guy, Artie, hadn't gotten a bad flu, delaying her order of one hundred bales, the barn would be gone.

When the dogs started whimpering for their breakfast, Gideon turned to her and asked, "What is it we're supposed to do now?"

Mona took a sip of her coffee, which had grown tepid. *Go to sleep and never wake up? Let the animals do as they please?* Eventually she said, "Same as we always do. Start feeding everyone their breakfast."

She saw the swastikas on her way to feed the sheep: one on the garage door, one on the shed, one on the windshield of Old Baby. Later, she would find a miniature one on the FOR SALE sign.

She discovered the mangled spray paint can in the pigpen, where her Yorkshire, Lady Madonna, had acquired the bright red mouth of a circus clown—she'd tried to eat the can. Also in red was the word *JEW*, painted hastily across Lady Madonna's mud-crusted back. There was a sick look to the pig's eyes and a puddle of vomit at her feet. As Mona washed Lady Madonna's snout with a warm rag, her barn still sending up thin ribbons of smoke into the morning's blue sky, she felt her anger bloom into something darker, more dangerous.

After this, life on the Bright Side seemed cracked—that was the only way she could put it, as if a container had splintered and all the light was now pouring out. For the past six years, she'd been fine living alone—a touch lonesome, but fine. Now she woke in the middle of the night, her sheets damp with sweat, a ringing in her ears. She would hold her breath and listen, an unwise habit to develop on an animal sanctuary, where strange sounds could be heard at all hours of the night. Even in silence, she could pull out a thread of sound—an owl hooting, a dog snoring, the metallic screech of a cat fight—and stitch it into a nightmare. How angry she was that Sydney had taken from her the one thing she'd always had: courage.

Ariel

For more than a week, Ariel couldn't bring herself to make the call. Each time she thought about it, a feeling of nervous dread would rise up so forcefully she sometimes had to bend over, put her hands on her knees. *SHE'S YOUR EFFING MOM*, Sunny texted her one afternoon. *JUST DO IT ALREADY.*

OK, OK, Ariel sent back. *Tonight—I promise.*

When she got home, Dex was on the couch, playing on his phone. Probably Candy Crush or Two Dots. She noticed the windowsill held a new succulent, a peach-colored flower pushing up through a spiral of dark, waxy leaves. Dex was obsessed with plants. He bought a new one every other week, imbuing their otherwise cramped and unextraordinary house with a lush, jungle feel. It was one of the many things she loved about him, how he could transform a space into something textured and alive.

"Good day?" he called from the couch.

"Not bad," she said, setting her things down. "Got peed on by a corgi."

"That's my lady." He was still looking at his phone. "Want to get food somewhere?"

"I thought you were making lasagna." All day, she had looked forward to a home-cooked meal. When he wanted to, Dex could be an excellent cook.

"I was going to, but then I started craving India Palace."

"I'm not hungry right now," she said, trying to mask her irritation. "Maybe later."

"When is later?"

She went to the kitchen table, where her laptop was. "If I had to guess," she said, starting up the machine, "it'll be sometime between now and the future."

She ignored his groan as she searched for the most recent article about the fire, a shock running up her neck as she found one dated just the day before. When she read the suspect's name, the world flickered, froze, and then grew fuzzy. Sydney Fuller. The same Sydney who taught her how to play Risk, who showed her how to dance the Macarena, who gifted her a package of strawberry-flavored reeds for her clarinet when Ariel's mom kept forgetting to buy them. The same Sydney she'd hurt all those years ago. He was now in jail, his bail set at $200,000. If sentenced, he could face up to fifteen years in prison. Arson. Hate crime. Cruelty to animals. *What I did was wrong,*" he was quoted in the article. *"I see that now and can only hope God will forgive me."*

She stared at his mug shot. Despite his shaved head, he had grown more handsome over the years, his chin stronger, his acne gone. She recalled the first time she ever saw him. It was seventh grade, third period, band class. He was short and scrawny, with red hair that stuck up in the front, stiff with gel, and elbows so dry they appeared gray. He'd dressed up for his first day at a new school: khaki cargo pants, Red Hot Chili Peppers T-shirt, and a hemp necklace with green-and-red peace-sign beads. Ariel was alarmed when Ms. Kahn assigned him first-chair clarinet, a distinction that had always been Ariel's. Jealousy soon gave way to pity when she learned Sydney's parents had died in a car accident that winter, while heading to church—that he and his older brother, Big John, had moved to St. Clare to live with their grandma Loretta. This was why he would sometimes tear up in the middle of band practice—this, and he'd hurt his neck in the wreck and sometimes felt a shooting pain in his upper back. As if things weren't hard enough, he was also first-chair clarinet in a town where boys, if they dared play an instrument at all, chose drums, tuba, or trumpet. In the hall, kids began to shout *faggot* and *fruitcake*. Watching the awkward drama of Sydney's bullying—the way he cowered, how kids threw balled-up paper at his back—horrified Ariel. Having always been the target, she had never witnessed this abuse from the outside. To her surprise, when she invited him to sit with her at lunch, he said yes. From there, a friendship unfolded. At first, Ariel assumed their connection was based on circumstance—they were both lonely band geeks who lived in St. Clare—but as they spent more time together, she began to genuinely like Sydney's company. He was funny, with a grim sense of humor like her father's, and often talked about the movies and shows his grandma let him watch—*The Matrix, American Idol, The Real World*. He had grown up in St. Louis and felt bigger than St. Clare, his life still tethered to the outside world. She was happy when, on his insistence, they began practicing clarinet together after school, in her mother's garage or sitting on metal chairs in the pasture, the horses pacing, curious, around them. Occasionally they would go to his house, which smelled of mothballs and Lysol and made Ariel feel inexplicably sad. Loretta would bring them crustless sandwiches or pouches of warm Capri Sun, kissing Sydney on the forehead whenever she left the room. Mostly, he was nice to Ariel, but sometimes, if he was having a hard day, he could be cruel. He'd ask if she was retarded when she couldn't figure out a line of music. Or he'd say she smelled like a barn—didn't she take showers? There was also the time he patted the top of her head, and when she'd asked, giggling, what he was doing, he said he was feeling for her horns. Still, she cared for him. He was her only friend, and despite his occasional unkindness, she believed that, deep down, he was good. She was the one who had hurt him in the end, and she wondered now, in a flash of anxiety, whether this hurt had something to do with the fire. If, all these years later, Sydney had wanted to hurt her back.

Ariel continued reading the article, anticipating whatever quote her mother had given the journalist. When she got to it, her heart wrenched. *"We're devastated,"* said Mona Siskin, owner of Bright Side animal sanctuary. *"All we want is our horses back, and that's the one thing even justice can't give us."*

She was gathering the courage to call when a text came through from Dex. He was still on the couch, just a few yards away. *Since my lady isn't hungry, would she care 2 bone instead?* Ariel ignored the text and put on her jacket.

"You going somewhere?" Dex leaned over the couch to look at her. A tuft of his copper hair flopped in front of his eyes in a way she had always found endearing.

"Just outside to make a call."

"Did you get my text?"

"I did."

"Would you say you're for or against boning?"

"Currently undecided."

"Who are you calling?"

"Nobody. I'm just—ordering more contacts." It was a dumb lie, but she was anxious. She grabbed a beer and went out onto the back porch. There was a bite to the wind, but the fresh air jolted her to attention. Her hands shook as she dialed the sanctuary's number, which she still knew by heart. When the phone started to ring, she nearly hung up but forced herself to keep going, gulping down as much beer as she could. She pictured the black cordless in her mother's kitchen, next to a stack of wholesale pet-supply catalogs and overdue vet bills. She was both disappointed and immensely relieved when the voice-mail picked up.

Her mother's voice, like a song she hadn't heard in years. The sound of it gutted her. *You've reached the Bright Side. If you're calling about adopting an animal, please leave your name and number and we'll get back to you as soon as we can.* For a moment, Ariel thought it was the same message from when she'd left. This would be just like her mother, keeping the same voicemail recording for nearly a decade. *Well, Ariel, if it ain't broke why fix it?* But the message continued. *If you're interested in the property, please call Shirley Donahue at Midland Realty to set up a showing. Thanks!* This last part made her stomach turn.

She considered leaving a voicemail, something short and small, a sentence or two to open up a channel of communication. Her voice would shake, she knew, and hearing the message would probably cause her mother to cry or gasp or unplug the machine for good, but it was the only alternative to showing up unannounced. And yet, a millisecond after the machine beeped, a robot voice took over: *We're sorry, but this voice mailbox is full.*

She startled when the porch door slid open behind her. Dex asked, "Are you hungry *now?*"

The next day, Ariel asked her boss, Dr. Nguyen, if she could take a short leave of absence at the end of the month.

"You're not moving to Canada, are you?" Dr. Nguyen asked, completely serious. He was on his third cup of coffee—she could tell he hadn't been sleeping well lately. Then again, nobody had been sleeping well lately.

She smiled. "No, it's nothing like that. It's a family matter."

"I see," he said, employing the same gentle voice he used to calm dogs before he pricked them with a needle or inserted a rectal thermometer. "Is somebody sick?"

"Kind of," Ariel said, feeling it was not totally a lie.

In the end, he gave her a whole week off. It was something she'd noticed since the election: everyone was eager to dole out little kindnesses wherever possible, as if, deed by deed, they might tip the scales of the world toward goodness and restore some measure of order. She sometimes wondered what would happen if people all over the world shouted *Peace!* at the same time. They could organize it through Twitter or Reddit, maybe—whoever *they* were. There'd be time differences to contend with, but surely people would wake in the middle of the night to promote peace on Earth. Or would they? This was the kind of thing she now found herself thinking about. This, and chocolate chip cookies.

That night, at dinner, she told Dex she was planning a trip home to see her mother.

Dex stopped chewing his leftover tikka masala. "Really?"

"Really." Ariel rarely talked about her mother, and Dex had learned, over the years, not to broach the subject; if he did, she would spend the rest of the day in an agitated silence, reading novels or taking long walks around campus. She often thought about sharing more details about the Bright Side, but each time she gathered the courage, the fear of his not understanding quelled her. Because how could he—a man who grew up in a gated community in Mission Hills, where his neighbors were, on either side, a professional golfer and the CEO of Hallmark—understand what it was like to grow up in a house that smelled of animal urine and mold and cat litter, and where nobody cared to do anything about it? And how could he, a man so squeamish he refused to handle sponges that smelled even remotely of mildew, understand that if you tilted your head just so, it was the loveliest place in the world? All he knew was that her mother had a lot of animals and that they'd had a falling-out when Ariel was eighteen.

"Is everything okay?" he asked gingerly. The look of fearful caution in his eyes made Ariel feel ashamed. She knew it was selfish, how little she'd told him about her upbringing, and yet she had never felt ready to discuss it. To discuss it was to think of it, and she tried to think of it as seldom as possible.

"Everything's fine," Ariel said. "I just need to go."

"But why now? Is there a reason?"

Ariel didn't want to lie, but more than this she didn't want to tell the truth, a truth that would require a hundred others. "I just got engaged," she said. "I want to tell my mother—I want her to come to the wedding. But before I do that, I need to mend some bridges."

A look of pleasure spread across Dex's face. "You know, I'd love to meet her. You can tell her I say so."

So he would not ask any more questions, she leaned over the table and kissed him.

She left Lawrence after work on the first Friday of December. As she drove west, the land flattened and the billboards began to ask more questions. IF YOU DIE TONIGHT, one cartoon-flame-engulfed sign read, DO YOU KNOW WHERE YOU'LL GO? Beneath this, in black spray paint, someone had written, confusingly: AMERICA #1.

She'd packed quickly, nervously, as if preparing for a week's worth of first dates. At the last minute, she'd thrown in a couple gifts for her mother. Peace offerings. One was practical: a cat water fountain she'd bought on sale at Petco (she recalled how much her mother hated when the cats licked the sink faucet). The other was a photo, taken a lifetime ago, on the day Ariel and her parents moved to the Bright Side. In it, the three of them stand on the front porch, Mona's arms wrapped protectively around Ariel and her father. They wear jeans and matching kelly-green shirts. Ariel, seven years old, holds a wooden plaque that reads: HOME SWEET HOME! What kind of family had they been, to take such a photo? To wear matching out-fits? Ariel had stolen the photo the night she ran away, perhaps sus-pecting, even then, that she might not see her mother for a very long time.

She crossed the county line at eleven o'clock, arriving to a house so dark it was nearly indistinguishable from the sky. Growing up, Mona had been militant about conserving electricity. At nine o'clock each night, she would unplug every appliance, lamp, and gadget, forcing Ariel to read by flashlight. When Ariel was a freshman at the University of Kansas, it had taken her a month and several tiffs with her roommate, Gwyneth, to break herself of the habit. *If you unplug my phone charger one more time*, Gwyneth had said, *I will end you.*

Before she turned into the drive, her headlights illuminated the sanctuary's sign: WELCOME TO THE BRIGHT SIDE, WHERE THERE'S LOVE ENOUGH FOR EVERYONE. If nothing else, the sign was true. Her mother may not have had enough time, money, or manpower for the animals, but she certainly had enough love. Perhaps too much. Like any other force of nature—rain, fire, wind—too much love did more harm than good.

So as to not wake her mother or the animals, she parked in the visitors' lot and walked the rest of the way. She was exhausted from a day of work followed by the five-hour drive but was overcome by a surge of adrenaline—she was home. Her head felt weightless, her legs like they might detach and carry on toward the house without her. She wondered if any of the animals sensed her return, if they had dreamed of her the night before the way she had dreamed of them. Around her, the sanctuary was all shadow and whisper: the silhouette of a horse, the soft bleat of a sheep. Sounds thin as crepe paper. Here it was, the stage on which her childhood had played out, the place where she had spent more concentrated time than any other in the world. Stupefied, she pressed a finger to the soil and then held it to her nose. Earth. A relief that it was all still here, still intact—the same, the same, the same. It made her want to cry for all she'd missed, and so, for the first time in a long time, she did.

Before she could even turn the spare key (hidden under the ceramic goose, as always), the dogs began to bark and whimper. As soon as she opened the back door, a group of them rushed her. She kneeled down and took the dogs into her arms, let them lick her face, their tails going wild. They smelled terrible—they were sanctuary dogs, after all—but this terrible smell was also the smell of home. The feeling of animals—their movement, the stink of them, the brush of wet fur on an ankle, the slick of slobber on an open palm—it was all synonymous with home.

"Hey, babies," she whispered. "Hi, hello, hello." She'd come prepared, with a baggie of Milk-Bones and Beggin' Strips. She doled out the goodies, letting the dogs lick her fingers clean. "I missed you, I missed you, I missed you."

She then flipped a light switch, exploding the living room into color. There was the Oklahoma-shaped stain on the shag rug, the bendy standing lamp that had always reminded her of a dejected old man. Across the room was the sunporch where her father had written poetry—a room Ariel had been prohibited from entering and which Mona had promptly packed with dog beds after he disappeared. On the mantel: a butter cookie tin filled with loose change, a mason jar of dog teeth, a pile of sun-bleached *Horse Illustrated*s. Here it all was. The same, but somehow both smaller and larger than she remembered, like a dream version of the house she once knew.

Ariel tiptoed down the hall, the dogs trailing excitedly behind her, and opened the door to her old bedroom. She expected to see her twin bed and the apple-crate desk her father made for her tenth birthday; her towers of novels and old journals; her Harry Potter poster and

Opal's hot-pink dog bed tucked into the corner. Instead, there were cats. A dozen, at least. Some sleeping, some playing, a pair hissing at each other, paws raised. A ragdoll scratched at a hole in the wall's plaster while a fat calico lazily licked the inside of its thigh. She recalled what Dr. Nguyen told patients whose cats were exhibiting signs of stress. *If there's more than one cat in the house, separate them. They're probably driving each other nuts.* Where her bed had been there was now a mound of towels and blankets. Shoeboxes and felt mice and scratching posts and a gigantic brown cat tree. A row of litter boxes occupied what had once been her closet. The odor was all-consuming, like a fetid scarf wrapped around her face. She felt a tingle on her ankle and realized it was a flea. As she turned to leave, gagging, she accidentally stepped on the paw of a terrier, who released a shrill yelp and then began to rapid-fire bark, its body jerking up with each cry.

"Fuck, I'm sorry," Ariel said, stooping down to calm the dog. "Shhh. Everything's okay."

Suddenly a German shepherd was bounding down the hallway, growling, teeth bared. Ariel closed her eyes, afraid the dog might actually bite her—she had been bitten by dogs several times before, and it was not an experience she wanted to repeat—but soon felt the dog sniffing her hand, a moment of cold wetness as its nose touched her wrist. She realized it was Katydid, who'd come to the sanctuary as a puppy, her ears the size of candy corn, her tongue the color of bubblegum. Over the years, Katydid became a sort of godfather among the house animals, arbitrating skirmishes between cats and dogs, offering protection for the weak. Once, Ariel swore she saw a cat paw a Milk-Bone to Katydid across the kitchen floor—payment for some unknown favor.

"Katydid," Ariel said excitedly, trying to keep her voice down. "How's it going, girl? Remember me?"

The dog cocked her head, as if to say: *Ariel? That is* so *weird! We thought you were dead!*

Ariel then heard the sound of someone coming down the stairs. A human someone. She took a deep breath, steadying her heart, and prepared to see her mother.

Dex

"A long weekend," Ariel had said. "If it's any longer, I'll call you."

She had too much luggage for a long weekend, but Dex said nothing. He understood that this trip was important to her and his job was to step aside and let her go. "I'll miss you" was what he'd told her.

She'd kissed him on the cheek. "I'll miss you, too. Be good while I'm gone. No parties."

"I'll try, Mom."

Part of him had been excited for the time alone—he could play his records as loud as he wanted, eat Oreos and string cheese for breakfast—but as soon as she was gone, he felt a pinprick of emptiness plunge through his middle. He missed her.

Over the years, he'd come to shape his week around Ariel—he woke when she woke, ate when she ate. Or maybe she woke when he woke, ate when he ate—there was no telling the difference. Sunday nights were movie nights and on Wednesdays they went to trivia at the Burger Stand, where Ariel dominated every subject except for music and pop culture, which were his domains. He was secretly grateful for the routine. For too many years, he'd lived as a bachelor, staying out as late as he wanted, drinking as much as he wanted, subsisting on toast and macaroni and cheese and shrimp ramen noodles, telling himself he had it good when all he really wanted was someone to tell him to come home and eat some fucking vegetables.

That he had found Ariel—a person whose sense of order balanced his tendency toward chaos, whose practicality kept his head from floating too far into the clouds—was a relief he felt over and over again each day. Before her, he'd been a puddle of warm Jell-O—messy, ludicrous, confused. She was his mold.

There were other things he loved about her, too. How she laughed a certain way only around him—a special laugh, with a rounded, buoyant quality, like a cluster of red balloons. How she noticed things he didn't: the iridescence of a housefly, the color of someone's eyelashes, how the pressed tin ceiling at their favorite brunch spot matched the pressed tin ceiling in the record store's bathroom. How she so rarely relaxed but when she did, she went all the way, burrowing into a couch or bed with so much abandon he worried she might dissolve. This happened when she danced, too—she would close her eyes, tilt her head back, disappear. He was always surprised by how much she liked to dance, despite the fact that she had no rhythm and always looked wildly out of control. She was *odd* despite wanting, desperately, to be ordinary, to fit in and be loved.

For as different as they were, there had always been an ease between them. They could talk about inane subjects with the conviction of political pundits (they'd once argued about the merits of sugarcoated versus plain gummy worms for more than an hour). Mostly, he loved that he loved her, that out of the world's seven-point-something billion people he had found his person, a person who surprised him as regularly as she disappointed him. (Of course she disappointed him, they had been together for almost six years.) And who, at the end of the day, went with him to bed and woke with him in the morning, proving, in this simple yet essential way, that she wanted to go through the world beside him, that he did not have to do it alone.

On Friday nights, he and Ariel usually ate dinner downtown.

Then they'd see a show or have drinks at Harbour Lights, playing foosball or darts until Ariel was ready to go home and watch exactly one episode of *The Office* before falling asleep, her head on his shoulder. Now he was hungry, bored, and lonesome. His main crew of friends was out of town for the weekend, at an EDM festival in Kentucky. He thought about calling Buddy, but this would be admitting defeat.

The problem with Buddy was that, two years before, he'd gone to the most beloved Thai place in Lawrence and ordered a plate of pad see ew in whose perfect golden noodles he'd discovered a piece of steel wool, an egregious breach of health code that resulted in a week of severe intestinal pain and "atypical" stools, or so he told his lawyer. When Buddy won the lawsuit, he quit his job scanning receipts at Best Buy and became something of a professional pothead. Meanwhile, the Thai place went out of business and Buddy became, overnight, one of the most despised people in Lawrence. While it was true that Buddy was annoying, arrogant, lazy, and crude, he was also terrifically fun. They had met their first day of college and, over the years, had endured more escapades together than Dex could accurately recall. At some point, during these escapades, they'd transitioned from being drinking friends to just friends.

Ariel couldn't stand Buddy—she called him the Tick. "All he does is take, take, take," she once said, "and what do you get in return? Lyme disease."

Insanely, Dex had replied, "Well, what if I *want* Lyme disease?"

On the other end of the phone, Buddy's words were muffled.

"Were you sleeping?" Dex asked.

"No thanks to you."

"Want to get a drink?"

"Let me guess. Ariel's gone?"

"That's not why I'm calling."

"Typical." A pause on the line, then, "I bought some weed yesterday, so things are a little tight, financially speaking."

"I'll get the first round," Dex said, knowing he would end up buying them all.

"Right on. Meet you downtown in twenty."

As Dex put on his going-out clothes and styled his hair, he thought about what Ariel had said: *If it's any longer, I'll call you.*

If it's any longer. What had she meant? Longer as in a day longer? Or two days? Or a week?

Whenever they visited his parents in Kansas City, their stay was calculated down to the minute, with escape plans and backup escape plans involving fake phone calls and imaginary migraines. Ariel had never felt completely comfortable around his parents, whom he loved deeply despite their suburban ridiculousness. They were boring and Presbyterian and had thrown away their vote in the election by writing in *Jesus Christ, Lord and Savior*, but all they ever said of Ariel, who hardly spoke a word around them, was that she seemed nice. *If you're happy,* his mother had said, *then we're happy.* Dex understood his parents were relieved he had found someone at all; they wanted grandchildren, and he wasn't getting any younger. The year before he met Ariel, they'd sent him a card containing a username (HandsomeProvider321) and password (WeLoveYouDex321!) to ChristianMingle.com.

Meanwhile, Dex knew little about Ariel's parents—her entire childhood was a half-formed question mark. He knew her mother lived on the western edge of Kansas and had given Ariel neither a phone call nor a nickel since Ariel moved to Lawrence. It was therefore surprising that Ariel was suddenly determined to bridge this gap, to forgive old grievances so that, when the time came, she could invite her mother to the wedding.

Before heading out, he spritzed Ariel's lavender-and-basil pillow spray onto his shirtsleeve, so that he might catch a whiff of her as he moved about his night. His *fiancée*. Was there a lovelier word in the world? He even preferred it, at least musically, to *wife*, a word like a starched white apron, unyielding and tight. *Wife*. It didn't suit Ariel at all, but that was part of the novelty, the thrill. As much as she was not a wife, he was not a husband. He liked to imagine that someday, when he and Ariel were shriveled old pumpkins, he would think *boyfriend, girlfriend* and laugh.

Ariel

Her mother stood at the end of the hallway in a ratty gray nightshirt. "Who's there?" she called. She appeared to be gripping a gun.

"It's just me," Ariel said, putting her hands up. The sight of her mother with a gun was so startling she forgot, for a moment, that they hadn't spoken in years. Her heart was beating so fast she could feel it everywhere: in her head, her wrists, her tongue.

Her mother let the gun drop to her side, put a hand to her heart. "Ariel?"

How long had it been since she'd heard her name pronounced that way—*are, ee, ell*? When she'd started school in Lawrence, she'd been too shy to correct her professors' mispronunciations, and so she'd decided to just go with it, accepting the new pronunciation of her name, the new pronunciation of her life. It sounded like the Little Mermaid's name. Like something that flies through the air.

"I thought someone was breaking in," her mother said.

"I'm sorry. I didn't want to wake you."

"What the hell are you doing here?"

She had rehearsed a hundred responses during her drive, but not a single one had felt right. "I just—I wanted to come back. So I did." She hoped her mother could hear how terrified she was, that this terror was a symptom of remorse. How does one apologize, in a sentence, for six years of pain?

Her mother stared at her, and so Ariel stared back. Her mother's dark hair, which she had always kept in a long braid down her back, now ended at her shoulders and was shot through with gray. She held herself like a soldier who'd gone into battle and returned only half-alive, eyes glazed with everything she couldn't unsee. She was barely fifty but looked a decade older. Ariel felt a pang of regret—she had missed the sunset of her mother's beauty. Here was dusk, the crickets chirping.

She wondered what her mother saw, what kind of daughter. Ariel was only twenty-four but could already feel the layers of her girlhood sloughing off, pooling at her feet when she showered. Dex had found her first gray hair the month before, plucking it from her head and then handing it to her, like a rose. *A crooked witch hair for m'lady.*

Her mother cleared her throat. "You could have called."

"I tried, but nobody answered, and the voicemail was full."

"Well," said her mother, and then there was nothing else to say.

Just then, a Scottie dog came skipping down the hall. An old-timer, with a gray muzzle and cloudy eyes. Strapped around its middle was a length of blue cloth—a diaper band. The dog hopped up and down at Mona's feet, asking to be picked up.

"Hey, Daisy Doo," Mona said cheerfully, clearly grateful for the distraction. Still holding the gun, she scooped the dog into her arms. "Daisy's got bladder issues. Don't you, Daisy?" She spoke in her animal voice, soft with a singsong lilt. "Aren't these diapers cute? They come in all sorts of colors and patterns. Bad news is the diaper rash. I have to put ointment on her twice a day."

As if on cue, Ariel saw a tiny stream of urine leak from the diaper and onto Mona's nightshirt.

"Oh, shoot," her mother said, setting Daisy down so the dog could finish her business on the carpet. "She must have gotten excited."

Ariel put a hand over her mouth to hide her smile. "Sorry, not funny."

"Yeah, yeah," Mona said, pinching her shirt away from her body. "They're putting on a show for you."

Ariel crossed her arms, felt her heart still racing. "Mom?" she asked.

Her mom looked at her. "What?"

"Do you think you could put the gun down? You're making me nervous."

"Oh, this thing?" Her mother opened her mouth and pointed the gun inside. Before Ariel could do anything, her mother pulled the trigger. Water squirted out.

Ariel had been ready to scream. "Jesus. You scared me."

Mona smiled, clearly pleased. "Looks real, huh? Gideon and I picked it up at the church rummage sale. You wouldn't believe some of the stuff there—bear traps, bowie knives. A pickled thumb in a jar. The people in this town, I swear."

"Wait, Gideon's here?" Around Ariel, the room shifted slightly.

"Where else would he be?"

"I don't know—I figured he would have moved on."

"Believe it or not, he likes it here."

Ariel felt dizzy. She needed to sit.

Her mom was still pinching her shirt away from her body. "Listen, I'm beat. And covered in pee. Can we talk in the morning?"

"Sure, that's a good idea." Morning. It seemed a million years away.

"I guess you can sleep on the couch. I'm not sure if any of the extra blankets are clean. I wasn't expecting you."

"It's fine. Really."

"I gave your room to the cats," she said, her tone brisk and unapologetic, proud almost, as if she were confessing to a crime she didn't regret.

"I saw—it's not a problem."

"It just seemed a waste, to leave it empty for so long."

"That's all right. I'm glad the cats like it."

"They do like it. It's their own space."

"That's good."

"And you weren't using it."

"I know."

"Well, all right, then."

For a moment they stared at each other, the last six years like a line of fire between them. Ariel remembered a time long ago, when her mother was braiding her hair for school and had whispered in her ear, *One day, when I'm a little old lady, you can braid my hair just like this.* At the time, Ariel had assumed this vision of the future would come true, that she and her mother would always be together. How could they not? Many nights as a girl, she would lie in bed, thinking about the death of her mother. The infinity of death. The infinity of infinity. It had panicked her, to think of a world that did not contain her mother, the person who most thoroughly knew the story of Ariel's life. Sometimes she would lie in bed, sobbing at the mere idea of it. Now the intensity of this feeling was so foreign as to be almost impossible. What had happened to all that love? Where did it go?

"It's good to see you, Mom," Ariel said. She thought of the photo in her bag, the cat water fountain, but the moment didn't feel right.

Mona hadn't moved from her spot at the end of the hall, and Ariel hadn't moved from hers. "If the dogs get fussy, you can unlock the dog door. I assume you closed the front gate?"

"I did."

"Good girl." With this, her mother disappeared up the stairs to her bedroom, Daisy and Katydid and all the other dogs trailing behind her like a tiny parade.

Deep down, she had known her mother would still be

angry—certainly, if she wasn't, she would have tried to contact Ariel by now—but a part of her, a small, secret part, had hoped, despite everything, that her mother would see her and forgive her, that she would take Ariel into her arms and say: *I'm so glad you're back—I've missed you every day.* She understood, now, that this dream was exactly that. A dream. They hadn't even hugged.

Ever since she'd left, Ariel had missed the sanctuary with a longing so severe it often felt like a kind of physical withdrawal, a tightness and irritation of the body she'd experienced only once before, when she'd tried to give up coffee. In Lawrence, she'd yearned for a dog. Just one dog, and then maybe a cat or two—a healthy, normal number of animals for someone in her early twenties. When she first raised the idea with Dex, he'd dismissed it. *I'm just not into them,* he'd said, by which he'd meant, Ariel assumed, *I don't want to be responsible for another living thing right now.* And that was that. She'd dropped it, worried that adopting a dog might activate a genetic chain reaction that would eventually manifest in the same sickness as her mother's. And what was Mona's illness, exactly? Ariel had never found the right words to describe her mother. She wasn't a hoarder, per se, because she only accumulated animals, and even then she didn't keep them in the house—at least not all of them. And it wasn't just that she loved animals. It seemed, at times, that Mona felt a religious impulse to help them, though she never talked explicitly about God. Ariel recalled a time her mother had nearly driven them into a ditch, to avoid hitting a baby raccoon. When Ariel accused her of almost wrecking the car, she'd said, *What if that had been a human baby crawling across the road? It's the same thing.* The logic had bothered Ariel for days until, like a gear clicking into place, she'd realized it troubled her not because she didn't agree with it, but because she did.

The three of them—Ariel, her mom, and her dad—moved to

St. Clare from Wichita when Ariel was seven. Mona had always talked about running an animal sanctuary, but Ariel figured it was empty grown-up chatter, like when her father talked about opening a café that sold ice cream and poetry. And yet, a few months after the death of her grandpa, a man she'd never met but whom she'd always pictured with a long gray beard and hair coming out of his nose, a moving truck appeared. Everything they owned was put into boxes and sealed with tape.

Weeks before the move, Ariel had gone into tantrum mode—she didn't want to leave Wichita, leave their house, their street, her school. She liked her teachers and had a best friend, Celia Bradbury, in whom she confided all her secrets and dreams. It was the only life she knew, and leaving it felt like a death. And yet, as soon as she and her parents loaded into her dad's old Windstar minivan, all the terror and sorrow turned to excitement. She'd recently finished *Little House on the Prairie* and realized she was just like Laura Ingalls Wilder, moving out into the grasslands, the place where the buffalo lived. Lying across the back seat, she closed her eyes and imagined the van was a wagon and Ma and Pa were taking her west.

The first thing she did after they pulled down the long, winding driveway was run straight into the grass, her arms outstretched, the sky an open page above her. A butterfly landed on her shoulder, and she took this as a sign of her life to come.

Those early days, before the animals arrived, she had her parents mostly to herself. The only dogs were Peanut Butter and Jelly, the gray-muzzled black Labs Ariel had known since she was a baby. After the move, the five of them would take long walks down Sanctuary Road, Mona teaching her bird calls and the names of different clouds, her father reciting lines of poetry he could never quite remember. At night, Mona would read to her, Peanut Butter and Jelly curled at her feet.

And then the first rescues arrived—four pit mixes from a kill shelter in Tulsa. Ariel's affection for the new dogs, like her affection for Peanut Butter and Jelly, was immediate and pure. She found herself drawn to the dogs at odd hours of the day, sneaking out in the middle of the night to visit them. She would slip into their pens and curl up beside them, rub her thumb along the soft pads of their feet. It was not just that she wanted to be with the dogs; she wanted to *be* a dog, to live among them, to spend her days running and rolling in mud, eating her food from a bowl, no hands. She wanted people to pet her, to coo over her, to brush the brambles from her hair. She wanted to cuddle at her mother's feet, roll belly-up for a tummy rub. She even tried the dogs' kibble, which was dry and chalky and tasted like old bread and dirt. When she requested to drink like a dog, Mona played along; for nearly a year, Ariel lapped her apple juice from a plastic saucer her mother set before her each morning. All the while, Ariel's father watched on, his mouth pinched with disapproval.

Ariel never knew quite how to read her father, who felt even more mysterious and inaccessible than the dogs; sometimes, she wished he had a tail to wag, so she could know when he was happy. He was a quiet person, requiring lots of alone time in which to read and write and stare into space, brow furrowed. This quietness did not seem to match his body, which was large and powerful, his torso as wide and sturdy as the grandfather clock in the living room, his hands thick and hard-knuckled, more like pieces of pottery than the hands of a poet. When Ariel was very little, this size translated directly to love— he was her safe keeper, her protector. He could swoop her into a hug so consuming that nothing, not even the light, could get in. They were family.

In the beginning, he had seemed happy with the move. He would wake early and drink his coffee on the porch, a notebook opened on his lap. In the afternoons, he would take the dogs on a walk down Sanctuary Road, going two at a time so that everyone got a turn. Eventually, when there were too many dogs, he stopped going for walks altogether. *If I can't take them all, then I won't take any.*

Over time, he grew more and more indifferent to the dogs— tolerant but not affectionate. He would allow them to sit beside him on the couch while he watched a baseball game, but he would no longer let them lick his face or rest their heads in his lap. After one of the dogs chewed up a manuscript he'd left on the table—he was always finishing manuscripts and then throwing them away in a huff of frustration—he stopped petting them completely.

A few months before he left, Ariel heard her parents fighting. They did not fight often, but when they did, it was like a thunderstorm, rolling in slowly, changing the quality of the air, and then filling the house with electricity.

"Why am I so cold?" her father had asked. "Maybe it's because my wife cares more about a bunch of dogs than she does about her own family."

"That is *not* true," her mother had said, but Ariel could hear the uncertainty in her voice.

"You certainly spend more time with them," her father had countered.

"If I was a doctor or a lawyer—if I was gone all day at a fancy office, nobody would say a word. Or if I was a man! If I was a man, nobody would say I work too much, that I don't spend enough time with my family. But because I'm a woman, because it's animals, because it doesn't bring in a big paycheck—suddenly I'm a heartless villain. I'm a bad mother. A bad *wife*." After a few beats of silence, she added, "I will not apologize for taking pleasure in my work. You get to hide out in your studio all day, writing poems you don't even let me read, but nobody calls you a bad husband, a bad father."

The house had gone quiet then.

"I never called you a bad mother."

"You certainly implied it."

"You're putting words in my mouth."

"And you," said her mother, "are putting an untrue story onto our lives."

Ariel had thought about this accusation for days. An untrue story. Wasn't it true that, once the animals came along, her mother had less time for Ariel and her father? After the first dogs arrived, her mother had stopped reading to Ariel at night. "You should practice reading on your own," she'd reasoned. Ariel didn't mind, at least not in the beginning. If she ever felt lonely or bored, she would join her mother in her chores: cleaning the dogs' cages, taking them for walks, brushing their fur and tossing the tufts of hair into the wind where, her mother teased, they would stick into the ground and grow a prairie of dogs.

But, over the years, her mother had grown more obsessed with her work, less interested in family life. When Ariel was ten, her teacher assigned a project in which everyone had to interview their personal hero. Ariel decided to interview her mother. When she told her mom about the interview, Mona said she was busy. She was taking a nonprofit management class at Middleton Community College; someone had left a pair of very sick goats tied to the sanctuary gate. The weekend would be better. When the weekend arrived, Ariel asked her mother again, and again it was not a good time. Mona now had a paper to write, and a meeting with an insurance agent, and a Girl Scout troop coming to volunteer. Things went on like this for another week, until suddenly Ariel's assignment was due. The morning before school, Ariel jotted off the interview herself, answering the questions how she imagined her mother might.

Q: What makes you different from other people?

A: I'm very strong, smart, and can speak to most animals, but especially dogs, who have no accent (unlike birds) and understand English perfectly. Sometimes the cats understand me but don't listen anyway, because they are snobs!

Q: If you had to give one piece of advice, what would it be?

A: If an animal bites you, squeeze the blood out a little before putting on a Band-Aid because that way the germs won't go back into your body.

A week later, her teacher confronted her about the assignment. "Ariel, did your mother really say these things?" she asked, standing with Ariel after the lunch bell had rung.

Ariel's cheeks turned red, her skin burning. "No," she whispered, for she was not, at that point, any good at lying.

"Did you write these responses yourself?"

Ariel nodded.

"And why did you do that?"

"My mom was busy," she said, wondering, for the first time, if there was something wrong with her mother.

"And what about your dad? Was he not around to ask?"

How could Ariel explain that her dad was not to be bothered with these sorts of things?

"I'm sorry," Ariel said to her teacher. "I didn't mean to cheat."

Her teacher frowned, a look Ariel interpreted as disapproval until she said, "It's not your fault, sweetie. You did a very nice job."

Now, in her mother's living room, she made a nest of blankets and pillows on the floor. She had always hated the plastic couch, which reminded her of a giant rubber dog toy, coated with dried slobber and who knew what else. For a while, she lay still, listening. A cat knocked something over in the kitchen and then skittered away. Something spooked a donkey, who brayed a long, soulful complaint. One of the dogs in the pens howled, sending a few others into a fit of concerned whimpering until the sanctuary finally settled into silence. She thought about Opal, her wolfhound. Her best friend, her sister. Heartbreak hounds, they were called, for they rarely survived into the double digits. Ariel knew Opal had likely passed away while she was busy partying her way out of college. What had she been doing, she wondered, the moment Opal died? Taking a shot of tequila with Dex? Singing karaoke with Sunny? She knew that if Opal were still here, she would have forgiven Ariel in a heartbeat.

She was nearly asleep when a dog came to lie beside her. Eyes closed, Ariel allowed herself to imagine it was Opal, with her pretty black eyes and her white-gray beard that smelled vaguely metallic. The serious way she would stare at Ariel, as if to say: *Human, do you know I love you?* When Ariel opened her eyes, she saw a cattle dog, small and brown with a rubbery nose like a bear's. He yawned and stretched his forelegs into Ariel's belly. She ran a hand across the dog's side, feeling the warmth of his body, the matted spots in his fur, the bumps of his ribs.

"Sweet boy," she said.

The dog licked his lips, as if trying to taste the last moment of the day, and then closed his eyes for sleep.

Ariel closed her eyes but couldn't sleep. She was anxious for the morning, to see her mother again. To see Gideon. To know that he was only a short walk away—out the mudroom door, past the barn, to the shady spot behind the crab apple trees where he kept his RV, the Man Van. Just thinking of it made her woozy. She wondered if she would still find him attractive, or if the years had worn him down like they had her mother. If he would still find *her* attractive.

Over the years, she'd checked the Bright Side's website to see if Gideon had stayed but could find no clues one way or the other. As she'd packed her bag in Lawrence, she'd found herself reaching for her lace underwear, her red bra, even, ridiculously, a black velvet skirt. The truth was that, on the slight chance Gideon was still at the Bright Side, she did not want Dex around when she saw him.

Dex

By seven o'clock, Dex and Buddy were three beers deep at the Replay, the bar where Dex sometimes deejayed and where Buddy tended bar. Buddy was a terrible bartender, known for doubling tips and letting pretty girls drink for free, but he showed up when he needed to and stayed past closing to clean—mostly because it made him feel like part of something—and so the manager kept him on.

Dex's secret was that he hated drinking in the early-evening hours, before the bar filled up with movement and sound. This time of night, when normal people were eating dinner, the Replay was not a funky, rollicking party den but a hovel that reeked of stale beer, the bathrooms of urine. Oddly shaped stains scarred the dance floor. Middle-aged men played pinball and nursed cans of Rolling Rock, slowly working themselves up to a state of drunkenness. As much as he loved the Replay, it sometimes depressed him.

Buddy, too, sometimes depressed him. He was known to go days in the same novelty T-shirt (among his favorites: a neon tank top that read *My favorite book is beer*). Today, he wore a green V-neck under the kind of nude, cable-knit cardigan favored by old ladies and Mr. Rogers. The V-neck was wrinkled, and something that may have been ketchup made a squiggly, heart-monitor line from one nipple to the other. His breath smelled like onion and peanut butter, but he was willing to slam tallboys until Dex felt less lonely, and so Dex told him he looked nice.

"I always look nice," Buddy said. And then, "Any updates on the wedding?"

Ever since the engagement, Buddy brought up the wedding constantly, perhaps hoping Dex might eventually say he'd called off the whole thing.

"It hasn't even been a month since I proposed."

"Don't people plan this shit years in advance?"

"We're both really busy right now."

Buddy looked at Dex and then examined the bar, as if to say: *Yeah, this is busy.* "You getting cold feet? Thinking about running off to Mexico with a good pal, opening a mango stand on the beach?"

Dex rolled his eyes. He thought about the brief thrill of their engagement (more than nine hundred likes on his Facebook post), followed by its sudden denouement. How disappointing, that the world went on regardless of their love. That the birds did not sing, that Big Carl the town madman was still mad, that the alleyway behind the barbershop still smelled like urine. But maybe this was just the way it went. He had been accused of taking his love, his feelings, too seriously, most often by the women who had refused to reciprocate said feelings. *You can't go around thinking your love is more important than everyone else's love*, a girl had once told him. *The world's just going to break your heart.* But who was she, anyway? A Wilco song? He'd recently seen a picture of her on Facebook in an Applebee's uniform.

"So where's Ariel?" Buddy asked.

"St. Clare," Dex said. "Some bumfuck town in western Kansas. She's from there."

"And she's just visiting?"

"I'm not exactly sure. She and her mom have been on the outs—they haven't talked in a while. She's there to make amends."

"How long's a while?"

"Like, since high school?"

Buddy took a swig of his beer. "Jesus. I call my mom like every day."

"I'm sure she loves that."

"She does. I'm her precious Baby Buddy Boy." Buddy pulled out a pack of American Spirits. "So what happened? With her mom?"

"I don't know the exact details, but I think her mom's an animal hoarder or something. They had a falling-out when Ariel was eighteen."

"About what?"

Dex shrugged. "Ariel doesn't like to talk about it, and I've learned not to ask. All I know is that she left and now she feels guilty about it."

"Huh. So they haven't talked for *years* and all of a sudden she's going home?"

"She wants to tell her mom about the wedding—she wants her to be there."

Buddy raised an eyebrow. "And she didn't ask you to come with?"

"I wouldn't have wanted to go." In truth, had she asked him, he would have been excited to tag along. This was his future mother-in-law, after all. He wanted to meet her.

"All right," Buddy said. "So she's visiting her mom."

"Would you stop it?"

"Stop what?"

"You know what. You're trying to get me worked up."

"I'm just making conversation, exploring the facts at hand."

Dex knew better than to buy into Buddy's paranoia, but Ariel *had* been acting weird lately. He blamed Donald Trump. Sometimes Dex would catch her looking at him, a shimmer of contempt in her eyes, as if his penis alone had engineered the electoral college. He understood that, in the circles they ran in, this was not a good time to be a man.

"You think she's hiding something?" Dex asked.

Buddy tilted his head back and released a snake of smoke—technically, smoking wasn't allowed on the patio, but Buddy had never been big on rules. He brought full pizzas into movie theaters, went to weddings in sneakers and jeans. When he ran out of clean silverware, he would walk into a fast-food restaurant, buy nothing, and leave with a handful of plastic cutlery. "I mean, maybe. I don't know. She's your girlfriend."

"Fiancée."

"Whatever. You know her better than I do. Does she usually make stuff up?"

"I don't know. No. Not that I know of."

"That's the crazy thing. It's worse if she's a liar and you don't know, because that means she's good at it."

"She's not a sociopath, if that's what you're saying."

"I'm just talking." Buddy waved a hand through the air, scattering his smoke. "I'm sure she's fine. And anyways, she's not gone for very long. So no matter where she is, what she's doing, *who* she's doing, she'll be back before anything too weird can happen. Right?"

"What do you mean *who* she's doing?"

Buddy laughed. "You're adorable, Dex. People cheat, you know? Happens all the time."

"No, it doesn't."

"Listen to me. It does. *All the time.* You think I don't know about these things? I know about these things. I know *people.*"

Dex understood that Buddy *was* the people. The only girl Buddy had ever truly loved, Miranda, had stepped out of his life without so much as a single red flag. One day she was there, the next she was gone. Abracadabra. She ignored Buddy's phone calls and blocked him on Facebook, where she had begun to post an avalanche of pictures of her new boyfriend, a clean-shaven flight attendant named Trevor. All these years later, Buddy had yet to move on. Instead, he'd become obsessed with his victimhood, distrusting all women but continuing to pursue them with a ravenous desire only Miranda herself could have slaked. He'd become the sleazy guy at the bar, the one with sour whiskey breath who tried to sneak glances down women's shirts. He pushed women to reject him, to validate his theory that all women were evil, not just Miranda, and therefore their breakup had nothing to do with him. Meanwhile, he continued to use Miranda's Netflix and sometimes forwarded spam to her email address. Like this, Dex had watched the long, slow drama of Buddy's downward spiral, knowing not at all how to stop it, grateful it wasn't happening to him.

Now Buddy had freaked Dex out. This was no great accomplishment, as Dex was often worried when it came to Ariel. Being with her felt like standing on the edge of a precipice, as if, at any moment, a gust of wind might send him toppling into an abyss much like the one into which Miranda had pushed Buddy. It was not that Ariel didn't love him but that he knew their loves were unequal. His love was a mountain; hers was a flower, timid and unfolding only when conditions were just right. Sometimes, when he kissed her on the cheek in the morning, she would keep her eyes on whatever novel she was reading, as if she were post–Novocain injection and hadn't felt the pressure of his lips. For her birthday, he'd bought her a pair of turquoise earrings. For his, she'd bought him a shot that tasted like vanilla cake.

He knew part of it was how she'd been raised. For instance, their first Christmas together, when Dex asked what she wanted, she'd looked at him, confused. "You want to get me a present?"

"Well, yeah. It's Christmas. And I love you."

"I've just never done the whole Christmas thing."

"Because you're Jewish? It could be a Hanukkah present."

"It's not that. We just never did that kind of stuff when I was a kid. I mean, we did when I was really little, but after we moved—" Here she had gone quiet, shrugged. "We just didn't do gifts. That's all."

He eventually learned that, growing up, she had not watched MTV or participated in sleepovers. She had never eaten a fast-food hamburger, ridden on a roller coaster, or flown on an airplane. They made a sort of game of it, called "What Didn't Ariel Do?" "Chuck E. Cheese?" he would say, and she would shake her head. "Laser tag?" *No.* "Pop Rocks?" *No.* "Pokémon cards?" This one made her laugh so hard she nearly spat out her La Croix. It sometimes felt as if she'd grown up in a hole and that Dex was a rung on the ladder leading out of it.

They'd met when she was a freshman and had been together ever since. Because of this, he often feared she was only with him because she had confused loyalty with love. Sometimes, if he was feeling down, he could think of nothing to justify her wanting to be with him. He had three jobs—spinning at the Replay, cutting hair at the barbershop, and tending to the garden at New Springs retirement home—but none were professionally impressive for a man of thirty. He had no benefits, no savings, no car. He was handsome, but not as handsome as he used to be. He was funny—yes. That was the one thing he had. He could make Ariel laugh and, by doing so, fend off the dark moods to which she sometimes fell prey. He could pop on a record, put a beer in her hand, and shimmy her around the living room until she had no choice but to smile, rest her cheek on his shoulder. He was *romantic.* And, God damn it, he loved her, which was no small thing in a world where many people went unloved. People like Buddy, he thought, and then felt ashamed for thinking it.

"So what am I supposed to do?" Dex asked.

Buddy shrugged. "Nothing, man. You drink beers with me, you wait for her to come home. As long as she left all her shit behind, you're in the clear. No woman runs off for good without her clothes. And like I said, she can't do anything too weird in a weekend. Right?"

Ariel

In the morning, Ariel found her mother in the kitchen making pancakes. Growing up, the choices for breakfast had been oatmeal, cereal, or yogurt—quick vegetarian meals that required little effort. Some mornings everyone just ate a piece of peanut butter toast on the way out the door. These pancakes were happening for Ariel's benefit. Her mother was trying to welcome her.

"Need help?" Ariel asked.

Mona kept her eyes on the griddle. "It's Bisquick, not astrophysics." Daisy danced at her mother's feet, toenails clicking against the hardwood, a fresh magenta diaper around her waist.

"How about coffee?"

"Already brewing."

"Anything else I can do?"

Mona glanced at her. "Go be helpful somewhere else—you're making me nervous."

Ariel turned to assess the kitchen. On the counter, she found her father's old Humpty-Dumpty cookie jar. When she lifted the lid, she discovered a layer of cookies so green with mold she could hardly tell they were cookies at all. She quickly replaced Humpty's head.

Mona eyed her. "Something wrong in the cookie jar?"

"Nope," Ariel said, clasping her hands behind her back.

It was this sort of detail that had prevented Ariel from inviting people over when she was younger. In the way children are prescient to the hardships of others, her classmates had understood the squalor of Ariel's home without ever having seen it: they could smell it on her, detect it from her clothes. Many of them were farm children, versed in the rhythms of hard labor and animal care, but while their parents' work turned wheat into bread, pigs into pork, and cows into beef, her mother's work amounted to nothing more than hard work, shit, and food stamps.

During recess, Ariel would sit alone, scanning the sky for birds or feeding saltine crackers to squirrels. At lunch, she read books in the counselor's office or hid in the smelly slice of darkness between the dumpsters. When her fourth-grade teacher asked her class to write an essay about their best friend, Ariel had composed a paper about Peanut Butter and Jelly. Only when it was her turn to read her assignment out loud did she understand the grave error she had made. By the time she was in middle school, her classmates were saying that her mother liked to have sex with animals, that her father liked to watch. That her mother fed Ariel dog food, and they all went potty in a baby pool filled with kitty litter.

"They're idiots," Mona said when Ariel told her what was going on at school, how in PE all the other girls had gotten together and written a note to Coach Kell, requesting that Ariel change in a separate locker room because of the ringworm on her ankles. "Just wait until you're older. Everyone will think you're cool because you grew up here."

Ariel had believed her mother, for she wanted, more than anything, to have friends—to go to football games and field parties and sleepovers, to walk down the hallway arm in arm with a line of girls, a matching friendship bracelet on her wrist. And yet, the more she wanted friends, the more vehemently her classmates denied her. When at last she realized the pecking order had been established and she was fated to remain alone at the bottom, she gave up altogether and doubled down on her studies. And then Sydney Fuller had arrived. Aside from the animals, he had been her first real friend in St. Clare.

At the stove, her mother turned to her. "You know, if it's money you're after, you're barking up the wrong tree."

Ariel managed to keep from laughing. "No offense, but this is the last place I'd go looking for money."

"Then why are you here?"

"I heard about the fire, about the sanctuary going up for sale."

Her mother was quiet. "Well, how long are you planning to stay? I saw your bags in the hall. Looks like you're ready to travel around the world."

"I don't know. I don't know how to do something like this."

"Here's the thing," Mona said, pointing the spatula at Ariel. "If you're here, you work. This isn't a bed-and-breakfast."

"So *that's* why there wasn't a pillow mint." She smiled self-consciously. This was the kind of thing Dex excelled at—awkward moments, jokes, apologies. People stuff.

"I'm serious, Ariel. We've got a lot going on—I'm at my breaking point."

Ariel swallowed her smile. "I'll help. Anything you need, anything the animals need, I'm here."

"All right," her mother said. "If you're here, you're here." She transferred a stack of pancakes onto a plastic plate. "Now come eat before Daisy gets any ideas."

The kitchen table was a mess of bills, receipts, old newspapers, and empty cans of cat food. As Ariel pushed everything onto one side of the table, she held her breath, waiting for a comment—*My house isn't clean enough for the college princess?*—but her mother said nothing.

"You're not pregnant, are you?" Mona asked, setting the pancakes onto the table. "Because there's a population crisis on this planet, and if we're not headed for nuclear apocalypse then we're certainly headed for water wars. This is no time to raise a child. If you ask me, it's the most ecologically irresponsible thing a person can do."

"I'm not pregnant," Ariel said. She put a hand on her stomach—she *had* been eating a lot of cookies since the election.

"Are you sick?"

"I told you, I saw about the fire and I was worried. I knew you must be terrified. And then seeing the sanctuary up for sale. Things feel—different." She wasn't ready to tell her mom about Sydney, about how she'd hurt him all those years ago. How she worried this hurt had led to the fire.

"Things are different," Mona said. "And I am terrified. Which is why you can't just waltz in here expecting everything to be all hugs and apologies. You left us. Left me." Her voice cracked, a crack that seemed to surprise her as much as it surprised Ariel. "And those post-cards you sent. As if that was some grand gesture."

She was referring to the cards Ariel sent each year on her birthday, each one inscribed with the same message: *I'm still alive. Please don't worry about me.* In the beginning, she'd sent one every week, per Gideon's suggestion. *If you're too afraid to call, you need to at least write her.* Each card was torn from a postcard book titled *Pretty Pigs Around the World.* Every year, Ariel grew dizzy as she slipped the card into the outgoing slot, wondering what exactly happened when it reached the Bright Side.

"I'm sorry," Ariel began. "Can we just assume that every time I say anything, I'm following it up with *I'm sorry?*"

"You know, my mom used to have this saying. She'd say: 'Mona, sorry is like a sponge. You can use it to clean up your messes, but the more you use it, the dirtier it gets.'" Mona cleared her throat, returned to the stove. "Do you have a job, then?"

"Yes," Ariel said, happy for the change of subject. "At an animal clinic."

Mona looked at her, a flash of pride in her eyes. "You're a vet?"

Ariel did not want to disappoint her mother, and yet she also did not want to lie. "I work at the front desk. I help with the animals when the doctor needs it."

"Oh," Mona said, her voiced edged with disappointment. "Well, it's good you're around animals."

What Ariel didn't tell her mother was that the job at the clinic was the best she could find without a degree. Occasionally, Dr. Nguyen let her help with sedations or vaccinations, but mostly she handled scheduling, billing, and cleaned up messes, walked dogs, changed bedding. She was careless about returning phone calls and would sometimes drift away while Dr. Nguyen was explaining something to her, but she was known for being able to calm even the most aggressive animals. "Go get Ariel," she would often hear Dr. Nguyen say, and one of the vet techs would appear in the lobby with a look of horror on her face, maybe a streak of blood on her hand or wrist, which meant that Ariel was to go into the office and subdue whatever animal was trying to bite them. Each time she felt a dog's heart steady beneath her palm, she thought of what her mother used to say: *An animal will never hurt you so long as it knows you love it.*

"Can I ask why you're selling the sanctuary?" Ariel asked cautiously.

Her mother wouldn't look at her. "I filed for bankruptcy in 2013, but my debt just keeps piling. I'm abandoning ship. Game over."

"What about the money from your dad?"

"Dried up a long time ago."

"There aren't any donors you can ask?"

"The donors are the problem—we've had some bad media. All these internet sites, I don't know what happens on them. Apparently, bad news spread about the sanctuary and now nobody wants to give us money. They think we're mistreating the animals."

Over the years, Ariel had googled the Bright Side and come across a few of these articles—bloggers writing about their time volunteering, how the animals were ill and underfed. How the pens were disgusting. *What would you rather be, dirty or dead?* Ariel had commented on one of the blogs, but then deleted it right away.

"So there's really nothing you can do?"

"I tried to make it work for as long as I could, but there's nothing left. The new name of the game is homing animals before the property sells. We've got an adoption fair next week—fingers crossed everyone wants a dog for Christmas."

"What about the rest of the animals? What'll happen to them?" She wondered, for the first time, if her mother actually *wanted* to sell the sanctuary. The thought was difficult to process, like imagining a clock that had grown tired of ticking.

"Suddenly you care?"

"I do," Ariel said, her heart sinking. "I do care. That's why I'm here."

Her mother looked at her doubtfully.

Just then, the door to the mudroom swung open and there was Gideon. Corduroy pants and a worn Yosemite National Park T-shirt. Red Wing work boots. Glasses, beard, sports watch. Time had touched everything but the details. He was almost thirty now, a grown version of the young man she remembered. His muscles had filled out, his facial hair had thickened. Ariel felt her chest turn to helium, her heart a hummingbird trapped in a hot balloon.

He stared at Ariel and then cleared his throat. "What's she doing here?" he asked Mona, as if Ariel were behind a soundproof wall.

Mona shrugged, slid the spatula under a pancake. "She says she's not pregnant."

"I'm not pregnant," Ariel said.

Gideon rubbed his chin. He would not meet her eyes. She noticed that his hand, ever so slightly, was shaking. "Mona, I think I'll go start feeding everyone if that's all right."

"You're not hungry?"

"I'll eat later."

Ariel heard the words he did not say—*when she's not here.* "I can help you with feeding," she offered, her body practically on fire. She could hear her heart pounding in her head. "If you want."

Before the screen door snapped shut behind him, Gideon called out, "Don't."

Like the rest of the animals, Gideon had come to the Bright Side because he had nowhere better to go. The day after Ariel's father left, Mona put an ad in a dozen papers within a hundred-mile radius. Because she had to pay by the word, the ad read only: *Help w/animals, room included.*

For more than a year, the Bright Side became a revolving door of workers. There were the free-love Burning Man types who thought working on an animal sanctuary meant smoking weed and cuddling kittens. They'd last a week, maybe two. Once, a woman named Thistle ate a handful of magic mushrooms and crawled into the sheep pen. Mona found her the next morning, naked and licking a salt block, her body covered in plum-colored welts from where the sheep had rammed her. "Euphoric," she kept repeating, as Mona dragged her back to the pea-green Volkswagen van in which she'd arrived. Then there were the hipsters who wanted to get in touch with the land, to replace their smartphones and tablets with shovels and pitchforks. At one point, Ariel developed a crush on a guy from Boulder who introduced her to indie music and Proust and who had a tattoo on his forearm that read, *If found, return to Walden Pond.* He was working on a screenplay and could often be heard crying at night. Whenever she heard him crying, Mona would roll her eyes. "You'd think we were beating him."

And then, the summer before Ariel's sophomore year of high school, the same summer she and Sydney stopped talking, Gideon rumbled up their driveway in an old Datsun that reeked of gasoline, wearing tan Carhartts and a baseball cap that read, *Potato Creek State Park*. He was nineteen but looked, to Ariel, like someone who had already lived a whole life. She would later learn that the day after he finished high school, his parents had moved back to Mexico, to be near their own parents as they aged. Instead of following them, Gideon set out to travel the country, working seasonal jobs in national parks, odd jobs in between. He picked oranges in California, harvested shell-fish in Washington. He considered moving to Mexico City, where his parents now lived, but he had never lived in a big city and the idea of it did not appeal to him. What he wanted was a place he could love as much as he loved his parents, a place that could feel like home, that could convince him to stay in America. Perhaps when he saw Ariel, not yet sixteen years old, quiet and dark-eyed in her mother's kitchen, he saw something else he wanted, too.

"Do you like animals?" was Mona's question.

"Do I like them?" Gideon had asked. "I am one. We all are." When he saw this did not impress Mona, he added that he knew horses—his dad, an elementary school teacher, had worked weekends at a horse barn for extra money. "I'm a trained farrier. I could trim your horses today if you wanted."

Ariel could see the interest pique in Mona's eyes. The horses and donkeys were due for a trim, their hooves oblong and thick, causing them to walk like drunkards. Still, she went ahead with the second part of the test. She held out her hand for a handshake. What she really wanted was to feel Gideon's palms, his skin. She was done with the vagabonds, the hippies, the undergrads. She wanted someone who would work.

Ariel could see in his eyes that he was a hard worker. They were eyes that wanted to be tired, to go to bed at night in so much physical pain there was nothing to think about except getting the body to sleep so that it might work again come morning.

After giving his hand a few firm pumps, Mona told him he could start right away; they needed help hauling donations. Gideon rolled up his sleeves and followed Mona down the driveway, where boxes of cat food sat baking in the midsummer heat.

Like this, Gideon became Ariel's coworker, twice as hardworking as they could have hoped for. Ariel sometimes wondered if her mother saw it as a productive business trade, Ariel's father for Gideon. Her husband for a ranch hand.

"I didn't sign up for this," her father had once said to Mona. It was the night before Ariel's first day of high school, and she was in her room, trying to find an outfit that wasn't coated in animal hair. "I signed up to be your husband and the father to your child, but not this. You wanted animals, I let you have them. But now look at this place. It's a zoo."

"You *let* me have them?" was all Mona had said in response.

When he came into Ariel's room to say good night—just good night, not goodbye—he asked if she wanted to know a secret.

"What is it?" Ariel had asked.

"I'm allergic to cats," he said. "Every morning, I take a pill. It makes me drowsy. Gives me headaches. Sometimes I can't do my work because my head is filled with fog—I just sit at my desk, staring."

As if summoned by the complaint, a kitten named Stripers jumped onto Ariel's bed and began to knead her quilt, a maneuver Mona called making biscuits. Her father simply stared at the kitten, as if considering a spider.

"I'm thinking of going on a little vacation soon," he said, staring at the cat.

"Where?"

"I don't know—where are there no cats?"

"Antarctica?"

"Too cold—but maybe."

"Can I come?" Ariel asked. She couldn't tell if he was joking—he was wearing a strange look, as if he'd rehearsed this conversation and it was going eerily as planned.

"You've got school," he said. "Next time."

"Promise?"

He smiled at her, a sad smile. "Promise." He kissed her on the cheek then, something he never did—he was a hugger, not a kisser. Without looking back, he left her room, Stripers following merrily behind him.

. In the morning, his earthenware coffee mug was on the table, his muck boots by the door, but his minivan was gone. Her mother was in the kitchen, drinking coffee, but when Ariel looked in her eyes, she could see a thunderstorm of fear, lightning crashing each time she blinked.

"Did Dad leave?" Ariel asked. At this point, he was already living in Blue House, the ramshackle tiny home he'd constructed on the opposite side of the property the year Ariel turned eleven. Although he claimed the space was a writing studio, Ariel knew it was really a haven away from the house. Still, he always joined them for breakfast.

Her mother traced an eyebrow and looked out the window, at the pasture, as if maybe he were out there, had been out there the whole time, walking figure eights like he sometimes did when he was stuck on a poem. She nodded.

"It's not just a vacation, is it?"

"I'm sorry, Ariel," she said. And then: "Come here." She opened her arms and Ariel fell into them. She was relieved to feel herself melt into her mother: the smell of her vanilla Suave shampoo, the familiar tang of her sweat. Ariel felt a sudden surge of longing, a bubble rising up through her chest and into her throat. They hadn't hugged like this in months.

"Don't let him ruin your big day," Mona said, squeezing back. "High school's a whole other world."

Ariel had nodded into her mother's shoulder, her tears staining her shirt.

Of course it ruined her day. She cried all through first period, then second. It was Sydney who put an arm around her during lunch, leading her outside so she could emote in the privacy of the small, grassy courtyard, and it was Sydney who brought her a stack of napkins so she could wipe her eyes. "Get it all out," he said, patting her on the back, somewhat roughly, as if burping a baby.

A week, then two, then three. There were no letters from her father, no phone calls. Ariel tried to look him up on the computer at school but could find nothing. Dozens of men shared his name.

It seemed impossible that he wouldn't return, but as weeks became months, she realized it was more than possible—it was reality. History was filled with fathers going out for cigarettes and never coming back. She had made the mistake of thinking her father was different.

She could understand why he wanted to leave the sanctuary; she could even understand why he wanted to leave her mother. But she could not, no matter which way she turned it, understand how he could want to leave her. She was his daughter, his only child. She was supposed to have been his world. She began to think that had she only been more intelligent, more beautiful, more likable, maybe then he would have stayed. Had she been a better writer, a better poet. Had she been more like him and less like Mona. Some nights, all of her self-loathing and fear and disgust would swirl in her mind until the only thing that brought relief was to take a hot match and press it into her wrist, where a tiny mound of scar tissue eventually formed. This was her ritual, how she kept her thoughts at bay.

And then, like a crack of thunder after months of drought, Gideon appeared.

On weekends, she would wake to find him making sopapillas in the kitchen, the radio burping up bluegrass. On these mornings, he was not a ranch hand. He did not live in the old camper van out by Blue House, the same van in which her parents had long ago driven all the way to the Grand Canyon so that Mona could mount an animal-rights campaign against the Park Service after watching a young boy kick a squirrel off the rim (or so her father had once told her). On these mornings, he did not receive an embarrassingly low paycheck that Mona delivered only after big donations, and only if nothing needed immediate fixing. On these mornings, Gideon was only himself, with his crooked black-rimmed glasses and a scar on his arm from where a swan bit him when he was a boy. He was the person who called her Kangaroo, because she wore loose hoodies with large pockets in the front where she could hide her hands, raw and bloody from where she gnawed her cuticles. On the sopapilla mornings, they were both their most basic selves. She would help him roll out the dough, and then they would stand together, mesmerized as the soft mounds of sweetness sizzled in oil. Later, she would think of sopapillas when they were in bed together—the popping of oil, the taste of fat and honey melting onto her tongue.

It was on one of these mornings that he'd looked at her and said, "One day you're going to leave here and make some guy really happy."

The words had startled her, both because they implied she would one day leave the Bright Side, and because it would be without him.

• • •

His prediction began to play out her junior year, when the school counselor, Mrs. Palmer, called Ariel into her office. The walls were covered in posters for colleges Ariel had never heard of: Northwestern, Duke, Pepperdine. Ariel was admiring the posters when Mrs. Palmer explained that Ariel's standardized test scores qualified her for a big scholarship. "You can likely go anywhere in-state for free," she said, "and possibly out-of-state, too. Do you know where you want to apply? What you want to study?"

"I'm going to Middleton Community College," Ariel said.

Mrs. Palmer had put her hand to her mouth, to hide her smile. "That's a perfectly fine school, Ariel, but with your test scores—what I'm saying is you can go *anywhere*. However, if you're thinking about Ivy Leagues, you might want to join a club or two—admissions offices prefer an active student."

This word, *active*, had confused her. Hardly an hour passed when she wasn't active in some way, be it mucking stalls or studying for a test or trying to beat back the cat and dog hair that threatened to overtake the house if she didn't regularly sweep and vacuum.

She was also confused because she and her mother had discussed college several times, and from what Ariel had gathered, her only option was Middleton. There was a sum of money saved for this purpose—to pay her tuition, to buy a clunker for her to drive to and from campus. But here was Mrs. Palmer, plum lipstick on her adult braces, repeating that word: *anywhere*. Ariel had spent little time thinking about anywhere, but she took Mrs. Palmer's brochures and read them that night, in her room, Opal snoring beside her.

Because the idea of leaving Kansas made her dizzy, she focused on the state schools. K-State was closer and had a good vet program, but Ariel knew a lot of kids from her class planned on going to K-State. If she went there, it would just be more of the same. Same people. Same ridicule. Same feeling of being on the outside, looking in. When she looked through the University of Kansas brochure, a kernel of excitement stirred in her stomach. In one picture, a girl with curly black hair lay in the grass, reading a book, a redbrick building rising in the background behind her. Ariel was overcome with the desire to be this anonymous girl, studying in front of the library, plans to meet up with friends later that night. For the first time, she wondered what it would be like to live somewhere other than the Bright Side. To have a new life.

People around St. Clare referred to KU as Gay U, a place where students ate tofu and cavorted with hippies. At Ariel's school, the gang of hair-netted lunch ladies would serve fried chicken the day after KU lost a basketball game, the meat representing a murdered Jayhawk—KU's mascot. Luckily, her mother did not subscribe to these prejudices—if anything, living in St. Clare had sculpted Mona's liberal politics to a fine point—and so, when Ariel was not only accepted to KU the following winter but also offered the big scholarship her guidance counselor had told her about, Ariel assumed her mother would be thrilled.

She decided to share her news the night after the winter adoption fair, which they held every December, before Christmas, to move dogs and cats before the coldest months set in. Mona was in a good mood. The fair had been a success—twelve adoptions and a generous heap of food donations. To celebrate, she made stuffed peppers and uncorked a bottle of Welch's sparkling grape juice. As the meal wound down, Gideon squeezed Ariel's knee under the table. *It's time*, the squeeze said. *Tell her.*

Ariel cleared her throat. "Mom, I have news." She wanted to speak up, to enunciate, but she was nervous—not for fear that her mother would be upset, but in anticipation of her mother's excitement. It was not often that her mother celebrated her; just thinking about it made Ariel dizzy.

"Well, spit it out then."

"I got into college," she said, her heart racing.

Her mother nodded excitedly. "Good for you. Although I'd have been surprised if you didn't get into Middleton. It's not exactly Harvard."

"I didn't get into Middleton." Her voice was louder now, more confident. "I got in at KU. With a full ride." She couldn't help but smile.

Mona froze, her mouth pinched into a line. "Pardon?"

"It's called National Merit. I get to go for free. They even give me money for books." There was a lifting sensation in her shoulders, her neck—she realized she was proud of herself.

Her mother looked at her, her eyes suddenly filled with a brand of panic Ariel had never seen before. "You want to leave?"

"I got a scholarship," she repeated. For a brief, senseless moment, she wondered if her mother knew what a scholarship was.

Her mother's fork was now trembling against her plate. She dropped it and put her hands over her face. "You're not going anywhere, Ariel," she said between her fingers. "You're staying here. End of discussion."

"But I got a full ride," Ariel said, her voice growing higher, more desperate. She glanced at Gideon. She didn't understand what was happening. "That means we don't have to pay anything."

"It doesn't matter, Ariel. I'm saying no."

"But why?"

"Because I say so is why. Besides, there's no such thing as a full ride. There's housing and food and campus fees and everything else."

Ariel tried to remain calm. If it was about money, she could find a way to make it work. "I can get a job in Lawrence. And then eventually I'll become a veterinarian and come back home and take care of the animals. Think of how much money that'll save you. See? It makes sense if you think about it long-term."

Mona shook her head. "Do you know how long it takes to become a vet?"

"Four years," Ariel said. "That's what the brochures said."

"That's just for the first part, Ariel. After that you have to go to vet school—that's another four years. And it's very expensive. How am I supposed to afford your replacement here for eight years? Who am I going to get to help me? I can hardly afford to pay Gideon." She took a deep breath, squeezed her temples. "You'll go to Middleton like we planned, and if you still want to be a vet once you graduate, we'll discuss it then."

Ariel felt everything sink in. "But I didn't even apply to Middleton." Alarmed, she looked to Gideon.

"Mona," he said, leaning forward. "You won't even think it over?"

"Oh, so you're in on this, too?" She tossed her napkin on her plate and stood up from the table. "I'm not talking about this anymore. Nobody's going anywhere. We're all staying right here, where the animals need us."

After a beat of silence during which Ariel could only stare at her stuffed pepper, Gideon put his hand on Ariel's back. "I'm sorry," he said.

Ariel shook him off and went to her room. She curled up on Opal's bed, pressing her ear against Opal's ribs so she could hear the sound of her heartbeat. Opal turned to lick her hand, frantically trying to fix whatever it was that had broken.

In that moment, Ariel missed her father more than ever. He'd gone to college; surely, if he'd been there, he would have supported her decision to go away. She felt a pang of longing, followed by a rush of anger. The sanctuary had never felt like a prison, but now, with the snap of Mona's fingers, she could feel the bars coming down around her, the definitive click of a lock.

After months of imagining her new life in Lawrence—a life in which she would have friends, and go to parties, and stay up late having heated discussions about science and literature and philosophy, and, in the end, come away with a vet degree—attending community college in Middleton seemed unbearable. She had developed an image of herself, in Lawrence, wearing stylish hoop earrings and faded jeans, carrying a suede fringed backpack filled with books. She would be pretty and mysterious-looking. She would go to poetry readings and attend lectures about psychology and evolution. As she walked through campus, girls who had been popular at their high schools would turn to look at her, wonder who she was. Now she imagined her life at Middleton: she'd be like everyone else—a farm kid who couldn't make it to university. A girl who got stuck in her mother's dream.

None of this was Gideon's fault, and yet, in the days following her argument with her mother, when he tried to kiss her, she would turn away. Eventually, after weeks of Ariel snubbing him, he cornered her in the barn. "You can pity yourself and you can hate your mother, but you will not block me out from your life."

Ariel stood there, trying to conjure anger but feeling only a deep frustration. She broke down and allowed him to hold her as she wept. "I want to go," she told him. "I didn't realize how badly I wanted to go until she said I couldn't."

"Then go," he said. "You already got in. What's stopping you?"

"I don't have any money—I don't even have a way to get there."

"I'll lend you whatever money you need," he said. "And I'll drive you. See? It's that easy."

She looked at him—he seemed to be serious. "Gideon, I can't take your money."

"You're not taking it, you're borrowing it. Once you have a degree and a big fancy job, you can pay me back."

"But what about your plans?" She knew he was saving up to one day buy his own land, his own horses. On the sanctuary, money came slowly.

"I'm happy here for now. I'll be fine."

"What about my mom?"

"What about her? She can't handcuff you to the kennels."

"If I leave, it'll kill her. She'll hate me."

"Maybe for a little while, but she'll get over it. She'll have to."

"And then what?"

"Then you'll be in school. And we'll be here. And you'll visit, and we'll visit, and it'll be fine. People do it all the time." He pulled her in tighter, rested his chin on her head. He'd been working all morning, and she could smell his skin—sweat and Irish Spring soap—through the fabric of his shirt. She'd grown to crave this odor—the animal musk of his body, the scratch of his beard. She tried to imagine her life without him, and it filled her with a fear so raw she had to catch her breath.

"You can't live your life for other people," he said. "Especially the ones who say they love you. If they really love you, they'll let you go. Understand?"

"I just don't want to lose you. Or the animals. Or my mom."

"You won't," he said, his voice so certain she made the mistake of believing him.

In the end, it was Gideon who paid the deposit on her dorm room and it was Gideon who drove her to Lawrence, the two of them slipping out before dawn, each carrying a duffel bag filled with Ariel's clothes. As his truck bumped across the final road out of St. Clare, she had imagined her life shedding behind her like the skin of a snake. She cried most of the way, leaning on Gideon's shoulder as he rubbed her back. By the time they pulled onto the campus, Ariel was shaking so forcefully that Gideon drove to a pet store so Ariel could watch a puppy-training class. After this, they went to Walmart, where Ariel bought a Tracphone—*So you have no excuse not to call*, Gideon explained—and then to a local credit union where Gideon helped her open an account into which she deposited a check for $7,000—most of his savings and ostensibly enough money to last until she found a job of her own. Because nobody had ever done something this generous for her, she didn't know how to thank him. There was also the distinct feeling that she was making a grave mistake.

"Gideon?" she'd said in the car on the way back from the bank.

"Yes?"

"I feel like I'm taking too much from you."

He was quiet for a moment. "That's half of what love is, Kangaroo. Taking."

She called Gideon the very next day. "I woke up and had no idea where I was, what I was supposed to do. I feel like I'm floating in space, like nothing here is real," she said. "I miss you so much it feels like not breathing."

"Give it time," Gideon said, his voice calm, soothing. And then, "I miss you, too."

She asked the question she didn't want to ask. "Did you tell my mom?"

A pause. "I did. She's pissed, but not so pissed she won't talk to you. If anything, the sooner you talk the sooner we can all move on."

"I'm not ready. Not yet." Even the idea of it sent a spike of nerves up her belly. "Maybe next week, once she's adjusted to the idea." She had a fear, silly as it was, that her mother might convince her to drop out of school and come home. Such was her mother's power.

"Okay," he said, a hint of impatience in his voice. "When you're ready."

For a while, at least, she would call in the afternoons, when she knew her mother was out doing chores. Gideon would update her on the animals, and if Opal was around, he'd put the phone to her ear so Ariel could tell her how much she loved and missed her, sometimes talking for so long that Gideon would pick up the phone and say, "Ariel? She went outside."

Ariel told Gideon about her classes and her professors, how she was studying French and reading Nabokov and learning about earthquakes and natural disasters, a class the frat kids called "E's and Natty D's." So he wouldn't worry, she invented stories about friends and parties. She couldn't bring herself to tell him the truth: that she hated Lawrence—hated the cars, the buildings, the noise. Hated that the mockingbirds sang car alarms and the squirrels were fat from junk food. Hated how the hills and trees made it feel as though the world were a heavy book that might snap shut at any moment. She didn't tell him that to save money, she alternated between peanut butter sandwiches and ramen noodles for dinner. Although she did tell him about her part-time job at the library, she left out that it was in a windowless room where she worked alone, scanning blueprints for architecture students. How sometimes the students yelled at her for making a crooked scan or accidentally creasing the delicate paper. How sometimes, watching the massive scanner flash and flash, she would cry.

She didn't tell him that she searched for animals wherever she went, her heart lurching each time she passed a dog or saw a cat spying on her from a windowsill. She realized, after a few weeks, that the floor of her dorm room was riddled with crumbs—she'd never had to pick up dropped food before. At night, she would watch YouTube videos of animals, sometimes devolving into hour-long compilations with titles like *Cutest Puppies U Will Ever See!!* or *Funniest baby animals that will make you say awwww!!!*, ignoring the looks her roommate, Gwyneth, gave her. Nearly everything she did invoked a look from Gwyneth.

She had hoped that being on her own in a new place might inspire the kind of extroversion that had eluded her in St. Clare, but she was still the same as she'd always been—soft-spoken, awkward, unsure of herself. Sometimes, while talking to someone for the first time, the person would snap, "I can't hear what you're saying," and Ariel would spend the rest of the conversation self-consciously monitoring the volume of her voice. Despite the many afternoons she spent reading on the grass, she never managed to feel like the girl in the brochure. Sometimes she felt so alone and out of place she wondered if her mother had been right. Maybe she would have been happier staying at the sanctuary, going to Middleton. Maybe she wasn't meant for the bigger world after all.

The only place she felt at ease was in class, and so she upped her course load to eighteen credit hours, the most her scholarship would pay for. She'd expected to like her science classes, but it was her English class she looked forward to most. She found herself initiating class discussions, her heart pounding as her classmates turned to look at her. Six weeks into the semester, she changed her major from biology to English, abandoning her dream of becoming a vet. At night, instead of watching animal videos, she began to write short stories, many of them about the Bright Side. It became yet another reason she wanted to delay talking to her mother, who would surely think English a waste of time. Ariel had run away from everything she knew and loved, and for what? To study a language she already knew. To read books. To follow not in her mother's footsteps, but her father's.

On weekends, she scoured the student events calendar for ice-cream socials, singles mixers, fraternity barbecues—anything where she might meet people. Holding a cup of punch or an off-brand cookie on a napkin, she would stand quietly in a corner until somebody spoke to her. Usually, this was a boy. Skinny, pale, clean-smelling.

His hair would be gelled back or combed neatly to one side, his shirt would have a collar or a tiny breast pocket with nothing inside. Sometimes this boy would ask for her phone number, but the next morning, her mind fuzzy, she would think: *Who even was he?* He was nobody.

The problem was that she had nothing in common with the people she met. She wanted someone who understood the peculiar satisfaction of stacking firewood, who enjoyed the sweet musk of a sleeping dog's paw. Someone who filled his pockets with wire cutters and work gloves. At the very least, a pencil. Someone who understood the pleasure of caring for animals. What she wanted was Gideon, but nobody on campus compared. Although she and Gideon hadn't explicitly broken up, she also understood they weren't still together.

And then, one night, while walking home from the library, she heard the sound of a party. She must have walked by the house a dozen times without noticing it. A sign on the front lawn read: FREEDOM HOUSE COOPERATIVE LIVING CENTER—EVERYONE IS WELCOME! She was surprised by how much the sign affected her—like a warm hand on her back. It reminded her of the Bright Side.

On the front porch, a couple of girls were eating potato chips and passing a cigarette back and forth, their flip-flops tossed onto the grass nearby. Mustering her courage, Ariel made her way into the house, quietly whispering "hey" as she passed the girls on the porch. It was one of the scariest things she'd ever done, and yet she also felt strangely free—inside, the lights were dim, everyone was drunk. The music was happy and loud. She could have been anybody.

After three drinks that were not really drinks but Dixie cups filled with spiked Jell-O, she was on the dance floor, having so much fun she could hardly believe it was real. This, she realized, was what people talked about when they talked about partying. Two Jell-O shots later, she was ejecting her dinner into a potted plant. And then there was Dex, tall and skinny with freckled arms and hair the color of a cinnamon stick. The scent of his jean jacket and minty hair gel as he helped guide her upstairs to a toilet. He was wearing a neon tank top that read, *Caution: Hot Meat.* On his feet were the most beautiful leather boots she'd ever seen.

In the morning, in a room she didn't recognize, he lay on the floor beside the bed, on a pile of blankets. She felt terrible, her head pounding, stomach hollow. She also felt guilty, as if at any moment Gideon might walk in on them. She hadn't *done* anything—this much she remembered. He had held her hair while she puked, had guided her into the bed, had given her cups of water. Still, she felt guilty. Dex looked older in the daylight, his eyes tired, the skin around his mouth dry and flaky. But when he smiled, she felt herself grow nervous. He was cute. Just looking at him, her head didn't hurt so bad.

"Morning, Drunky," he said.

She had smiled, embarrassed. "Thanks for taking care of me."

He waved a hand, brushing away the comment. "I was known as Party Doctor in college. It's sort of my thing."

She accepted his invitation to brunch, letting him lead her downtown, the day syrupy but bright. Her first college hangover. On the way, they stopped at a gas station where Dex bought her a travel-sized toothbrush and toothpaste. She brushed her teeth and tongue in the bathroom, desperate to scrub away the taste of puke. In the mirror, she was alarmed to find that her hair was a mess, the skin under her eyes puffy and dark. When she was done, Dex asked if he could borrow the toothbrush. "But I just used it," she said. He shrugged and took the toothbrush from her. "No grosser than kissing," he said. She tried to conceal how greatly this sentence bewildered her.

He took her to a brightly lit restaurant called the Mirth Café. Inside, he hugged the blond ponytailed hostess, fist-bumped two of the busboys, and high-fived the gray-haired woman behind the pastry counter.

"Did you used to work here or something?"

He waved at someone in the back. "No, why?"

He ordered orange juice, hash browns, blueberry pancakes, and a plate of bacon to share. Ariel had never eaten bacon before—the flavor was so overwhelming she began to cough.

"You okay?" he asked, patting her gently on the back. "You need the Heimlich?"

"I'm fine. It's just so . . . *potent*." She thought of her mom's pig, Lady Madonna, and felt a tug in her chest.

As they ate, three more people stopped by their table to say hello, to tell Dex they had missed him at this or that party, to ask about his next gig at the Replay. Dex was clearly *someone*, and it occurred to Ariel that if she stuck by him, perhaps she could be someone, too.

Their first weeks together felt like exploring a great mansion. She wandered down hallway after hallway, no idea how she'd gotten there, but excited that she had. Each door opened to a new room of experience: her first joint, her first margarita, her first time watching the sunrise from a rooftop. In the mansion, it didn't matter that she was shy. Dex was a talker and could single-handedly keep the conversation afloat, drifting from topic to topic with such ease that Ariel soon found herself joining in, adding an opinion here, asking a question there. Laughing so hard that once, in a booth at a diner, she released a trickle of pee. He never asked her to talk louder; instead, he leaned closer. He listened. He did not seem to realize she was shy and awkward, perhaps because, around him, she no longer was.

She began to think of him at odd times of the day: in the shower, while watching the scanner at work, during the middle of a lecture about Marxist literary criticism. At the base of her stomach, a bed of coals would burn orange each time she imagined his face: the electric blue of his eyes, the stubble on his chin. The way his tongue would poke out when they had sex.

Sex. Of all the rooms in the mansion, this was her favorite. Sleeping with Dex made her feel like an entirely different person—not shy, nervous, or fearful, but sexy and brave. An animal. His bed became an expanse of land where she was free to run wild, exposed to the elements, vulnerable. In this way, Dex taught her how to let go of something she didn't know she'd been protecting. Even with Gideon, she'd been reserved.

By November, her calls to Gideon became more and more sporadic. She realized the sound of his voice only amplified her homesickness, and so, just as the maple trees on campus began to turn, she asked if they could take a break from talking, so she could focus on school. "Just for a couple weeks, until I settle in a bit more. I need to try and really be here."

The line was quiet.

"A week or two," she said. "That's all."

"I don't like this, Ariel."

"I don't, either, but it's something I need to do."

"And what about your mom? When are you going to call her?"

"Soon. I promise."

"You say that every time."

"Please, Gideon."

There was a long silence, and then he said, "Okay."

She spent Thanksgiving alone, in her dorm room, reading *Jesus' Son* and eating a frozen Hungry-Man dinner of turkey and mashed potatoes, occasionally texting Dex, who was in Kansas City with his parents. She tried not to think about Thanksgiving at the sanctuary, where each year her mother arranged a veggie platter into the shape of a turkey and plopped a tray of foil-wrapped baked potatoes onto the table. Even after Ariel's father left, Mona still read from the short blessing he'd written years before when they were newly married, and which he had, before his exodus, recited himself. *Tonight, we partici-pate in a holiday that has, at its heart, a historical lie. A holiday that cel-ebrates an imaginary friendship between settlers and indigenous peoples, that erases all mention of the genocides exacted upon this land's rightful stewards. Tonight, in defiance of this lie but in reverence to its themes of gratitude and comradery, we celebrate not the people who stole this land from those who called it home long, long before us, but the land itself, land that has sustained us and our fellow animals despite the atrocities committed upon it.* It was a speech Ariel had memorized years before, and whose opening line she found herself whispering over her frozen dinner.

When Gideon called, she let it ring.

A month became two months became three until—how had it happened?—a year passed without her hearing Gideon's voice, with-out her visiting home. The longer she waited, the guiltier she felt and the greater she knew her mother's wrath would be, and so she waited even longer, putting it off until eventually she gave up the idea al-together. Sometimes she would think of Gideon or her mother or Opal and a pang of anxiety would course through her, as if she'd just remembered an important deadline that had passed. But this was life, wasn't it? One chapter gave way to another that gave way to another. If she focused too much on what had already happened, she'd never get around to turning the page. She had made a decision and could either move on or drive herself mad wondering if it was a mistake. In the end, she decided to move on, to come unglued from yesterday in order to see what tomorrow had to offer.

Like this, she understood how her father had slipped away.

• • •

The grand consolation was Dex, who quickly filled the cracks the sanctuary had left behind. Whenever she walked into a room with him, people would perk up, as if they'd heard a song they liked.

"People smile at you," she once told him. "It's the strangest thing."

He'd looked at her like she was crazy. "What else are they supposed to do? Gag? Weep?"

There was also an illicit feeling to hanging out with Dex. She felt, for the first time, like a rule breaker. Life with Dex meant bars and parties and jam sessions and potlucks and drag shows and movies and game nights and long, cursive walks through Lawrence, some of which lasted until sunrise, when they would order fresh cinnamon rolls from WheatFields and eat them under the campanile. Falling in love with Dex meant falling in love with Lawrence. He showed her it was a place worth loving, a place she could learn to call home.

Her sophomore year, he gifted her a fake ID—her ticket into an even larger world, one filled with kaleidoscopic nights that left her hungover and unmotivated, her eyelids so heavy it felt like someone had lined them with metal. She began to sleep through her classes, to turn in unedited or unfinished papers, some ending midsentence.

She had grown up thinking the world was running out, but with Dex, the world felt suddenly limitless. She began to frequent the vintage boutique downtown, combing for the kind of clothes she saw on Dex's friends: brightly patterned skirts, oversized sweaters, bohemian-looking blouses stitched with chevrons and flowers. In her bank account, Gideon's savings dwindled.

She was on academic probation by spring and lost her scholarship the next fall. Dex offered to help pay her tuition, but she refused, understanding that she could not take Dex's money after squandering Gideon's. She looked into loans, but without a cosigner the interest rates were exorbitant. In the end, she decided to take a break from school and save up the money herself. Dex tried to console her, pointing out that half his friends had master's degrees and still worked as baristas or bartenders. The economy sucked. He himself had a music degree he never used. And yet, no matter how generous his comfort, she couldn't help but wonder what her life would look like had she never met him. This, she supposed, was the price of love. You gained a partner—in her case, someone kind, generous, and patient. Someone who could make her laugh, who had never been anything but supportive—but in exchange you gave up a piece of yourself, the piece that would have gone on to live a different life without them.

Aside from Dex, Sunny was the first person she told about her decision to drop out. It was early in their friendship and they were drinking coffee at La Prima Tazza, where they often studied together on Sunday afternoons.

"Wait," Sunny had said, leaning over the table. "You had a full ride?"

Ariel nodded, her cheeks suddenly burning. Dex had made it seem like it was no big deal, like lots of people had full rides and lost them.

Sunny leaned back and shook her head. "That," she said, "is a real fucking shame, Ariel. I figured you were going into debt like the rest of us assholes."

Ariel had started to cry then. She tried to be quiet, but she was on her period and all the anger and frustration of the past few months— the past few years—was mounting inside her. When the guys at the adjacent table turned to look at her, with their perfect beards and their immaculate Carhartt jackets, she'd wanted to shout, *You don't even work outside! Get a normal jacket!* Instead, she'd sat quietly, hands around her mug, trying to calm herself.

"Hey, it's all right," Sunny said, taking Ariel's hand. "You'll figure it out. You'll be okay."

"I gave up everything to come here," she said, wiping the snot from above her lip. "And I blew it."

"Yes," Sunny said, "you did blow it. And you did give up everything. But think of all you've gained, too. You have to focus on that, or you'll never forgive yourself." Then, noticing the guys with the perfect beards were still staring at Ariel, she turned to them and said, "Fuck off with your lattes, will you?"

Dex

After a few more drinks with Buddy, Dex stumbled home. Maybe he was drunk. So what? Maybe he popped a Hot Pocket in the microwave and forgot about it. Maybe, when the smoke alarm went off, he simply removed the batteries and threw the Hot Pocket into the yard, so the resident squirrels could feast. Maybe, because there were no more Hot Pockets, he settled for refried beans, plain, cold, straight from the can.

What he wanted was a cigarette, or Ariel. Sometimes, if he came home drunk, she would rub his back and bring him water, wedge an extra pillow under his head so he wouldn't snore. Sometimes she would run her hand down his belly, slide it under his briefs. *It'll help you sleep.* Of course, *sometimes* hadn't happened in a while. Over the past couple years, she'd grown more serious, less interested in staying out late and partying. When she did go out, she rarely had more than two drinks and usually walked home before midnight. He had once taken great pleasure in showing her how to have a good time, but it seemed they no longer shared the same definition of *fun*. She liked staying home and reading or watching movies. If she went out on her own, it was to have dinner or drinks with Sunny or attend a poetry reading at the Taproom. Gone were the days of concerts and 2:00 a.m. burritos, the days that defined their years of falling in love. Sometimes he felt like he was stuck in the past while she had leapfrogged into middle age. More than a few of his friends had pointed out how different they were, and he couldn't disagree. But it made sense to him, to seek out someone different. What was a partner except for the person who, when combined with oneself, created a whole? Yin and yang and all that jazz.

The problem, of course, was that he loved her—so much that it sometimes made his stomach ache and he would sit on the toilet, waiting for something gastrointestinal to happen, to prove that he wasn't hopelessly whipped but rather experiencing a mild case of IBS. When they'd first met, he'd found himself constantly breathless, his heart beating so fast he worried it might require medical attention. Certainly, this phase would pass, he'd thought. Time would dull his feelings, his hormones would level out. And yet, all these years later, he could bring himself to a cold sweat just thinking about how much she meant to him. She was his best friend, his partner, his family. Rather than die, the butterflies in his stomach had turned to hawks.

When the beans were gone, he made his way to bed. Questions circled his mind. What was she doing? Who was she with? Why, for the love of God, had she taken so many bags?

At last, he decided to text her: *Did you run away with a flight attendant named Trevor? Ha Ha JK, but really, what's my lady up to?* It was no good. He deleted it and wrote: *Did you make it to St. Clare okay? Miss you.* After reading it a hundred times, checking for errors, he pressed send. Then he drifted off to sleep.

When he woke a few hours later, covered in sweat from a drunk nightmare involving Tom Cruise and a talking Hot Pocket, he checked his phone, where he had a new text message. The text was not from Ariel but from Buddy, who had sent him, at 3:34 in the morning, a link to a YouTube video of a pretty girl farting onto a cake. The video was called *Cake Farts*. Dex watched the video five times in a row. There was something soothing about it—the curve of the woman's rear end, the cake's vanilla frosting rippling beneath her flatulence. It was the kind of internet curio he wanted to share with Ariel but knew he never could. She would find it vulgar and a waste of perfectly good cake. He felt a sudden rush of frustration, that the woman he was about to marry didn't even attempt to appreciate the things he appreciated. But perhaps he was being unfair. Perhaps, if he gave her the chance, Ariel might surprise him. *What a strangely beautiful little film,* he imagined her saying. *In this increasingly vitriolic political climate, it's important to take a break and enjoy whimsical, semipornographic You-Tube videos. Maybe we could try this sometime, with a sheet cake? Thanks for sharing, baby. I love you dearly and am coming home right now to express this love through sex.*

Feeling brave, he copied the video's link and pasted it into a message to Ariel. "This made me think of you," he wrote, and pressed send before he could ruminate on the matter any longer.

His regret was large and instantaneous, like a blast of flatulence on a cake.

Ariel

She'd forgotten that her mother couldn't eat a meal without simultaneously completing a peripheral task or three. This morning, after making pancakes, Mona sat down to address a Chihuahua who'd cut his rump on barbed wire. After feeding him part of a Benadryl and numbing the area with Orajel, Mona held the Chihuahua between her legs and began to close the wound with dental floss. The Chihuahua hardly seemed to notice—he actually appeared to be falling asleep, his wet eyes slowly closing.

"So what are you going to do if someone wants to buy the sanctuary?" Ariel asked. She was eating her pancakes one tiny, sugary triangle at a time, watching as her mother's became soggy with syrup. Her thoughts kept drifting outside, to Gideon, but she told herself to focus.

"Sell it to them," Mona said, not looking up from the Chihuahua. "Any other brain teasers?"

"I mean what will *you* do? Where will you go?"

"That," Mona said, "would be putting the cart before the horse."

"You haven't even thought about it?"

Her mother ran her fingers over the dog's silky ears to calm him. "Sometimes I think about Florida."

"Florida?" It was like imagining a wild horse in the Louvre.

"You know how I don't like the cold—and there's lots of Jewish people there."

"Since when do you care about being around Jewish people?"

"Since I woke up to my barn on fire. That's when." She flashed her eyes at Ariel, then returned her attention to the dog. "I'm tired of this backward town and everyone in it. I'm sick of them all."

You don't even talk to the people in town, Ariel wanted to say, but managed to keep the sentence to herself. "It just seems strange is all. Florida."

"It's an idea, Ariel. Without the Bright Side, there's nothing keeping me in Kansas. I can go anywhere—what's the difference if it's Florida or Alaska or Timbuktu?"

She felt a pinch in her chest—all these years, she'd taken comfort in knowing her mother was in the same state. Before she could ask any more questions—*Where in Florida? Would you need help moving?*—a pair of texts came in from Dex. According to the time stamps, he'd sent them the night before, but cell and internet reception at the sanctuary was spotty, existing in random pockets around the house, or, as it sometimes seemed, whenever a breeze pushed them along.

The first message said: *Did you make it to St. Clare okay? Miss you.* The next was a link to a video that had something to do with cake— the thumbnail was too small to make out. When she clicked on it, the page took a moment to load, but eventually there came the sound of moaning and farting.

"What in the hell is that?" Mona asked.

"Just spam," Ariel said, closing out of the page as fast as she could. She knew he'd sent it to get a rise out of her. He often poked fun at her for having puritanical tendencies, and while it was true she did not like dubstep or action movies and had, more than once, used the phrase *Idle hands are the devil's playground* in earnest, it did not make it okay to pass gas onto a perfectly viable baked good. But there she went again. Even the phrase *pass gas* was reason enough for Dex to razz her. Once, after he found a Werther's Original in her purse, he subscribed her to AARP's magazine so that, every two months, there appeared in her mail a glossy publication filled with coupons and advice on how to treat arthritis. She secretly enjoyed some of the articles, like how to safely fall on ice or make soups from expired canned goods. There was also, to her delight, a two-for-one coupon for Werther's Originals.

"I hate those damned things," Mona said, nodding at Ariel's phone. "Last winter, Puck Doddy, the kid from the Patterson Ranch, he ran his dad's truck off the road, straight into a cottonwood. Last thing he ever did on this earth was fiddle on his stupid face booklet or whatever it's called. He was sending some girl a profanity."

"That's terrible," Ariel said, putting her phone on the table facedown.

"Natural selection is what it is." She was tying her finishing knot, the thread squeezed between her fingers. When she was done, she kissed the Chihuahua on the nose and set him onto the ground, where he stood blinking. "Poor thing'll probably go straight back to the barbed wire. But what can you do?"

Ariel was reminded of a feeling she'd often had when she was younger—jealousy, thinly lined with shame, for wanting her mother to stop paying attention to the animals and instead pay attention to her.

"Listen, I have to run some errands. Bank business and the post office and all that."

"Can I come with?" Ariel dreaded the idea of running into people she hadn't seen in years, but she wanted to continue their conversation.

"You'll be more useful here, helping Gideon."

"He said he didn't want my help."

"Men say all sorts of shit. It's our job not to listen." With this, Mona gathered her keys and the gallon Ziploc bag that served as her wallet. "I'll be back when I'm back. Don't go running off again while I'm gone. But if you do, turn off the lights behind you."

Ariel watched through the window as her mother climbed into Old Baby, a pair of dogs jumping into the truck bed behind her. Mona started the engine, waited a beat for it to warm, and then was gone. Ariel felt her heart sink—how was she supposed to make things better if her mom wouldn't sit still?

Alone in the kitchen, she wondered what Dex had been doing when he sent the cake video. Most likely he had been drunk. Probably with Buddy. And what was he doing now, without her? Perhaps he was at home, trying to figure out why she had not invited him along for the weekend. She reminded herself that she had done nothing wrong aside from withhold information about her past—about her mother and the sanctuary. And Gideon. But why should Dex know about Gideon? Certainly, there were girls from Dex's past she didn't know about—one-night stands and summertime flings. Of course, Gideon was neither a fling nor a one-night stand. He was Gideon.

When he first started working at the sanctuary, Gideon would find ways to speak around Ariel. "I'm thinking of changing out the sheep bedding today," he would say, his eyes locked on Mona. "Maybe your daughter could help." *I'm right here*, Ariel would think. *Look at me, look at me.*

Every morning, she would watch as he brought the horses their hay, the muscles in his arms tightening as he urged the pitchfork forward. She would watch him brush the knots from their manes, occasionally slipping them one of the soft peppermint candies he kept in his pocket. He would whisper in their ears, close his eyes, and press his forehead to theirs. Ariel would wonder what it felt like, to be the horses. To turn to putty under his touch.

Everything changed one morning in October, while Mona was delivering a dog to a family in Lark City. Ariel was doing her homework at the kitchen table when Gideon burst into the house.

"I need help," he said.

Ariel closed her calculus book and followed him, running, out to the sheep pen. Inside, an ewe named Minnie Mouse lay pinned beneath a wooden support beam.

Ariel went in and crouched beside Minnie. "It'll be all right, girl," she said, although, judging from the way Minnie was breathing, she knew it wouldn't be. "We're here."

"Help me lift the beam," Gideon said, his voice panicked.

Ariel positioned herself on the other end of the beam, and on the count of three, they lifted it a few inches from the ground. Sensing she was free, Minnie scrambled to her feet, only to discover her limbs wouldn't operate as normal. She collapsed, and then tried again, in vain, to stand. Once they had righted the beam, Gideon went to Minnie, who was now on her side, a bead of blood forming at her nose.

"I was trying to do too much at once—I was carrying two bags of feed. I knew it was too much, but I thought I could do it, and I had it, for a little while, but then I tripped over a salt block—"

"Why didn't you ask for my help? I was right inside."

"I'm sorry," Gideon said, and when he looked at her she could tell he really was.

By now, the other sheep were making the rounds, coming over to see what had happened to their friend. Minnie Mouse was a rescue from a hobby farm whose owner had retired and moved to Las Vegas. She had no blood relatives at the sanctuary, a fact that now saddened Ariel.

"We could call Doc Powell," Ariel said, although at this point they both understood it was too late.

"I'll stay with her," Gideon said, "for however long it takes. It's the least I can do." He ran his hand over Minnie, whose breath was growing more and more labored.

Ariel went inside and returned with a thermos of lukewarm coffee, a heavy Pendleton jacket that had belonged to her father, and a quilt. She put the quilt over Minnie Mouse and handed the coat and thermos to Gideon.

"Thanks," he said, not meeting her eyes.

She sat down across from him, on Minnie's other side, the wind whipping her hair. What she hated most about dying was how long it took—the slow unfurling, like a flower losing its petals. She and Gideon kept quiet, both of them watching, willing the process to be over. Twenty minutes passed, then thirty. Neither of them said anything, just listened to the wind, to the scratch of Minnie's breathing. As painful as it was, Ariel relished the uninterrupted time with Gideon, both of them experiencing the same bite of sadness. Finally, after more than an hour, Minnie's hoof twitched one last time.

"There she goes," Gideon whispered. He looked up at Ariel, his eyes red-rimmed. "Please don't tell your mother how it happened," he said, his voice thick, clotted with guilt.

Ariel put her hand on Minnie's side, feeling her warmth beneath the quilt. "I'll say you came out and found her under the beam."

Gideon nodded.

"For the record, I don't like lying to my mom."

"I'll make it up to you—is there something you want? Something I can do?"

"Maybe next time you can ask for help sooner rather than later." It felt good to say what she was thinking. She wondered if this was how her mother felt all the time.

"That was dumb of me to ask," he said, his voice low. "It's just that I really like it here. I don't want your mom to fire me."

Beneath her palm, Minnie was now cold. How unfair, that something as dense and important as life could slip away so easily. She wanted Gideon to say something to make this feeling of sadness smaller, but he remained silent, and so the feeling grew. Before she knew it, she was crying, great sobs rising up in waves. Even after all her years on the sanctuary, after witnessing the death of dozens of animals, she was not immune to the blow. Every death felt like the first, like nature was reinventing the premise.

"She was a good sheep," she whispered. "She was never mean."

She was startled to feel Gideon's hand on her back, electrifying every muscle in her body. "She doesn't feel anything now," he said.

Ariel had always hated this brand of consolation, one Doc Powell often employed in the cold moments after an animal had passed. Of course Minnie Mouse didn't feel anything—that was exactly the point. Sure, she no longer felt pain, but she would also never again feel the quiet peace of a sunrise, or the rush of eating a bowl of grain, or the refreshment of a cold drink of water on a sun-scorched day in July. The simple pleasures of life were over for her now—they had been taken from her. In her last moments, she must have wondered what she had done to no longer deserve them.

"I want you to come with me to a football game," Ariel said. "That's what I want." That she had thought of the idea so easily, and that she had the courage to ask him for it, surprised her. It was something she'd asked of Sydney many times during their friendship, and which he'd always denied her. He thought football was stupid. "It's not about the football" had been Ariel's argument. "It's about being there—that's how people make friends, they go to stuff. They try." Sydney had given her a look like: *Who are you, to think you can try?*

"Whatever you want," Gideon said.

She felt silly, but suspected it was the only way out if she wanted any of the good feelings to remain. If she wanted to keep thinking about him as she had over the last months.

"Go finish your homework," he said. "I'll take care of her body."

She gave Minnie Mouse one last kiss, petting the soft skin around her eyes, and then left, the cold air growing colder around her.

Mona had believed their story. The beams were old, after all, and had endured almost a decade of hard winters and spring rains. She thanked Gideon for burying Minnie and for offering to take Ariel to the football game that afternoon. "Why she suddenly wants to watch a bunch of meatheads slam into each other is beyond my comprehension, but I'm happy not to drive her."

Ariel spent hours trying to figure out what to wear, only to decide on her standard uniform: jeans and a gray secondhand Old Navy hoodie two sizes too big. Gideon was waiting for her out by his Datsun, What-the-Truck. He wore dark jeans and a green cargo jacket she'd never seen before. In lieu of work boots, he wore black sneakers. This, she understood, was his version of dressing up.

What-the-Truck smelled of oil but was otherwise in good shape. On the dashboard stood a plastic figurine—Darth Vader in a bright green hula skirt. Instead of music, they listened to NPR turned low. Ariel grew more and more nervous as they approached Middleton. She was eager to see the look on everyone's faces when she showed up with a good-looking guy who had a truck with Texas plates. But as they walked up to the bleachers, where rows of familiar kids sat drinking from Styrofoam cups filled with Coke and vodka, she understood that she could have arrived with a three-headed giraffe and still nobody would have looked twice. She would always be the weird, quiet girl whose mom hoarded animals.

They sat behind a clique of popular girls. "That's Elysia Maloney, the quarterback's girlfriend," she whispered to Gideon. "And Jen, the blond one, her boyfriend is the third-best wrestler in the state."

Gideon raised his eyebrows—it was clear he didn't care who any of these people were. If Ariel's high school was a prairie fire, Gideon was a faraway tropical island. One had nothing to do with the other. At one point the girls turned around to look at Ariel. They then whispered something to each other and burst out giggling.

Gideon scooted closer to Ariel so that their thighs were touching. "What if we left?" he asked.

Her heart sank. "You want to go home?"

"Not home. Somewhere else."

Now her heart was beating so loud she worried he would hear it. "Where?"

"It's a surprise. But trust me—it'll be more fun than this."

Back in his truck, Gideon cranked the heat and rubbed his hands together, blew into his palms. Even this, Ariel enjoyed watching. The way his hands came together. The thickness of his fingers. "It's kind of far," he said. "But we should make it back before your curfew."

"It's your skin if we're late." She felt equal parts giddy and nervous. She hoped he wasn't taking her somewhere like an arcade or a bowling alley. She'd never been and wouldn't know how to play any of the games. Or what if he was taking her somewhere adult—like a bar? Or a strip club? He didn't seem the type, but then again, she didn't know what type he was. There was a shard of fear in her stomach, one that made everything feel heightened, as if she were in a movie. *Maybe this was love*, she thought. Like starring in your very own movie.

When they pulled onto the highway, heading west, he turned the radio to a classic rock station. "This okay?" he asked.

"Sure," Ariel said, trying to sound confident, cool.

After a couple commercials, a song came on—something about a landslide. She felt at once calm and melancholy, as if remembering something nice that would never happen again. "Who is this?" she asked.

Gideon looked at the stereo and then to her. "Fleetwood Mac?"

"Oh, right," Ariel said. "She's great."

"You mean Stevie Nicks?"

"Yes," Ariel said, her cheeks on fire.

"You've never heard of Fleetwood Mac, have you?"

"I mean, the name sounds familiar."

Gideon turned up the volume and glanced at her. "We'll work on getting you out from under that rock."

Twenty minutes later they were approaching the border. "Are we going to Colorado?" she asked.

He gripped the steering wheel and smiled at the road. "Have you ever been?"

Ariel shook her head. Her mom often picked up or delivered animals to towns on the Front Range, but Ariel had never gone with.

"Have you ever seen mountains?" he asked.

This, then, was the real surprise—mountains. "I haven't." It was like admitting she was a virgin, which, of course, she was. She felt small. Sixteen years old and she'd never seen mountains.

They kept driving until they reached a town called Limon. The sun was nearly setting, the sky a child's erratic drawing of pink, lavender, and orange crayon strokes. It was her favorite thing about the prairie—the grandness and melodrama of the sky, how it constantly churned above like a mood ring, stagnating then simmering then eventually boiling over into a deep purple temper tantrum, throwing out fistfuls of lightning and hail, the occasional twister, only to clear out the next morning, contrite and bashful, smiling a uniform blue as if nothing had happened. *Who, me? I would never.*

They were still hours from Denver, from the Rockies themselves, but from here the mountains were visible beneath the sunset's soft colors—a dream of a mountain range.

Gideon pulled down a country road and parked. "What do you think?" He gestured to the sky, as if he'd painted it himself.

Ariel held very still and considered the horizon. "To be honest, they kind of scare me." She looked at him. "Is that stupid?"

"It's never stupid to feel something. It's just not what I expected you to say."

"I mean, they're beautiful—but they're also awful. It's like seeing a dragon or something."

Perhaps unsure what to say, Gideon only nodded. She kept staring at the mountains, as if they might, under enough concentration, come into greater focus, or begin to move, like an actual dragon stirring from a nap. They were absolutely silent and yet they roared, their snowy peaks biting the sky. They seemed somehow related to the knot of nervous fear in her stomach, the pinch she felt each time she looked at Gideon. She thought of what he'd said. *It's never stupid to feel something.*

After a few wordless minutes, Gideon reversed his truck and they headed back the way they'd come, the horizon gulping down the mountains in the rearview mirror. Gideon turned up the music. She'd heard the song before—*Say hey, good lookin', whatcha got cooking?* She didn't dare ask who it was.

They made it home fifteen minutes before her curfew. She wondered if her mother would ask her about the football game, if Ariel should prepare a fake final score, but then realized a million lifetimes could pass and her mother would not once, in any of them, ask about a football game.

They were still sitting in the car when Gideon turned to her. "Did you have a good time?"

Part of her was ready to be alone in her room, to digest the evening's events, but another part wanted to pause the moment forever, to stay there, in the car, with Gideon. She was not ready to say good night. "I did," Ariel said, her voice sadder than she intended it to be.

"You don't really seem like it."

"It's just that I feel silly."

"Why?"

"Because I bribed you into hanging out with me—it's pathetic. I feel a little pathetic."

"You shouldn't."

"Why not?" Already, she ached at the thought of interacting with him the next morning, and each morning after that, knowing she'd embarrassed herself in such a way. Somehow, she would have to conceal this embarrassment from her mother.

"Because I spent all day looking forward to this. I mean, not the football game, but this." He gestured to the empty space between them. "You know what I mean."

She examined his face, to see if he was telling the truth. Was it possible he actually liked her? That he had been watching her in the same way she had been watching him?

"Really?" she asked.

"Yes," he said. "Really."

"How come you never talk to me?"

"Because you're young—and my boss's daughter. There's red flags everywhere I look."

Ariel had to close her eyes. As soon as she did, she felt his lips on hers. Despite all the times she'd practiced on her stuffed penguin, she had never been kissed before. It felt, a little, like dreaming. She thought of the animals, how unfortunate it was they didn't kiss the way humans did, how they could never really hold a loved one in their arms. So few animals even had lips. When she opened her eyes, she half expected to find that nobody was there, that she was alone, in a daydream. But there was Gideon, a goofy smile on his face.

"Hey there," he said.

"Hey," she said back.

Like this, the world cracked open.

Mona

She didn't need to go to the bank or the post office. What she needed was a goddamn moment to think. She needed someone to talk to, someone to help her make sense of Ariel's return. She needed someone to tell her exactly how she was supposed to react now that the thing she'd been wanting to happen for the past six years had finally happened.

Coreen lived a few miles away, in an ostentatious colonial Daniel had referred to as the Little Mansion on the Prairie. The house had belonged to Coreen's late husband, Beau, who had inherited it from his father, a cattle rancher turned dog-food tycoon. Beau had abandoned his father's line of work to become a doctor and full-time drinker, taking to the bottle with a brand of determined self-annihilation Mona hadn't seen in anyone since her own father. When Beau was alive, Mona would sometimes catch him blasting down Sanctuary Road in his Ford F-350, one big hairy arm hanging out the window, platinum wristwatch throwing off sparks of sunlight. Only once did he hit a dog—a mutt named Macaroni who'd gone after a deer near the culvert—but once was one time too many.

Nobody was surprised when Beau died of liver failure. The real wonder was what happened to Coreen in his absence. Formerly a discreet woman, Coreen began inserting herself into the town and its webs of gossip and business. She started a women's poker club, a

children's clothing swap. She even ran for treasurer. Perhaps most surprising of all was the way she appeared in Mona's life, demanding they
finally act like neighbors. She was lonely, she said, and began inviting
Mona to eat lunch, take walks, make supper. Mona was surprised to
discover she not only *could* make room for this new person—who
knew, all this time, there was room?—but that she also wanted to. She
didn't realize how badly she, too, needed a friend.

They were still friends, or something like it. Whatever happens
to friends once love gets involved, they were that. Everything was
fine until the afternoon Coreen put a hand on Mona's knee and said,
"Maybe I'm wrecking everything, but here I go." She'd leaned in,
the floral scent of her perfume thick as morning fog. Out of shock,
Mona had kissed her back, her body going electric with nerves as
Coreen walked a hand up her T-shirt, causing Mona's back to arch.
There was an uneasy feeling in the pit of her stomach, one that said:
This will be complicated, and we don't have time for complicated. But
as Coreen pushed a hand through Mona's hair, fingernails raking her
scalp, Mona felt a roar of hunger that was many times louder than
the whimper of her fear. She hadn't been touched since Daniel left.
And yet, after three confusing and anxious weeks in which Coreen fell
deeper and deeper while Mona clung to the surface, unable or maybe
just unwilling to let go, Mona realized it wouldn't work. What she
needed was a friend. "Honestly," she'd told Coreen, "I'm not even sure
I like men these days." Coreen had only nodded, her face pale with
disappointment.

She knew Coreen was still in love with her, an unbalance that
made Mona uneasy. Still, she found herself migrating toward her in
times of trouble. When she decided to sell the sanctuary, Coreen was
the first person she told—a mistake.

"I'll give you the money," Coreen had said. They'd sat in Coreen's
kitchen, early-autumn light pouring in through the bay window.

Knowing something was wrong, Coreen had made oatmeal raisin cookies and cinnamon tea. She'd also straightened her hair and put on a sheer white blouse—habits Mona wished she'd give up.

"I won't allow it," Mona had said.

"This isn't the time for pride, Mona. The animals are on the line."

"It's not pride, it's common sense. It's also highly inappropriate." How could she explain that if she let Coreen help with the Bright Side, she would feel indebted for the rest of her life? How could she also admit that she was tired—not of helping the animals, but of being in debt, of being poor, of knowing that, in some countries, the amount of money she paid in interest each month could feed an entire community. She was tired of herself, for letting herself get so far in the hole, for feeling like a failure. She was tired of saying goodbye to animals, of burying them, of yielding to the endless cycle of love and loss, love and loss, love and loss. She was tired of always trying to try harder. She was getting older, too, and was simply feeling *tired*. Ever since the idea appeared in her mind, giving up the sanctuary felt more and more like setting down a horse she'd been unknowingly carrying across her shoulders for the past fifteen years. She was curious what it would feel like to finally set it down—to watch it run from her, full speed. To finally straighten her spine.

"There wouldn't be any strings," Coreen said.

Of course there would be strings, Mona had thought. There were always strings when it came to love and money. "I won't do it" was all she said. "End of conversation."

"Then you'll put the animals on my land—we can build pens here."

"And then what? I live here, with you?" *Sleep in your bed?* she wanted to say but didn't. "It's all the same thing. It's all a dead-end road, and it's my burden to find a way out."

"This isn't about us," Coreen said. "You're being unreasonable."

"And you," Mona had said, her tone meaner than she'd intended, "are sticking your nose where it doesn't belong." She'd left her tea and cookies on the table and stormed off, driving too fast down Sanctuary Road. Had it not been for the fire, it might have been the last time they'd spoken.

Mona knew the door would be unlocked, but she rang the bell anyway.

"Come in," Coreen called.

Mona found Coreen in the kitchen, eating a bagel with strawberry cream cheese. She wore stretchy black capris and a floral cardigan with buttons shaped like ladybugs. In the living room, *Dr. Oz* was muted on the TV.

"Hey, stranger," Coreen said, her eyes lighting up. "You hungry? I could put another bagel in the toaster—they're sesame. I know you like sesame."

"I already ate, but I wouldn't turn down a cup of coffee."

Coreen sprang to action. When they first started spending time together, she'd had one of those Keurig contraptions; Mona had convinced her to get a drip maker. "So what's up?"

Mona took a deep breath, sat down at the table. "Ariel came back last night."

Coreen stopped what she was doing. "Excuse me?"

"You heard me."

"What does she want?"

"I'm not sure."

"Well, what are you doing over here?"

"That's the thing—I don't know what to do. I don't know what to say to her."

"Well, what do you *feel*?" This was typical Coreen—feelings this, feelings that.

"I just— I feel— I don't know. That's the problem. That's what I came here for."

"Huh," Coreen said, bringing the coffeepot over. She'd chosen Mona's least-favorite mug, an ungodly pink thing with the words *I'm a mom. What's your superpower?* written in white bubble letters. "Well, what are you going to do?"

"Kick her out, probably."

"What are you talking about? She's your daughter."

"But after what she did to me?"

"You mean go to college?"

She and Coreen had never agreed on the terms of her and Ariel's rupture. Coreen agreed it was hurtful that Ariel had run away, but she thought Mona was petty for not letting her go in the first place. Every few months, Coreen would encourage Mona to track Ariel down, send her a message. Mona adamantly refused.

"You know it's about more than college," Mona said. "She left, just like her father did, knowing exactly how much it would kill me. After all that, I'm just supposed to open my arms and let her in?"

"Yes," Coreen said. "That's exactly what you're supposed to do. You're the mother."

"Well, I just can't," Mona said. "Besides, all she's doing is stirring up trouble. You should have seen the look on her face when Gideon came in this morning. Like a chocolate cake walked through the door."

"Does she know about him and Joy?" It was the other thread between them—Gideon was dating Coreen's daughter.

"I don't know—but I'm sure she'll find out soon enough." She looked at Coreen, at this woman she had hurt without meaning to. "I just wish she either would have shown up six years ago or not at all. It's like, just when I feel like I've moved on, there she is in my living room."

"Listen. I was mad as hell when Joy left. And it took Beau cough-ing up blood to get her to come back. But did I waste even an hour contemplating my ego when she did? Did I waste my breath saying, 'I told you so?' No, I just put clean sheets on her bed and moved on."

It was yet another thing they had in common, although only on the surface. After high school, Joy moved to Los Angeles, to try her hand at acting. She came home after a year, to be near her father as he was dying.

"This is different, and you know it. Joy and Ariel—it's apples and oranges."

"You can tell yourself that, but it's the same thing in the end. They both needed to go, and so they went. It just took Ariel longer to come back, probably because she was so scared of what you'd do to her when she did."

Mona said nothing.

"You need to try to forgive her. Think of how hard this must be for her. How scary. The least you can do is give her a chance. Give *yourself* a chance. You'll regret it if you don't." She poured Mona's cof-fee and then added a splash of hazelnut creamer.

"You know I hate that artificial creamer stuff," Mona said. "Makes my tongue feel weird."

"Well, I already put it in. So deal."

In moments like this, Coreen reminded Mona of her mother. They were both practical, no-nonsense women with the kind of do-what-you-have-to-do attitude most people associated with men but which, Mona knew, was more typical of women.

Mona's mother had appeared in her mind more often in recent years, perhaps because Mona had reached and then surpassed the age at which she'd died. Lung cancer, at forty-seven. An unfair way to end. *I only smoked one cigarette in my whole life,* her mother said after the diagnosis, *and I didn't even inhale.* Mona's mother was familiar with this brand of injustice, having worked for twenty years as a nurse in a psychiatric ward. Some nights, she would return home pale and shaky, strange fluids on her white Danskos, unwilling to talk about the day's events. Still, she loved her job—just as Mona loved hers—not because it was interesting or rewarding but because caretaking seemed like the only reasonable occupation in a world that needed so much care. It was also in her blood. Her own mother, Mona's grandmother, had famously cared for her sick bunkmates at Bergen-Belsen.

Months before her diagnosis, Mona's mother brought home a dirt-caked puppy, perhaps knowing, on a cellular level, that Mona would soon need him. The puppy was black with scraggly fur and a flat, abbreviated nose, like a hog's. "A birth defect," Mona's mother explained, "but that doesn't mean he isn't perfect." Then, addressing the dog, "How did you find us when we needed you most? How did you become so adorable?" It was Mona's idea to name him Howie.

As her mother's condition worsened, Mona's love for Howie became desperate, boundless. She found herself pining for him during school, the way she had once, as a little girl, pined for her mother. Each morning, she would leave hungry for her return, when Howie would come scrambling to the door, collar jingling, and jump into her arms for kisses.

To nobody's surprise, her father never took to Howie. Sometimes Mona would catch him looking at the dog with a cruel sheen in his eyes, as if Howie were a walking manifestation of Ariel's mother's illness, a tumor with a heartbeat, legs, and tail. He knew the dog was meant to replace his wife, and he did not appreciate the gesture.

For many years, Mona had wondered: *Why not her father instead?* He had been the unhealthy one: the smoker, the worrier, the kind of hard-bellied man who could devour a whole pint of Moose Tracks while watching the six o'clock news. He was a drinker, too. A beer with dinner, whiskey if he'd had a bad day or a really good one. After

Mona's mother died, when Mona was sixteen, his drinking took on a new shape. In the mornings, he would nurse a bottle of brandy. By the time he came home from work at the Boeing plant, he reeked of booze. One night, Mona came downstairs to find him chugging cinnamon mouthwash.

Her father changed in other ways, too. Most notably, Mona's voice began to pain him. She would whisper, and still her father would squint, press a hand to his forehead. "Do you have to shout?" he'd ask. Some days, her voice would induce in him migraines so severe he would lie for hours in his bedroom, a warm towel across his eyes, whimpering like a kitten.

"There's to be a new arrangement," he said one day, his breath heavy with alcohol. "No more talking."

"What do you mean?" Mona asked.

"I mean what I said. You don't talk anymore. At least not in the house. Not to me."

"You can't be ser—" she began, but he had clapped a palm across her face and was digging his fingernails into her cheeks so that, when she looked in the mirror later that night, she found little parentheses etched around her mouth. The smell of his palm—salt, garlic, cigarettes—lingered on her lips for days.

During these long voiceless nights at home, Howie became her closest friend. He was there when she came home from school, when she woke each morning. He knew she sometimes stole sandwiches from the school cafeteria to eat for dinner and that her greatest fear was that she would grow up to be more like her father than her mother, a tangle of anger instead of a ribbon of light. He knew she sometimes woke in the night, calling her mother's name, drowning all over again in the knowledge that she was gone, that she was not coming back to save her. When she cried, he licked her tears.

On Mona's seventeenth birthday, her father bought her a sweater that was too small, the bottom hem ending above her belly button. She looked down at the sweater and then toward her father, as if to say, *It doesn't fit.*

"What damn size are you anyway?"

Because she could not answer, she made an *L* with her thumb and forefinger, realizing a beat too late that she was also giving him the *loser* sign.

"Take it off," he slurred.

She began to remove the sweater when suddenly her father's hands were on her, forcing her arms up and over her head, pulling the fabric over her face with such force that it caught against her throat. When he noticed she was crying, he grabbed her by the wrist.

"What are you sad about? You've got a perfect life."

Even Mona was shocked when Howie, normally a gentle, passive dog, lashed out, biting her father's hand. Her father cursed and then kicked Howie in the stomach, hard. "Goddamn animal."

Howie slunk toward the door, whimpering, a look of terrified disbelief in his eyes. Before he left, he glanced at Mona, as if to ask: *Aren't you coming with me?*

"Don't you *ever* hurt him," Mona said, her voice a whisper. She was trembling.

Slowly her father came toward her and yanked her to the ground. He then cupped the back of her head and pressed her face into his jeans so that she smelled the cold metal of his zipper. "It's a fucking dog," he said.

She was afraid of what he might do next, but he only pushed her away, rough, so that she tumbled to the ground. As soon as he was gone, Mona crawled beneath her bed. She was nearly too big to fit underneath, but she lay there, her chest wedged against the springs, trying to ignore the dust bunnies and dead brown recluses. The only other thing under the bed was a sock, soft blue with a lime-green toe, from a pair her mother had given her years before. She'd thought she'd lost it. Lying there with the sock, she felt as if her father had carved the spirit from her body, like the flesh of a cantaloupe from its rind. Not a minute later, Howie appeared in her room and army-crawled under the bed to be with her. She wept as quietly as she could while Howie nuzzled her, pressing the top of his head against her neck. Limb by limb, she felt herself return to the world. As long as she had Howie, she did not have to be alone.

Had anything like this happened again—even once, or twice, or on a regular basis—she could have developed a routine of fear, rather than the unorganized paranoia that consumed her. It would take her eight more months to graduate from high school and gather the courage to leave; to find an apartment on the other side of Wichita, near the university; to get a job at a coffee shop on campus where she would meet a handsome undergrad named Daniel who was earning a degree in literature; to begin the rest of her life. Until then, her father owned her.

Coreen and Daniel were the only people who knew about her childhood, about her father and why she'd felt so indebted to Howie, why she'd wanted to start the Bright Side in the first place. Even Ariel didn't know. Mona had never found a good reason to tell her.

Ariel

Before going outside to help Gideon—her mom had told her to, so that's what she was going to do—Ariel washed her face with lemon hand soap. More than ever, she saw her mother in the mirror: her long nose and deep-set eyes, the diamond shape of her face. She had inherited her mother's hair—dark, cumbersome curls that compelled people to reach out and say, *It's so thick.* Sometimes, if she stood close to a mirror, she liked the way she looked. Other times, she didn't. One of the best parts about growing older was that she'd begun to care less and less what she looked like, which she realized had something to do with caring less about the opinions of men. Today was an exception. In the bathroom with the ceramic frog Kleenex holder and the water-stained mirror—the same bathroom where, upon the occasion of Ariel's first period, her mother had stood outside the door calling, *Are you putting it all the way in? It goes all the way in!* The same bathroom where she had given countless bubble baths to dogs, toweling their quivering bodies only to have them immediately shake water all over the tiles—she now bit her lips and pinched her cheeks, to give them color. She ruffled her hair, did a sexy duck face, and then went outside. Whatever she looked like would have to be good enough.

In the daylight, she found everything in its place. Across the driveway was Dog Town, a row of heated kennels capable of holding more than fifty medium-sized dogs. Beyond this was Catalina Island, an old shed where the cats liked to hang out, and beyond this the petting zoo, where the sheep, goats, chickens, and pigs lived. Down the narrow creek that ran dry in the summer was the barn, home to the horses, mules, and donkeys, as well as any exotic animals that found their way to the Bright Side before Mona could relocate them. At different points in Ariel's childhood, the barn had hosted a serval, an alpaca, and a fifty-year-old African gray who could recite the first line of the Declaration of Independence and who was so neglected in his previous home he'd plucked himself nearly bald. Now the barn's western wall was charred, shiny black detritus littering the perimeter. It was impossible to imagine Sydney creeping around in the dark, pouring gasoline, lighting a match. She recalled a clock in his room, with fish for each number, wooden paddles for the minute and hour hands. A collection of Beanie Babies sat on his bookcase, legs dangling over the edge. When he caught Ariel eyeing them—she had always wanted Beanie Babies, but Mona adamantly refused—he'd snapped, *My mom gave them to me. We'd get one every Christmas.* He'd thought she was judging him.

The barn was also Gideon's favorite hangout. Whenever he used to have a bad day, Ariel would find him mulling around with the horses. Sometimes he'd saddle Mona's mare, Ginger, and disappear into the fields around the Bright Side. Everything Ariel knew about horses, she'd learned from Gideon, who'd learned it from his dad: that the tough, V-shaped mass on the soles of their feet was called a frog; that they could see nearly 360 degrees; that their hearts weighed more than a newborn baby.

As she suspected, Gideon was in the paddock just outside the barn, brushing Ginger. Ariel had always felt a touch self-conscious around Ginger, as if the horse could see through to all the selfish and petty parts that made Ariel who she was.

A lump of emotion rose in her throat as Gideon leaned into Ginger's side, brushing her slowly from head to rump. "Hey," Ariel said, breaking the moment. She reached out to pet Ginger's nose, but the horse whinnied and jerked her head away.

"Easy girl," Ariel said. "It's just me."

"She doesn't remember you," Gideon said. He would not look at her.

"Don't say that."

He put his hand on Ginger's neck, to calm her. "I thought I said I didn't want help."

"My mom said I should come anyways."

"Since when do you listen to her?"

When he turned to walk away, Ariel reached out and grabbed his arm. "Will you just talk to me for a minute? I came all this way."

He shook her off. "For what exactly?"

"I saw about the fire—I was worried."

"Well, fire's out."

"Gideon."

"What, Ariel? What is it you want me to do? Give you a hug? Throw you a welcome-home party?" Over the years, she'd recalled the way he would look at her—eyes filled with affection, almost twinkling. Now there was this. Anger.

"I'm sorry, okay? That's part of why I'm here. To say sorry."

"I'm not the one who needs an apology."

"Of course you do."

Turning from her, he ran the brush through Ginger's mane.

For her seventeenth birthday, he'd gifted her a bracelet made from Ginger's hair. Ariel had cherished the bracelet. One night, while dancing downtown with Dex, the bracelet caught on her jacket's zipper and broke, the hairs unraveling and scattering around her feet, lost in the shuffle of bodies. Dex had been alarmed when she began frantically searching the ground on hands and knees. "It's just a bracelet," he kept repeating. "We can get you a new one, okay?"

"You want to know something funny?" Gideon was saying. The tone in his voice had changed.

"What?"

"I tried to come find you once, the spring after you left."

"You came to the dorms?" All these years, she figured he'd given up once she stopped calling. To think that he had come after her—it was like finding a love letter a decade too late.

"I'd worked the whole morning, got up extra early so I could finish everything and leave after lunch. I remember I was so tired during the drive. I had this idea that I'd find you and we'd take a nap together. Sounds ridiculous now, but that's what I kept thinking. How we'd take a nap in your dorm. I don't know what I thought would happen after that, but that was the plan as far as I knew it."

"What happened?"

"The door to the building was locked, so I waited until some girls came up with their key cards, and I snuck in after them. Then I realized I had no idea where to go. So I went upstairs and started asking around, seeing if anybody knew your room number. I must have freaked out one of the girls, because eventually your RA showed up and started to interrogate me, like maybe I was a stalker or something."

"Janet? I haven't thought of her in years—everyone hated her. She wouldn't let us have candles."

"Well, she was all right once I told her I was your boyfriend come to surprise you. She brought me to your room, and when nobody answered she told me I could wait in the common space. So I just sat there like a dope, waiting, nervous as hell, but eventually I got so tired I just fell asleep right there on the couch. When I woke up, there were a bunch of girls wanting to watch a movie. They needed the couch. When I asked for you they told me you'd gone camping. In Missouri."

Ariel flinched—she remembered that weekend. "So what'd you do?"

"Left. Got myself a coffee and drove back home." He looked at the ground and rubbed the back of his neck.

"I'm so sorry, Gideon."

"Nothing to cry about now. Here I am. Good as new."

Ariel thought about that weekend, the camping trip. She'd gone with Dex and some of his friends to Mark Twain National Forest. She'd looked forward to hiking, but all Dex and his friends wanted to do was get high and watch the trees blow in the wind.

Gideon reached into his pocket and pulled out a peppermint candy. "Here," he said, putting the candy in Ariel's hand. "Try this."

Ariel held out her palm. Without hesitating, Ginger took the bait, her gums tickling Ariel's hand. "Good girl," Ariel said, stroking Ginger's long nose. She smiled at Gideon.

"Don't get too excited. She'd take a mint from a wolf."

"Whatever," Ariel said. "She loves me." She watched Ginger happily crunch the mint, her pink tongue flashing as she chewed.

"Aren't you hungry, too?" she asked Gideon. "You never ate breakfast." She wanted to sit down with him, to talk. So long as they were outside, half his attention would be on the horses.

Gideon shrugged. "I could eat."

In the house, he put a slice of sourdough in the toaster and scrambled some eggs. Sourdough was his favorite, as were root beer floats, watermelon Jolly Ranchers, and rice pudding. Ariel remembered that he sometimes put a bag of Lipton tea in his coffee if he was feeling especially tired.

"So what's the deal? Are you staying for a while?" He brought his plate to the table and began to eat. She hated how happy it made her, to sit and watch him eat. So long as there was food on his plate, he would sit still with her.

"Just the weekend, I think."

"Do you work?"

"Of course I work."

"Doing what?"

"I work at an animal clinic." She anticipated the same reaction her mother had given her, but Gideon's expression remained neutral. "Just office stuff," she added. "I'm at the front desk."

"And what was your degree in?"

"English," she said, her heart skipping a tick.

"And now you're a receptionist? At a vet's office?"

"Don't do this," she said.

"Do what?"

"Make me feel bad for going to college." She could never tell him that she hadn't actually graduated—that she had run away from the animals, from him, for nothing. That she had wasted his money so she could stay out and party with Dex. The truth of it nauseated her.

"It just seems silly is all. If you wanted to work with animals, you could have stayed here."

"It's only a temporary thing, until I find something better. It pays the rent, and it's something I know how to do. I'm good at it." What she did not say was that it was also boring, tedious, and low-paying, and that what she really wanted was to finish school and become an English teacher, to know that she was actively doing something good in the world.

"I know I'm being hard on you," Gideon was saying. "It's just that when you left . . ." He looked outside, where a pack of dogs were play-fighting, taking turns wrestling one another to the ground.

"When I left, what?"

"Nothing," he said. "It was just hard. I was very angry at you, even though I wanted you to go—I hope you know that, that I wanted you to go, wanted you to do your own thing, and I'm glad if I helped make that possible—but still."

"Look, Gideon. I was young and selfish. If I could do it again, I'd do everything different."

"Like what? What would you do different?"

She had forgotten this about him, that when you showed him a door, he pushed on it. "I would have come home during winter break, like I said I would. I would have told my mom I was leaving instead of making you sneak me away. I wouldn't have taken your money. Maybe I would have even stayed here and gone to school in Middleton—maybe that was the right thing to do."

"So you regret leaving?"

The question surprised Ariel, for she had made it a rule, over the years, never to ask it of herself, for fear of what she might answer. "No—yes. No. I don't know. It's hard to regret something so fundamental to what my life is now. But do I regret how I did it? Yes. I do."

"Well, you did it." There was bitterness in his voice. She understood a part of him had not forgiven her, might never forgive her, and that this was the part that mattered.

"The thing is, a lot happened while you were gone," he said. "Things are different now. You understand that, don't you? I'm not the same person. Your mom's not the same person."

"I've changed, too."

"I can certainly see that."

She wasn't sure if it was an insult, but she felt a sting in her chest.

His eggs gone, he was sopping up the yolk with his crust. He always ate his crust last, a habit Ariel had forgotten. When the crust was gone, he brushed the crumbs from his pants and stood up. "All right. Time to get back out there."

"Could we talk while we work?"

"Sure," he said. "Mona-style. Killing two birds."

"You mean feeding two birds." She caught him smiling as he brought his plate to the sink. This was a joke, something Mona had come up with back in the day, saying, *Killing two birds is so violent. Why not feed them instead?*

Just then, a gang of cats raced into the kitchen, followed by a pack of dogs. "Hey," she said, watching the cats speed toward her old room, "do you know what happened to my bed?"

He turned from the sink to look at her. "You really want to know?"

"I mean, I get that my room belongs to the cats now. But where'd my bed go?"

"She burned it," Gideon said.

"She *burned* it?"

"That first Thanksgiving you didn't come back, she hauled the mattress out into the pasture, doused it with gasoline, and set it on fire. Scared the horses half to death."

"You're not serious, are you?"

"As a heart attack." He was washing his plate—he'd always been good about cleaning up after himself. "She said she was cleansing the bad energy."

"Jesus. She didn't dance around it, did she?"

"I'm not going to tell you she didn't."

"Now you're joking."

He smiled, a mischievous smile—he was fucking with her. Or was he?

"It had bedbugs," he said, drying his hands on his pants. "That's why she burned your bed."

Ariel felt the knot in her chest untie itself. "Don't fuck with me like that. I have no idea what's been going on here."

Gideon smiled. "Couldn't help it. I mean, she did say something about cleansing negative energy—but mostly, I think, it was the bed-bugs."

Together, they headed out to feed the animals. This had been the ritual of her life for years—every day, the same thing, with the same person, in the same way. This was how life with animals worked best: If you repeated the same procedure, no stomachs would go empty. No chicks would freeze for lack of a heat lamp. Nobody would go without their medication.

Ariel volunteered to feed the dogs while Gideon finished with the equine chores. She had always enjoyed feeding the dogs, the way they danced in circles and yipped as if each meal were the first they'd ever had. She had always loved the sound of animals eating.

"You remember how everything goes?" Gideon asked.

"It's dog food, not astrophysics," Ariel said, and then realized she was parroting her mother.

She went to the old storage shed, where the kibble lived. This was the verbiage of the sanctuary—everything *lived* somewhere. The scissors lived in the junk drawer, the hay pick lived on the hook, the wood-splitting ax lived on the back porch. Everything was given a life, a home, a reason to be. A bucket of kibble in each hand, she waddled toward Dog Town, the metal handles biting into her palms. She set down the buckets and examined her hands, soft and pale from her days spent filling out spreadsheets and updating Dr. Nguyen's sched-ule. Her fingernails were clean and she noticed the blank space where her engagement ring had been. She'd put it in her car's center console, for safekeeping.

She decided to let some of the dogs run around before she fed them. In groups of three, she emptied the cool pens, where the well-behaved dogs lived. The hot pens—identified by a stripe of red duct tape on the latch—were home to the Hot Dogs, the vicious and unruly dogs who might shred another dog's throat if given the chance. These dogs didn't get to go to the dog run. For the most part, they didn't get to go anywhere.

With the Cool Dogs in the run, Ariel cleaned their pens, removing the blankets, towels, and pads so she could shake out whatever had collected there and hose down the cement floor beneath. Everything reeked. She thought of a song Gideon used to sing to the dogs—*Me oh my, did someone bake a chocolate pie?*

"Good to see you still know how to clean a pen," Gideon said, startling her. How long had he been standing there, watching her work? In his hand was a milk jug of water. He offered it to her, and she took a long drink—she hadn't even realized she was thirsty.

"How could I forget this much fun?" she said.

"Let me help. It'll go faster."

It felt good, this flicker of camaraderie. Like the old days, when they could blow through an entire day of work having so much fun they hardly noticed they were covered in shit, their clothes sticky with sweat.

Gideon helped her clean the rest of the cool pens, the two of them working in what Ariel considered affable silence. When they were finished, they decided to let the Cool Dogs play a little longer while they fed the dogs in the hot pens.

"Is that your car in the visitors' lot?" Gideon asked. They were carrying buckets of food from the shed, Ariel still straining, Gideon carrying his with ease.

"It is." Ariel loved the car dearly. It was a piece of shit, but it was her piece of shit. It was also the one thing she didn't share with Dex, who, in an admirable but frustrating display of environmental activism, had allowed his driver's license to expire, opting instead for a car-free life. What this really meant was that Ariel gave him rides whenever the weather was bad or he felt too lazy to bike. "You like it?" she asked Gideon.

"I do. Can I see it?"

"Right now?"

"Sure. What else do we have to do?"

"Only about a million things."

Gideon waved a hand. "There's always a million things. As soon as we do a million, there'll be a million and two more. Besides, the dogs are having a good time in the run. We should let them stay out a little longer."

They started down the drive toward the visitors' lot. When they reached her car, Gideon etched a smiley face into the dust on her back windshield. Then he started on a pair of boobs.

"Would you quit that?" Ariel said. Did drawing boobs count as flirting? Even the idea of it made her heart race.

"Such a prude these days."

She spit onto the hem of her flannel and used it to erase the boobs.

In the car, Ariel turned on the battery so they could listen to the radio. "Pick something," she told him, pointing to the dial.

"What'll it be," he asked, "Christian or country?"

"I forgot about the radio out here."

"You got any CDs?"

Before she could stop him, he'd opened the center console and was rummaging through the CDs. "Jesus," he said, pulling out a series of emo albums. "Did you turn into a thirteen-year-old boy?"

"What can I say? I just can't get enough Good Charlotte." When he didn't register that she was joking, she explained that the CDs belonged to the teenage boy who'd sold her the car the year before. "I haven't gotten around to really cleaning it out." In truth, she'd spent a good hour of the drive rocking out to Fall Out Boy.

"This his ring, too?" he asked, holding up her engagement ring.

Ariel's stomach dropped. "No, that's mine."

Gideon eyed her but put the ring back with the CDs. For the first time, Ariel was glad Dex hadn't given her a fancier ring.

Gideon turned on the radio and started going through the stations, sifting through static. Eventually an old John Prine song came through, one Ariel hadn't heard in years. Something about sitting on a rainbow.

He let his head go back against the seat. There was his neck, creased with dirt. Ariel stared at his Adam's apple, remembering how she used to trace it down to his chest. "I could imagine a road trip in this," he said. "How about the Grand Canyon? Or Yellowstone?"

"That's where everyone goes."

"Fine, how about . . . Turkmenistan?"

"Maybe we could just sit here," she said. "I drove a long way just to be right where we are."

"And why did you do that?" He grabbed the cherry air freshener and gave it a yank, so that it snapped back to the mirror and bounced.

"I told you, I read about the fire, about my mom selling the sanctuary. I knew I needed to come back."

"Not good enough."

"What if nothing I say is good enough?"

"Try me."

Ariel grabbed the steering wheel and squeezed. "I was homesick?"

"Lame."

"I wanted to help my mom?"

"Still lame."

"I discovered my true calling is shoveling shit and I wanted to come back and reclaim my destiny?"

"Better, but not quite there." She didn't want to talk about Sydney, about how she felt responsible for the fire, or how she'd missed everyone—her mom, the animals, *him*—with a longing so extreme and protracted it often felt like a wedding dress train, made of stone, that dragged behind her wherever she went. Only now could she feel the train lifting, as if someone had finally picked up the tail end to help her.

"Let me ask you something," she said.

Gideon looked at her. He was tapping out the tune on his knee.

She breathed in, let it out. "Are you seeing anyone?"

"Like a therapist?" He smiled evasively.

"You know what I mean."

His gaze went out the window. The winter sun was high overhead, making water mirages against the horizon. This far into the season, all the fields had dried to a unified gold. At night, the air would smell like smoke. Wood stoves and bonfires and the hollow song of mourning doves.

Gideon turned down the music. The song was almost to the chorus, and she wanted to turn it back up, but she didn't dare. She'd look up the song later, if she had to. For now, she held her breath, not wanting to disrupt the atmosphere lest it somehow alter what he was about to tell her.

"I am," he said. "For about five years now."

She felt her heart constrict and then loosen, as if having withstood a punch. All this time, she'd blamed herself for their drift. It had never occurred to her that maybe he had wanted her to stop calling, that he, too, had wanted to move on. "I'm happy for you," she said. "Can I ask who?"

He cautiously met her eyes. "Her name is Joy—I think you know her."

"You mean Champ? You're dating Joy Champ?"

"Does that surprise you?"

"I thought she moved to California to be an actress. She was in a toothpaste commercial. I saw it."

Gideon smiled. "Yeah, I've seen it. Cracks me up every time. She was out there, in LA, but she moved back. She volunteers here now, a few times a week. She's good with the dogs, especially the abused ones. They trust her."

"She volunteers here? You mean she *works*?"

"Why's that so surprising?"

"I just remember her being so . . . rich."

"Turns out you can be rich and work."

"I guess," Ariel said.

Joy had been in the grade above Ariel's at school, but the two never became friends. When the county bus driver got fired for getting a DUI, Mona and Joy's mother, Coreen, had taken turns driving the girls to school in Middleton. Ariel had dreaded the arrangement. Her mother's truck, Old Baby, smelled like dog shit and was coated in a fine layer of dirt and animal hair; on a hot day, the odor could make her gag. The first time Joy rode in Old Baby, she had simply sat there, quiet and smiling, her eyes watering from the stench. As soon as Mona cracked the windows, Joy began gulping for air, but she never said one word about it. On the days when Coreen drove, Ariel closed her eyes and breathed deep the smell of new leather, the skin on her knees going numb from the powerful air conditioner.

"I'm happy for you," said Ariel.

"You already said that."

"It's because I mean it."

"Why wouldn't you?"

Ariel forced a smile. "I'm just saying. I'm glad you found someone out here."

"What about you? Are you seeing anyone?"

She thought of Dex, of his curly hair and how he always sang Marvin Gaye in the shower. She thought of his shoes, always in piles, always multiplying and in her way. The mole on his chest, the exact size and color of a chocolate chip. He had a serious nose—aquiline with a slight twist from where he broke it as a kid—and Ariel would often find boogers clinging to the outside of his nostrils. *A nugget of gold has escaped the mine!* she would say, and he would know to wipe his face.

"I've been dating," she told Gideon, "but nothing serious."

They sat together, neither of them saying anything. Years ago, they had spent many good hours in What-the-Truck. They would tell Mona they were going to town for ice cream sandwiches, and instead would drive out into the cornfields, the sky cracked open and dripping stars above them.

She traced the steering wheel, the very instrument that had brought her back to him, and then dialed up the radio. John Prine was still singing: *There won't be nothing but big old hearts, dancing in our eyes.*

As the song kept on, Gideon closed his eyes and started to sing. His voice was like everything else about him: sturdy, humble. Practical, but driven by emotion. It started soft but gained traction until Ariel could feel it in her collarbone, in the muscles beneath her neck. She remembered then how he used to sing to Opal. Sometimes, if he found the right song—something high-pitched, crooning—Opal would howl along with him, eyes closed, black lips turned to the sky. Ariel would howl, too, and if they were loud enough, they could stir up the rest of the sanctuary dogs and sometimes even the resident coyotes until the sky filled with the sound of howling and shivers ran up and down Ariel's spine, little electric pinpricks saying: *Hold on to this; hold on to this.*

Gathering her courage into a knot she could hold on to, Ariel asked the question that had been tugging at her for the past few years. "Will you tell me how Opal died?"

Gideon swallowed the song and turned to her. "You're not going to like what I tell you."

"Tell me anyways."

He laced his fingers together in his lap. "Bone cancer."

"Okay," Ariel said, stomach still clenching. "When?"

"That's the part you're really not going to like."

"*Tell* me."

"Last week," he said. "Well, nine days ago now."

She felt dizzy, as if the car were suddenly floating. "Last week?"

Gideon nodded.

"She must have been what? Twelve? Thirteen?"

He looked at her, eyes heavy—just talking about Opal clearly caused him pain. "Thirteen. Your mom started calling her Methuselah. She's the one who woke her the night of the fire."

"Nine days," Ariel repeated, feeling her heart fold in on itself. Years ago, she would have sobbed, but it had been too long now. She didn't even know what Opal had looked like in her old age. She still pictured her clear-eyed, a bounce in her step. "If I'd just come back a little sooner . . ."

For a moment they sat there, not saying anything. Eventually Ariel said, "I missed her so much. And not just her. All of it." She looked at him, to see if he believed her. She wanted desperately for him to believe her.

"I know," he said.

He then started to sing again, perhaps to comfort her. Listening to him, she was overcome with a sensation of having remembered something she'd once loved deeply but had somehow forgotten. The sensation was neither good nor bad, but ached slightly, like when a limb awakens after falling asleep.

This had been her life—her animals, her mother, her boyfriend. The place where she learned how to be a person, where she'd learned not only how to care for animals but how to care for others as well. How had she forgotten it so completely? She wanted to reclaim it, to put the halves together and produce a whole that she could hold to her chest, feel its heart beating against her. She was hungry for it.

Gideon closed his eyes. "Man, this song."

When she leaned over to kiss him, Gideon's eyes popped open. He put a hand on her shoulder and pushed her away. The look in his eyes screamed, *What the fuck are you doing?*

Ariel fell a hundred stories and then a hundred more. Tumbling and tumbling. Down and down and down. "That was very stupid of me," she said.

"I'm not going to tell you it wasn't."

She was still falling when Gideon clicked off the stereo, flooding the car with silence. He coughed, looked out the window. "We should probably put the dogs up now," he said.

Dex

In the morning, his first without Ariel, Dex lay in bed, regretting the cake-farts text. He hugged Ariel's pillow, smelling the coconut scent of her shampoo. For the past few months, she'd been obsessed with coconut everything: coconut lotion, coconut face wash, coconut granola. In the mornings, she massaged coconut oil into her face and onto the ends of her hair. She often boasted about being immune to these kinds of trends—acai bowls and kale smoothies and AcroYoga—but for some reason this coconut one had gotten her. He thought it was cute.

When he finally got up, he paced the house, head buzzing. He wanted to call Ariel, who had yet to reply to his message—undoubtedly because of the cake-farts video—but decided to text instead. Calling would seem desperate, paranoid. *Sorry to bug,* he wrote, *but can you text me when you see this? Just hoping you made it home okay.* He added a smiley-face emoji to conceal his panic. He then sat and waited for a response.

While waiting, he thought of what Buddy had said—how everything was okay because she hadn't taken all her stuff with her. The thought then occurred to him: What if she *had* taken all her stuff with her? Snooping was not a practice he condoned. He had never looked through Ariel's phone or tried to read her email. But, as someone smart once said—was it JFK? Rihanna?—extraordinary times called for extraordinary measures.

Casually, as if someone were observing him, he went into their closet and removed the wicker basket where Ariel kept her underwear. His heart sank: the basket was nearly empty. All that remained were the worst of the granny panties, their graying cotton tattered as an old war flag.

Fuck, he thought. *Fuck. Fuck. Fuck.*

Two breakfast beers later—still no response from Ariel—he opened her laptop, an old white MacBook with a worm sticker coming out of the apple. He knew he needed to work quickly, lest his conscience catch up to him. On her desktop, he found a few old poems, some tax documents, and recipes for lentil soup and blueberry pie. There was also a word document called *Bright Side*. When he opened it, he found a list of links. The first one he clicked on pulled up an article from the *Middleton Gazette*. The headline read, *Area Grocery Store Cuts Ties to Animal Sanctuary*. In the article was a picture of a woman standing next to a horse, her face partially concealed by the brim of an enormous lime-green sun hat. The article was about a grocery store that had retracted its biweekly food donations to a local animal sanctuary called the Bright Side. The store manager was quoted: *"After careful consideration, we've determined that Ms. Siskin's sanctuary does not meet the standards of ethical treatment of animals that our company seeks to uphold. Although we are disappointed, we hope to find a more suitable candidate for our proposed food donation program."* The journalist, who had been sent to inspect the sanctuary, went on to describe the animals he'd encountered there. Among them were a sheep blinded by an eye infection, a dog with a missing limb that had yet to receive medical attention, and a horse that could barely move due to severe malnutrition. The sanctuary's owner—clearly, Ariel's mother—did not support euthanasia. The article ended with a quote from Mona, who seemed only slightly peeved by the grocery store's retraction. *"I'm not in the business of making capitalists feel good about themselves. I'm in the business of helping animals."*

The next article was dated just after the election. *At two in the morning, Mona Siskin of St. Clare, Kan., woke to the sight of flames outside her bedroom window.* Dex kept reading, although he could guess how the story would end. He'd read somewhere that, in the week after the election, more than eight hundred hate crimes were reported—people harassing gay men and women in hijabs. People calling in bomb threats to mosques, schools, and black churches. Stabbings and fires and beatings. *Is this the new normal?* Ariel had asked one morning, while reading the news on her phone. Dex hadn't known what to say.

Now he felt a rush of emotion. He wanted to feel angry at the person who'd done this horrible thing to Ariel's mother, but instead he felt angry at Ariel. Why had she kept the sanctuary a secret from him? Why hadn't she told him the real reason she needed to go home? If she'd kept something this fundamental from him, what else might he not know?

The more he thought about it, the more sense it made that Ariel had grown up on an animal sanctuary. Each February, she forced Dex to watch the Puppy Bowl. Once, while watching a squirrel eat a hot dog downtown, Ariel had said, *Sometimes I miss animals so much it makes me want to die.* Confused, Dex had offered to take her to the zoo. Another time, while out to eat at India Palace on their anniversary, she'd started an argument about the superiority of plants and animals over humans. Her personal theory was that should aliens ever come to Earth, they would not identify humans as the superior lifeform but would assume it was something else: trees, birds, maybe insects.

Dex had vehemently disagreed. "But we've built everything here" was his argument. "Every structure and tool—the aliens would understand that right away. We'd be driving cars, drinking beers, using scissors. It'd be obvious that we're the ones in control."

"But think about it," Ariel had said, her frustration visibly mounting. "There would be birds shooting around in the sky, and when the aliens come down in their spaceships, what's the thing they'll notice first? Trees, mountains, water. Remember, the aliens aren't necessarily like us. They wouldn't look at a tree and go: *Oh, look, it's an elm.* They would look at everything and think: *Is this the supreme and most intelligent ruler of this planet?* And trees are fucking *everywhere*, and they're tall and strong and cover massive swaths of land—I mean, one of the largest organisms on Earth is a grove of aspens. They come in numbers we humans just don't have. Same goes with insects—spiders alone could eat every single one of us in a year."

Dex had shaken his head. "But the aliens would be arriving on Earth with transportation that requires *technology* and would therefore be able to identify other forms of technology. How are you not getting this? Show me a tree with an iPhone and then we can talk."

"Show me a person with a vast underground root system whose skin can convert sunlight into energy and whose corpse supports an entire ecosystem for decades and then maybe I won't think you're such a small-minded asshole."

This had been the end of their conversation. Ariel had stormed out of the restaurant, past the alarmed faces of the family in the booth behind them, leaving Dex to cover the bill.

His research answered every question except one: Why had Ariel taken a month's worth of sexy panties?

When his phone vibrated an hour later, he was only half-surprised by what it said. *Looks like I'll be here a little longer than I planned. I'll call you when I can. Love you.* She, too, had added not one, but two emojis—a pair of hearts. To his dismay, the hearts were not red but blue—a sign of certain doom.

Ariel

Growing up, Ariel had worked on her birthdays, on New Year's Day, on the Fourth of July. When the twin towers fell and Ariel was sent home early from school, Mona used the day as an opportunity to rebuild the fence around the pigpen. Today, the work would certainly not stop for the flame of embarrassment that roiled in Ariel's gut each time she thought about what happened in the car, each time she thought about Joy. It was hard to imagine Gideon with anyone, but harder still to imagine him with Joy Champ. Like a Bernese mountain dog with a teacup poodle.

The problem with Joy was that you wanted to hate her but couldn't—she was too nice. Ariel especially wanted to hate her, since Joy's life was nothing if not a fairy-tale version of her own. Whereas Ariel's mother's animals turned into food stamps, Joy's grandpa's cattle had turned into premium-grade dog food, which turned into money, which turned into clothes from Abercrombie & Fitch and a big maroon Lexus that Joy and her family drove to Wichita once a month to shop and eat at restaurants. It seemed both absurd and unjust, that murdering animals made you rich while caring for them made you poor.

The Cool Dogs were still in the run; her and Gideon's job was to return each dog to its pen, thus ending the morning of freedom and play. Like her mother, she'd once had a working knowledge of every animal on the sanctuary. She knew that Emily Chickenson laid oblong eggs, that Aladdin the boxer had some kind of beef with Cocoa Crisp the cat. She knew that Clancy the mule had high blood sugar and shouldn't eat the sweet alfalfa, and that Opal liked bananas so much she could smell it if one was opened in a different room.

"Will you tell me their names?" she asked Gideon, hoping to ease the awkwardness. Since leaving her car, they had worked mostly in silence, walking in wide arcs around each other.

"Okay," Gideon said. He started with the dogs in the run, who were playing a massive game of tag. "The golden is Rey, chasing her are Goof and Pongo. Over there is Luna, Mindy, Honey, and Romeo. The min pin with the zoomies is Jazzy Jo."

"What about the beast over there?"

"The mastiff?"

Ariel nodded. The dog was beautiful, with milky brown fur and soulful eyes. She must have weighed 150 pounds. Adorably, she was bounding around with the other Cool Dogs, many of whom were smaller than her head.

"That's Xena. Got dropped off last month with a note tied to her collar saying, *She likes chicken and is afraid of thunder. I love her to death but my new boyfriend doesn't like dogs so I have to say goodbye.*"

Ariel clicked her tongue. "What is wrong with some people?"

Gideon shrugged. "Lately, I've been trying to focus on what's right. Happier story, the one over there, the rat terrier? His name's Wooster. Rescued from a meth house not too far from town. When we got him, he wouldn't let anyone touch him. He'd just cry and cry, this terrified look in his eyes. It was awful. He was so scared of people he jumped out of Old Baby while Mona was going seventy-five on the highway. He was bone-thin and had these nasty wounds on his back, like someone'd been cutting him with glass. Took Joy nine months of constant work, but he's like a whole new dog now. A little wary at first, but he'll let you pick him up and everything. Still doesn't do well around men, especially bearded ones, but we're working on it. I just can't imagine what happened to him—what he must have gone through."

"It gets old, doesn't it?" Ariel asked.

"Some days are better than others." Gideon made his way to the run, double-checking that the gate was latched behind him before he leashed a mutt and a pair of pit bulls. This was another rule of life on the sanctuary: latch your gates and check them twice.

"Has anyone shown interest in the house?"

Gideon wiped the sweat from under his eyes. "Just Big John. It's been crickets since."

Ariel balked. "Big John wanted to buy the sanctuary?"

"I figured your mom told you."

"No—she didn't tell me anything."

"Well, yeah. He even offered to keep the horses and the rest of the big animals. I guess he also mentioned keeping me on, letting me work for him." Gideon's lip raised in a half smile. "Said he'd give me a raise."

"That's a good deal, isn't it?"

"Probably won't be a better one."

"What happened?"

Gideon gave her a look. "What do you think happened?"

"Oh, right," Ariel said, her cheeks warming.

"He tried to come over a few days after the fire, but your mom went ballistic. It was a whole scene—she was bright pink, shaking. She tried to throw this little clump of dirt at him, but it was windy as hell and the dirt blew back in her face. Any other time it would have been hilarious."

"Why was she so mad at Big John? The fire was all Sydney, right?"

"She thinks they both had a hand in it. You know how she is. She'd blame the whole town if she could."

Ariel understood that, to her mom, the fire was more than a fire—it was a symbol of every little grievance she'd ever had with St. Clare. The time the guy at the gas station asked for Gideon's green card; how every Fourth of July, families gathered to set off fireworks in the neighboring field, despite her asking, even posting signs downtown, that people find another spot—the sound drove the dogs wild.

"What'll happen when the sanctuary does sell? What will you do?"

He paused. "I guess I'm hoping we figure something out." He began to lead his dogs back to the cool pens, leaving Ariel at the dog run. She had managed to leash Jazzy Jo, Honey, and Wooster, but was still trying to get Xena, the mastiff, to sit still.

Ariel couldn't believe her mom and Gideon didn't even have a plan. Maybe they were in denial. Maybe they, too, couldn't believe it was real. "You could always go to school," Ariel said.

"So I can sit in a chair with a bunch of rich kids while an even richer guy tells everyone how to think? No, thanks."

"That's not what it's like," she said, and then reconsidered. "That's not *always* what it's like."

"Either way, I don't want school. My life is here, with the animals."

"Gideon, there's a for-sale sign on the gate. You should have a plan. An idea at least. You can't just pretend it's not happening."

He stopped what he was doing to look at her. "Look, I don't want to listen to this kind of thing the whole time you're here. All this talk about leaving and school and abandoning the animals. You already did it, and we all had to pay the price."

She froze where she stood, the dogs pulling on her leash. "I didn't abandon anyone, Gideon."

He looked at her, incredulous. "What would you call what you did to your mom, then?"

"I moved on, and clearly she has, too."

"You really believe that?" He'd taken his dogs to the cool pens and was coming back to the run for more, walking in a wide curve around her.

"I mean, you told her where I went and she didn't do anything about it—she never tried to find me. I'd call that moving on."

"Are you serious?"

"Even when I was here, she hardly noticed me. She was always too busy. Don't pretend it's not true."

"Of course she was busy! If you haven't noticed, she's running a million-dollar shelter project on pennies and dimes." He took a breath, his face growing red. "Did you know there's a shelter in Missouri that has nearly the same animal count, and guess how many people they have on staff? *Thirteen.* The other day your mom spent an hour chewing up a T-bone steak for a dog with bad teeth. She's out of her mind, Ariel. You know that just as much as I do. But just because she loves the animals so much it kills her doesn't mean she doesn't love you, too. You should have seen her after you left. She was a *mess.*" He was breathing hard, his eyes bearing down on her. "A woman can't lose her whole family and just keep on smiling, pretending everything's all right. And you shouldn't have expected her to."

She'd forgotten how worked up he could get over the things he loved. How she was once this way, too. "I figured you would have called if things were really bad," she said. "I would have come back."

"She's your mother, Ariel, and you left her without even saying goodbye."

"And who's the one who drove me? Who's the one who paid for me to go?" As soon as she said it, she knew it was the wrong thing to say. "I didn't mean that, Gideon."

Contempt glazed his eyes. "You shouldn't have come here," he said, and then threw open the gate to one of the cool pens.

Maybe Xena sensed Gideon's aggression, because as soon as Ariel got her on leash, the dog began pulling toward him. Ariel saw it almost before it happened: Xena tearing loose, her big brown head connecting with the back of Gideon's knee. No teeth were involved, just force. Gideon fell backward, catching his fall with his elbow. Ariel watched as the leash he was holding flew from his hand and the pit bull on the other end ran off after Xena. Because Gideon hadn't latched the pen, the other dogs inside quickly squirmed out: a beagle, a terrier, and a Chihuahua. Before Ariel could do anything, they were gone, a pack of five, Xena leading the way, going as fast as a dog her size could go. There must have been something good—a deer, maybe a family of them—because the dogs were on a tear, disappearing through a hole Xena widened under the pasture fence before Ariel had time to process what had happened.

Meanwhile, Gideon was still on the ground. Ariel wrapped her remaining leashes around her hand and went over to see if he was okay.

"I'm so sorry," she said, her heart pounding. "Are you all right?"

"Don't come here! Go get them!"

Ariel backed off. "They'll come back."

"Would *you* come back to this shithole?" He was on his feet again, frantically looking around. The dogs were gone, had turned a corner and disappeared. Gideon kicked the empty pen, which made a metallic wobbling sound that sent the dogs in the adjacent pens barking.

"Gideon, you're scaring them."

"What do you care?" He gave her a mean look. "This is your fault. Can't even keep a dog on a leash."

"She was huge, if you didn't notice. Her name's Xena, for Chrissake."

"You should have been able to control her."

"Well, I couldn't, because I'm so weak. Is that what you want to hear?"

He wiped the dust off his jeans. "Get over yourself, Ariel."

With this, she threw her remaining leashes down so hard that the metal claws hit the cement and bounced back. Wooster took a step and, realizing the resistance was gone, began to bound away from the pens, his tongue flopping wildly. Honey the pug followed after, her pudgy legs working double-time to catch up. The dogs took turns looking back, to see if they were being pursued, their leashes trailing awkwardly behind them. In Ariel's arms, Jazzy Jo kicked and wiggled until Ariel finally allowed him to leap from her arms, her final act of capitulation. How many dogs was that? Seven? Eight?

Gideon took a step toward her, his fists balled. She waited for him to do something—to touch her. "Give me your keys," he said.

"You're taking my car?"

"I'm making sure you don't go running off again."

How had he known? The thought was already in her head, a sprouting seed. She could get in her car, drive back to Lawrence, pretend like none of this ever happened. It would put her right back where she was a day ago—in bed with Dex, still pissed about the election. She realized, since coming home, she'd hardly thought about the news, about the state of the world. She felt a tremor of guilt, but then Gideon was grabbing for her belt loop, where her keys dangled from a carabiner.

"Is this all a big joke to you?" he asked.

"Does it look like I'm laughing?" She stared at him, this man she once knew down to every freckle and scar. It was terrifying, how completely love could transform into something else.

"Those dogs—most of them were on hold."

"*Most* of them?" When she had lived there, it was a good week if they homed a single dog.

"We've been pushing adoptions—advertising out of state, trying to move animals before the property sells. Some of those people are heading out here next week for the adoption fair. Those dogs—they were *on hold*." He was growing frantic, perhaps realizing just how much shit they were in. "Some people already put a deposit down. Your mom—she's going to freak."

"Just calm down, okay? I'm sure they'll come back once it's dinnertime, once they're hungry."

"And if they don't?"

"I don't know, Gideon, but they're dogs—they'll figure something out. Or someone will find them."

Had that many dogs gotten loose when she was younger, Ariel would have been in tears, already running out onto the road to chase them. Now she couldn't help wonder: What was the point? At least they were out, getting exercise, exploring. This was probably the most fun they'd had in years. Of course, they could also get hit by a car or wander into someone's livestock, provoke some nut with a shotgun. Her mom and Gideon had worked hard to find the dogs loving homes; in a burst of anger and ego, she'd undone this work and put the dogs in danger. Maybe Gideon was right. Maybe she shouldn't have come back.

There was a sadness to this realization, that she no longer cared about the animals the same way she once had. She had clearly lost something over the years—her unfaltering dedication to the animals. Behind this sadness was the relief of knowing that she was, at least in this way, unlike her mother. She still loved animals, but she loved people more.

Gideon clipped her keys to his own belt loop. "Maybe you should take a walk," he said, already turning away.

Seeking quiet, she went to the barn. Inside, everything looked soggy, lifeless. There were box fans everywhere—to dry things out, Ariel assumed—but none of them were running. Someone, maybe the volunteers from the Methodist church in Middleton who'd come to help clean after the fire, or so an article online had said, had applied a sheet of tin over the hole in the roof. The air smelled of shit, smoke, and mildew.

She sat on a bale of new-looking hay and tried to slow her breathing. She knew she wasn't supposed to be in there—nobody was supposed to be in there—and yet it was the one place she'd always felt safe.

She rewound the scene at Dog Town. If only she'd put a different dog on leash or asked Gideon a different question. The dogs would run back to the sanctuary, slip easily into their pens. The gates would lock. The day would remain level. She and Gideon would finish their chores and then go inside to have lunch: iced tea and fried egg sandwiches, like old times.

Before she had time to talk herself out of it, she removed her phone from her pocket and, finding a bar of service, texted Dex. *Looks like I'll be here a little longer than I planned. I'll call you when I can. Love you.* For levity, she added two heart emojis. Ten seconds later, her phone rang. Dex. She ignored it and turned off her phone. She didn't want anyone to reach her.

She knew that, eventually, her mom would return from her errands and learn what had happened. And what would Ariel tell her? That it was an accident? No matter which way you spun it, Ariel had let the dogs go.

When she heard the clang of the paddock gate, she held her breath, figuring it was Gideon, coming back to chastise her. But when the door to the barn creaked open, it wasn't Gideon. It was Joy Champ.

Dex

Dex needed a ride. The trouble was, he didn't have a car. Or a license. Years ago, during a phase his parents now referred to as his "tie-dye years," he'd sold the beloved, reliable 1997 Camry he'd driven throughout high school and replaced it with a secondhand Schwinn so shoddy the pedals sometimes flew off mid-ride.

While his other tie-dye-year convictions had faded over time, he had never returned to the world of cars. He wouldn't admit it to anyone—especially not Ariel, who was often inconvenienced by his lack of a vehicle—but his reasons were no longer environmental. Rather, he liked being the guy who biked everywhere, the guy who had ideals and stuck to them. Aside from Ariel and his plants, cycling was the one thing he'd truly committed to, and he was afraid what it would mean—to his ego, his sense of self, and his calves—to give it up. Besides, he liked that Ariel was the driver of the relationship. Without fail, watching her parallel park—the determined look on her face as she gazed over her shoulder while reversing, hand gripping the edge of his passenger seat—always turned him on.

But now he needed a ride. Luckily, he knew someone with a car and plenty of time to burn. Buddy lived a short but stressful bike ride away, in a sprawling, booger-colored complex on the corporate side of town. He'd been in the same apartment for years, and yet it always looked like he'd just moved in. The cabinets were mostly empty, the walls bare except for a cross-stitch that hung in his bathroom and read: *For those with courage, everything is a dildo.*

"What do you want?" Buddy asked when Dex opened the door. The apartment smelled of weed and popcorn. In the background, Dex could hear the soundtrack to *Harry Potter.*

"Wanna go on a road trip?"

"Where?"

"Western Kansas?"

Buddy scratched his chest. "This for Ariel?"

"Yes," said Dex. "And for fun. It'll be for fun, too."

Buddy yawned so deeply that Dex could smell his breath. "Look, I just woke up. Let me have some juice and think for a second."

Dex followed Buddy into the tiny kitchen, where empty pizza boxes and cans of Natural Light crowded the counter. Long ago, he'd gifted Buddy a peace lily, thinking even someone as careless as Buddy could keep it alive. Each time Dex visited, he was alarmed to find the plant in a deeper state of decline.

"So what happened?" Buddy asked. "Did she call you or something?"

"Kind of the opposite—she ignored me all last night, and then today she texted saying she's staying longer. And I found this article online—I guess her mom runs an animal sanctuary. Why would she have kept something like that from me?"

"Huh," Buddy said. "Animals."

"It's weird, right?"

Buddy opened the fridge and produced a gallon of SunnyD, which he chugged for an uncomfortable amount of time.

"Can I have some of that?" Dex asked.

"This is my juice. You can have water." Buddy opened the dishwasher and removed a plastic cup with cartoon dinosaurs on it. After picking something hard off the rim, he filled it with water from the tap and handed it to Dex. "So when would we need to leave?"

Dex took the kiddy cup, observed something brown and feathery float to the bottom, and set it back down. "Maybe soon? Like, now?"

"Is this an overnight thing? Are we talking clean underwear?"

"I don't know. I guess you could just drop me off. Actually, that would be best. We could have a good time driving out there, and then you could just leave me at the animal place, go on to somewhere else that's cooler. You could even go to Colorado if you wanted—I don't think it's too far. You could visit some dispensaries. How's that sound?"

"No deal. If I'm driving you there, I want a ticket to the freak show."

"What freak show? Who said anything about a freak show?"

Buddy gave him a look. "If I can't stay, I'm not going."

"Fine," Dex said, knowing he'd regret it later. But that's what later was for: everything he didn't want to deal with now.

"And you pay for everything."

"Obviously."

"Including snacks. And car beers."

Dex stared him down. "I could purchase a few select items."

"Even peanut butter snack?"

Of all Buddy's annoying habits, Dex despised peanut butter snack most of all. PBS, as Buddy sometimes called it, involved a jar of peanut butter—creamy, never crunchy—whose center Buddy would carve out (eating the peanut butter along the way) so that he could fill the empty space with chocolate chips and crushed-up pretzels. When he ate it, the smacking, sucking sounds could be heard in other rooms, through closed doors, over the sound of music. The idea of enduring these noises in the close quarters of a car was enough to make Dex teary-eyed.

"Sure," he said, "even peanut butter snack."

"Right on. I've been craving chocolate."

"Is that a yes?"

Buddy patted his belly. "Why not? Isn't that what the under-employed are supposed to do? Travel? See the world?"

Dex reeled, remembering he had a nine o'clock at the barbershop the day after next, and a full shift at the bar later that night. A popular punk band from Fayetteville was coming to do a set. He'd been looking forward to the show, to meeting the band, whose drummer was a buddy of a buddy of his and whose father had toured with Sonic Youth when he was younger. This was why Dex loved working at the bar; he could meet one person and suddenly know six. But he was willing to give this one up.

"So we're leaving now?" Buddy asked. "Like, now now? This present moment?"

Dex figured he could make some phone calls on the road. People owed him favors and he knew he was the kind of guy people liked to do favors for. It wouldn't be hard. "Yeah. You ready?"

Buddy looked down at his outfit, then inspected his hands, which were covered with what looked like orange Cheeto powder. "I think I'm good to go."

"You're not going to bring anything? An extra shirt? A toothbrush?"

Buddy shrugged. "I've probably got stuff in the car. I'll be fine." He petted his beard, as if thinking. He then retrieved the Altoids box in which he kept his weed. From the counter, he grabbed a tattered copy of *Frankenstein*. "All righty. Off we go."

Buddy drove a 1987 Volvo wagon he'd inherited from his great-aunt Caroline, a cantankerous woman who, during the early stages of dementia, used the car to frequent casinos in Oklahoma. To everyone's surprise and confusion, Caroline dominated the blackjack tables, once bringing home $4,000 in a single night. When Buddy's parents finally put her in a home, they found chips hidden all over her apartment—in the refrigerator, the toilet tank, her cat's litter box. Now the car's interior stank like cigarettes and hamburgers. Eau de Buddy. From the rearview mirror hung a pine-tree air freshener procured from some long-ago car wash, the paper sun-bleached and cracking. Buddy refused to remove it. "Everything about this car is good luck," he explained. "How else would my aunt have won all that money? She was out of her goddamned mind." And so the air freshener remained, as did the grocery bag of Aunt Caroline's dirty pantyhose, which lived in the back seat next to a hair dryer and a stack of Bibles.

The problem was that Buddy couldn't keep a consistent speed. He'd unknowingly accelerate until he saw the speedometer was nearing ninety, at which point he'd slam the brakes.

"Either you put on your cruise control or you let me drive," Dex eventually said. He'd been nauseated for the last hour.

"Cruise control is how people die," Buddy said. "They let the technology take over and then *bam*, they're dick over tiptoes in a ditch. Haven't you seen *Blade Runner*?"

"Do you mean ass over teakettle?"

"What teakettle? It's dick over tiptoes. Think about it—it's basic anatomy."

Dex attempted the imagery but was overcome by another wave of nausea. This time, he emptied his stomach into an old Burger King bag. Beer, Cheerios, water.

Buddy said, "Disgusting."

"Pull over, will you? I need to drive or I'll just keep puking."

"You don't have a license."

"What do you care?"

Buddy finally agreed, but only because he wanted to roll a joint.

Soon the car was thick with smoke and Dex was at the wheel, setting the cruise control to ten, then twelve, then fifteen miles over the speed limit. This was Kansas; if a cop was out there, Dex would see it in time to slow down. According to his GPS, they would make it to St. Clare around five o'clock. If Dex hauled ass, he could probably cut twenty minutes off that time.

"Just to be clear," Buddy said, sprinkling weed onto a rolling paper, "if we get pulled over, you're paying the ticket."

Annoyed, Dex eased up and set the cruise control to eighty-two. Buddy handed him the joint. He didn't want to be high when he saw Ariel, but they were still hours away. The joint would relax him until they got there, wherever exactly *there* was. He'd googled St. Clare and found a few grainy pictures of a gas station, a post office. The population, just as Ariel said, was barely more than four hundred. When he searched the animal sanctuary, he was directed to a website that had a gallery of animals available for adoption—a sheep with no eyes, a half-dozen horses, and what seemed like a thousand dogs and cats— but no pictures of the sanctuary itself. When he'd clicked on the STAFF link, he was directed to a cartoon picture of a hog and the message, *Oops, something went wrong! Error 404.*

He'd been driving for less than an hour when he pulled behind a semi going ten miles under the speed limit. Every so often the truck would drift into the left lane and then overcorrect onto the rumble strip. HOW'S MY DRIVING? asked a plaque on the back. From the trailer hitch swung a pair of blue truck nuts. For too long, Dex tailed the truck, mesmerized by the plastic testicles. When he emerged from his hypnosis he gunned it into the left lane. Just as he was passing the truck, the highway turned. Dex hated these moments—sandwiched between a semi and a guardrail, the only option to keep accelerating until the whole thing was over with. Driving on the highway for the first time in years, he imagined the collision: he and Buddy on fire, smashed beneath the truck, truck nuts dangling above them as they bled out onto the asphalt. When Ariel learned about his death, she would piece it together and understand that he had been coming to find her. She'd feel horrible.

Perhaps sensing Dex's panic, Buddy woke from his nap, assessed the situation, and began to shout, "You're turning with a truck!"

"Quit it," Dex said.

"You're turning with a truck! It's so precarious! Inherent risk! Turning with a truck!"

"Fuck you," Dex said, trying to hide his fear as they came nose-to-nose with the semi.

Buddy drummed on the dashboard. "Turning with a truck! Turning with a truck!" Only once they were safely beyond the truck did he collapse into a fit of laughter.

"You do realize," Dex said, "that this is your car? And that you're in it?"

For a moment, Buddy seemed to genuinely consider this information. "Better speed up, asshole. There's another truck up ahead."

"I hate you," Dex said.

"Liar," he said, pinching Dex on the elbow. "You love me."

When they first started dating, Ariel made an effort to accept all of Dex's friends. Her dislike for Buddy, however, was immediate and unmoving. Before Buddy knew Ariel was Dex's girlfriend, he'd hit on her, hovering too close while she was pumping a keg at a party. *Is it hot in here, or is it just you?* Once he discovered she was Dex's new love interest, he was all faux respect, telling Ariel what a great guy Dex was. "He's just so *real*, you know? There's no one like him. Not a soul in the world." And then, staring her down, "Don't you fuck with his heart, you hear me? Don't you dare hurt my friend."

Over the years, Buddy had tried to win Ariel over, but her opinion of him had remained fixed. Now, as the hours passed in the car with Buddy, Dex realized the severity of his mistake. Not only was he going to show up at Ariel's childhood home uninvited, using information he'd pilfered from her computer, but he was also going to do so with her least favorite person in tow. Was he insane? For a moment, he considered ditching Buddy—leaving him at a gas station or booting him out at a McDonald's. But then he recalled the time he got the flu freshman year of college, how Buddy had brought him chicken soup and saltines every night for a week. How Buddy had also written an essay on the Roman Empire for Dex's Western civilization class—the only essay for which Dex ever received a perfect score. He couldn't ditch Buddy because Buddy would never ditch him. Those were the rules of friendship.

It seemed the only solution was to give up altogether—turn around and head back to Lawrence, wait patiently for Ariel to return home. What he should have done all along.

"You know, I'm not so sure about this," he said, easing up on the gas.

Buddy startled from another nap. He had been snoring for the past half hour, his face smashed against the window. Asleep, he almost looked sweet. "Huh?" he said, prying his cheek from the glass. "What'd you say?"

"I said I have a bad feeling about this. Showing up at Ariel's house."

"You're serious right now?"

"The more I think about it, the crazier it seems. So what if she is fucking some random guy? How's my showing up going to make that better?"

"You come to my house in the middle of the day, ask to borrow my car, drive me three hours into the middle of nowhere, smoke my weed, and now all of a sudden you don't want to go through with it?"

"Come on. It's not like you were doing anything else."

"I was watching *Goblet of Fire*."

"Who cares?"

"You know what? Fuck you. You owe me twenty dollars."

"Buddy, calm down." He was used to Buddy's mood swings. Usually, they meant he was hungry, thirsty, or tired. Perhaps he needed a juice.

"Fuck that. You owe me twenty dollars *an hour*. This is basically a job, what I'm doing for you right now. I could have been out earning money today, but instead I'm sitting here with you. Wasting my time. And we didn't even get peanut butter snack, which makes you, in addition to everything else, a liar."

"All right," Dex said, deciding that, at least for the time being, it was easier to commit to the plan than deal with Buddy's temper tantrum. "We'll get you peanut butter snack soon—I promise."

Buddy sat quietly for a moment. Eventually he said, "Peanut butter."

"That's right, we'll pull off at the next town. Promise."

"Snack tease," Buddy murmured, before resting his head against the window and once again closing his eyes to the road.

Mona

On the way back to the Bright Side, pumped up on Coreen's advice, Mona rehearsed what she would say to Ariel. *We can't undo the past, but we can try to make things better going forward.* Or maybe: *I don't forgive you for leaving, but I don't need to forgive you—you're my daughter. I love you.* All of it sounded Hallmark, but maybe that's what she needed. Some Lifetime channel. A sprinkle of cheese. Maybe that's the ingredient they'd been missing all along—the ability to say the squishy stuff other families had no problem tossing around. Maybe the whole problem was that Mona would never buy a mug that read, *I'm a mom. What's your superpower?* Her mug would say something like, *Fuck off, I'm busy,* or *Look at me funny and I'll smack you.*

She repeated the words until they sounded natural, genuine: *I love you, I love you, I love you.* And it was true, wasn't it? She loved her daughter. Even in her moments of greatest anger, behind the flames there was always love. If anything, love was the air that stoked the blaze. She was angry at Ariel *because* she loved her so dearly, because Ariel had been the most important thing in Mona's world, and knowing this, Ariel had removed herself, kicking the keystone straight from Mona's life and turning away before she could see the structure crumble.

She was still practicing the words—*I love you, Ariel*—when two dogs, a min pin and a pug, shot from the grass and ran across

Sanctuary Road, tongues flapping. The pug was limping, its hind leg swinging above the ground, and both dogs were coated in grime and dirt. Mona slammed the brakes and blinked a few times. It was Jazzy Jo and Honey, she was sure of it. She'd been fawning over them the past few days, preparing them for adoption: no fleas, no eye boogers, no dingleberries.

She hopped out of the truck, but by then the dogs had disappeared into the grass on the other side. "Fucking fuck," Mona shouted to the empty road. She kicked Old Baby's front tire, a bolt of pain shooting up her big toe and through her ankle. Old Baby stared back at her, and so she patted the truck's wheel well. "I'm sorry, I didn't mean to take it out on you," she said, realizing she sounded just like the crazy person everyone in St. Clare thought she was. But she was pissed.

There was no way for her to know it was Ariel's fault, and yet somehow, she did.

Ariel

In high school, the boys had gone brain-dead in Joy's presence, stumbling over their words, nervously fiddling with their hair. The years had dialed down Joy's good looks, leaving behind the kind of pretty, rosy-cheeked cowgirl found in FarmersOnly.com commercials. She wore a navy flannel shirt and, over this, a mustard-yellow down vest. Jeans. Chunky leather belt. Strawberry-blond hair in two thin braids that ended just below her shoulders.

Joy stepped into the barn's darkness and squinted. "Holy shit—Ariel?"

"Hey, Joy." She felt nervous, as if they were still in high school and somebody might see them talking.

"Nobody told me you were coming back."

"I got in late last night—I didn't exactly warn anyone."

"What are you doing here?"

Ariel squeezed her forehead. "God, everyone keeps asking me that. I just saw about the fire—"

"No, I mean what are you doing in the barn?"

Ariel picked at the bale of hay beneath her, not wanting to meet Joy's eyes. "There was an accident. Some dogs got out."

"They ran off?"

Ariel nodded. "You should probably know that it was my fault. I let a few of them go."

"On purpose?"

"No, it was an accident. Sort of." She finally looked up at Joy, who was eyeing her suspiciously.

"Did Gideon go after them? I couldn't find him just now."

"I don't know, probably. I'm sure he did."

"Should we see if he needs help?"

"Sure, that's a good idea." Ariel stood carefully, worried she might become light-headed. Motes of dust floated through the air. She was cold. And thirsty. And tired. Behind Joy, the light of the day came rushing through the barn door. There was so much to do. She was glad Joy was there, that she didn't have to do it alone. She wondered, had Joy not appeared, how long she would have sat in the barn, thinking herself into a hole.

"You know, I saw you in a toothpaste ad a few years ago," Ariel said, following Joy into the paddock. "I figured you were living in a city somewhere."

"Oh God, you saw that?" Joy kept her eyes to the ground, half smiling, maybe proud or embarrassed or both.

"It was good! I mean, it was a commercial, so it was annoying, but *you* were good." She felt stupid, like she was fourteen again, trying to flatter one of the popular kids.

Joy bared her teeth and turned her head back and forth. "Nothing says clean like Denta-Clean."

"Why'd you come back here?"

"My dad got sick," Joy said. "That, and things were getting weird in LA. I didn't have any money and was living with this guy who was going through some stuff. I figured I would come home for a week or two, see how my dad was doing, and get my head on straight. Reboot before figuring out the next move. And then I met Gideon. I don't know if he told you."

"He did." Ariel forced herself to think of Dex. *You're engaged,* she told herself. *You're in love.* "I'm glad you two found each other. I know how it can be out here. Lonely."

"It's true. I think my mom's happiest of anyone. I'm not sure how she'd fare out here by herself, with my dad gone."

"I didn't know about your dad," Ariel said. Beau Champ had been a fixture in St. Clare—he had money and was known for giving it to anyone who flattered him. As one story went, he lent the owner of the hardware store $10,000 to fix his roof, all because the man said Beau looked like Clark Gable.

"Liver failure," Joy said. "No surprise there."

"I'm so sorry." She had known Beau was a drunk—everyone in town knew that—but half the men in St. Clare drank beer like it was water. Nobody used the word *alcoholic.*

"He drank himself to death, so I suppose he deserved it."

"Don't say that."

"I can't help it. I was so angry at him, but all he could say at the end was that he was sorry—just repeated it over and over—so now I'm not so sure what to do with all my anger." She looked at Ariel, as if apologizing for going so deep so fast. "That's just life, I guess. Nobody wants to hear about it."

"I don't mind," Ariel said.

Joy gave her a weak smile. "You should know that your mom's been really great through everything. My mom would be pretty lost without her."

"I didn't know they even talked." They were almost to the driveway now. Ariel noticed their steps were in sync.

Joy paused and put her hands on her hips, made a visor with her hand. "After my dad died, your mom and my mom became close. My mom—she sort of fell for your mom."

Ariel was having trouble digesting this news. "What are you saying?"

"You know, it happens to women as they get older. They realize they want certain things."

Ariel had spent little time thinking about her mother's sexuality—who *wanted* to think of their mom's sex life?—but had always assumed, perhaps naively, that her mother was asexual. Or at least too busy to bother with sex. She could hardly recall her parents holding hands. There was also the fact of Coreen—not just that she was a woman, but that she was a certain kind of woman, one who wore animal print blouses and Pandora bracelets, who kept her nails long and painted and always smelled clean, like expensive shampoo. She was rich—that was the difference.

"So you're saying your mom . . . and my mom. They were involved?"

"Your mom says nothing ever happened between them, that they were always just friends, but I'm not so sure. Either way, they've been hot and cold for a while." There was a tiny smirk on Joy's lips—the pleasure of delivering gossip. "Sorry, I realize it's a shock."

Ariel felt as if the whole earth had shifted ten inches to the right. The news saddened her—not because her mom had dated a woman, but because her mom had fallen in and out of love without Ariel even knowing. "Honestly," she said, "I'd have been less surprised if you told me my mom found Jesus."

"Like I said, I don't know what all happened. Only that, whatever was going on, my mom was pretty upset for a while. But she's moved past it now, or at least she's trying. They still see each other pretty regularly. I'm sure you'll see her soon, if you're around. Do you know how long you'll be here?"

"I was only staying for a couple days. But now—"

"Now what?"

"Seems like it may be longer, with the dogs and all." The hollow feeling in her stomach grew each time she thought about what she'd done. "I just feel so embarrassed. It's like I'm ten years old, throwing tantrums."

Joy elbowed her. "Hey, what else is coming home for?"

There was something about Joy, about the way she walked and moved and spoke, that made Ariel feel at ease. She had always admired this type of woman—women like her mother, like Sunny—who naturally exuded authority. They navigated the world with confidence, looking for things to improve, whereas Ariel moved through the world on tiptoes, expecting someone to reprimand her, to tell her she was doing something wrong.

"Looks like he left," Joy said, gesturing to where Gideon usually parked his truck. "Should we go out, too? See if we can wrangle some dogs?"

Ariel still felt tired—a no-no word on the sanctuary—but straightened her spine, lifted her chin. *Wake up*, she told herself. *Fix your mess.*

"Let's do it," she said. "At least then we can say we tried."

They took Joy's truck, the heat turned high, a hundred bugs meeting their end against the windshield. This sort of thing had bothered Ariel, growing up—how, on the way to get the dogs' heartworm medicine in Middleton, they would kill an entire kingdom of butterflies. How most of the dog and cat food contained meat.

After flipping through a few stations, Joy settled on a Kenny Chesney song. *She's the only one who really understands what gets me*, Kenny sang. *She thinks my tractor's sexy.* "Tell me you love this song," Joy said.

"It's all right," Ariel lied. She could imagine Dex putting a finger-gun to his head, pulling the trigger. And yet, a moment later, she found herself tapping the tune on her knee. *Stop it, body*, she thought. *We don't like this.*

"You know, you can sing if you want to," Joy said.

Ariel felt her neck grow warm. "Oh, I don't know the lyrics."

"It's not Shakespeare. You can practically guess what's coming." She nudged Ariel on the shoulder. "Loosen up. If we're going to drive around we should at least have some fun."

"You can't just tell someone to loosen up—that's not how it works."

"Then how does it work?"

"If I knew that," Ariel said, "I'd be more like you."

As they drove, passing the landmarks of Ariel's childhood—fields dotted with cows and irrigation systems and old barns so rotted they leaned toward the ground—Joy told Ariel about her time in Los Angeles, how her parents had refused to send her money and so she'd lived on whatever she could scavenge from the sushi restaurant where she worked. If she wanted a proper meal, she would go onto OkCupid and wait for a guy to ask her out. On these occasions, she ordered drinks and appetizers and fatty desserts. Into her purse, she slipped rolls and saltines, french fries folded into napkins. She tried to eat enough calories to last the weekend.

"Once, I was out with this guy and I ordered an insane amount of food—and this was not a cheap restaurant. Like, fifteen-bucks-for-a-drink kind of place. So we get to the end of the meal, and the guy asks the server for separate checks. He looks at me and goes, 'God bless feminism, am I right?' So I just smile and excuse myself, say I have to use the restroom, and sneak out the back door. It was so embarrassing, but I was also pissed. What kind of guy doesn't pay for a first date? And I was dressed up and everything—lipstick, heels, the whole shebang." Joy laughed. "You probably think I'm a total bitch."

"You're sort of my hero," Ariel said. She was surprised by how comfortable she was around Joy, despite the twinge she felt each time she thought of her with Gideon.

"Trust me, I feel a lot more heroic out here."

"Do you ever miss California?"

Joy tilted her head. "Sometimes I miss the weather and the flowers. The ocean. You know that feeling when you're by the water—like nothing you're worried about could possibly matter?"

"Not really," Ariel said. She had never seen the ocean in real life.

"Well, it's a cool feeling. I used to go out to the beach at night and get right up against the water, pretend like there was nothing behind me—it makes you feel like you're just standing in the middle of the world, completely alone. It's something else. Oh, and the salads—the salads in California are excellent. None of the dinky iceberg and runny tomato stuff we have here."

Ariel had never thought one way or the other about Kansas salads.

As they got closer to town, Joy pointed out all the ranches that had been bought or sold, who all had divorced or remarried or died. She explained that more than a few families had moved—Mexican farmhands who didn't feel safe in St. Clare. "Before the election, everyone in town starts getting out their pitchforks, saying the Mexicans need to go, that they're here taking our jobs, that we're building a wall. Blah blah blah. And then when the Mexican families *do* leave, everyone's pissed because now they have to pay their white workers minimum wage, give them benefits." Joy shook her head. "Morons. And don't even get me started on the Fullers." She looked over at Ariel cautiously. "You were friends with Sydney, right? I remember you two eating lunch together."

"We were both in band," Ariel said, her heart skipping a tick.

"Was he crazy back then, too?"

"He was pretty sweet, actually." She paused. "For the most part."

"Huh. You should see this blog he started. Some of the stuff he would post—really fucked-up rants about immigrants and gay people."

Ariel rubbed her eyebrow, looked out the window. "That makes me really sad."

"He actually asked me out one time," Joy said.

Ariel felt her stomach tighten. "Really?"

"He came to my mom's house and asked if I wanted to watch a movie. Except he basically stared at my boobs the whole time. When I told him I was dating Gideon, he started going off, yelling about how the Mexicans were taking our jobs and our women."

"What'd you do?"

Joy's face cracked into a smile. "You're not going to believe me."

"Tell me."

"I booped him on the nose." Joy reached out and tapped Ariel's nose with her finger. "Like that. I even said it. *Boop.* It was something my dad used to do whenever I got mean with him. You should try it sometime. It completely disarms the enemy."

"What'd he do?"

"He kind of blinked a lot and swatted my hand away. But I think he thought it was kind of fun, because I touched him."

Ariel forced a hollow chuckle, but then grew quiet.

Suddenly, Joy hit the brakes. "Son of a bitch," she said, and pointed across the road. Wooster the rat terrier was trotting merrily through a ditch.

"I've got the treats," Ariel said, shaking off thoughts of Sydney. She hopped out of the truck and brandished one of the stale hot dog buns they'd brought for this purpose. Like a miracle, Wooster came running toward her, as if this were all part of the plan: escape the sanctuary, take a stroll in the free world, catch a lift back home with some ladies hawking hot dog buns.

Ariel looked at Joy, so happy she could have cried. "How easy was that?"

Joy gave her a look. "Not easy. Lucky."

Wooster made a beeline for Joy. "Wooster?" she said. "Is that you?" When he was close enough, he sprang into her arms, so that

Joy stumbled back, laughing. "Holy hell," Joy said. "You're not that small, Woosie." The dog went wild, licking her face, his feet kicking streaks of dirt onto Joy's vest. Ariel remembered what Gideon had said, how it had taken six months of training before Wooster would let Joy hold him.

"We have a special bond," Joy explained. "If I'd known he was one of the dogs that got out, I would have flipped. He's got a family coming for him from Wichita."

"Good thing we got him, right?" Ariel smiled nervously, feeling guiltier than ever.

Joy put Wooster in the truck bed, where he set to work sniffing his new surroundings, tail beating against the plastic floor. Joy poured him a bowl of water and he drank it frantically. When they were back in the truck, Joy took a breath. "It's a good thing I don't know which dogs are out there, or I might not be so calm about this."

"Don't worry," Ariel said. "We'll get them."

"You don't know that."

Because it was true, Ariel said nothing.

As they resumed their drive, Ariel's thoughts wandered back to Sydney. She wondered if he'd really stared at Joy's boobs when he asked her out. It had always been his habit to gaze into the middle distance, as if worried people might find something incriminating if they looked into his eyes. That he had found it necessary to ask Joy out at all made Ariel deeply sad.

All these years later, if she felt like blaming someone else for what happened between her and Sydney, she would blame Kimber Matthews, a popular girl famous among the upperclassmen for having blow-job lips.

It was spring of freshman year, and Ariel was sitting alone in the cafeteria when Kimber walked by. For a brief moment, Ariel had the crazy idea that Kimber was going to sit down with her. In that instant, an entire future unfolded in her head, one filled with pool parties and late-night phone calls and notes left in her locker, signed *LYLAS*.

Instead, Kimber sneered, "Where's your sidekick, Pigsty?" popping the dream in Ariel's head like a needle to a balloon.

"Just leave me alone," Ariel said, her appetite suddenly gone. Sydney was home sick again, which had been happening more and more lately. Some days, she knew, he couldn't get out of bed. Ariel always marveled at how Sydney could stay home whenever he wanted. Once, after Ariel started her period, she'd told her mom she was too tired to go to school. "Tired is not an excuse for anything," Mona had said, and began piling cats and dogs on Ariel's quilt until, hysterical with both laughter and irritation, Ariel had given in and gotten dressed. She wished she could go over to Sydney's house now and tell him to get up, to try. But he was home, and Ariel was here, in the cafeteria, under what felt like a spotlight. Sweat was pooling under her thighs as kids at nearby tables turned to watch Kimber in action, a snake unhinging its jaw before a mouse.

"Uh-oh, did I hit a sensitive spot?" Kimber asked, jutting out her bottom lip in mock sympathy.

Ariel sat very still, a carrot pinched between her fingers. She could feel her heart begin to gallop with a type of anger she hadn't felt before.

"Did you finally figure out he likes boys?" Kimber asked. "Took you long enough."

The question would have irritated Ariel anyway, but lately she'd started feeling strange around Sydney. They'd been friends for two years at this point, but suddenly, whenever she looked at him, she found his pale eyes beautiful, his sloppy haircut (his grandmother's doing) endearing. Suddenly, looking at him made her stomach float.

Now, as Kimber smiled—perfect teeth, dimpled chin—rage filled

Ariel's chest, moving up from her sternum to her neck, her face, her ears. A thought appeared in her mind, like a firework: if only she looked like Kimber, her father would have stayed. Her mother would pay more attention to her. Sydney would look at her the way she now looked at him.

"Actually, yeah," Ariel heard herself saying. "I caught him sucking your boyfriend off the other day." The words fell out, unstoppable. She didn't know where they'd come from.

Kimber's face lit up. "Oh, shit!" she cried. And then, to her group of equally beautiful friends at the popular table: "Everyone, we have it on record! Pigsty says Sydney Fuller sucks dick!"

The depth of Ariel's error felt immediate and irrevocable. The carrot in her hand grew heavy, and she had the sensation of falling and rising toward the ceiling at once, as if watching the moment unfold from a spot on the wall. From this spot, she saw Kimber stride back to her table, she and her friends pulsing with laughter.

The next day, Sydney returned to school to find that someone had written I ♥ DICK on his locker. Ariel was too scared to explain what had happened with Kimber, so she just shook her head and gave him a hug he did not return. Knowing Sydney would be too embarrassed, she asked the maintenance guy, Mr. Shore, to clean Sydney's locker. As he rubbed the metal door with a rag dipped in alcohol, Ariel heard him whisper, "Fucking kids."

The following day, in English, Ariel overheard something about Kimber's boyfriend cornering Sydney after school. Her stomach filled with ice, the words in her book blurred into unintelligible squiggles. As soon as the bell rang, she rushed to Sydney's locker, where she found him standing with his head against the metal. "Sydney, are you okay?" He turned to her briefly, his blue eyes muted. She'd heard this before, that you could see pain in people's eyes, but she hadn't understood, until now, that it was literal, that the quality of light in someone's eyes could actually dim, as if a cloud had moved across the surface. She saw too that his lip was swollen, the inside of his nostrils crusted with blood. He'd combed his hair in a funny way, so that it fell over his right ear. She put a hand on his shoulder, but he brushed her off.

"Sydney, I'm so sorry," she said, but he was already walking down the hall. When she called out his name, he gave her the finger, a gesture she'd never seen from him and which felt infantile, as if he were a kid mimicking something he'd seen on TV.

Soon after this, Sydney stopped showing up to school. By April, he'd missed so many days that Mr. Pembroke, the high school band teacher, promoted Ariel to first chair. Taking Sydney's chair felt like the greatest betrayal of all, and so she began to play out of tune, to enter songs too late or too early. Two weeks before the end-of-year recital, Mr. Pembroke demoted her back to second chair. Ariel could have hugged him, so great was her relief.

Then, like someone turning on the lights in the middle of a movie, it was suddenly, garishly summer. The horses rolled in the dirt and the pigs caked themselves in mud. The fields hummed with bugs, the humidity like a terrible song that wouldn't stop playing. She tried to talk to Sydney several times, but he always refused, either not answering her phone calls or sending his grandma Loretta to answer the door and say he wasn't feeling well. At the height of Ariel's frustration, Gideon washed onto the sanctuary's shore, a treasure from another world, and eased the hurt and guilt of losing Sydney.

In September, she learned that Sydney had dropped out of school. Each time she saw him after this, he looked smaller, sadder, his shoulders more stooped. His hair grew long, his pants baggy. One day, a tattoo the shape of a hammer appeared along the length of his forearm, a grinning black skull on the nape of his neck.

"Thank God you stopped hanging out with that boy," Mona said one afternoon, as they drove by and saw him sipping a can of beer on his porch.

"Yeah," Ariel responded quietly. "Thank God."

One morning, while reading *Giovanni's Room* months later, Ariel startled as if from a bad dream. She thought of a time Sydney had gone into her closet and removed a light purple cardigan. He'd rubbed the fabric between his fingers and whispered the word *soft*, his voice so sad Ariel had figured the color reminded him of his mother. She thought of the Alex Rodriguez poster in his bedroom, situated right above his bed, and the time they'd danced madly to Mika's "Grace Kelly," Sydney's eyes squeezed shut as he gyrated and pumped his fists, giving Ariel the acute sensation that he was imagining himself somewhere else, with someone else. Afterward, they'd dropped onto his bed—his mother's childhood bedframe, with the floral carvings in the posts— and he'd asked her, an elbow thrown over his head, "Do you ever feel like you're a different person than everyone sees?" and she'd replied, "Always," not understanding the magnitude of his question.

Now, driving with Joy all these years later, she felt a familiar swelling of shame. Sydney had tried to let her into his world—in turn, she had failed him.

Dex

As the land became redder, Buddy narrated the scenery. "Church. Church. Cross. Trump sign. Church. Antiabortion billboard. Church. Burger King. Church. Trump sign. Arby's." At one point they passed a giant billboard painted with a mysterious, sexy-looking Jesus brandishing a bundle of wheat.

"Is it advertising Jesus?" Buddy asked. "Or the wheat industry?"

"Maybe both?" Dex said.

Twenty miles outside of St. Clare, they passed another billboard: JESUS CHRIST HEALS AND RESTORES. PORNOGRAPHY DESTROYS! The orange paint was sun-bleached and peeling. Some brave revolutionary had crossed out JESUS CHRIST and written MY COCK.

"How did Ariel grow up in this shit?" Buddy asked.

"I imagine it's part of why she left."

"Is her mom super Christian or something?"

"As far as I know, her mom's Jewish. At least by blood or whatever." He thought of the article he'd read, how the arson guy had painted swastikas all over the animal sanctuary.

Buddy rubbed his chin. "Why would she want to live out here?"

Dex shrugged. "Why does anyone live anywhere?" He figured if Ariel's mom chose to live out here, there was probably a good reason why.

• • •

It was not yet five o'clock, but the sun was already setting when the sign for St. Clare appeared beside the road. Dex tried to rehearse what he would say to Ariel. He would explain that he was worried she was in some kind of trouble. Yes—that was the proper angle. He had come as a hero, not as her paranoid, insecure fiancé, the same fiancé who once showed up at her job because she mentioned the clinic had hired a new veterinary assistant named Marco, who, until Dex saw his gangly limbs and braces in person, he'd pictured as Inigo Montoya from *The Princess Bride*.

"I was worried about you," Dex would say when he saw her. "You sent me those blue heart emojis, and I knew I had to come."

She would also wonder how he'd found her mother's address, but that could be easily explained. It was an accident. An honest, innocent accident. If anything, Google was to blame.

The sign said: WELCOME TO THE BRIGHT SIDE, WHERE THERE'S LOVE ENOUGH FOR EVERYONE. Surely *everyone* must include him, too, Dex thought. It was nearly dark, a gauzy sliver of moon pasted to the sky. From the entrance gate, he could see a pair of horses walking through a field. There was a barn near the house and a few beat-up-looking trailers by the detached garage. It was all a little underwhelming; he realized he'd been imagining animals running wild—rhinos and peacocks and puppies and turtles—but what he saw seemed more like a farm.

"Is this like some Sarah McLachlan PETA shit?" Buddy asked.

"I don't know," Dex said. "Maybe."

"So we're just gonna knock on the door and see what happens?"

"*We're* not going to do anything. You're going to stay in the car until I give you further instruction."

Buddy saluted him. "Aye aye, asshole."

They pulled into a small lot with a sign that read: VISITORS, PLEASE PARK HERE. There, like a miracle, was Ariel's car. Down the driveway stood a narrow two-story house with a wraparound porch. From this vantage, it looked normal enough. The lights were on, and Dex could see shadows moving inside.

"You stay here," he reminded Buddy.

"If you're not back in twenty, I'm coming in." He removed his Altoids box from the center console and began to roll a spliff.

Dex was nearly to the house when a squat, muscular dog ran out and began barking so forcefully his front paws left the ground. "Whoa, friend," Dex said. "Calm down. Everything's good." Cautiously, Dex continued down the driveway. The dog looked like one of those Michael Vick fighting dogs. Ariel had followed the trial closely, going off on emotional tirades about the injustice of it all. "You just watch," she'd said. "Michael Vick is going to get off on a tiny sentence, meanwhile those dogs are going to have health issues for the rest of their lives. Five years from now, he'll be drinking champagne in one of his mansions while those dogs die alone in a cage, unable to find a home because they can't look at another dog without going berserk." He knew better than to say what he had been thinking—*But people really, really like football*—and so had let her rant, nodding and saying, "So true." Now this tirade made a whole new kind of sense.

The dog was still barking at him, blocking Dex's route to the front door. He'd never been afraid of dogs, but this one seemed interested in ripping his throat out. *Let him come to you first*, Ariel had told him once, when their friend's Doberman, Ditto, growled at him at a party.

He crouched down, put out his hand. "It's all right, dude," he said. "Come sniff my anal glands or whatever." He was shocked when the dog approached him warily, one step at a time. Soon the dog was sniffing his hand, then his wrist, then his arm. Before Dex could stop him, the dog was licking his face. "That tickles, bud. And your breath smells like ass."

The dog was actually kind of cute, if he thought about it. When he stuck his tongue out, it looked like he was smiling. He was gray with a stubby tail and a hard, round belly. The hair on his snout was so patchy Dex could see the soft pink skin beneath. "You're like a little hippo," Dex said. The dog seemed to approve of this comparison; he wagged his tail and went in for another round of licking. When Dex made his way toward the house, Hippo happily followed after, toddling along on his muscular arms, his butt wiggling back and forth.

Look at me, Dex thought. *I've been here a minute and already I'm king of the dogs.*

The front porch was covered in *stuff*—rawhides, tennis balls, Frisbees, muddy bath towels, brushes, water bowls, shovels, brooms, dead potted plants, foam dog beds, shredded tennis shoes, decapitated teddy bears, and a mop so old and dirty it was hard to the touch. The air smelled like shit and pee, potting soil and citronella. On the far side of the porch, a harem of cats lifted their heads but did not bother to get up. Dex pressed an ear to the front door and heard voices. He took a deep breath, looked down at Hippo for courage, and then rang the bell. Immediately, the house exploded into an uproar of barking. Dex braced himself, waiting for Hippo to join in, but the dog came over and sat politely at his feet, leaning his weight into Dex's leg as if to say, *Don't worry, guy, I'll vouch for you.*

The door opened not on Ariel, but a man—a handsome man. Thick hair, good jaw. Had he been in a commercial, he would have been driving trucks up winding mountain roads, smiling into the horizon at all the good fortune and low APR financing that awaited him. His face suggested a history of hard, respectable labor, something both patriotic and adventurous, perhaps a stint in the marines. Yes—now that Dex saw it, he couldn't unsee it. This was a man of the water, a man who had risked his life to protect his nation at sea. He had a working knowledge of maritime knots and could navigate by the light of the stars. Sometimes, when he closed his eyes, he could still hear the sound of waves lapping at the ship's hull. What was that rhyme? *Red sky at night, sailor's delight . . .*

Dex stuck out his hand, which the marine squeezed with such force Dex could feel his knuckles slide over one another. "I'm Dex," he said, pumping the marine's hand.

"How can I help you, Dex? You looking for an animal? Or did you happen to find one?" An eagerness flashed in his eyes.

"I'm actually looking for Ariel. Is she home?"

"You mean *Ariel*?" he asked, pronouncing her name incorrectly.

"Tomayto, tomahto. Is she here?"

"No, but she should be back later. I think." The marine's face suggested something bad had happened. "And you are?"

"I'm her fiancé."

The marine raised his eyebrows. "I see."

In Dex's heart, a tiny red flag began to climb up a pole. "Would it be okay if I came in and waited for her?"

The marine stepped aside so Dex could enter. The door led into a mudroom that smelled of cat pee and mildew. Bags of cat food slumped against the wall. Like the porch, the room was a mess of chew toys, bath towels, and empty water bowls collecting dead flies.

In the living room, a few grimy dogs approached him, sniffed his crotch, and retreated. There, like a celebrity from a movie he'd never been allowed to watch, was Ariel's mother, sitting on a plastic-covered couch. His instinct was to rush up to her, wrap his arms around her and say *Thank you for making my favorite person.* But she did not look like the type of person who wanted to be rushed up to and hugged. She had the same face as Ariel—long nose, wide eyes, thin lips— but her hair was cut short, the ends flying up every which way, as if she hadn't brushed it in weeks, or maybe years. How satisfying it would be, Dex thought, to wash it, run a comb through it, drench the ends with argan oil and a keratin cream. She wore jeans and a denim shirt—a Canadian tuxedo—a silver watch on her wrist, the clasp held together with duct tape. Her hands were Ariel's hands, the fingers long and bony with big knuckles that bulged out. She was crouched over a phone book, the old-school yellow kind. Dex didn't realize they even still made phone books.

"Mona, we've got a visitor," said the marine.

Mona looked up with wide eyes. "Has he got a dog?"

"No, it's not that—"

"Then tell him to come back. I've got too many calls to make." She picked up a cordless phone—Dex hadn't seen one of those in years, either—and began to punch in numbers.

"Mona," the marine said. "This is Ariel's fiancé."

Mona stopped what she was doing, put down the phone. "Fiancé," she said, as if trying out the word for the first time. "Jesus Christ on a cross, what's wrong with that girl?"

The marine offered Dex an apologetic look. "Don't worry. It has nothing to do with you."

"Did something happen? Is Ariel okay?"

Mona gave him a funny look. "Why are you saying her name like that?"

"Like what?" Dex asked. "That's how you say it—you're the ones—" He realized, then, that he was talking to the woman who had given Ariel her name in the first place.

The marine and Mona exchanged looks. "Maybe I should get some coffee going," Mona said. "Seems we've got things to discuss." When she stood up from the couch, all the dogs in the room rose to attention, their metal collars tinkling. It was then Dex noticed just how many animals there were in the house. They congregated at the end of the hallway, where a series of dog beds and pillows lined the floor. He counted six dogs, four cats, and something that looked like a gremlin. In the kitchen, there was a Lassie dog under the table and a Chihuahua sitting on one of the chairs, licking its privates. When Mona walked in, they began to wag and whine, as if the Queen of England had entered the room. *Oh my God, it's her, it's really her, oh my God.* Dex wondered where Hippo had gone to.

"Everybody cool your jets," Mona said, petting the dogs as they came to greet her. "It's just me."

The coffee was Folgers, weak but hot. Mona poured mini twist pretzels into a white cereal bowl with ivy painted along the rim. Dex ate one, discovered it was so stale it had become almost moist, and then took another, to prove he wasn't too good for old pretzels.

"Does Ariel know you're here?" Mona asked.

"Not exactly." Dex popped another pretzel in his mouth. "I'm sorry to intrude on you all—it's just that she hasn't told me much about this place. And I wanted to see it, to meet you—to be here with her."

Mona wrapped her hands around her coffee mug and leaned in. "What all did she tell you?"

"Not enough. Just that she left when she was eighteen. I'd love to know the whole story—if you don't mind."

Mona and the marine exchanged looks. "You tell him," she said, elbowing the marine. "I don't want to talk about it."

The marine took a big drink of coffee and then started in, explaining how Ariel had gotten a scholarship to KU, how Mona had wanted her to stay, how Ariel had left. How the past six years had been filled with radio silence. Then, finally, Ariel's return. The loose dogs. The upcoming adoption fair. The fire.

By the time the marine finished talking, Dex had reached the bottom of the pretzel bowl. When he removed the last two twists there lay a dead spider, its body a crisp tangle of legs.

"Winner winner chicken dinner," the marine said, nodding to the spider. "Free protein."

Uncertain whether he was actually expected to eat it, Dex was relieved when the marine started to laugh. "Relax. I'm just messing with you."

Dex pretended to laugh, too. "Not to change the subject," he said, pushing the bowl away, "but did Ariel not tell you about me?"

"She told me she was single," said Mona.

The marine nodded. "Dating around is the version I got."

Dex felt a pulse of dread and quickly tried to reason himself out of it. Maybe Ariel didn't want them to know she was engaged until she'd mended the bridges she'd burned. Maybe she was just waiting to tell them when the time was right.

Mona picked up the coffeepot and sloshed the remaining liquid inside. "Gideon, do you want more coffee?"

Dex choked on his own breath.

The marine looked at him, as if sensing something was wrong.

"Sorry," Dex said, "you're Gideon?"

"I am." Gideon smiled, and a cleft appeared in his chin. A deep cleft. "Ariel's mentioned me?"

"She has."

"Only good things, I hope."

Dex thought then about the sexy panties, about what Buddy had told him. *People cheat. Happens all the time.* He could feel how intently both Gideon and Mona were staring at him, awaiting his answer. "Of course," he said, forcing a smile. "All good things."

Ariel had only mentioned Gideon once, on the night she and Dex first met. The party was at Freedom House, the funky co-op where Dex had lived all through college. The house was an old candy-colored Victorian with four stories and a zillion rooms. The thrift-store furniture was frayed and stained, the air perpetually spiced with curry and weed. He was getting too old for these parties, but he loved the old house. Being there was like walking the halls of his memory.

He met Ariel because she was vomiting into a banana plant. The plant was a holdover from the days of old, when Dex had lived at the co-op and his good friend Frederic, an impossibly good-looking exchange student from Germany, would take women on a tour of his greenery before leading them into his bedroom. When it was time for Frederic to go back to Germany, Dex asked if he could be left in charge of the plants. Frederic agreed. *Be good to the plants,* he'd told Dex, *and the plants will be good to you.* Dex could barely do his own laundry, but he found himself tending to the plants like he'd never tended to anything before. He did some research and learned how to make compost, how to trim back growth and transfer seedlings to larger pots. And now here was some lightweight undergrad, retching into a plant that had somehow survived a decade of house parties and Kansas winters.

"Hey, how about we do that in a toilet," he'd said, taking Ariel by the elbow. His first words to her. Their first touch.

"But that's where people go *poop.*" She spoke so softly he could barely hear her.

Dex led her up the stairs to an empty bedroom with a relatively clean-looking toilet. When it seemed like she had thrown up everything she possibly could, Dex helped her to the bed and set a trash can beside her. "I'm going to go find your friends now," he said.

She looked at him intently, as if she hadn't properly seen him until just now. "Friends?"

"Who did you come with? I'll go find them."

After a moment, she said, "Gideon. Gideon Gonzalo."

Of course she had a boyfriend. "I'll go find him, then. You stay here, okay?"

She found this hilarious. "No, I think I'll go for a jog. Maybe make a pizza, run for Congress, take a quilting class . . ."

He could hear her as he left the room, listing things. Weird girl.

In the basement, he called out Gideon's name. No answer. After he'd asked in every corner of the basement, he decided to take a break and drink a beer. Then a Bowie song came on and he had to dance. (It was a rule he'd made for himself, years ago: if Bowie came on at a party, he danced, no excuses or exceptions.) He'd almost forgotten about the girl when the sound of someone else puking reminded him. He ran upstairs and found Ariel asleep on the bare mattress. It was cold in the room, so Dex found her a blanket. As he was spreading it over her, she startled. "What are you doing?"

"I couldn't find your boyfriend."

"My what?"

"I asked around, but I couldn't find anyone named Gideon."

"Gideon's here?" She spoke with her eyes closed.

"No, that's what I'm saying. I couldn't find him."

"I can't sleep here," she said, but then put her head back against the mattress, made a sound like a pig snorting, and fell instantly back asleep.

Dex was ready to call it a night but worried it might be irresponsible to leave a drunk undergrad alone in a room. What if she threw up in the night? He'd heard of people dying this way—choking on their own vomit. But wasn't it also creepy to sleep in the same room as a girl he didn't know? He wasn't sure how old she was, but she looked young. Deciding that creeped-out was better than dead, he stole more blankets and made a bed on the floor. As he drifted to sleep, his back already hurting from the hard floor, he imagined accepting a diploma before a crowd of roaring fans: DEXTER DONNELLY, DOCTOR OF PARTY MEDICINE, EMPHASIS IN PUKE.

In the morning, he woke to find her staring at him. "Thank you," she said, "for taking care of me." In the light, he saw that she had the kind of eyebrows that looked boorish on men but made women look powerful—a Frida Kahlo effect. Her face seemed to change the more he looked at her, a quirk that would continue long after they started dating. Her hair was a mass of crazy black curls, and there was dried drool on her chin, but she was cute, in her own way. She looked kind.

It was then he remembered Gideon Gonzalo. "Hey, your boy-friend," he said.

"My what?"

"Gideon—I couldn't find him last night. He's probably worried about you."

Her cheeks turned red. "I made him up."

"Why?"

"Because I was drunk, and I didn't want you to think I came here alone."

"Really?" he asked.

She'd looked at him, her gaze unwavering. "Really."

Sitting in Ariel's mother's kitchen, Dex could still recall with pre-ternatural clarity the afternoon that followed: their tired, headachy brunch, how Ariel agreed to come over the next night and watch a movie at his place. How they'd fallen asleep on his couch, *Almost Famous* playing so quietly they should have used subtitles. How, when they woke up, she'd pressed a finger to his third eye and said, "I feel good around you." He'd also remembered that name—Gideon Gonzalo. He'd once searched the name on Facebook but had found only two candidates: a white-haired insurance agent from Key West and a high school anime geek from Maple Grove, Minnesota. The more he tried to forget Gideon, the more Gideon appeared in his mind. When he was not wearing a suit, he wore a tight white V-neck, skinny black jeans, and crocodile boots so pointy they could pierce a hole through a coconut. Professionally, he was a pediatric oncologist who moon-lighted as a model for Ralph Lauren. Ariel loved him not because of his good looks or charm but because he'd once hauled her from the underbelly of a burning streetcar just moments before it exploded. Where or when Ariel would have ridden a streetcar, Dex couldn't be sure, but his paranoid daydreams were not limited by details of geog-raphy or chronology.

That morning after the Freedom House party was the last time either of them spoke of Gideon Gonzalo. Ariel never brought him up again, and so neither did Dex, who feared that to speak the name— such a strange name for her to make up on the fly while drunk— would be to revive the man who had passed like the silhouette of a shark beneath their first night together. Over the years, he couldn't help but feel that Gideon was real. Now, he knew, he was right.

Ariel

Night was falling as Ariel and Joy returned to the sanctuary. Joy had been right—finding Wooster had been a matter of luck. They'd spent the rest of the afternoon fruitlessly combing the county, talking and listening to the radio to distract themselves. Ariel had memorized the lyrics to several country songs. There was one she kind of liked, about a guy wanting to check his girlfriend for ticks—something Gideon had once done for her.

At one point, while driving down a wide gravel road, flanked by fields of yellow grass, the sky an empty thought bubble suspended overhead, Ariel felt a spike of happiness—in that moment, she was glad she'd let the dogs go, if it meant she could ride in the car with Joy, watching Kansas unfold, acre by acre, around her. She felt immediately ashamed of the thought, knowing it would infuriate her mother. There was pleasure in this line of thinking, too. How long had it been since Ariel edited her thoughts to please the imaginary audience of her mother? It was something she'd done as a little girl, when she suspected her mother really could read her mind.

As they pulled through the sanctuary's gate, Ariel could practically feel the heat of her mother's anger radiating from the house. By now, Gideon would have told her mother what had happened. She felt amazed with herself, then, for how much damage she'd caused in so little time. She could feel this amazement billowing inside her mother, taking the shape of rage.

They were passing the visitors' lot when Ariel noticed a beige station wagon parked next to her car. "Do you know whose car that is?" she asked Joy.

"Nope. Never seen it before."

Ariel couldn't decide whether company would work in her interest. Maybe the owner of the car was there to adopt an animal or had come to return one of the missing dogs. Maybe Mona would, despite everything, be cheerful.

Outside the house, a man was sitting on the porch. Gideon. Ariel steadied her breath, prepared for whatever was to come. She would start with an apology and go from there. She would promise to stay until they found all the dogs. She wanted to help—she had come, after all, to help. Not to hurt. She would fix her mess. She would not mention the kiss, of course, not with Joy around, but perhaps later she could apologize more fully—she could promise it would not happen again, that she had been confused, overwhelmed. That she had confused the sensation of missing home with the sensation of missing him. But the person on the porch seemed to be smoking a cigarette, an orange bead of light moving against the dark of the porch.

"Gideon smokes now?" Ariel said.

"That's not Gideon," Joy said. "I'm not sure who it is."

Ariel had to blink to make sure she was seeing right.

"Welcome home," said the smoking figure.

Ariel dug her fingernails into her palm. "I don't know what you're doing here," she said to Buddy, "but you need to leave. Now."

"Keep your panties on," Buddy said, twisting out his cigarette on her mother's porch. "We just got here."

· · ·

Inside, Dex was sitting on the living room couch, chatting with her mom as if they were old friends. This was typical Dex—she'd often find him engaged in a conversation with someone at a bar, both of them leaning so close their foreheads nearly touched (*So your grandmother never loved your father and that's why he smothers you?*), only to find out he'd just met the person. Her mother, to Ariel's relief, didn't seem to mind. She was nodding along as Dex talked, her hands busy petting an orange cat on her lap. Dex wore a look of pure amusement. He'd dressed the part—faded blue jeans and a chambray shirt with pearl-snap buttons, white flowers stitched on the breast pockets. Ariel could tell he was in full-on schmooze mode, his smile even wider, more ingratiating than normal. Seeing him here, in her mother's living room, in the space where she'd grown up, was unnerving. She wanted him gone, for her two worlds to remain separate.

"Dex," she said.

"Ariel! You're home." He stood and came to her. He looked taller than normal, in her mother's living room. He was wearing his dancing boots.

She saw her mother grimace at how he pronounced her name—a new name, different from the one she had given Ariel. "Dex, what are you doing here? And why is Buddy with you?"

"Shoot—I told him to stay in the car."

"Well, he's on the porch. Smoking."

"You want me to go smack him on the nose with a newspaper?"

There it was: everything that annoyed her about Dex, drawn out like a floor plan. How he talked too loud in public, the way he let messes accumulate, how he tried to argue about current events when he'd read only the headlines of articles. How, whenever she was angry, he tried to defuse the situation with a joke.

"Answer me," she said. "What are you doing here?" Only once

she said it did she realize she too had shown up at her mother's house uninvited, without concern for how it would affect anyone else. At least Dex had arrived at a reasonable hour.

Mona was standing now, a hand on her hip. "He's not a burglar, Ariel. He's your fiancé." She looked at Ariel as if to say, *Anything else you want to tell me?* She looked exhausted, as if she'd spent the last few hours running in circles. Of course, Ariel realized, she probably *had* been running in circles, trying to catch the dogs Ariel had let loose. She narrowed her eyes at Ariel. "I leave for one little errand and when I come back, everything's in chaos."

"Your mom told me what happened with the dogs," Dex said. "I can stay and help. We can work together. I'll reschedule all my cuts and find someone to cover for me at the Replay. Buddy can go back in the morning and I can drive back to Lawrence with you, whenever you want to go home. It's perfect, right?"

Clearly, he either did not want her to be here alone or he didn't want to be alone in Lawrence. She wondered if he'd met Gideon, if that had anything to do with the anxiety in his eyes. "Dex, I appreciate that you want to help, but I think it'd be better if you went back home."

He came closer to her, so that her mother couldn't hear. "You took all your underwear," he said into her ear. "Even the sexy ones."

She looked at him, this man she was going to spend the rest of her life with. "Dex, why were you looking through my underwear? I've only been gone a day. *One day.*"

"But you left with so much stuff—and you didn't say when you'd be back." He put his hands on her shoulders. "I love you, Ariel. That's why I came here."

"How did you even find this place?"

"You had some articles on the computer. See, I was just clicking around, and then before I knew it—"

"*Dex*," she said. She had never suspected him of snooping.

"I'm sorry," he said.

She thought of what her mother had said about *I'm sorry*. Perhaps it really was a kitchen sponge, a limited resource that eventually became dirtier than the surface it was meant to clean. Or perhaps in this case, she knew she was the one who should be apologizing, not Dex. Had he left on a mysterious trip, she too would have worried what he was up to. Maybe she would have snooped, too.

"I think you should go," she said.

"Gideon Gonzalo," Dex said quietly. He was talking through his teeth. "You packed all your sexy panties, and you're out here with Gideon Gonzalo." His eyes bore into her. "I'm not leaving."

For years, Ariel had wondered if Dex remembered this detail of their first night together. Afraid of what doors it might open, of what her voice might reveal if she said his name, she'd never brought it up.

As if they'd conjured him, Gideon appeared in the living room, Joy at his side. He met Ariel's eyes but she couldn't interpret the look. He was mad at her, but how much of his anger was about the dogs and how much was about everything else? About her barging back into his life? About the kiss? She had thought coming home would fix the damage she'd caused upon leaving, but so far, she'd only made things worse.

"We're going to make pasta," Gideon said matter-of-factly.

Dex looked first to Ariel, as if for permission, and then to Gideon. "Let me help. I make a mean red sauce."

Before Ariel could react, Dex followed Gideon and Joy into the kitchen, glancing back at Ariel as if to say, *I'm making sauce, and I'm not going anywhere.*

When they were gone, Mona said, "I want to talk to you. Now. In private."

Ariel had no choice but to follow her mother onto the back porch, a gang of dogs scrambling excitedly at their heels. Despite the knot in her stomach, it was also strangely wonderful, to follow her mother outside for a scolding. It meant her mother was still her mother, that they were still capable of inhabiting their old roles. It meant they were still a family. For a moment, Ariel wondered if part of her had done it on purpose—let the dogs loose, tried to kiss Gideon. *Nothing bonds people like drama*, Sunny once told her. If drama was what Ariel wanted, then she had certainly succeeded. Rather than hold the screen door open, her mother let it clap shut in Ariel's face.

Mona

She led Ariel onto the back porch, where the steps opened onto a field of prairie grass. It was the same place where they used to carve pumpkins in the fall and eat watermelons in the summer. She could recall Ariel's face perfectly: her gap-toothed smile and frizzy hair, chin dripping with watermelon juice. Her little girl. Some nights, when the field lit up with fireflies, she would watch Ariel run through the grass.

"Can we catch them in a jar?" Ariel once asked—a trick she must have learned in school.

"They're alive, just like you and me," she'd explained to Ariel. "Let's let them stay in their home."

Ariel's eyes had widened, as if, for the first time, she understood that everything—*everything*—was just as real as she was.

Mona had never told Ariel, but when she and Daniel were trying to get pregnant, she'd wished every night for a little girl, a daughter with whom she could share her life the way she and her mother had shared theirs. Eventually her wishing felt empty, and so she'd checked out a book from the Wichita library titled *Folk Wisdom for Mothers*. She learned that if she really wanted a girl, there were things she could do: eat lots of fruits and vegetables, make love on even-numbered days, initiate sex. When she found out she was having a girl, she did something she never did: she thanked God, or whatever God might be—the sky, the earth, the invisible everything and nothing around her—for answering her tiny, selfish prayer.

Now night had fallen in earnest and Ariel was pretending not to be cold. She was wearing all the wrong clothes—no hat, thin pants, and a pair of those silly leather slippers like the hippies used to wear. She had her arms crossed and was trying not to shiver. When one of the donkeys began to bray, she startled. Who was this girl? The girl Mona remembered would have gone wild with worry if even a single dog got loose. A memory rushed at her: Ariel, nine years old, declaring it was spa day on the sanctuary, going around giving hip massages to the dogs, brushing the horses and cats. It seemed like another life entirely.

"Let me start with a question," she said, trying to keep her anger in check. "Did you come back to give me a heart attack?"

"It was an accident," Ariel said, her voice low, already contrite.

"That's not the way Gideon told it." She would not tell Ariel, but Gideon had also told her that Ariel had tried to kiss him. *She was just caught up; it wasn't anything.* But Mona knew well and good about trying to kiss someone who did not want to be kissed. It was the same thing she had once done with Daniel, something Coreen had recently done with her. Part of her felt sad for Ariel, for wanting something that was no longer hers. "He told me you let a few dogs go on purpose."

"Well, it started as an accident. And then I just got mad. Or frustrated. Or something."

"About what?"

Ariel wouldn't meet her eyes. Mona remembered what Coreen had said: *Think of how hard this must be for her. How scary.*

"I don't know," Ariel said. "It's a lot to take in, coming back. Seeing everyone. You and Gideon. The animals. I guess I'm only now realizing what I did—that I'll never get back the years I was gone."

Mona felt an ache in her chest. This was it, wasn't it? Hadn't she been waiting years to hear Ariel say this very thing—that she regretted leaving? And yet, somehow, it wasn't enough. Not anymore. "There's good dogs out there, probably hungry and thirsty or flattened by a semi." Her heart was in her throat now. She could hear Coreen in her head: *Be gentle. This is your daughter.*

"I'm sorry. I wish I could undo it."

Mona heard what Ariel didn't say: she wished she could undo all of it, turn back the clock and start over.

"There's something I want to ask you," Mona said.

Ariel nodded. "Okay."

"Why did you leave like you did? What did I do to deserve that?" It was a question that had tormented her over the years. Gideon had tried to explain as best he could—she wanted to go to school, to live her own life—but Mona had never understood why Ariel had to run away like she did. Mona was stubborn, but she wasn't completely unreasonable. Had Ariel tried harder to explain herself, they could have found a middle ground. She was sure of it.

"I'm sorry, Mom."

"Sorry isn't an answer."

Ariel squeezed her temples and looked out, beyond Mona. "It was hard here," she said, her eyes meeting Mona's. "I had no friends. My whole life was the animals. And just when it was time for me to go off on my own, you wouldn't let me. It was like you just wanted me here to work. That's what it felt like, at the end—that I was free labor."

"Free labor?"

"I'm just telling you what I felt."

"I thought you liked working with the animals. You never complained, never said no. Every morning, you got up and started chores on your own. I figured it was every little girl's dream to play with ponies and puppies."

"But I didn't have ponies and puppies. *You* had ponies and puppies."

"It's not about *having* the animals, Ariel. They're not furniture."

"I know, Mom. That's not what I meant. I meant it was your dream. All of this was yours." Ariel spread her hands out to the deck, the prairie, the night sky with its skimpy little moon.

This, more than anything, Mona felt in her heart. "But it was yours, too. I always figured one day you'd take over, help the animals when I couldn't." A lump rose in her throat, but she forced it down. "How could you not have gotten that?"

"Because you never told me. You never told me anything. We hardly talked once the animals got here."

She couldn't look at Ariel and so she looked away, toward the field and the miles of cold, flat earth that had always echoed back the same word: *home, home, home.* "You had me, Ariel. Every hour of every day, I was right here with you. I thought I'd given you a good life. I thought I was a good mother."

"You were," Ariel said.

"Well, it doesn't matter now." There was a feeling she had that as soon as she sold the sanctuary, her ties to Ariel would dissolve completely. It was a terrifying feeling. Perhaps Ariel felt it, too.

"You know, Joy and I were talking earlier," Ariel said, shifting her weight. "She told me about you and her mom."

Oh boy, Mona thought. *Here we go.* "Coreen and I are just friends."

"Right. But I was thinking—what if Coreen gave you the money? Or bought the sanctuary herself? You wouldn't owe anybody anything."

"Any way you slice it, I still owe her something." All these years, she'd needed more help than she could ask for, and now, as soon as she was ready to give up the game, here came everyone stampeding in, telling her to keep trying. Work harder. Think of the animals. She'd done nothing these past fifteen years but think of the animals, and what had it gotten her? "I'm tired of talking about it."

"But you need to talk about it."

"Why? So you can feel involved?"

"So you don't lose the sanctuary."

"It's already lost, Ariel. There's nothing you or I or anyone can do—it's over."

"But it doesn't have to be. There has to be a way. But not if you don't talk about it."

"I just told you," she said, her frustration mounting, "I don't *want* to talk about it."

"Because it hurts?"

Mona stamped a boot into the deck. "Because I want to lose the sanctuary, Ariel. Okay? I'm ready. I'm done." She realized her hands were shaking. The tips of her fingers were numb—she put them under her armpits, to warm them.

"Really?" Ariel said, a look of mild alarm in her eyes. She had taken a micro-step back when Mona stamped her foot.

"I can't do it anymore. I'm so tired, Ariel. I gave it everything I had and now I just—I just can't. I'm done."

They stood in silence then, the night pressing in around them. Mona had anticipated feeling ashamed of admitting her failure but found she felt good. Lighter and alert, like the moment after a big sneeze.

"Okay," Ariel said carefully. "I understand. But what are you going to do? What are the animals going to do? Where will they go?"

"Look," Mona said, "I know you're trying to help—I get it. But I'm figuring it out. I have a list of sanctuaries to call, to see if anyone has space."

"You're going to transport the animals by yourself?"

Mona ignored the pinch of stress she felt each time she thought of this process—she knew how much work it would be. How much money and time it would require—the two things she never had enough of. "I'll figure it out, Ariel. I always do."

"It just seems like you're all in denial. Nobody's making plans. Nobody wants to talk about it. And then this whole thing with Big John—I just don't get it. It's like you're drowning and someone comes by with a boat, and you refuse to get in just because you didn't build the boat yourself."

"Who told you about Big John?"

Ariel shifted nervously. "Gideon mentioned it earlier."

"Well, it's out of the question. Another buyer will come along. I'm patient. The animals, God knows, are patient."

"But why? Maybe he's a bad person, but at least you'd know the animals are safe. You wouldn't have to worry about rehoming everyone."

"I said, it's out of the question."

"But *why?*"

"Because even if I still wanted him to buy the sanctuary, he wouldn't want it. Not anymore."

"Because of the fire?"

"Because I stole something from him, okay?"

"What are you talking about?"

She looked at Ariel, expecting disapproval but finding only confusion. "He had one of those Trump signs, with the slogan. I took it from his property, and then he saw it in my truck."

"This was before the fire?"

Mona nodded. "A couple weeks before. I'm sure it's what set Sydney off—that and the election and everything else."

Strangely, Ariel's eyes began to lighten, a smile on her lips.

"What's funny?" Mona asked.

"I just—I didn't know about the sign. I thought the fire was my fault."

"How on earth could it be your fault?"

Ariel grabbed her own elbows and pulled them to her chest, a mannerism from her girlhood, when she'd walked around as if the world was trying to hurt her. "I thought Sydney did it as revenge, for something that happened between us."

"You thought he set fire to my barn because you were mean to him a decade ago?"

"When you say it like that—"

"Is that why you came back? Because you felt responsible?"

"No—I mean, yes, I felt guilty. I still feel guilty. But it's more than that. I wanted to see you. To help you."

"And Gideon, right?"

"What are you talking about?"

"I saw how you looked at him this morning. And then your poor fiancé shows up, no idea what's going on, where you are or what you're doing."

"I didn't come back for Gideon, Mom. I didn't even know he was here. I came back for *you*."

There was a strain in Ariel's voice, one Mona wanted to believe, to feel in her heart, but couldn't. "You say that, Ariel," she said, "but look at what you've done." Her words hung in the air—she wasn't sure if she meant letting the dogs loose, or the fact that they were standing there, six years later, the silence between them still solid as a wall. She could tell Ariel was about to say "I'm sorry," and so she put up a hand, to stop her. Exasperated, she turned to go inside, leaving Ariel out in the cold.

What Ariel didn't know was that, a month after she left, Mona had driven to Lawrence. She was tired of waking up with a pit in her stomach, remembering all over again that Ariel was gone. She was tired of checking Ariel's bed, as if Ariel might finally be there, proving the whole thing was a bad dream. She was tired of waiting, and so she decided to act.

When she got to campus, she'd looked up at the dorm—seven stories high, boasting a hundred windows through which Mona could see pastel curtains and twinkle lights and psychedelic tapestries—and realized that one of those windows belonged to Ariel, that this was Ariel's new home. She sat there for a minute, paralyzed by the truth of it. Not only had Ariel left, but she had also not come back; she'd chosen this life over the one Mona had made for her. She was about to leave when she saw Ariel walking with another girl, both of them wearing jean shorts, carrying backpacks, their faces turned down in conversation. Like a crack of lightning, Ariel laughed, threw her head back in pleasure. It was the first time Mona had ever seen Ariel laugh like this with a friend, and her immediate reaction was joy. How good it felt to see Ariel happy, free. She looked like an entirely different person than she'd been at the Bright Side. As Ariel and her friend drew closer, Mona felt dizzy—she couldn't imagine what she would say. What had she been thinking, coming all this way to confront someone who didn't want to be confronted? And so, she went home. By the time she got to St. Clare, her face was salted with tears. Just like Daniel, her daughter had left her for a better life.

Mona had wondered, over the years, whether she overreacted the night Ariel told her about wanting to go away to school. Coreen had certainly scolded her for it—*The girl gets a full ride and you say she can't go? Of course she ran off!*—but Mona still believed that as Ariel's mother, the person who had provided for her and loved her every day for eighteen years, she had a say in what Ariel did with her life. Was it so much to ask that Ariel stick around the sanctuary for another few years? To go to college—a perfectly decent college that Mona had planned and prepared and saved for Ariel to attend—that was near her family rather than clear on the other side of the state? According to Coreen, it was, and there must have been truth in it; Ariel had left, after all, causing the thing Mona had feared most—the reason she'd put her foot down in the first place—to happen: just like Daniel, Ariel had disappeared.

At least, in the beginning, Gideon had shared her grief. For months, he would stare at the telephone, the front door, the novels Ariel had left on the coffee table—*Lolita, The Bell Jar, Ceremony*—books Mona would eventually box up and put in the attic. She suspected Ariel and Gideon were still in contact, that they spoke whenever Mona was out of the house, a suspicion that was as comforting as it was maddening. At least if Gideon was still talking to her, she might return, and for a while it seemed like Gideon expected her to. At any sudden noise, he would perk up, as if Ariel might walk through the door. This pained Mona more than anything—to see her hurt and desperation manifested in another person. Sometimes, she wanted to shout, *Go get her, you idiot. You know how to bring her back. Tell her I love her. Tell her I miss her. Tell her I'm angry as hell.* But she knew, deep down, that nothing could make Ariel return except Ariel.

At last, on a morning that would have been ordinary had it not been Ariel's twentieth birthday, Mona woke and decided enough was enough. From then on, whenever she thought of Ariel—which was every day, even if just for a passing moment—she would force herself to imagine a wall. She could look at the wall for however long she wanted, but she could not look beyond it, or through it, or around it. Those were the rules. She had learned, from losing Daniel, the importance of letting go. Of recognizing when to stop waiting. A woman could waste a perfectly good life thinking about the people who left her, and Mona couldn't afford the distraction—she had animals to take care of. Mouths to feed and wounds to clean. She worried, too, that if she focused too much on what she had lost, she would eventually become like her father—bitter, hateful, so obsessed by what was gone that she couldn't appreciate what remained. And so, she focused on the animals.

The animals—thank God for them. She wondered, for the millionth time, what it would be like without them, whether she would feel the way she had before the Bright Side, that there was an emptiness in her life that needed filling, that there was an entire world she was meant to inhabit that had nothing to do with people, and that this world, and only this world, would make the other one—the world of people—tolerable.

Ariel

Ariel's face was numb, her fingers stiff with cold, but she wasn't ready to go inside. The conversation with her mother had not gone well. She'd said some stupid things that already made her cringe. Had she really used the words *free labor*? What was wrong with her? She'd sounded so selfish, so spoiled. There was also the matter of Sydney. Despite what her mother said about the sign, Ariel couldn't help but feel that her past with Sydney still played some part. Sure, her mother stole a sign, but Ariel had stolen something much bigger from him, something that had followed him through his life.

Maybe her mother was right, though. Maybe she was putting herself in the middle of business that was no longer hers. She felt sorry then, for her mother, that her behavior had sabotaged the best offer she was going to get, had played a part in her barn burning, her horses dying. Yet, more than this, she was in awe of her mother. She'd seen a few Trump signs around Lawrence, little dinky ones planted in people's lawns, and the most she'd done was smack one with an umbrella. (After which she felt immediately guilty and speed-walked away, cheeks burning.) In the end, no matter what had happened to inspire Sydney's anger, it was nobody's fault—not hers, not her mother's, not even Trump's—but his.

She thought about what her mother had said, about how she'd imagined Ariel taking over the Bright Side someday. Ariel tried to imagine what it would be like to run the sanctuary, to know that the animals would live or die by her hand, that they would eat only if she fed them, that they would survive only if she took them in and gave them shelter. The thought of it overwhelmed her. There were too many animals, too many moving parts. Anything less than total dedication, total sacrifice, would result in chaos—like running a country, Ariel thought. In the wrong hands, for the wrong reasons, it would be madness.

Ariel was glad when the cattle dog who'd slept with her the night before came to lay beside her. She put the dog's head in her lap, feeling a surge of gratitude. She rubbed his velvety ears, trying to warm them. She'd forgotten how a dog could make anything better. Dog medicine, her mother had called it, to which Ariel would always respond, *No such thing as an overdose.*

When she could stand the cold no longer, she went inside, the cattle dog following after, his nose gently bumping the back of her knee, trying to herd her. In the kitchen, the air smelled of garlic and onion and she could hear laughter. Dex's phone was playing something twangy by Trampled by Turtles. Perhaps he thought this was a crowd that appreciated twang. The clutter from earlier had been collected and stacked on the countertop and replaced with a vase of dried flowers—Joy's doing, Ariel was sure.

"There you are," Dex said, looking at Ariel. He was slicing lemons for water. "Dinner's almost ready." All this time, she had worried about Dex accepting and fitting into her past, and yet here he was, getting along just fine with everyone. She was the one who no longer belonged.

"It smells great," she said, feeling a pang of sadness she identified as the feeling of being left out. Despite everything, the mood in the kitchen was festive. Perhaps this was also Joy's doing. Ariel knew a few women—Sunny was one of them—who could single-handedly alter the mood of a party. They'd put on the right song or tell the right joke, and suddenly everyone would be dancing or laughing, having a good time.

Dex finished slicing the lemon and came to her. "Guess what?" he asked, putting his arm around her, drawing her close.

She allowed herself to melt into him, to smell the lemon on his fingertips. She wanted to match the mood in the kitchen, to feign cheerfulness despite the dark feeling that sat in her stomach like a stone. "It's not chicken butt, is it? Because there are actually chicken butts here."

"Gross," he said. "Also, wrong. I met a dog named Hippo. We're basically best friends now."

"You? And a dog?"

"His name is Hippo because that's what he looks like and also because he's extremely cool—like *hip*. Get it?"

She couldn't help but smile. He was in one of his goofy moods. Maybe he was stoned. "That's great," she said. "I'm happy for you."

"I'm happy for me, too. For *us*."

When dinner was ready, they sat down at the table as if theirs were a normal family and this a normal meal. The pasta was over-cooked, but Ariel ate two helpings, covering each bowl with a layer of Kroger Parmesan cheese. Dex called it Italian cocaine, and when Mona chuckled—she was being nice, Ariel realized—he repeated the joke so many times that Ariel wondered if he actually thought it was funny. He even went so far as to make a line of cheese on the table and pretend to snort it. He was nervous, trying too hard. Each time Dex opened his mouth, Gideon would look up at her, trying to transmit a message.

You don't get to make fun of my fiancé, she wanted to say, among a hundred other things. *He's normally funnier than this—he can be hilarious. In Lawrence, everyone loves him. You couldn't even believe how many friends he has.* But she just continued eating in silence as Joy and Mona took turns asking Dex questions. How did he learn to cut hair? Did he like being a DJ? Did he like animals?

When Dex said he liked animals just fine but didn't consider himself an *animal person*, Gideon looked at Ariel one last time, a look she had no problem translating: *You know he's not the one. I was the one, and now you have this—this city boy who doesn't know animals.*

Or maybe it was all in her head. Maybe Gideon wasn't thinking anything of the sort. Probably he was thinking about the dogs.

Mona quickly turned the subject to business. "We have what, seven dogs missing?" She looked at Ariel.

"Six, now," Gideon said.

"We've got a haul of donations coming in on Monday," Mona said, "which means the storage container needs to be cleared out tomorrow. I don't want boxes sitting out for a week, especially if it decides to snow. We want things to look nice for the adoption fair."

"What's in the container right now?" Ariel asked.

"Just some old donations."

Gideon cleared his throat. "Very old."

"It's not that bad," said Mona, which was how Ariel knew the donations were ancient.

The plan was for the boys to tackle the container while the girls went out to look for the remaining dogs. Ariel caught Gideon and Joy exchanging a look that said: *Can this hipster handle it?*

"I want everyone up early," Mona said. "Those dogs will be half-way to Colorado by sunrise—if they make it to sunrise."

Gideon began to clear the table. "Where are Ariel and Dex supposed to sleep?"

Ariel assumed they'd sleep on the floor. Dex would just have to deal with the dogs and cats wandering around.

"What about Blue House?" Joy said. She had gotten up to help

Gideon with the dishes. When he thought nobody was looking, Gideon pinched Joy on the hip.

"Is Blue House livable?" Ariel asked.

The last time she'd been in Blue House, her senior year of high school, it had been infested with mice and brown recluses. The air smelled like mildew, the windows were cloudy with mold. Her father had left behind a package of unopened undershirts, a Nescafé tin full of pennies, and a cardboard box of *New Yorker* magazines with the cartoons cut out. She and Gideon had used the house early in their relationship as a place to hook up when they worried Mona might catch them in the RV. Once, just after they'd gotten undressed, Ariel had stepped on a pregnant spider, and thousands of babies, none larger than the dot of an *i*, had exploded beneath her feet. As the tiny spiders swarmed around them, Gideon picked her up and carried her outside, both of them butt-naked. From there, they sprinted to the RV, dying of laughter along the way, a gang of Free Dogs chasing them.

"We've been fixing it up, Gideon and I."

"You're going to live in there?" Ariel asked.

"That's the plan," Joy said. "Progress is slow—there was a lot of mold and water damage. But we're aiming for spring. Unless, you know, the sanctuary sells."

Everyone went quiet. "Good for you," Ariel eventually said, choosing to ignore the part about the sanctuary selling. "I would have counted it as a lost cause."

"These two could turn dog shit into diamonds," said Mona. "You won't believe it when you see it. They should be on one of those TV shows."

Joy was blushing. "The water's not on yet, but it's fine to sleep in for a few nights. There's a pellet stove. And a bed."

Ariel did not like the idea of sleeping in Joy and Gideon's future bed, in their future house, the house her father had built out of sadness.

"That's really generous," Dex said. "Thank you."

He then leaned into Ariel and whispered, "You think Buddy could crash with us, too?"

Dex

While everyone else was doing dishes, Dex took a plate of food onto the porch.

"Seriously?" Buddy said, taking the plate. "I watch you guys in there, eating dinner all Norman Rockwell, and nobody comes out to invite me in? It's fucking cold out here, man. I can't feel my nose."

Just then, Hippo came over and pressed his side into Dex's shin. Dex reached down to scratch him behind the ears—he'd heard about dogs liking that. "I'm sorry—I just needed some time to talk to everyone. It's been a weird night."

"Yeah, for me, too, asshat. I got cats rubbing up on my face. And this donkey over there keeps honking at me."

"I don't think it's called honking."

"He's honking." Buddy loaded a forkful of pasta into his mouth, dripping sauce onto his shirt. "Hey, knock knock."

Dex sighed. "Who's there?"

"Fuck you. And fuck you's cousin, suck my dick. I drove you all the way here and then you leave me outside in the cold. You're a shithole of a friend."

"Earmuffs," Dex said, putting his hands over Hippo's ears.

Buddy rolled his eyes.

"You're right. I'm a shithole."

"Shit canyon."

"Yes, I'm a shit canyon."

"Shit crevasse. Shit pit."

"Are you done now?"

"Yes," Buddy said. "You can take the stupid earmuffs off."

Dex released Hippo's ears and sat down beside Buddy, his back stiff from the drive, his brain buzzing. "I'm sorry, all right?"

Buddy slurped a noodle and said nothing. Eventually he asked, "Who's the blonde?"

"Her name's Joy. She's dating that guy, who I'm pretty sure used to have a thing with Ariel."

"So there is a guy." Buddy smiled, food in his teeth.

"Yes," Dex said. "There's a guy."

"Didn't I tell you there'd be a guy?"

Dex looked out onto the sanctuary, where animals of anonymous species moved in the night. Far off, a pair of bright green eyes paced the length of a wire fence. Buddy was right; the donkey tipped his muzzle to the sky and honked. In response, Hippo barked twice, as if to say, *Quiet, donkey. Men are talking.*

Buddy said, "Clean-plate club, motherfucker," and Frisbee'd his plastic plate onto the grass.

"Don't do that," Dex said, but did not get up to retrieve the plate. Hippo had already gone after it and was licking the oil and leftover sauce.

Buddy lit a cigarette and passed it to Dex, who took it without thinking, his eyes trained on the plate.

"That was shitty of me," Dex said, "to leave you out here during dinner. I should have asked if you could come in and eat with us."

"You know why I agreed to this trip, don't you?"

Dex shrugged. "You were bored?"

"I did it because I've been in your shoes. With Miranda."

Dex passed the cigarette. This was the one thing Ariel didn't know about Buddy—that, once upon a time, before he was the way he was (selfish, crass, a walking dumpster fire), he'd been different, *happy*, and it was because of Miranda. She was funny and ambitious, a strong-willed girl who was studying to become a chemical engineer and who had used her long, beautiful legs to run track for KU until she tore her ACL sprinting drunk through a cornfield her junior year. She was known for her plume of squiggly, rose-colored hair. According to Buddy, her hair had materialized for months after she left—in his coat pocket, in his peanut butter snack. On occasion, Dex would still find a strand of the stuff plastered to the molding in Buddy's bathroom, woven into the fibers of the bathmat.

"I'm sorry I wasn't around more when she left," Dex said. "I know it was hard for you."

"The hardest part was knowing it wasn't hard for her."

"You don't know that. I'm sure she was sad about it, too, in her own way."

"No, she wasn't." The certainty with which he said it made Dex wonder if it was true. "Sometimes I think about it and it feels like it's happening all over again. Like it was yesterday. Or today. Like it's right now. It just makes me feel so *shitty*, you know? Like, why would anyone ever want to be with me? I'm useless."

"She wasn't the one, Buddy. That's all."

"But she *was*. I know she was. Which is why I wanted you to prepare for bad news with Ariel. These things happen, you know. To everyone. Not just other people. Sometimes we *are* the other people."

"But it's Ariel."

"Yeah," Buddy said. "And it was Miranda. We were supposed to get married, too. We had names picked out for kids. And that's the thing—there's no rules. No promises. They can say one thing and be thinking something completely different. One night they can be in your bed, saying they love you, and the next thing you know they're on a red-eye to New Orleans so they can spend Mardi Gras with their new boyfriend."

Dex stood up. "I don't think I can talk about this right now." He was remembering a conversation he'd had with Ariel, years before, in which they exchanged their favorite baby names. He liked Arnold for a boy; she liked Piper for a girl. Dex had committed these names to memory, so that he would be able to recite them when the day came. On this day, he would quit drinking and smoking. He would also forfeit his job at the Replay and take up a full-time slot at the barbershop. That was his plan, one he hesitated to share with Ariel, for he worried she wouldn't believe him. He made a mental note to wash his hands, so Ariel wouldn't smell the tobacco on his fingers.

"Don't get all worked up," Buddy said. "I'm just trying to help."

"I know. I'm just not in the mood to hear this kind of story."

Just then, the mudroom door opened and Ariel came out onto the porch. "You missed all the dishes."

"Sorry," Dex said. "We got to talking." He stuck his fingers into his mouth, as if he might suck away the smell of the tobacco.

"Are you ready for bed?" she asked. "I'm beat."

Dex said, "Never been readier."

"I can come, too?" asked Buddy.

"Sure," Ariel said, defeated. "You can come, too."

Dex took a moment to say good night to Hippo, who was still licking Buddy's plate. He scratched behind Hippo's ear, hoping Ariel was watching him, that he was gaining kindness-toward-animals brownie points. The truth was that he wasn't just doing it for her benefit; he genuinely wanted to say good night to the dog. "Sweet dreams, funky disco dude. See ya tomorrow." Hippo wriggled his butt, as if to say, *Peace out, reggae papa.*

When Dex looked up, Ariel had already set off down the drive. He jogged to catch up with her and saw that they were headed toward a small house, a bouquet of floodlights illuminating the exterior. The house was the exact color of Kurt Cobain's Mustang guitar, an egg-shell blue that had become, in Dex's mind, the same color as the song "All Apologies." Just looking at the house depressed him, but when Ariel opened the door, he followed her into the darkness. The air smelled of new paint and bleach. Behind him, Buddy put a hand on his shoulder and squeezed.

Ariel

Ariel's dislike for Buddy was a paper swan, one she had crafted meticulously, fold after fold, starting with an unblemished sheet of paper and working toward something sharp and clean, an aversion so perfect it could practically take flight. There was much to dislike about Buddy. He was crude and careless, lazy and arrogant. She once saw him throw a half-eaten rotisserie chicken from the window of a moving car. On Election Day, he stayed home with "loose stools" and worked a two-thousand-piece glow-in-the-dark jigsaw puzzle. When Trump won, he collected $1,200 in a bet, the bulk of which he blew on a round-trip ticket to Miami, where he spent a long weekend drinking margaritas and sending Dex pictures of women in bikinis.

Ariel had tried to give Buddy a break, but over the years, he'd only reinforced her original opinion of him. There was the time he'd drunkenly urinated on her bookshelf (hitting, to her dismay, her entire collection of Alice Munro) and the time he ate the entirety of a coconut cream pie she'd baked for a work potluck. The time he put a foil-wrapped burrito in their microwave, and the time he clogged their toilet and tried to blame it on Ariel. The time he cornered Ariel at a bar and tried to kiss her, and the time she slapped him and he called her a succubus. Like all people, he had his good moments, too. But even a million good moments couldn't make up for the fact that his default setting was destruction.

Now, in the kitchenette where her father had, years ago, read Ariel his poems and allowed her to microwave marshmallows until they inflated to the size of soup cans, Buddy lit a cigarette with a white Bic lighter. His fingernails were stained a bold, putrid yellow.

Ariel plucked the cigarette from his mouth and put it out in the sink. "Are you insane? This isn't your house."

"It isn't yours, either. Chill out."

She dug her fingernails into her palm.

"So, your mom runs a zoo." He smiled at her with his beautiful white teeth. Teeth he had done nothing to earn.

"It's an animal sanctuary."

"Seems a lot like a zoo to me."

"Why are you even here?"

Buddy's smile unnerved her. "Better question. Why are *you* here?"

She turned away, not wanting him to see that the question upset her. Dex was in the other room attempting to figure out the pellet stove. She understood why he'd done what he'd done, but she was still angry that he had the nerve to snoop through her computer and follow her, Buddy in tow.

"I want you both to leave," she said. "First thing in the morning."

Dex looked up from the pellet stove. He was always more handsome than she remembered him. "But I'm supposed to help clean the container thing tomorrow," he said. "Your mom said so."

"It's a bad idea, Dex, and you know it."

He abandoned the stove and went to her. "I want to help." He kissed her on the forehead. "That's what I'm here for—to help you through the rough stuff."

She was exhausted—it had been a long day, and the days ahead were sure to be longer. "I'm here because this is something I need to do. And I know you want to help, but you're making everything more confusing. More complicated."

"You mean because of Gideon." The look he gave her explained that he had figured something out—exactly what it was and how much of it he'd untangled, Ariel couldn't be sure.

"It has nothing to do with Gideon. You don't even know Gideon."

"Well, I've seen him. And I know you two lived here together when you were younger."

"That was years ago. And besides, he's with Joy now." The word *now* was heavy with all the emotion she wanted to hide from Dex. "I'll be home in a few days. We can talk about everything then."

"I'm not leaving without you."

Looking at him, this man who so clearly loved her more than she loved him, she felt a plume of sadness rise so quickly in her body she was afraid she might choke on it. She did not want to cry—to cry would be to invite another conversation, one that required energy she did not have. "That couch pulls out," she said. "I hope you have a safe drive back to Lawrence. I'll see you in a few days." She kissed him then, and when he tried to hold on to her, she gently pulled away.

The house was too small for dramatic exits, and so she simply turned around and slipped into the bedroom—her father's old bedroom—and closed the door behind her. She took in the blessing of four walls, the miracle of a door. Where her father's twin mattress had been, there was now a full-sized bed that took up almost the entire room, draped in a quilt the color of honey. A lamp. A dresser. A mirror. Everything her father had needed but failed to buy, opting instead for a mattress on the floor and a few wooden crates for his belongings. Perhaps even then, after spending more than a year and countless hours of labor building Blue House, he had known he would not stay. He had already fallen out of love with her mother; it just took his body a few years to catch up.

Ariel stripped her clothes, crawled into bed, and fell asleep.

Dex

Buddy demanded $300 and a cat. As they passed a bottle of whiskey back and forth (Buddy had rooted around in the tiny kitchen until he discovered a half-empty pint of Jameson), Dex talked him down to $200. "Half now and half later," Dex said, handing over a fold of twenties.

Buddy pocketed the money. "I'm a good friend to you. Remember that. Most people would have said 'screw you' from the very beginning. You'd still be in Lawrence and Ariel would be nipple-deep in that cowboy."

"That's not a phrase, *nipple-deep*."

"Says the man with no imagination."

Dex watched as Buddy gathered his things, which included his cigarettes and the cat he'd befriended earlier on the porch. The cat had no tail and an infected-looking bald patch just above his left eye. He had followed Buddy from the porch to Blue House, where he had apparently scratched at the door, eager to gain entry or, as Buddy interpreted it, become best friends forever.

"I'm taking the cat," Buddy said. "He loves me, and I love him, and I've named him Bill Clinton."

"Take all the cats. What do I care?"

Buddy cradled Bill Clinton against his chest. "If they start looking for him, say you saw an eagle swoop down and nab him."

"There's a thousand animals here. They're not going to notice one nasty old cat. Besides, that's the point of this place, remember? To get rid of all the nasty old cats?"

"He's right here," Buddy said, putting his own pair of earmuffs over the cat's small, gnarled ears. "Take it back."

"Fine," said Dex. "I take it back. He's not nasty. He's handsome and refined and a master saxophonist. Just go already, please?" He was worried Buddy might suddenly change his mind.

"You sure you don't want to come with? Ariel seems pretty pissed."

"I'll be fine. But only if you leave."

Buddy shrugged. "Your funeral."

Dex watched with relief as Buddy disappeared down the drive-way. There, at least, was one problem solved. When Buddy was out of view, Dex sat on a patch of grass, a good distance from Blue House. Above him, the sky was loaded with stars. There was the Milky Way, and the moon, grinning like a raver with a miniature glow stick on his tongue. He could easily picture Ariel here, with the animals, could see her sprawled on the grass in the summertime, watching for shooting stars. Focusing on a distant cluster of darkness, Dex felt a sudden ex-plosion of perspective, apprehending just how tiny he was. A terrible feeling. What a blessing, he now saw, that Lawrence's modest light pollution concealed the truth of the sky. He didn't want to feel small. He wanted to feel important.

"Can't sleep, either?"

It was the girl, Joy. She was the kind of moon-faced blonde Ariel loved to rag on in Lawrence. *I bet she does so much yoga*, Ariel would say, walking past one of them downtown, *and is, like, super conscien-tious about charging her crystals.* He suspected that, deep down, she wanted to be one of these girls but was too awkward for yoga class, too sensible for crystals. It was why she'd glommed onto Sunny—they were each as practical, as no-nonsense as the other, and had found, in the other's company, permission to finally let loose.

"My friend just left," Dex said.

"That's too bad. He seemed nice."

"He's not."

"Why did he leave?"

"Ariel wanted him to go—wants me to go, too."

"But you didn't go."

"I realize it was stupid to come here without asking. But I'm here now, and I don't want to leave yet—I want to see what it's like. It's important to her, so it's important to me, too. She just can't see that right now. And that's fine. I'm patient."

Joy sat down beside him, cross-legged, and picked up a handful of dirt. Slowly, she let it fall back to the ground. "Cold out here."

"Could be worse." He wanted her to think that he was rugged, that he often spent time outside in extreme weather. "What are you doing up?"

"Gideon snores. Camper's tiny."

"That's rough." It made him a little happy, to hear that Gideon snored.

"It's all right. Sometimes I go to my mom's house. Other times I walk around, check on the animals. It's a good excuse to get out in the night. Most people go their whole lives without ever really seeing the stars. That's part of why Mona keeps all the lights off—so the animals can see the stars, too. She says it's important for their spiritual health." She took a deep breath and surveyed the sanctuary. "At first I thought she was crazy, about the spiritual health thing, but I get it now. The animals are weird at night. You'd be surprised how many of them are awake—like they're all dressed up and ready for church."

He followed her gaze and saw a dozen eyes staring back at him from the far end of the sanctuary, where darkness met more darkness. Were they dogs? Sheep? Goats?

"Does it ever make you sad?" he asked.

"What?"

"The animals."

"Why would they make me sad?"

"You know, because of their life here. What's their reason to live?"

"Mona always says it's not our place to decide who gets to live or why. Everything deserves a chance."

"And this is their chance?"

Joy grabbed another palmful of dirt. "I think if you spent a little time out here, you'd understand it better. People are always looking in from the outside and making judgments. Nothing good ever comes from that." She looked at him, her eyes two spots of white in the darkness. "They still feel joy, the animals—they're happy when you feed them, when they get pets. They're just like us. Even if you were stuck in a cage, you'd still want your life. You'd want people to be kind to you."

"I guess," Dex said, although he wasn't sure.

"Just because you don't understand it," she said, "doesn't mean it's not true."

Dex felt a spike of something—shame? Guilt? He realized he was being reprimanded. "So you like living out here, in the middle of nowhere?" he asked.

"Would I be here if I didn't?"

Dex shrugged. "People do all sorts of things they don't like."

"Well, I do like it. I was living in California for a little bit, after high school, and I couldn't understand what was wrong with me, why I wasn't happy. Everyone's supposed to be happy in California, right? But I was miserable."

He himself was guilty of the error, assuming that, at their very saddest, the average Californian was still happier than the average Kansan. They were the blessed people, living in the place where oranges, wine, and movies came from. He knew many people who thought of California the way some thought of heaven—an easy, comfortable place you went to if you behaved well in your previous life. "Why were you miserable?"

"I didn't realize it until I came back, but I was physically sick for this place. Everything out there just felt so ridiculous—the traffic, people running around with spray tans and purses that cost more than a cow. Even the environmentalists didn't understand nature the way people do out here. Out here, we have to work with nature. It's our boss. Our livelihood. Out there, people see nature as this dying thing they need to protect—this thing totally separate from themselves, from the world of people. A few of the hippies I knew had worked on organic farms here or there, but mostly they were about smoking weed and going to protests. Hula-Hooping and eating chia seeds and rock climbing. All that stuff. They had clean hands. Clean hair. Clean shoes. Over time, it wore me down. You know what I mean?"

"Totally," Dex said, although he had no idea what she was talking about. He had notoriously clean hands—Ariel often teased him about it—and spent little time thinking about the natural world. Whenever he heard the word *nature* he imagined the kind of picture you'd get with a Google search: A mountain looking over a lake. Green trees and a sunset.

"You think Ariel misses it out here?" he asked.

"I don't see how she couldn't."

"Do you think she wants to move back?"

She smiled and pulled up another handful of dirt. "Definitely not."

"Even if she misses it?"

"Have you ever broken up with someone you still loved?" she asked.

Dex had to think about it. "I guess I was always the one who got dumped."

"Well, it's the same thing. You can miss something like crazy and still never want to go back. Some things, no matter how much you want them to work, or think they should work, just aren't meant to be."

Dex listened as something howled, a gut-sharpening sound. "That's the most terrifying thing I've ever heard," he said. "Is it a wolf? Do we need to go inside?"

"Dogs," she said. "Then coyotes. They sing to one another—they flirt."

"Doesn't sound like flirting to me."

"Well, most men don't know what good flirting sounds like, do they?"

A breeze picked up, making him shiver. He was surprised to feel a pang of concern about the dogs who had gotten loose. What if it had been Hippo? Sitting in the dark, in the chilled air, he finally understood the danger of the night—the exposure of darkness. An image came to his mind of him rescuing all the lost dogs. In the morning, Ariel and her mother would find him surrounded by dogs setting white roses at his feet. A few would feed him grapes or fan him with a palm frond. Ariel would run to him, through the throng of grateful animals, and throw her arms around his neck. *My hero!*

"I should probably go in," he said.

Joy was still looking out at the stars. "Yeah, me too."

"See you in the morning?"

She nodded. "See you then."

Before heading into Blue House, he glanced back and saw that Joy was still sitting there, a faint shadow among shadows. He wondered how long she would sit there and what exactly she would think about as she did. He wondered whether Gideon would wake and find the space beside him empty. Whether he would turn away from it or reach his arm across it, knowing that the person he loved would eventually return to fill it.

In Blue House, Ariel was only a shape in the dark. Normally, she would curl into a shrimp formation, hands tucked under her head, knees up to her chin. Now she was sprawled out starfish style. He considered going back to the living room, leaving her to sleep, but he wanted to be with her too badly. She was usually a sweet sleeper, so it was a risk he was willing to take.

When he pulled back the covers, she startled.

"It's just me," he said, slipping under the covers.

"Dex," she said, her voice small. "Is Buddy on the couch?"

"He left," Dex said. He was about to add, *And he took Bill Clinton*, but figured now was not the time.

"You didn't go with him?" she asked.

He put his arm around her. She was warm. "I love you, Ariel."

There was a moment of silence, and then she grabbed his finger, squeezed. "I love you, too." And then, related to nothing or perhaps everything, she added, "I'm sorry."

Related to nothing and everything, he said, "Me too."

He woke to the sound of a knock on the window. The room was black; he had no idea what time it was, whether he'd been asleep for an hour or five. Beside him, Ariel grunted. When the knock came again, Dex pulled back the curtain. There was Mona, a fuzzy shape behind the glass. "Time to get up," she said, and then, as quickly as she'd appeared, she receded from the window, ghostlike, the night gulping her down.

Startled, he turned to Ariel and gently shook her shoulder. "I think it's morning, Ariel," he said. "Wakey wakey."

She rolled her face into her pillow, mumbled, "No—sleepy."

Dex worried about being late for the day—he didn't want Mona to think he was lazy—and so, unsure what else to do, he began to tickle her. Ariel kicked her legs and flung an arm toward him. "Stop, stop—I'm up." She clicked on the bedside lamp, washing the room in buttery light, and turned to squint at him, her eyes puffy and crusted, filled with drowsy confusion and a hint of rage—she hated being tickled.

"Sorry," he said. "I didn't know what else to do."

"Is it really morning?"

"I think so—that was your mom knocking."

"Oh God," she said, burying her face in her hands.

He wished they had more time in bed together, to smooth out the wrinkles of their argument the night before. They always did well in bed, when it was just them, some sheets, a quiet room.

"You look beautiful," he said, hoping to restore some semblance of good feeling before the day began.

"I'm not," she said, wiping the gummy stuff from the corners of her mouth. She smiled faintly at him, a tinge of playful sadness in her eyes. The mornings turned her into a different creature—half monster, half child, quick to anger but also eager to be complimented and soothed. He kissed her on the forehead, where a pimple was growing.

"I'm scared of today," she said, reaching for her clothes on the floor. "I feel like I've fucked everything up."

Dex pulled her back to bed, feeling his heart steady when she didn't resist. "Don't be scared," he said, running his fingers through her hair, which was greasy at the roots. "I'm here, and it's going to be okay."

After a quick breakfast of Grape-Nuts and coffee, they separated. Before piling into the truck with Joy and Mona, Ariel whispered to Dex, "A nugget of gold has escaped the mine." Dex touched his nose. Sure enough, there was a booger.

Once the girls were gone, Dex followed Gideon into the mud-room, to get outfitted for the day ahead. From a closet that smelled of mothballs and cat piss, Gideon removed two pairs of khaki overalls and rubber gloves. One for him, one for Dex.

"Twinsies!" Dex said, ignoring the look Gideon gave him. He stepped into the overalls and felt like a little boy trying on his father's uniform.

"You can roll up the pants if you want," said Gideon. "Or we could get some safety pins."

"No, it's fine. They're not that big."

"They look too big."

"Well, they're not," Dex said. "They're just right."

Gideon held up his hands. "If you say so."

"The real problem is my boots. Mine aren't exactly . . . work appropriate. Is there an extra pair I could borrow?"

Wanting to look nice for Ariel's mother, he had worn his favorite pair of vintage wingtip boots. How could he have predicted a weekend of manual labor? The boots were everything he wanted in a boot, and there was a lot in a boot that he wanted: comfort, style, and an aura of nostalgia so palpable that to touch the leather sent you whooshing back to the days of Hendrix on a cloud of funky psychedelic time-travel smoke. A real boot made you think of sex, drugs, and rock and roll, but also tobacco pipes and Hemingway and summertime bullfights in which men were willing to die for their honor. Ariel would be the first to point out that everything on this list reeked of hypermasculinity and bravado. Well, that was fine with him. What man didn't want to be hypermasculine, to own boots forged from the flames of testosterone? On his feet were these very boots, and now they were going to clean out a storage container, whatever that entailed.

Gideon examined Dex's feet and frowned deeply, as if Dex had shown up to mow a lawn with a pair of nail clippers. "What size are you?"

"Ten, give or take."

"Sorry, bud. I'm a twelve."

Dex nearly combusted with shame as Gideon laced up a pair of Soviet-era submarines—ugly and old, entirely indestructible. All this time, Dex had thought his boots were masculine, but now they felt like ballet slippers. It occurred to him that, on this side of Kansas, real men wore shitty, gigantic, mud-encrusted machines with steel toes and rubber soles and laces thick as eels. Real men treated their footwear like an extension of their already valiant feet—hard, calloused instruments intended to clobber the earth. And here was Dex with his precious baby booties, not wanting to muddy them up.

He thought of an article Ariel had once read to him, about a writer who, as a graduate student, overheard his mentor calling his son "dear," and how it was the most masculine moment the writer had ever witnessed. Until now, Dex had never understood the story. How could calling someone "dear" be masculine? Sentimental, maybe, but not masculine. The story seemed to have absolutely nothing to do with masculinity until now, when it seemed not only possible but entirely likely that, in actuality, masculinity was a small, quivering thing with little hands and even littler feet that did nothing all day but close its eyes and hope for love and a pair of shoes that would make other dudes think it was cool. For a moment the revelation took shape in his mind, but was gone as quickly as it appeared. He really didn't want to fuck up his boots.

He followed Gideon out past the barn to the storage container. When he heard something trotting behind him, he turned to find Hippo.

"Hey, my man," he said, crouching down to greet the dog, who licked both of Dex's cheeks and, briefly, his lips. After wiping his mouth, Dex picked up one of Hippo's front paws and gave the dog a high five.

"Looks like you have a shadow," Gideon said.

"I have to admit, he's pretty cool."

"Yeah, Bam-Bam's a good guy."

"Bam-Bam?"

"Like from *The Flintstones*?"

"Right," Dex said. *Don't worry, bud*, he thought to the dog, who was still happily trailing behind them. *I know you're really a Hippo*.

"He's a fixture around here," Gideon was saying. "We've been trying hard to find him a home, but pit bulls are especially difficult to adopt out. Everyone thinks they're mean and aggressive, but really, most of them are sweethearts. They just want to be loved."

I could love this dog, Dex thought. The truth of it startled him. "I like the little white spot on his forehead."

Gideon smiled and looked back at Hippo. "Yeah, he doesn't even know it's there."

They reached an open field, where the container sat rusting in the wind.

"Thar she blows," said Gideon.

On the side of the container, someone had spray-painted: TRUMPETER SWAN. Beneath it was a crude outline of a swan, its neck raised proudly in the air. "It was *Trump*," Gideon explained. "We couldn't get it off, so we decided to enhance it—that was Mona's word. *Enhance*."

Dex admired the container. "Clever."

From a nearby shed they retrieved a green wheelbarrow into which they threw two brooms, a pile of rags, two contractor trash bags, a series of spray cleaners, steel wool, three sponges, a tub of Clorox, and dust masks.

"What's with the masks?"

"Hantavirus," Gideon said, explaining that it was a virus transmitted via rodent urine. "Survival rate is one out of three."

"We should have gotten a third person then, huh?"

Once again, Gideon did not laugh. "The truth is, I don't really like mice." His voice had a hint of shame, as if he had admitted to not liking peace on earth.

"Nobody *likes* mice," Dex said. "They caused the plague—you can't just forget about something like the plague. *Children* died."

"That was rats, not mice. And if we want to get technical, it was actually fleas."

"Whatever—rats, mice, fleas. It's all the same."

"Don't let Mona hear you saying this kind of stuff."

"What, she gets warm and fuzzy over mice?"

"The garage over there is where the rodents live. She goes over there and tickles them."

"Tickles them?"

Gideon nodded. "Rats, they love to be tickled." He then lifted the door to the container, putting an end to their conversation.

Dumbstruck, Dex blinked into the container. All at once, the stench surrounded him. Through the mask came an odor of rotting food and dead animals and mold.

"Holy. Shit," he said, clapping a hand over the mask.

In the container were boxes that appeared to have melted and solidified into strange shapes. Could cardboard even melt? Pressed against the nearest corner of the container was something furry and deflated. There were dark beady eyes and yellow teeth, the crooked angle of a foot. Hippo went over to inspect it and quickly backed off; it was too disgusting even for him.

"Rule one of the sanctuary," Gideon said. "If Mona says something isn't that bad, it's probably a nightmare."

Ariel

Had someone asked, Ariel would have said that home was the sound of horses crunching carrots, or the smell of hay on a hot summer afternoon. Her old bedroom, her bed. The way light filtered through the window above her dresser, throwing a box of pale blue light onto the carpet where a cat would undoubtedly lay napping in the warmth. Home was the rhythm of Opal's breath and the sound of dogs growling as they tussled in the yard. It was the smell of dog breath and cat urine, but also citronella candles and lemon carpet shampoo. It was the feeling of waking up in a warm bed, covered in animals, as the first winter snow fell softly outside, coating the horses with a layer of powdered sugar, painting their eyelashes with delicate crystals of ice. Never would she have predicted that home was also the pressure of her mother's shoulder against her own, their knees connecting and disconnecting each time Old Baby dipped into a pothole, or the crack in the windshield that looked so much like a squid it was hard to believe an artist hadn't chiseled it there. Home was driving in Old Baby with her mother, something they had done so often that Ariel had not, until now, appreciated its import.

Every Sunday afternoon, Ariel and her mom would drive the half hour to Middleton to run errands. After loading the truck with groceries and supplies, they would drive through the Dairy Queen and get two small Oreo Blizzards—the only civilian luxury Mona allowed.

One time, "Tiny Dancer" came on the radio and Ariel watched as tears slid down her mother's face. When it was over, Mona turned off the radio, as if whatever followed might contaminate the air. "That," she had said, "is one of the finest songs ever made."

All of it came back to her as she counted cows and churches on the side of the road, trying to keep her eyes open. She had slept too hard the night before, falling into a pit of darkness so deep she had to crawl from it on elbows and knees when Dex woke her to say Buddy had left.

"Dex seems like a sweet guy," Joy was saying. Despite the cold air, she hung an elbow out Old Baby's window.

"Yeah, everybody loves him. It's the most irritating thing about him."

Her mother clicked her tongue. "Can't you give anyone credit for anything? The boy drove all the way here just to be with you."

"He *followed* me," said Ariel.

"Can you blame him? You didn't tell him where you were going. He didn't even know about the Bright Side." She leaned her head past Ariel to look at Joy. "Did you know that? The man she's going to marry didn't know she grew up on a sanctuary."

"I sort of get it," Joy said. "When I was in LA, I stopped telling people where I was from. Explaining St. Clare was too hard. People thought I was a farmer. Or a polygamist. This one time, I went on a date with a guy, and when I told him I grew up on a cattle ranch in Kansas he asked if I needed help reading the menu."

"Okay," Mona said, "but this is her fiancé. It's different. And besides, he's from Kansas, too."

"The Kansas City suburbs are a whole different Kansas," Ariel said.

"I'm just saying it's a bad sign that you're not honest with him."

"Like you were always honest with Dad."

Her mother was quiet for a moment. "I never lied to your father.

We knew everything about each other. That's one thing we did right, and we did a lot of things wrong. I'll admit to that."

"He didn't know you wanted a sanctuary—he was allergic to cats."

Mona looked over at her, astounded. "He was not allergic to cats. Where did you get that idea?"

"He told me is where."

"Well, that's just not true. He loved cats. And of course he knew I wanted the sanctuary—he helped me every step of the way. It just didn't turn out the way he expected. I don't think he ever believed I'd actually go through with it. Or maybe he didn't imagine what it would be like, actually having so many animals around. But I never lied to him. Not once."

Before Ariel could say anything else, Joy turned and leaned out the window. "Dog," she shouted. "I think it's Bagel."

Mona hit the brakes and brought the truck over to the shoulder, where a tan-and-white beagle was nosing something in a field. His entire lower body was encased in mud, as if someone were trying to make a clay cast of his legs. "Must have gotten a rabbit," said Mona. "Get the leash. And the treats."

Ariel grabbed a leash and followed her mother and Joy out into the field, where Bagel ran away from them, abandoning the dead rabbit. After running a few yards, he stopped and turned, as if to assess whether returning to his prize would result in his capture. Mona stood near the dead rabbit and talked sweetly to the dog. "Here, Bagel. Come on boy. That's a good boy." As if suddenly recognizing her, Bagel trotted over and, after a short game of chase, let Mona leash him while Joy fed him treats.

"Good boy," Joy said, inspecting to see whether Bagel was hurt. "He's dirty as hell, but he looks fine, thank God."

"Let's just hope he hasn't gotten into any trouble. Not all these dogs have their shots."

"What do you mean they don't have their shots?" Ariel asked.

"I mean what I said. Most have the first two rounds but nothing more."

"So no rabies?"

Mona shook her head. "I didn't have the money. What was I supposed to do?"

At the clinic in Lawrence, Dr. Nguyen refused to board any animal that hadn't been properly vaccinated, with all three rounds of shots, and here were dozens of dogs, some of them susceptible to rabies. Anything could get them—a bat, a raccoon, a skunk—and soon the whole sanctuary would be at risk, humans included.

"You've never had anyone get rabies?" Ariel asked.

"There was one episode," said Mona, "but we nipped it in the bud."

As soon as Mona was busy giving Bagel water and kibble, Joy leaned in and whispered, "When she says we nipped it in the bud, she means Gideon had to shoot a retriever in the head."

Once they were back on the road, Ariel couldn't bear the feeling of her mother's shoulder against her own. "I'm feeling a little woozy," she said, and asked Joy if they could switch seats so Ariel could have the window.

Joy agreed, and soon it was Joy's shoulder pressed against Ariel's, the wind whipping their hair as they drove deeper into the country, Bagel happily biting the cold December air as they went.

Mona

As they drove, one dog down and five to go, Mona couldn't stop thinking about what Ariel had said about Daniel being allergic to cats. Mona had once watched him rub his eyes until they were bright pink, the fine skin under his eyelashes swollen.

"Are you allergic to cats?" she'd asked.

He'd looked at her, dead-on, and said, "Do you think I'd have agreed to all this if I was?"

Yes, Mona had wanted to say, *Actually, I do*, but she'd held her tongue. Over the years, she had learned that his unconditional generosity wasn't always unconditional. Whenever he yielded to something he didn't actually want, he would eventually make her pay for it—with his brooding, his passive-aggressive sighs, his silence. It often played out in silly ways—after agreeing to watch a chick flick, or when sitting down to one of Mona's salad-only dinners—but Mona understood it could also happen on a grand level, that she should be cautious.

They'd been married for twelve years when Mona received a phone call saying her father had died. A heart attack while mowing the lawn. Despite all that had happened between Mona and her father, hers was the only name in his will.

She'd discussed the sanctuary idea with Daniel before. He'd been open to it, saying that if they ever had the money, why not? He could do his editing work anywhere, after all, and there was nothing tying them to Wichita. If Mona was going to do anything with her father's money, she was going to spend it on animals. There was a feeling she had—a certainty—that the animals would finally fill the space in her heart that had opened when her mother died. She wanted something that would force her to rise above her ordinariness, to become the kind of woman her daughter could one day admire. She wanted to be responsible for something big.

After two months of fruitless hunting, her Realtor told her about a parcel of land in a town Mona had never heard of, several hours west of Wichita, nearly all the way to the Colorado border. The thirty acres came with a farmhouse, two outbuildings, a tool shed, a detached garage, a sizable pasture, a creek that ran in the spring, and a barn painted the color of a stop sign. At this point, Mona imagined the sanctuary for dogs and only dogs, and yet the barn served as a question mark. Who knew what might happen over the years? She'd always loved horses. And sheep. And pigs. All animals, really. Who was to say she wouldn't one day need a barn? It was true that the town, St. Clare, was smaller than she would have preferred—Ariel would have to bus to school in the next town over—but the cost per acre was so cheap Mona drove there to have a look. She was alone when she stood in the middle of the pasture, eyes closed to the smell of wet grass and dirt. The house was on Sanctuary Road—what greater sign did she need?

"Are you sure you want to do this?" Daniel asked after the moving van had already come and gone.

Mona did not want to admit that she had never been more certain about anything in her life. "I'm sure," she said. "Are *you* sure?"

He'd looked away. "If nothing else, it'll be good for my writing."

In her stomach, a warning bell rang. She ignored it.

Mona had hoped the sanctuary would bring her family closer together, give them a common passion and purpose, but as the dogs arrived, she could feel Daniel slipping away. Within months, he began hiding out in his office, sometimes eating his meals at his desk. He seemed uninterested in the dogs, a fact that bothered Mona deeply. She feared her dream was already making him miserable. *Come back to me*, she would think each time she looked at him. *I miss you, I miss you, I miss you.* Parallel to this sadness was a growing anger—that he had once again agreed to something he didn't want. That he was going to punish her for it, this time slowly, with calculated force.

One night, when she was in bed, petting a dachshund named Luca, Daniel had looked at her and said, *You never touch me that way anymore.* It had broken Mona's heart, because it was true. She still loved him as much as she always had, but she was busy now. The exhaustion she felt on the sanctuary was even greater than the unrelenting fatigue she'd felt during Ariel's first years, when she had been certain she could never feel so tired again. Now she was exhausted in both body and mind, the muscles in her upper back tender to the touch, her brain a hamster trapped on a wheel of to-do lists. Gone were the days when she and Daniel would reach for each other in the middle of the night, hungry. Now when she was in bed, she wanted to sleep.

Once, a few months after Mona began taking in cats, a foul odor overtook the house. For days, they tried to locate its source. Eventually they realized it was coming from a closet in the basement, where Daniel had, a couple weeks prior, stored away a few boxes of old books. It was there they found the cat, Seymour, his brown body stiff and eerily flat from dehydration, the wall scarred with scratch marks, piles of filth in the corner.

"Jesus," Daniel said, his eyes watering, hands trembling. Then, turning to her. "I swear I didn't know he was in there when I closed the door."

"I know that," Mona said, a hand over her mouth. "Of course I know that."

After this, he grew even more distant. Sometimes he would ignore Mona altogether, a brand of behavior that drove Mona mad, for Daniel knew it was what her father had inflicted on her all those years before. Some nights, she would lay beside him, trying to hold in her tears.

"Daniel?" she asked one night, her voice clotted. "Can I ask you a question?"

He was facing her, but in the dark, she couldn't make out his features. "You just did."

"I'm serious."

He sighed. "What is it?"

Her heart sped up, a feeling like falling. "Are you going to make me choose between you and the animals?"

The room had stayed quiet for too long. Eventually he said, "Have you not already?"

When he built Blue House, she knew that something had broken beyond repair. She'd hated the house, the stupid wicker welcome mat, how the sky-colored paint made it glow against the grass like an Easter egg. Hated watching him carry his books and manuscripts, stack by stack, across the property, as if it really were a writing studio and not something else entirely. Hated that, on some nights, Ariel went over there for dinner, as if she were already the child of divorced parents. But Mona had also loved Blue House, because it meant that he was still there. That he had not yet given up.

When he finally left, she was so heartbroken she could hardly speak, her tongue a useless lump inside her mouth. Even the animals, when she looked at them, seemed uglier, less kind. She wanted to run away then, too, but of course she wouldn't. Couldn't. She had responsibilities: the property, the animals, and Ariel, who was hardly a teenager, that most difficult of ages. Ariel looked so frightened the first morning Daniel didn't show up at the breakfast table, and so Mona tried to stay strong, concealing from Ariel the loneliness that followed her to bed each night and woke beside her each morning. She made a vow to only cry when alone in the barn or the pasture. When Ariel asked, she told her the truth: she didn't know where Daniel had gone, or how to reach him. She had no idea when or if he would return. He was a man of words, and yet he hadn't even left a note. This, out of everything, infuriated her most. Twenty years of marriage and he couldn't write the word *goodbye*.

Dex

After an hour of steady work, he and Gideon had barely made a dent in the container. Dex's boots were covered in dust and mold and dirt, a stray thread along the toe from where he'd nicked it on a wire.

At one point, Dex found three dead mice—cute ones, like dinner buns with tails—that made Gideon visibly shudder. A few minutes later, Dex uncovered a cardboard box containing a dozen bags of pork-flavored dog treats. When he picked up a bag to look for an expiration date, the paper on the bottom disintegrated and the bag exploded into a cloud of mold.

"Don't breathe," Gideon said, sprinting from the container as the mold dispersed through the air. They stood together, a few yards away, until the toxic cloud had settled.

"This is fucked," said Dex.

Gideon returned to the container, now coated in a film of powdery mold that soon tinted their rubber gloves green. "I'd give it a six out of ten."

"If this is a six, what's a ten?"

Gideon kept moving, tossing cans of cat food into the salvage pile. "Ten is a puncture wound, or any day that ends with stitches." He kept tossing cans, two at a time, onto the pile. His aim was impeccable. "There's also the killing days."

"What happens on the killing days?"

Gideon looked at him. "We eat ice cream and watch Disney movies." When Dex didn't respond he added, "What do you *think* happens on the killing days?"

"But I thought this was a no-kill shelter?"

"Technically yes, but sometimes I take things into my own hands. Mona doesn't know, or at least she pretends not to."

"You mean you kill the animals yourself?"

"Only if it's absolutely necessary. Otherwise I have Doc Powell put them down. Joy usually foots the bill."

"That's nice of her—and you."

"You'd do it, too, if you had to."

"I don't know," Dex said. Once, in the fifth grade, a bully had dared Dex to feed an antacid tablet to the class bird, Mr. Beakers—a crime that still haunted him. He knew how it affected Ariel on the days Dr. Nguyen put down animals at the clinic. She'd be morose for a day, sometimes a whole week, turning from Dex in bed or pushing her dinner around her plate. Dex hadn't thought much about what it would actually be like, to take an animal's life, or to be in the room while it happened. He tried to imagine Hippo in a vet's office, a needle in his little foreleg, his watery eyes closing—just thinking about it upset him.

He and Gideon fell into a comfortable silence. Dex enjoyed the flow of labor, how it streamlined the chaos of his thoughts, braiding them into a rope he could grab whenever he thought of Ariel. Their wedding felt far away, an unlikely mirage in the distance, but so long as he was in the container, everything was fine. He and Ariel would return to their normal routine soon enough, resume the life they had worked so hard to build. And it was a happy life, wasn't it? They had good friends, a nice house, decent jobs. It wasn't at all like the life she had lived here, on the sanctuary—this much he now understood. He wondered, then, if this was what Ariel had come back to reclaim—a kind of atavistic fulfillment he would never be able to give her.

Unable to restrain himself, he turned to Gideon. "Did you and Ariel ever, you know?"

Gideon continued throwing tins of cat food into the salvage pile. "Is it going to drive you crazy if I say yes?"

Dex felt his heart sink.

"Look, it was years ago—we were kids. She was in high school, and I had no clue what I was doing. I mean, don't get me wrong. I cared for her. But I was young."

"None of this makes me feel better."

"It should."

"You're telling me you were each other's first love."

"But nobody stays with their first love—that's why it's the first and not the last. It'd be like listening to the same music you liked in middle school. Nobody should have the same taste for that long. It's a sign of stunted growth."

This only made Dex feel worse, since, for all intents and purposes, Ariel was his first love. All of the girls before her had been flings—one-night stands or relationships that lasted two or three months before imploding or fizzling out. He sometimes wondered if, because he was so well-known around town, women thought of him more as a character than a real person. They had heard stories about him, knew the other people he'd dated. They wanted to be with the idea of him. Before Ariel, he'd accepted that he might grow old and die alone, a bachelor with a hundred friends but nobody to spoon. And then, out of nowhere: Ariel. Sometimes he imagined her like a bag of gold falling from the sky. Or maybe like a bag of gold regurgitating Jell-O shots at a party.

"Were you upset when she left?" Dex asked.

"Yes," said Gideon. "But, like I said, this was a long time ago."

After a few beats of silence, he asked, "Are you worried about why she came back?"

"Honestly? I'm always worried when it comes to her."

"Worried she'll cheat on you?"

Dex considered the question. "Not that, specifically. But about her realizing she doesn't love me. That she'll leave me." He wiped his forehead with the back of his wrist. "Sometimes I think she blames me for the way her life turned out—like I'm the reason she didn't finish school."

Gideon raised an eyebrow. "She didn't finish school?"

Dex felt a shift in the air. "She lost her scholarship, so she quit."

"Huh. Was it too hard for her or something?"

"No, nothing like that. I think it was a lot for her—Lawrence, college life. I think, when I met her, she was really lonely. And then all of a sudden she started having fun—maybe too much fun. She stopped focusing on school."

"And she blames you?"

Dex shrugged. "She's never said as much, but it's like this vibration that runs through our relationship—I can just feel it sometimes. That I'm the one who corrupted her. Who ruined her education." He'd never told anyone this, not even Buddy. "I guess it's not normal, when I say it out loud."

"Then why put up with it?"

"Why put up with anything? I love her."

If Gideon had something to say, he was choosing not to say it.

Feeling brave, Dex asked, "Do you think, if she wouldn't have left, you'd still be together?"

Without missing a beat, Gideon said, "No."

"You're that sure?"

"I didn't exactly realize it until later, but when I was with Ariel, there was always a cushion between us. Despite everything we went through together, she never let me all the way in. I could tell there were things she wasn't telling me. I don't think I could have done that forever."

Dex knew this cushion, too. It was not a large space, but it was a persistent one, and inside it was everything Ariel refused to share with him: her childhood here with the animals, her mother, Gideon. Her past. In the beginning, this space added mystery, but Dex no longer wanted mystery. What he wanted was Ariel—all of her, down to every last secret and scar.

"Do you think it's unhealthy to still have a distance like that after five years?" Dex asked.

Gideon picked up a bag of soggy-looking kibble and tossed it into the trash pile. "Yes," he said. "I do."

At noon, they broke for lunch: tomato, cheese, and pickle sandwiches arranged between thick slices of sourdough. Gideon slathered the bread with a peach-colored sauce he kept in a glass jar labeled: FUCK YEAH SAUCE.

After the first bite, Dex said, "If you sold this sauce in Lawrence, you'd be famous."

"Probably," said Gideon, "but then I'd be famous."

They ate slowly, chewing contemplatively and sucking their thumbs clean. The kitchen window faced the barn, where the horses roamed nearby, ripping up pockets of grass. "Isn't it weird they just eat from the ground all day?" Dex asked. "Can you imagine if people did that—just ate whatever grew around them?"

"You do know how farming works, right?"

Dex could feel himself going red. "Right. Didn't think that one through." He leaned back in his chair and put his hands over his belly—he wanted another sandwich. "You know, you guys have some weird-looking horses."

Gideon squinted at the pasture. "Those are mules."

"Is there a difference?"

"Honestly, I can't tell if you're joking."

To keep from saying anything else stupid, Dex took a big drink of his water. When he looked closer, he saw that one of the donkeys had a boner. "Oh my God," he said, pointing. "That one's got a hard-on."

Gideon didn't even bother to look. "That happens a lot."

"You serious?"

"Yes. Especially in the morning."

"And they just stand around like that? With their things out?"

"Why not?"

"Huh." Dex felt a sudden connection with the donkeys—who knew morning wood spanned the animal kingdom?

"You haven't had a tour yet, have you?"

Dex wiped pickle juice from his chin and shook his head.

"How about I take you around so you can meet everyone?"

"This is going to sound bad," Dex said, "but I don't really *like* animals."

Gideon looked at him suspiciously, as if to say: *How are you and Ariel even possible?*

"You know what? Sure," Dex said, shamed. "When in Rome, right?"

After touring the petting zoo, Gideon said their next stop would be Dog Town. Dex imagined a miniature metropolis with dogs driving taxis, wielding briefcases, and pushing puppy-filled carriages. In reality, Dog Town was a covered area with two rows of chain-link pens, a cement aisle in between. When he walked in, a few of the dogs clambered to their feet, barking. Some stood on their hind legs and pawed the door of their pen. Some were missing eyes or ears or tails. Others had tumors or painful-looking bald patches. In Dex's heart, a flicker of pity.

"What do you think?" asked Gideon.

"There's a lot of them." Many of the dogs were still barking, asking for something. Others licked their own genitals or ran in hyperactive circles. "What happens to them all?"

"The goal is adoption, but it's hard to keep up. A lot of them come from abuse and have behavior issues. They're aggressive, or they're timid, or they're bad with kids or other dogs. Everyone wants a happy little puppy, but for every happy little puppy we have three unfriendly mutts."

"Wouldn't it be easier to put them down? The ones that don't have any hope?"

Gideon's eyes went soft. "It's not their fault, what they've been through. People failed them, so it's our job to stand up for them now. To take care of them. For a lot of them, this is heaven compared to where they're coming from. They still enjoy their lives."

Dex looked at the pens, thinking nothing had ever looked less like heaven. A little Taco Bell dog was nibbling the fur of its pen mate, who flashed its teeth, as if annoyed but too resigned to do anything about it. Dex thought about Hippo, whom he hadn't seen since they started working on the container. He wondered what Hippo was up to, if maybe he was thinking about Dex. He was glad Hippo didn't have to stay in a cage like these dogs.

"What do they do all day?" Dex asked.

Gideon shrugged. "Eat. Drink. Sleep. Same shit we do."

"Don't they get bored?"

"Don't *you* get bored?"

"Sometimes—but I have television. And work. And music. How could anyone live without music?"

"I bet the dogs are thinking: 'Look at those stupid humans, staring at a box all day. Listening to all that noise.'"

"True, but they don't know about beer."

"You're not wrong about that," said Gideon.

Now that Dex was thinking on it, a drink sounded glorious. "You wouldn't happen to have anything to drink, would you?"

"Do you know how mad Mona will be if the container's still a wreck and we're drunk?"

"Who said anything about drunk? Just one drink. To fortify us."

Gideon rubbed the back of his neck and looked off, toward the road. "I guess one drink wouldn't ruin the day. But if Mona finds out, it's on you." He punched Dex lightly on the shoulder, instilling in Dex a familiar brand of comradery. Following Gideon to the RV, he felt the same relief of being picked for the basketball team in junior high gym class, or receiving an invitation to the secret scout bonfire at Camp Fire Bird when he was twelve, or winning homecoming king his junior year, the auditorium roaring with applause as he accepted his plastic crown and proceeded to do a backflip off the metal bleachers. The relief of having an ally no matter the situation. This had always been his greatest talent: to arrive a stranger and leave a friend.

Ariel

They stopped for lunch in a town called Lark City. It was understood that the chance of finding more dogs had plummeted drastically once they crossed the county line, but they couldn't give up—that was the tacit agreement.

The deli was a small operation: three card tables, aluminum folding chairs, and a refrigerator stocked with cans of pop. Above the counter hung a dry-erase board on which someone had written the entire menu in green marker. The daily special was corn chowder and a Cobb salad for $5.75. There was only one other person in the restaurant, a gangly teenager who sat in the corner, eating Fritos and macaroni salad and playing on his phone.

Without asking Ariel or Joy what they wanted, Mona ordered three egg salad sandwiches with Sunchips. The three stood waiting as the woman behind the counter wrote their order on a piece of paper, which she then handed off to the cook, who stood on the other side of a small window peeking into the kitchen. The cashier wore a gold cross necklace and stretchy jeans that came over her navel. A skunk-stripe of gray bisected her brown hair. She swiped Mona's card once, then twice, then apologized and said she would have to enter the numbers manually. "These things," she said, hitting her palm against the card reader. "Maybe Mercury is in Gatorade."

Mona chuckled at this and told the woman to take her time. "Whatever you need to do. We're patient."

While they waited, they watched a television mounted in the corner of the restaurant. The channel was turned to Fox News. The sound was off, but the captions told the story of coal workers in West Virginia who were eager for the new president to take office.

Mona pointed at the TV. "Aren't they in for a rude surprise."

"And what's that supposed to mean?" asked the woman behind the counter, a sheen of angry excitement in her voice, as if she had been waiting all month for someone like Mona to come along.

"Hey, let's not," Joy said, touching Mona on the arm.

"It means ten years from now when everyone figures out coal is dead, these loonies will not only be out of a job, but they'll also be sick from huffing all those chemicals their whole life. And guess what? Their health care will be gone. Kaput." She snapped her fingers for emphasis. "They're all fools if they think he's going to do all the great stuff he says. You think Mexico is going to pay for a wall? It's all nonsense, but these people have been waiting all their lives for a president to give them permission to be as hateful as they've always wanted."

The woman clicked her tongue. "Do you hear yourself? The man isn't even in office yet and you're already acting like it's Armageddon. You people won't even give him a chance."

"Some people don't deserve chances," said Mona. "Like men who go around bragging about grabbing women by their privates."

The woman smiled and nodded as if to say, *Oh, you're one of those feminists, aren't you?* "You know, when Barack Hussein Obama got elected, we didn't make half the fuss. You people are acting like this isn't a democracy. Well, this is how democracy works. This is how *America* works. Sometimes you win, sometimes you lose. Personally, I've never felt more hopeful."

"Well, of course some people feel hopeful. I'm sure when Hitler came to power there were many Germans who felt—"

"Mom," Ariel said. "Stop it." She noticed the teenager had put down his phone and was watching them.

"I'm talking here, Ariel. If you want to see democracy, this is it. Civil discourse. The polite exchange of opinions."

"It's not polite or civil when you're over here making treasonous comparisons about the next president."

"That's a funny word for someone who didn't actually receive the most votes."

The woman threw up her hands. "I just can't get over you people. Whining and crying, crying and whining. The only reason he lost the popular vote is because the system is rigged. You've got illegal aliens out there casting votes three times a person, and in different counties, too."

"You've been watching too much of this trash," Mona said, gesturing to the television. "They depend on people like you—people who can't think for themselves."

"I'll have you know I just earned my bachelor's degree."

"In what? Spreading mayonnaise?"

"That's it," the woman said, her cheeks flushed. "I'm packing your food to go."

"I'm sorry," Mona said. "That was out of line. I shouldn't have said that."

"The reason I'm here spreading mayonnaise is because I can't get a better job, so don't you come in here, making fun of my livelihood, insulting the president who's gonna get us all out of this mess. I'm packing your food and I don't care where you eat it, but you can't eat it here."

"Now, listen. I said I'm sorry. There's no need to go kicking us out."

"Mom," Ariel said. "We can eat in the truck. What's it matter?"

"What matters is that we're paying customers. We'll eat our lunch inside like everybody else."

The teenager in the corner cocked his head, understanding that he was the everybody else.

"Ma'am, I don't want you in this restaurant for one more second. You can take your food and go."

"I will not."

"Then I'm calling the police," the woman said.

"And saying what? That we had an uncomfortable conversation?"

"That you're disrupting the peace." There were tears in her eyes now. "And threatening me."

"I've done no such thing."

"There is a particular tone of voice you have employed."

"Careful you don't choke on those big words."

"Mom, can we just go? You're making a mountain out of a molehill."

"This is not a molehill," Mona said. "This is why a skinhead came to my house and set fire to my property. This is why I have to sleep with a weapon under my bed."

"Oh, it's *you*," the woman said, her face breaking into a mean smile. "You're the one with all the animals, from St. Clare. I saw you on the news." She looked Mona up and down. "My husband says you're an abomination—hoarding all those sick animals."

"I'm sure your husband is a man of fine education, just like you."

"Least he don't have sex with goats." The woman narrowed her eyes and looked at Mona dead-on. "Now get the hell out."

"I'd like to see you make me."

The woman tried to spit on Mona, but her trajectory was off and the little wad of mucus landed on the counter between them. For a moment, Mona simply stared at the saliva, as if trying to translate a message in its bubbles. Then, without warning, she reached out and grabbed the woman by the hair. The woman shrieked, summoning the cook from the back, a stained white apron tied around his belly.

"What in the hell?" he said, and then pulled Mona's hand from the woman's hair.

Straight-faced, he said, "Girls, I suggest you take your mother elsewhere."

"She spit on me," Mona said, her face pink, mottled. A wild look in her eyes.

"I have no doubt that she did," said the man.

From the corner, the teenager simply stared, a deep sadness in his eyes. His expression made Ariel think of a YouTube video Dex showed her a few days after the election, of two Latvian men coming upon a pair of swans whose necks were tangled together. The swans had flapped across the pond toward the men, as if asking, even begging, for help. Tears had welled in Ariel's eyes as one of the men gently separated the swans' necks, as if untangling the chain of a necklace. *People are good*, she thought. *All over the world, people are decent.* Once free, the swans spread their enormous wings and parted ways. She had felt a swelling of love for Dex, for recognizing the video's poetry and wanting to share it with her. But then, as if shooting down a crystal chandelier with a machine gun, he had asked: "You think the swans were fucking or fighting?" The question had gutted her. "Sometimes you ruin things that seem impossible to ruin," she had said.

Perhaps realizing she'd gone too far, Mona left the deli, her hands balled into fists, her mouth twitching.

The whole thing left Ariel shaken. Her mother had always had a streak of bold behavior. When Ariel was in middle school, Mona would drive around town the night after Halloween and make her steal pumpkins from people's front porches so they could feed them to the pigs—*Better than letting them rot out here until Christmas*—but it was never anything like this. As far as Ariel could remember, her mother had never done anything more violent than slam a pickle jar against the countertop. Now she was starting fights with strangers, pulling their hair. Not to mention the matter of stealing the Fullers' sign.

Back in the truck, they sat quietly until Joy asked, "Are you all right, Mona?"

"No thanks to you two," Mona snapped. "Just standing there, letting that woman spew nonsense."

Ariel wanted to say something but didn't know what. She waited to see what Joy would do, but Joy just kept her eyes on her lap. When it was clear nobody was going to say anything, Mona cleared her throat. "We didn't even get our damn sandwiches." With this, she started Old Baby and sped back onto the highway, in the opposite direction of St. Clare, which Ariel took to mean they would not be eating lunch anytime soon.

They drove through miles of prairie—skinny trees and dilapidated barns and old road signs gone to Swiss cheese from gunshots. There were no dogs out this way, that much was clear. Her mother was driving just to drive.

"I guess if there's a silver lining," Mona was saying, "it's that if these dogs don't come back, they're that much less to worry about. A few adopters will be disappointed, but we can set them up with another dog. Maybe it'll all work out for the best."

Joy said, "Don't think that way. We got Bagel, didn't we? We'll find the others."

"And then what?" Mona asked, her voice cracking. "What's the goddamn difference?"

"You know the difference," Joy said softly.

"We can't give up on them," Ariel added, knowing, deep down, that all of this was her fault. Before she could decide against it, she reached out to put a hand on her mother's shoulder. Her mother flinched, her body retracting. Ariel tried to ignore how much this hurt her, that the woman who had made her, who had given Ariel her hands, her bones, her skin, now felt wary of her touch. Swallowing this hurt, she put her hand on her mother's shoulder and squeezed.

Dex

From the outside, Gideon's camper looked like crap. The wheel beds were rusted, the windows murky and yellowed. So when Dex stepped inside, he was surprised by the funky black and white checkered tile and mint-green walls. Covering the large back window was a worn American flag, faded to a vintage softness. Beneath the window sat a pullout sofa with corduroy throw pillows. An old-timey AM/FM radio, shiny as a cherry lollipop, sat on the linoleum counter, its long antenna tapping the frosted window pane.

Gideon opened a cabinet and retrieved a bottle of Wild Turkey. "This good by you?"

"Absolutely," Dex said. He was trying to imagine life in such a place—waking up in the lofted bed, climbing down the short ladder into the kitchen, where he would brush his teeth at the sink and watch the horses move across the pasture. He would fill a pea-green bowl with Cinnamon Toast Crunch and then begin his day with the animals. It would be a quaint but enviable life, the kind people would follow on Instagram. *#simple. #vanlife. #blessed.*

On the counter stood a pyramid of mason jars filled with red and pink jelly. He picked one up and inspected it. "Did Joy make all this jelly?"

"I did. And it's not jelly. It's preserves."

"I didn't know there was a difference."

Gideon gave him a sympathetic smile. What kind of man didn't know the difference between jelly and preserves? Between horses and mules? Dex felt himself flush with shame, overcome by the feeling that perhaps his life was smaller and more pitiful than he could have ever imagined. There was something admirable in a life like Gideon's, a life in which you could identify animals and make whatever you desired. Dex had once tried brewing his own beer. Two weeks in, his apartment filled with a yeasty smell so noxious his neighbors called the landlord, worried someone in the building had died.

"You know, this is really something," Dex said, gesturing to the camper.

"You think so? Sometimes I feel like I'm living in a toaster oven."

"Not at all. It's got character. It's *cool.*"

"Thanks. Mona gave me the title, years ago, when she couldn't afford to pay me." He reclaimed the bottle from Dex and took another pull.

Gideon was still drinking when someone knocked on the door. Dex looked through the dusty window and saw a man: cowboy hat, khaki outfit, radio clipped to a thick leather belt. With him was a rust-colored dog with floppy ears and an American flag bandanna tied around its neck.

"Oh, boy," Gideon said, setting the bottle on the counter.

"Who is it?"

"The sheriff."

Like a character from a movie, the sheriff held his hat as he ducked into the RV. Once inside, he tipped the brim at Dex.

"Howdy," Dex said, the alcohol warm in his blood.

"Hello," the sheriff said, one skeptical eyebrow raised. The dog skittered in behind him, the giant red fan of its tail beating back and forth. The dog made a beeline for Dex and dug its snout into his crotch.

"Hey, dude," Dex said, trying to pry the dog away. "Nice to meet you, too."

"That's Red Dog," the sheriff said. "He doesn't mess around with hellos."

Dex stroked the fur on Red Dog's forehead, and the dog looked up at him with big inky eyes. He wondered, again, where Hippo had gone off to.

"Is something the matter?" Gideon asked.

The sheriff took a big breath in, as if preparing to blow out birthday candles, and then leaned against the counter. "I just got a call from a lady in Lark City, saying Mona assaulted her." He ran a hand over his face, as if trying to wipe off the bad news. "I called Mona but her cell's off."

"She *assaulted* someone?" Dex asked.

The sheriff picked up a saltshaker, inspected it, and set it back down. "Who knows—people around here, they're bored. They can find drama in a sugar bowl."

"Did the woman say what happened?" Gideon asked.

"Yes and no. Hard to understand half of what she was saying. She was hysterical, yelling about hair pulling and spitting. Jerry Springer stuff. Whatever happened, says she has the whole thing on tape, that some kid recorded it on his cell phone." He looked off toward the back of the camper. "The thing is, she's threatening to press charges, so I thought you all might want a heads-up, considering recent events."

Dex wanted to ask about these recent events but figured it might be rude. He felt like a little kid, listening in on a conversation between adults.

"Should we be worried?" Gideon asked, already looking very worried.

"Chances are it'll fizzle out once the woman calms down, but I just wanted to let you know." He was eyeing the bottle of Wild Turkey. "Mind if I tasted some of that?"

"By all means," Gideon said.

Dex watched the sheriff take a long pull of liquor, as if it were apple juice. "All right. I better be off. You boys have a good rest of your day." He shook Gideon's hand, tipped his hat at Dex, and was gone just as swiftly as he'd arrived. When Red Dog failed to follow him, he called out, "Red Dog! Roll out!" and the dog sprang to attention, bounded out the door.

"Jesus," Gideon said. He was squeezing the bridge of his nose, so that his glasses momentarily popped away from his face.

"Is this kind of thing normal?" Dex asked. "Mona getting in fights?" He wondered if there was a side to Ariel's childhood he didn't know—a violent one.

"No, not at all. But nobody's acting normal anymore."

"What'll happen if the lady presses charges?"

"I think it means she'll go to jail." Gideon stared out the window toward the barn. "You know, suddenly I'm a little buzzed. How do you feel about hot tubs?"

"Hot tubs?"

"Yes. Hot tubs."

Sometimes, without Ariel knowing, he and Buddy would hop the fence of an apartment complex on Iowa Street and spend the night drinking PBR tallboys in the hot tub, arguing over whose toes were more shriveled. "Hot tubs are good," he said.

"Joy's got one at her house. We could finish up the container and head over for a soak. How's that sound?"

"I didn't know relaxing was allowed here."

Gideon took a final swig of alcohol. "Only if you earn it. But it's important to dangle a carrot in front of your face. Give yourself something to work toward."

Dex liked this image—the hot tub dangling before them, roots growing out of its base. He realized that, at one point, years ago, Ariel had likely been Gideon's carrot, and Gideon had likely been hers.

Ariel

They killed the remaining daylight hours driving through neighboring towns, spotting deer and hawks and, come dusk, a little red fox that emerged from the tallgrass and crossed the road, but not a single dog. In the back of the truck, Bagel settled down, having already forgotten the day of freedom and dead rabbits behind him.

At one point, Mona said, "Maybe I'm a prude, but I've never understood that rumor. How could any female have sex with a goat?"

Other than this, the events of the deli went unmentioned, although the scene continued to replay in Ariel's mind: her mother lashing out, the look on the woman's face, as if she really were afraid for her life. That her mother—a women who once let six baby turtles live in her bathtub and who once carried around an injured miniature schnauzer in a BabyBjörn until its broken legs healed—could threaten someone in such a way was a hard truth to swallow.

Ariel had forgotten that this was a symptom of life with her mother. Each day was a Rubik's cube. You could be on the cusp of figuring the thing out, and then one twist of the wrist could change everything. One moment her mother would tell her she couldn't go out driving with Gideon until she gave the ducks a bath, and so out to the ducks she would go, enraged, only to melt a moment later when the ducks began to kick their bright orange feet against her stomach, relaxing into her hold as she soaped their bellies and then toweled them dry. The boiling heat of a summer afternoon would make her cranky to the point of tears, but then, just as quickly, an iced tea and a puppy would undo the knot of her temper, retying it into a bow. Every bad moment was her mother's fault, but so was every good one. In the back of her mind was Mona's scene at the deli, but here was the falling sun, a Nina Simone song coming through the radio, the sweet sight of Bagel closing his eyes to the wind, ears flapping as he sniffed the twilit air. If she closed her eyes, the world was a baby blanket. She was home. And yet she knew if she looked closer, the fabric was full of brambles and fleas, in desperate need of washing.

By the time Mona decided they could give up looking, it was dusk and all of their stomachs were growling. As they pulled into the Bright Side, they decided they'd make a big pot of veggie chili and jalapeño cornbread.

"One dog isn't so bad," said Ariel. "It's better than zero, right?"

Her mother looked at her as they pulled up to the house. "Tomorrow we go again, but earlier."

Rather than argue, Ariel hopped out and returned Bagel to his pen, giving him an extra serving of food and bonus kisses. Meanwhile, Mona and Joy made the rounds, making sure everyone had what they needed—water, food, medicine.

Ariel was still tending to Bagel when she heard a cry from the petting zoo—a human cry. Heart racing, she ran over and found Mona and Joy near the sheep pen, where Honey the pug and Jazzy Jo the min pin were drinking from a bucket of water, leashes still dangling from their necks. The dogs were filthy, their paw pads cracked and bleeding, but they were alive.

"They came back," Mona said, tears in her eyes. She quickly filled a pair of rubber bowls with kibble and watched, smiling, as the little dogs scarfed their dinner.

"Thank God," Ariel said, feeling a chunk of her anxiety drift away. She quieted the cynic in her head, the one saying: *All that time looking, and they came back on their own.*

Mona gave Ariel a cautionary look. "Xena's still gone. And Luna and Mindy. But it's better than nothing." After a moment of quiet, she added, "We're doing the best we can, aren't we?"

Ariel felt a swelling of tenderness rise in her chest. Before she could reach out and touch her mother, Joy beat her to it. "We're doing just fine," Joy said, resting a hand on Mona's back. Ariel noticed her mother did not flinch.

Back in the house, they expected to find the boys in the kitchen, but nobody was there, save for a pair of cats fighting over a dead mouse that Joy swiftly took by the tail and tossed onto the front porch. On the counter was a note that read: *Sore from work—went to hot tub at Joy's house. P.S. Sheriff Donner was here—said something about Lark City. He wants you to call him back. —Gideon & Dex*

For a long moment, Mona stared at the note, the color draining from her face. Eventually she said, "That container better be clean enough to lick." She then disappeared upstairs and did not come back down, even when Joy and Ariel called up to say that dinner was ready.

"I'm not hungry," she called back. "Go on and eat without me."

Ariel and Joy did as she said—they were ravenous. The chili was good and spicy. Joy brought out the milk and they took turns taking long dramatic gulps straight from the bottle. Ariel could not remember a better meal in her life.

After dishes, Joy suggested they go meet the boys at her house for a soak. "Could be a good way to forget about all this for a second," she said. "You can borrow one of my suits."

"I think I'll pass. Thanks, though."

"You sure? I know everything's crazy, but there's no need to punish yourself."

She didn't say it, but she wasn't in the mood to watch Gideon and Joy in the hot tub together—her sitting on his lap, his arms around her middle. Dex would want to ape whatever they did, and she wasn't in the mood for that, either. "You go ahead," she said. "I'll see you in the morning for another day of fun and adventure."

"All right. Suit yourself."

Ariel chuckled. "You made a pun. Swim*suit*."

Perhaps because she was exhausted, Joy began to laugh—first a snicker but then a genuine belly laugh that made Ariel laugh harder, too. Eventually they were both cracking up.

"Thanks for being so nice to me," Ariel said. "It's made a huge difference, having a friend here." She was thinking, *Why couldn't we have been friends when we were younger?* She suddenly felt terrible for trying to kiss Gideon. He was Joy's person now, not hers.

"I've been where you are before. I mean, not exactly, but close. I know what it's like to come home and have everyone mad at you. It's not easy." She then gave Ariel a hug, a hug Ariel had not realized she needed. "I'm really sorry about what happened at the deli. That can't have been fun to watch."

"It's like I came back and made her even crazier."

"You think that was because of you?"

"Well, yeah," Ariel said. "Don't you?"

Joy looked at her sadly. "Your mom's been through a lot these last few weeks. Maybe you're a straw on the camel's back, but I don't think you're the one that broke it."

Ariel realized she had, once again, put herself at the center of a large and complicated world. "You think the sheriff will do anything?" she asked. She was worried for her mother in a way she had not been earlier.

"I think it depends."

"On what?"

"How big of a fuss the Lark City woman makes—and Big John. He told the sheriff he wanted to press charges for the stolen sign, but we haven't heard anything about it one way or the other since the fire."

"Even after everything, he'd do that?"

"I'm not sure," Joy said. "I don't really know Big John. But I know your mom's worried about it."

"Well, what'll happen if they both press charges?"

"I don't know that, either," Joy said. "But whatever it is, we'll handle it."

"My mom used to say that all the time—in just that same way. *Whatever it is, we'll handle it.*"

Joy nodded, a sadness to her eyes. "She still does."

Mona

Mona could hear the sound of spoons scraping bowls, could smell the tomato sauce and spices from the chili the girls had made. Someone had started a fire in the woodstove, and she could smell that, too, could feel the heat radiating up through the floorboards, into her room. She could hear the girls talking but could only pick out certain words. *My mom. Animals. Sheriff.*

What a novelty, to lie in her bed and hear her daughter's voice. It was something she'd taken for granted for years. Something she wished, now, to hold on to.

She was restless, but she didn't want to go downstairs, didn't want to talk to Ariel or Joy or anyone else. The scene at the deli replayed in her head. She shouldn't have grabbed that woman by the hair. She shouldn't have said the mean thing about spreading mayonnaise. It was foolish. And yet, she knew if plopped into the same situation, she'd do it all again. It all boiled down to that comment: *sex with goats.* The rumors had always incensed her. Here she was, trying to do a decent thing, and other people had to twist it apart, turn it into something vulgar. Something they could wag their finger at, gossip about with their friends. That's all anybody wanted anymore. A scandal. Something they could post about on the internet.

When she could no longer stay still, she got up. Katydid and Daisy followed her into her closet—dim explosion of clothes and towels—and watched as she pulled a cord dangling from the ceiling. Mona had always liked the way the attic stairs came down, gently, with caution, like an old woman toddling down from a bus. Mona's life had few hiding spaces, but this was one.

Once in the attic, she pulled another cord, this one attached to a yellow light bulb fixed to a dusty eave overhead. All these years, the light bulb had never gone out. Each time it flickered into life, she breathed a sigh of relief. She had no idea what she'd do when the light finally gave out—the bulb was too high for her to reach.

The attic was crowded with boxes, each one containing what remained of the people who'd left her. The eastern wall was for everything Daniel had left behind: his baseball cards, his encyclopedias (*A–W* only; *Nothing too important happens after W*, he'd said), his box of random electronic accessories that by now were certainly obsolete. The western wall was for Ariel. Her stuffed animals, her baby shoes, her clarinet.

The north and south walls were for everything she'd salvaged from her father's estate, mostly her father's belongings but also, to Mona's surprise, some of her mother's. Things her father had held on to. In the attic, Mona had made a point of separating their things. For once, her mother deserved a space of her own.

Exhausted, she sat in Daniel's old reading chair, a squishy rocking recliner with a cupholder in each arm. Beside the chair was a stack of his audiobooks. There was a stretch of years, toward the end of their marriage, when he'd become obsessed with audiobooks, buying a dozen at a time from the Goodwill in Middleton. He'd walk around the house with his headphones on, lost in a story. He never would tell Mona what he was listening to—whenever she'd ask, he'd mumble, *A book.* Only once he left did she find out, rummaging through the boxes he'd left behind in Blue House. To her surprise, most of the audiobooks were romance novels. Nicholas Sparks, Nora Roberts. Books with titles written in flowery cursive, the cover image a single rose on a nightstand or a couple grasping each other in a strong wind. The book he'd been listening to before he left was *The Bridges of Madison County*.

She inserted disc one into the old Sony Discman, arranged the foamy headphones over her ears, and pressed play. *There are songs that come free from the blue-eyed grass, from the dust of a thousand country roads. This is one of them.* She closed her eyes, settled further into the chair, and imagined that Daniel was sitting beside her. That if she only reached out, she would feel him there, a body that was once so familiar she could identify it by smell alone. It was a fact she'd grappled with over the years: the missing of a person and the missing of their body. She missed Daniel's corny jokes and his gentleness, but she also missed his hands, his chin, his morning breath. The way he would rake his fingers through her hair at night. The way, when they hugged standing up, her ear rested against his chest in exactly the place where his heart beat. He was a large person, with wide shoulders and long legs, and Mona sometimes imagined that if she hugged him hard enough, his body would crack open to reveal not a man of bones and muscle but a collection of powerful birds. He had been her everything: her first love, her partner, the father of her child. All these years later, despite her depthless anger, she missed him.

She was still thinking of Daniel when a calm voice alerted her that it was time for disc two. She opened her eyes, half expecting to see Daniel sitting casually beside her, legs crossed, a smile on his lips. Instead, there was only darkness, sudden and complete. The bulb had finally gone out.

Dex

Joy's house loomed against the night sky like an alien spaceship—long and glowing, appearing to hover just slightly off the ground.

"You sure it's okay if we use the hot tub?" Dex asked.

"I've got an open invitation," Gideon explained. "Not to brag, but Joy's mom loves me."

Dex felt a prick of envy. It was something he could never say—that his mother-in-law loved him. "Is it an optical illusion or is this house gigantic?"

"Ever heard of Champ's dog food?"

"Can't say I have."

"I keep forgetting you don't know dogs."

"Does Hippo—I mean, Bam-Bam—does Bam-Bam like it?"

"Sure," Gideon said. "I don't know if he's had it, but I bet he would like it if he tried it. I mean, it's dog food, and he's a dog, so."

"Then I bet it's pretty good stuff."

Gideon smiled, as if he'd seen this whole routine before: a man falling in love with a dog. "Anyways, Joy's grandpa started Champ's. Had a rendering plant, a packaging and shipping warehouse. The whole thing. Before he died, when he realized Joy's dad, Beau, wasn't going to take over the company, he sold his stake and left the money to Joy's family. Not that they needed it, since Beau was a doctor. But still. Point is, they're loaded."

"How did he die? Joy's dad?"

"Liver failure. Wasn't a single time I saw that man he didn't have a drink in his hand. He started getting really bad Joy's senior year of high school—hiding bottles in the toilet tank, and in Joy's room where her mom wouldn't think to look. It's part of why Joy wanted to leave Kansas so badly. They'd find him passed out in the middle of the yard, covered in his own vomit. Eventually he lost the clinic in Middleton because he kept showing up drunk. I think, when he died, everyone was a little relieved. I know that sounds terrible, but it's the truth."

"So what does Joy's mom do now?"

"Tries to stay busy. Volunteers with the church. Keeps a garden, reads a lot—right now she's on this baking spree. The problem is that she and Joy could live a hundred lives with what Beau left them. She even offered to buy the sanctuary, but of course Mona won't allow it."

"Why not?"

Gideon explained the relationship between Mona and Coreen. "Every few months Coreen makes anonymous donations through our website."

"Huh," Dex said. "And it doesn't make you mad?"

"What?"

"That you're going to lose your job, all because Mona's too proud to take help?"

Gideon kept his eyes on the road. The lights of Joy's house were growing closer, brighter. "You know, Mona has a way of presenting the facts—I was on her side, I guess. I didn't want us to take pity money, either. But Joy and I are finding a way around it."

"What do you mean?"

"Mona won't take money from Coreen, but I think she'd take it from me. We're figuring out a way to make it work—a way for Joy and me to buy the sanctuary."

"That's pretty big, isn't it?"

"It is."

"Does Mona know?"

"We're still crunching the numbers. We don't want to make any promises, get anyone's hopes up, until we're certain it'll work."

"Is that what you want? To own the sanctuary?"

"The Bright Side is my life—my home. It's the only thing I know."

"It just seems so *hard*."

Gideon looked at him quizzically. "Of course it's hard." With this, he went quiet as they turned onto the dirt road. A green street sign flashed in the truck's headlights: CHAMPION STREET.

"They named the street after themselves?"

"If there's one thing I've learned," Gideon said, "it's that when you're rich, you can do whatever the fuck you want."

Despite what seemed like a quiet night indoors, Coreen wore crisp black slacks and a red floral blouse, a gold necklace, and just enough makeup to make you wonder what she looked like without it. On her feet were short leather boots with modest heels that clicked across the hardwood floor when she walked. She was not a small woman— sizable chest, heavy around the middle—and yet her face was slender and young, her skin tanned. She had Joy's smile, the same lightness around the eyes.

She kissed Gideon on the cheek and then shook Dex's hand as if the lives of many small children depended upon it. "And you are?" she said.

"Oh, I'm Dex," he said. "Ariel's fiancé."

"Is that right?" Coreen said, glancing at Gideon.

"Dex just got in last night," Gideon said. "He's been helping around the sanctuary."

"How interesting," said Coreen, emphasizing *interesting*. She put a hand on Dex's back. "Well, come in. No use standing in the cold." She led them past a curved staircase and into a kitchen so tidy and bright it felt like the set of a sitcom, as if at any moment the walls might erupt with canned laughter. Above the kitchen table hung an owl-shaped plaque that read, OWL YOU NEED IS LOVE!!

There was a chocolate cake on the marble island, with small pink roses made of sugar. "That's a beautiful cake," Dex said, his mouth already watering. "What's it for?"

Coreen was already busy retrieving a pair of plates. "Isn't it strange, that we need a reason for cake? Do we need a reason for cookies? Or muffins? This cake," she said, cutting them each a generous portion, "is for the love of cake. Tomorrow, I'm making peanut butter pie."

She placed a massive slice before Dex. "You know, I saw Mona yesterday morning. She was in a *state* about Ariel coming home. And then Joy told me about the dogs getting loose." She shook her head and looked at Dex. "You're engaged to her—she's not pregnant, is she?"

Dex nearly choked on his cake.

As Gideon filled in Coreen about the day's events—sans the visit from the sheriff—Dex tried to imagine this woman falling in love with Mona. What could they possibly have in common? Perhaps when people lived in the middle of nowhere, they learned to make do. The more he thought of it, the more small-town life made sense. Lawrence was crawling with potential partners, and yet so many people were alone, their phones filled with dating apps that only made them feel lonelier. Perhaps Buddy should move out to the sticks, find a nice country girl who could look past his flaws. Buddy. Dex had hardly thought of him since the morning. He wondered if he'd made it back to Lawrence all right. Dex hadn't received any texts or calls—cell service was sparse, the Wi-Fi nonexistent. At the Bright Side, he had been too nervous to ask anyone for the password. He imagined Gideon shaking his head in disapproval. "How could you care about Wi-Fi when there are starving donkeys with boners?" And so he hadn't asked.

Coreen led them out to the patio, where the hot tub sat on a raised platform. Above them, paper lanterns hung from a canopy woven with ivy. The tub was large, with seating for five, and began to bubble and hiss when Gideon pressed a button on the side.

"Don't you just love a winter night?" Coreen asked. She lit a long, skinny cigarette and looked up to the sky, where the stars were gathering in numbers. "I don't know how you can live in the city, Dex. There's no such thing as real happiness in a city."

"Dex likes it in Lawrence," Gideon said. "Don't you, Dex?"

"I love it, actually. Funkiest town in the world—or at least in Kansas."

"Maybe you love it," Coreen said, "but are you at peace there?"

The question surprised him. "I guess I haven't thought much about peace."

Coreen gave him a wry smile. "I recommend you try."

When the tub was warm enough, Coreen went inside and Gideon took off his clothes—boxers included. Dex kept himself from looking, lest he discover another point of envy. As he removed his pants, he felt for his phone in his pocket. He suspected this was a house of open, password-less Internet, and he wanted to make sure Ariel had not called or texted. The night was growing late—surely the girls had returned to the house and found the note. He hoped Ariel would come over, that they could sit in the tub and soak away the past twenty-four hours. From experience, he knew that a tub of hot water could cure just about anything. Once a month, he and Ariel took a bath together, agreeing to wash away whatever stresses they'd incurred during the weeks prior. Theirs was a small, rusting claw-foot tub, but they made it work, both of them sitting at opposite ends so they could face each other. Dex had a rubber ducky and they would sometimes play a game called Quest to Booby Island in which Dex would propel the rubber ducky from his end of the tub, trying to make it "dock" on Ariel's chest. The game had once made her laugh uncontrollably, but the last time they'd taken a bath, she'd said, *Can we not with the bath toys?* and tossed Mr. Ducky from the tub. He hoped Ariel would come over, but when he checked his phone, there were no notifications from her. Instead, there were three missed calls and a voicemail from Buddy.

The calls were from five thirty that morning. They hadn't gone through at the sanctuary, but there was strong cell service here, and so they arrived all at once, along with a handful of missed calls from friends in Lawrence.

Expecting an angry rant (*I'm out here, bored out of my fucking mind, driving through the middle of fucking nowhere . . .*), he nearly deleted Buddy's voicemail without listening. But he let the message play. As he listened, he could feel the air grow colder.

"Is something wrong?" Gideon asked, seeing the look on Dex's face.

"Can you give me a ride back to Ariel's?"

"Everything okay?"

"Not exactly," Dex said.

Gideon rose from the water. "Let's get going then."

Gideon was a good guy, Dex thought. Other men—men like Buddy, for instance—would have razzed him. *But we just got here. I just opened a beer.* Not Gideon. He was solid. Someone you could rely on. Dex could see why Ariel had loved him—why she might, after all these years, still love him.

Ariel

Eager for time alone, Ariel retreated into Blue House. On the sofa was a copy of *Frankenstein*, one of her all-time favorite books. It occurred to her that the book might be Buddy's, left behind the night before. A sudden frisson of fondness rose in her, to think of Buddy bringing a novel with him on what was likely to be a short journey. She, too, liked to carry a book with her wherever she went. In all her anxiety, she'd forgotten to bring one to the sanctuary.

Or perhaps the copy of *Frankenstein* was Joy's, left there during her and Gideon's renovations. Now that she thought of it, of course the book was Joy's.

Burrowing into the couch, she felt a wave of relief flow through her, to be alone, at last, with a story. She was only ten pages in when the door opened. There stood Dex, his clothes filthy, his favorite pair of boots caked in dust, as if Dr. Frankenstein himself had emerged from the page, fresh from his epic pursuit on Mont Blanc. "Buddy had an accident," Dex said, his voice panicked. "We have to go."

"Slow down. What happened?"

"He hit a deer early this morning, just outside of Salina. I didn't get the message until now."

"Is he okay?"

"I mean, he's alive. But he broke his collarbone. Got a concussion.

I'm not sure what kind of state he's in. The hospital called because I was the last-used number in his phone."

Ariel was silent. She'd always assumed Buddy was indestructible—once, at a barbecue, she'd watched him punch his thumb through a watermelon, pry open a bottle of beer with his teeth.

"I'm so sorry, Dex. That's terrible."

He looked at her expectantly. "Do you want to go get your things together?"

"What are you talking about?"

"I'd like to leave soon. It's already late."

"I can't go anywhere, Dex. Not right now."

"But Buddy—"

"Buddy's *your* friend, Dex." She knew it was the wrong thing to say—what did it matter that Buddy wasn't her friend? Dex was her fiancé. She should have wanted to go for him. A weight suddenly fell onto her shoulders. She was so *tired*. Tired of the day, tired of the world. Tired of herself.

When Dex looked down at his hands, Ariel noticed his fingernails were lined with dirt—he'd worked all day, cleaning the container. He'd done that for her, to make a good impression on her mother, and yet she would not make the same effort for him.

"You really won't do this for me?" Dex asked.

"I'm sorry," she said, "but I have to stay."

"Can't you come back, though?"

"The problem isn't coming back," she said, "it's leaving. I can't go running off again."

"Then can I take your car?"

"Dex, you don't have a license."

"Really, Ariel? You know I know how to drive—I drove Buddy's car yesterday. I'll be careful."

"I'm sorry, Dex." She did not want to tell him that Gideon had her keys, or that she did not trust him to drive her car.

"Ariel, he's all alone in a town he doesn't know. He's hurt. The only reason he was driving so late was because of me." After a moment he added, "And you, too. You're the one who made him leave."

She felt a sudden tick of anger. "Are you trying to make me feel responsible?"

"Not responsible, but something. I want you to feel *something*. I know Buddy's annoying, but he's my friend, and he's hurt." He looked at her, and she knew what he was thinking: *How could she be so cold?*

"I never said he had to go in the middle of the night, Dex. And I certainly didn't put that deer in front of his car. He could have left in the morning. He could have driven more carefully. We both know he was probably stoned. And in case you don't remember, I didn't ask for you to come here. You did that without my permission."

"I wouldn't have had to if you'd been honest with me. You're out here with some guy you fucked through high school, and did you even tell me about him? No. You didn't tell me about any of it." He was almost yelling now. She could see the muscles in his neck.

"That's not why I'm here, and you know it," she said, angry in earnest now. "Maybe you should go to Buddy. But I'm staying here. With the guy I fucked through high school." The words seemed to hang in the air between them. She understood that something irreversible had happened. She'd gone too far.

Dex stared at her. She would have rather he looked angry—instead, he looked hurt. Injured. When he spoke, it was softly. "What's happening, Ariel? It's like you don't even care."

She opened her mouth as if to say something, but then closed it. Dex stared at her, jaw clenched, waiting for something she wasn't sure she could give him. Eventually, he walked past her and out the door. He tried to slam it, but the door was made of cheap, light wood and merely floated toward the frame without closing so that Ariel had to get up and properly shut it.

For a few minutes, she sat on the couch with the book, Dex's words looping in her mind. *It's like you don't even care.* Sunny once told her that people consistently rate themselves as being funnier than they actually are. Perhaps it was the same with kindness. Sure, Ariel thought she was a good enough person, at least she was *trying* to be good, but what did she know? She was, more likely than not, a bad person. A selfish person. She sometimes felt superior to Dex, because she followed the news more closely and read novels written by people from other countries, but what did any of that really get her? While Ariel walked through the world identifying and critiquing the darkness, it was Dex who actually made it brighter.

She thought of Frankenstein's monster, how all he wanted was somebody to talk to, somebody who understood him. Someone who cared about his needs and feelings. She knew if Dex had been in the book he would have befriended the monster; she would have shied away.

Closing the book, she got up and went outside. "Dex?" she called, "are you out here?"

"I'm here," he said, his voice soft, defeated.

He was sitting on the grass near the driveway. She went to him, the wind picking up and stinging her ears. "Gideon has my keys," she said. "You can go get them from him. You can take my car."

He looked up at her, his face only a pale shadow in the dark. "But you won't come with?"

She held her elbows close to her chest. "I'm sorry."

"I need you to understand something," he said, rising to his feet.

She was afraid of the look in his eyes, a look that said she had finally damaged something beyond repair. "What?"

"I came here because I love you. Everything I do, I do because I love you. Because I want to keep you. But sometimes it feels like you don't want to be kept—like you'd rather I let you go."

"Dex," she said, but then wasn't sure what to say. She knew there was at least a kernel of truth in what he said—a truth she didn't want to acknowledge. The only words she could find were "I'm sorry."

She stood there, her body numb. She wanted him to kiss her goodbye, but instead he clicked his tongue and began to make his way toward Gideon's camper. She thought about calling after him but couldn't figure what to say, and so she said nothing. Eventually she went back into Blue House, turned off the lights, and lay in bed, knowing she wouldn't be able to sleep.

After an hour or so she got up, left Blue House, and crossed the Bright Side, the moon a sharpened sickle overhead. The wind was blowing in earnest now—one of those wrathful prairie winds that used to capsize trash cans and coat the animals with dust. When she saw that her car was no longer in the visitors' lot, she felt a tug in her stomach. Dex was gone.

In the mudroom, the broken light created a momentary disco before dumping her into the kitchen. The smell of chili and cornbread still spiced the air. She could hear the sound of animals moving, their nails clicking against the floor.

The door to her mother's bedroom was open—it was never closed, so dogs could come and go as they pleased—but Ariel knocked anyway. When nobody answered, she turned on the lights. Like the rest of the house, her mother's room was the same as she remembered—the sagging queen bed messy with sheets and dog toys. Piles of books and newspapers and dog collars on the bureau. Near the door was a ceramic flowerpot filled with desiccated soil, the shriveled brown fist of a long-dead plant. The only new addition was a gigantic metal sign that leaned against the wall opposite her mother's bed. The sign came up to Ariel's neck and was longer across than her mother's bed. When she pulled it away from the wall she saw, in great chunky letters, the words MAKE AMERICA GREAT AGAIN. She couldn't help but laugh. Her gaze lingered on the sign, an idea forming.

She found the spare key to Old Baby where her mother had always kept it, in an old Dannon yogurt container next to the cookie jar. It had been years since she'd driven stick, and yet she was going to have to try. The hardest part was getting the sign into the truck. It was too big to lift and carry, and so she had to slide it down the carpeted stairs, bypassing the curious dogs and cats who came to see what she was up to. She worked quickly, her heart racing lest her mom come back from wherever it was she had gone to—on a late-night pasture walk, Ariel assumed, her usual practice in times of distress.

Getting the sign into the back of Old Baby was difficult, and yet she managed it, summoning the same strength that had once allowed her to throw a sixty-pound bag of horse feed over her shoulder, no problem. Once, when one of the sheep began to pant and foam at the mouth from bloat, Ariel had scooped her clean off the ground and carried her, nearly running, all the way to Gideon's truck so they could rush her to town and watch, gagging, as Doc Powell drained putrid green rumen from her side. Now Ariel's arms were tired, but the burn of work felt good.

She started Old Baby and sat with her head in her hands, waiting for the engine to warm up. If she could make it off the property without anybody noticing, she would take it as a signal that she was doing the right thing. She hadn't come back to kiss Gideon or make a mess of letting the dogs out—she had come back to do what daughters were supposed to do. She'd come back to help her mother. She'd come back to set things right.

Big John's house—Sydney's house, as she still thought of it—was only a few miles down Sanctuary Road, but by the time she reached the front door, her hands were slick with sweat, her heart in her throat. Stacked by the floor mat were a dozen newspapers, still in their blue plastic sleeves. Moths circled above her, hurling their small bodies against the porch light. When she finally gathered the courage to ring the doorbell, she was surprised to hear a dog bark.

When the door opened, Big John was standing with Xena the mastiff. "Can I help you?" Big John asked. He was holding Xena by the scruff of her neck, to keep her back. He wore blue cotton pants and a gray sweatshirt that hung loose over his belly. On his nose sat the same pair of frameless glasses he'd always worn, now ten years out of style, the lenses visibly scratched and dirty. She had remembered him being taller. She could see, in his high forehead and rounded nose, the face of Sydney. They were both redheads, with light eyes and freckles that made their faces look dirty.

"Hi," Ariel began, her voice unsteady. She tried again. "I don't know if you remember me. I'm Mona Siskin's daughter, Ariel." She took a deep breath. "Sydney and I used to hang out, when we were younger."

His eyebrows lifted. "I know who you are. Didn't you run off?"

"I did." She hated the way it sounded—*run off*—like she, too, were a dog who'd gotten loose.

He looked beyond her, as if searching for another person. "Does your mom know you're here?"

"I mean, she knows I'm here, but not *here* here."

"Let me guess—you heard about the fire and had to come back?"

How strange, that he was the first one to understand her. She nodded.

"Why don't you come in. I've got this dog—she's kind of a spaz but she's all right. Fair warning, she's a licker."

Ariel reached down to pet Xena, who stuck her wet nose into Ariel's palm and began to lick her slowly, with great concentration. "She's one of my mom's dogs, actually."

"I figured that might be the case. Crazy thing showed up this morning, trying to get into my garbage bin—I'd just put chicken bones in there last night. She seemed hungry, so I gave her some hamburger and now she won't leave me alone." He looked at Ariel. "Your mom told me to stay away, so I wasn't sure what else to do. I tried to call, but the voicemail was full." Xena was leaning against Big John now, her tongue happily hanging from her mouth. "Do you know her name?"

"It's Xena."

"Wouldn't you be damned. I've been calling her Naomi."

Big John led her through the kitchen where he filled two plastic cups with tap water. The sink was so stuffed with dishes that he had to angle the cups under the faucet. Ariel glanced around. There were Styrofoam take-out boxes stacked on the table, empty cans of Campbell's Chunky soup collecting dead flies by the stove. She wondered if she should feel nervous or afraid, but for now she felt only pity. From behind, she saw that a perfect circle of baldness was forming on the back of Big John's head.

"Sorry about the mess," he said, handing her a cup.

"It doesn't bother me."

"Sydney used to take out all the trash—I didn't even realize it until he was gone. It's funny, isn't it? What you don't notice till it's gone?"

For as much as they hung out, Sydney had invited her over only a couple of times. She figured he was ashamed of something—living with his grandma, maybe. His room had once been his mother's, and the furniture was clearly meant for a little girl—the bedposts carved with flowers and ivy, the dresser topped with a vanity mirror. Even the light fixtures attached to the ceiling fan were made of frosted-pink glass.

Now Big John led her into the living room, which was as clean as the kitchen was dirty. There were framed photographs all over the walls, photos she didn't remember. A black-and-white field of sunflowers. A rusted R2-D2 sitting in the back of an even rustier Ford pickup. Loretta in a rocking chair, drinking a Diet Coke. They were the kind of quiet, rural photographs that coffee shops and bars in Lawrence liked to display, suspending them from the ceiling with lines of invisible wire. In one photo, a boy in a hooded sweater walked down a train track, his back turned to the lens. Sydney.

On Big John's wooden coffee table was a stack of books, most of them related to photography—*A Photographic Journey Through Our Country's National Parks*, *America's Dust Bowl in Photos*, *RUST: Abandoned Factories of the United States*. Across the room, a small television sat on a wooden stand. The Weather Channel was playing on mute.

Big John sat down on the other end of the couch. Xena came over and put her front legs up, so that half her body was on top of Big John and the other half was on the floor. Ariel waited for him to push the dog away. Instead, he played with Xena's ears.

"Did you take those?" Ariel asked, gesturing to the photos.

Big John surveyed the walls, as if this were his first time noticing them. "I did. Long time ago. I don't shoot as much as I used to."

"I didn't know you were a photographer."

"It's just a hobby. My grandma Loretta, she was the only one who ever believed in me."

"I'm sorry she's gone," Ariel said.

Big John kept playing with Xena's ears, flipping them back and forth. "Me too."

When Ariel remembered Loretta, she remembered the shirts she wore, always decorated with sequins or beads, the beige strap of her bra peeking out from the neckline. The bra strap had terrified Ariel. Only now did she appreciate how hard it must have been for Loretta to take in two teenaged boys while still mourning the loss of her daughter and son-in-law. Ariel wondered what else she hadn't noticed, growing up, how many people zoomed by her girlhood periphery without qualifying for deeper consideration.

"Did you come here to yell at me?" Big John asked.

Ariel startled. "No, it's nothing like that."

He seemed genuinely relieved, his body relaxing into the couch. "That's good—I don't think I could take any criticism tonight."

"Actually," Ariel said, "I came to return your sign."

He gave her a funny look. There were purple bags beneath his eyes—he was clearly exhausted. "Oh, I don't want that thing."

"It's mostly just a gesture," she said.

"That's nice and all, but I think we're far past gestures."

Ariel set her water glass down on the table, making sure to use one of the coasters. "The thing is, my mom's in trouble. She got in a fight earlier today, with a woman in Lark City. I just thought maybe I could come over and convince you to drop any charges about the sign."

His thick fingers were still working Xena's ears. "Honey, I'm not pressing any charges." He squeezed the bridge of his nose, lifting up his glasses, and took a deep breath. "What my brother did—" he started, but couldn't finish. He turned to Ariel, his brow furrowed so that a line neatly bisected his forehead. "I'll never forgive myself for what happened. I should have known he was going to try something. I should have been able to stop him, but I didn't."

"Everyone's been wondering whether you knew about it before-hand."

"I mean, I had an inkling he was going to do *something*—he was pissed when I told him about your mom taking our sign. That was my mistake, getting him all worked up. I figured he might egg your mom's truck or something. But the fire—" He turned to look at Ariel. "I mean, you were friends with him. You know how he could be. But deep down he's good." Big John looked at Xena, as if she had known Sydney, too. "He's always had a good heart."

Ariel could only nod.

"I tried to be a good brother. Now I'm all alone in a town full of people who think I hate Jews. They think I wanted to kill your mom's horses, to burn down her barn, when all I wanted was to buy some land. My grandma always liked your mom. Said she was good people. I thought I was doing something kind, offering to take your mom's animals. Helping someone like her. And then all this stupid stuff with the sign." He closed his eyes. "I don't want to see that sign ever again. You can take it right back with you."

Ariel felt foolish. What had she thought she was doing, coming over here with the sign? "My mom—she thinks you had a hand in the fire."

He looked at her, his eyes red. "Who do you think called nine-one-one?"

Ariel remembered her mom saying the firefighters had gotten to the sanctuary eerily fast. She'd figured someone driving by had called—but who drove down Sanctuary Road at three in the morning? "So you did know. You knew Sydney was going to attack the Bright Side."

"No—I mean yes, eventually. I saw him packing the truck with gasoline the night before. He told me he had a plan to burn some of our grandma's old furniture in the pasture—he hated the furniture in his room, always complained it was old-lady stuff. But then when I heard him leave in the middle of the night—when I saw his truck heading in the direction of your mom's place—I just knew. But it's not like he told me anything."

"My mom needs to know this," Ariel said.

"Well, I tried to come explain it to her, but she freaked out and threatened to sic her dogs on me."

"She's pretty rattled."

"I can imagine," he said. "But I'm not sure what to do here. I tried." He looked at Xena, who had closed her eyes, her enormous, cream-colored head still in his lap, drool dripping from her jowls. Big John ran a finger down the dog's nose, forcing the fur in the wrong direction. Xena sighed, licked her lips. "Look—I know she probably won't want to hear it, but you're her daughter, so maybe she'll listen if it's coming from you. You can tell her everything I told you. That I didn't have anything to do with it. That I'm not pressing charges about the sign."

"I'll tell her." Ariel noticed how calm she felt, despite everything that had happened. She focused on a photo at the far end of the room, of Sydney. "I was wondering—do you still want the Bright Side?"

Big John rubbed the back of his neck. "What with Sydney gone, I don't need the house. Maybe if he gets a short sentence, but things aren't looking that way." He turned to Ariel. "But I feel responsible. I really do. I'd like to help your mom, if I can."

Ariel realized she had imagined Big John scooping up the sanctuary, relieving the burden from her mother's arms (and her mother, in turn, thanking Ariel for brokering the transition). Happily ever after. The end.

"Help how?" she asked.

"This might sound silly, but I've been thinking, these past few weeks, about how I could take photos of the animals. No offense, but that website she has is garbage. I was looking at other sanctuaries and they've got these beautiful photos of dogs, with descriptions about their personalities, where they came from, what kind of home they're looking for. I think that type of thing really helps."

"It's true," Ariel said. "The website sucks." She was already planning—Big John could take the animals' photos and she could write the descriptions. They could keep pushing adoptions, posting about the animals on social media. She could use her connections in Lawrence, Dex's connections, too. She would keep working, keep helping, so her mom could feel comfortable leaving the Bright Side when the time came.

"You can tell her I'm here to help, whatever I can do. Even if she doesn't want to hear it, I'll at least know I tried."

"That's generous of you," Ariel said.

He pressed a finger to his tear duct. "What your mom does—that's generous. I'm just trying to sleep at night."

Ariel fiddled with the edge of a throw pillow. "There's something I want to tell you, about Sydney."

Big John raised his eyebrows.

A part of her wanted Big John to tell Sydney that she would never forgive him for what he did to her mother, to the horses, to her home. But what good would it do? It wouldn't change anything, and it certainly wouldn't make her feel better. She'd hurt him, too, and it was at least in her power to make good on that.

"When we were younger—in high school. I think I did something really mean to him." She swallowed the lump in her throat. "It wasn't intentional, exactly, but it caused a lot of the other kids to bully him. I think it's why he eventually quit school."

Big John nodded. "He did have a rough go of it in Middleton. I always wondered if something like that was going on. And why you two stopped being friends—he'd never had a friend the way you two got along."

"I just wanted to say I'm sorry. If you could tell him that, the next time you talk to him, I'd really appreciate it."

"That'll probably confuse the hell out of him, but sure. I'll let him know."

"Thank you," Ariel said. After a moment of awkward silence, she stood. "I should get going."

Big John nodded, lifted Xena's paws from his legs. "Sorry, girl. Time to get up."

Ariel was nervous to broach the subject of Xena, but knew she needed to. "I should probably take her home with me," she said, gesturing to the dog.

Big John's face fell. "Oh, right."

Ariel approached the dog, hand outstretched. *It was you who started all this,* she thought, looking at the dog. *I hope you at least had a good adventure.* She startled when Xena bared her teeth, saliva pooling at the corner of her lips.

"Hey, now," Big John snapped. "None of that." Xena turned her head slightly toward him but kept her eyes on Ariel, teeth still flashing.

"It's all right, girl," Ariel said, "I just want to take you home." She offered the back of her hand to Xena to sniff, but without warning the dog lashed out, her teeth connecting with Ariel's knuckle. Ariel pulled her hand to her chest. The bite wasn't anything much—a scrape the size of a staple—but it was on thin skin and so a line of bright blood rose to the surface. Heart thumping, Ariel glanced at Xena, whose eyes were still locked on her.

"Christ," Big John said, leading Ariel to the kitchen sink. "Let's get it cleaned out. Is it bad?"

"No, it's just a nick. Really."

"I'm so sorry. I swear, she's been nothing but gentle since she got here."

Ariel remembered her mom's mantra: *An animal will never hurt you so long as it knows you love it.* She felt her cheeks go hot as she held her hand under a stream of cool water. "It's my fault. I shouldn't have forced it."

"Maybe I should just hold on to her," Big John said. He looked at Ariel with pleading eyes. "If that's all right?"

She knew she shouldn't leave the dog there—Xena might have been one of the dogs on hold—but she didn't have the heart to deny him. It was clear Big John was lonely, and Xena had clearly voiced her opinion on the matter. "I guess that wouldn't hurt."

Looking at Xena, Big John put his hands over his forehead and squeezed. After a few deep breaths, he said, "Thank you." He offered Ariel a paper napkin for her hand and then showed her to the door.

When Ariel pulled back into the Bright Side, her mother was standing on the porch, hands on her hips, the porch lights deepening the shadows on her face. She was an angry mother from a TV show, and Ariel was the daughter coming home past her curfew. Ariel swallowed her nerves and parked Old Baby. During the drive over, she'd started to feel hopeful—giddy, even—that she'd done exactly what she'd wanted to do. She'd made peace with the enemy, a peace that might help her mom home more animals. But now, as she sat in the car, the engine tinkling, she couldn't help but wonder if she'd made a huge mistake. What had she really done? The sanctuary was still up for sale. The animals were still in jeopardy. The horses were still dead, the barn still burned. The closer she got to the porch, the more certain the doom feeling became.

"Where were you?" her mother asked. "And where's your car? I was worried you'd run off again."

Ariel's heart leaped at her mother's phrasing—she was *worried* Ariel had left. One had to care to feel worried. "Dex took it. His friend, the one who drove him here, he had an accident. Hit a deer." She held her hand behind her back, so her mother wouldn't see the napkin around her finger.

"Is he all right?" Mona said, her voice softer.

"I'm not sure. He broke his collarbone. Got a concussion."

"And the deer?"

"I don't know," Ariel admitted. "I didn't ask."

"I hope they're both okay."

"Me too," Ariel said, feeling a little like a fraud.

"Well, where were you then?"

She squeezed the napkin against her finger, to feel the hurt. "I went to take the sign back to Big John."

Mona jolted. "You what?"

"I was worried, after what happened in the deli. I thought I could convince him to drop any charges about the sign—but you don't need to worry, because he's over all that. I know you don't believe him, but he feels terrible about the fire. He's torn up about it—you'd see for yourself, if you'd just talk to him." She was talking too fast, tripping over her words. "He wants to help in whatever way he can. He says he'll take pictures of the animals for the website—"

"The last thing I want to do," Mona said, "is have a photo shoot with the monster who killed my horses."

"But he didn't. He was the one who called the fire department—he figured out what Sydney was doing and he called right away. If anything, he saved the barn."

"Do you think this is helping me, Ariel? You trying to play peacekeeper?"

Ariel swallowed the knot in her throat. "Yes—I do."

"Those men killed my horses, set my *barn* on fire, and tried to poison my pig. They painted hate symbols all over my property—" Mona choked on her words.

"Big John didn't do any of those things. He wants to help you." How could her mother not see the situation for what it was?

"He's playing innocent so people in town will stop looking at him funny."

"Sydney's going to be in prison for a long time—do you understand that? Big John's all alone. It's just him. He wants to *help* you."

"I don't want his help."

"Then what about Coreen? Why won't you let her help you? Why won't you let anyone help you? I don't get it."

"Because it's my life, Ariel. It's my animals, and it's my problem to figure out. You're back one day and you think you can solve all our problems. But it's not your business. Not anymore."

Ariel was growing more frustrated by the second—she wanted to shake her mother. "You act like there's only one way to do anything, and if anyone comes along with another way, you write them off as if they're trying to hurt you. It's just like when I wanted to go to school—you were so stubborn you couldn't even let yourself imagine it. All you could see was that I wanted to leave you. All you could see was yourself."

Ariel could feel that something was slipping further and further away, out of her grasp. The frustration in her mother's face was written in bold, radiating in waves so thick Ariel could almost taste them. It was then she recalled Joy's advice. *It completely disarms the enemy.* Figuring she had nothing more to lose, she took a deep breath, reached out, and tapped her mother on the nose. "Boop?" she said.

For a moment there was only silence, and then her mother jerked away, as if a wasp had landed on her face. "Have you lost your goddamn mind?"

"Shit," Ariel said. "I'm sorry." She could have slapped herself. She could have turned and run away.

"Is this funny to you?"

She could feel a burning sensation steadily walking up her throat, pinching the back of her tongue. She shook her head.

Her mother was breathing so heavily Ariel could see the fabric around her shirt's button separate slightly each time she inhaled. "You know, we've been perfectly fine without you here, and we'll manage fine without you again."

"What are you saying?"

"I'm saying it's time for you to go home." With this, Mona turned and stormed into the house, the screen door snapping shut behind her.

Unsure where else to go, Ariel went to Blue House, her eyes stinging. She was pissed, and embarrassed, but it was also a relief. At least now she could say she'd tried, that she hadn't sat by and watched her past slip away forever. She could return to Lawrence and resume her life with Dex. She would go back to her job, keep trying to work toward an indeterminate future in which she might finally feel fulfilled. The problem was that when she thought of her and Dex's house in Lawrence—a house filled with plants, sunlight, and music—it no longer felt like home. Not completely.

There was also the problem of leaving—where could she go now, at this hour, with no car? She couldn't call Dex to come get her, and she certainly didn't want to ask Gideon for a ride.

She was sitting on the couch, still stunned from the conversation with her mother—had she really booped her on the nose?—when she heard a noise at the front door. She sat up straight, hoping it was her mother returning to talk things out, to say she'd overreacted, that she wanted Ariel to stay. Maybe, for once, they would really *talk*. Instead, it was Gideon who walked in, the cattle dog following at his heels. Ariel deflated.

"I've been looking all over for you," he said.

"Well, here I am."

"Are you crying?"

Ariel put her hands over her face. "Maybe."

"What happened?"

"Nothing—don't worry about it."

"I just wanted to tell you I gave Dex your keys—he said you were okay with it, but I figured I should tell you."

"Thanks."

"Do you want me to go?"

It was her least favorite thing about life—how people could come and go, that not everybody could be in the same place at once. "Please stay," she said.

He came over and sat beside her, crossing his leg over his knee to reveal a puck of manure on the bottom of his shoe, latticed with hay and grass. Ariel figured the cattle dog would sit by Gideon, but instead he jumped onto the couch beside her. Ariel pet the dog's back, encouraging him to lay down and cuddle. It was the same dog who'd slept beside her two nights before, the one she'd imagined as Opal. The same dog who'd sat with her on the porch when she'd argued with her mother. She'd forgotten this about the sanctuary dogs—how sometimes one would pick you.

"What's this guy's name?" Ariel asked.

"That's Old Crow."

"Like the whiskey?"

"That's right." Gideon scratched near Old Crow's tail and the dog thumped his leg. "He's a good boy."

Ariel had a memory of drinking Old Crow with Dex years before. He'd poured shots into a bottle of Coke they snuck into a movie theater, along with a Ziploc of pretzels and M&M's. Halfway through *Gravity*, Dex slipped his hand into Ariel's skirt and whispered, *Are you as turned on by space as I am?* Now she raked her fingernails down the dog's spine. Old Crow licked her wrist and then worked his nose under her thigh, closed his eyes.

"Are you still pissed at me?" she asked Gideon.

"For trying to kiss me?"

"For that," she said, embarrassed all over again. "And for the dogs. And for leaving. For all of it."

Gideon kept his eyes on Old Crow. "Is it important to you that I not be?"

"Of course it is. That's part of why I came back."

"Okay," he said. "Then I'm not mad at you."

"Don't say it if you don't mean it."

"I'm not sure how to win here, Ariel. All I can say is that I'm not mad. Rattled, maybe. But not mad."

She understood what he meant: he was not mad because he no longer cared. She felt her heart wrench in the same way it had when Gideon first told her about Joy. Perhaps the trick was not to eliminate this feeling, but to accept it. To know that she could feel it and still move on.

Gideon met her gaze. "Dex told me something interesting today. He told me you didn't graduate. That you lost your scholarship."

She felt a wave of shame wash over her. Her first instinct was to be angry at Dex, but she understood he had no way of knowing this was a secret he was supposed to keep for her. "I don't know what to say."

"You don't have to say anything. I just wanted you to know that you can stop pretending. At least around me."

"I feel awful about wasting your money. I think about it a lot."

"It's not about the money, Ariel. I just don't understand. What happened?"

She refused to bring up Dex, to blame him. "I don't know. Things just got out of hand. I'd never had that kind of freedom before—I couldn't handle it. I stopped going to class, stopped trying."

"So, you don't have a degree?"

She shook her head.

"Do you still want one?"

She felt a lump of emotion rising in her throat. "I don't know what I want, Gideon. I think that's another reason why I'm here. It's like the world's on fire, and what am I doing to help anyone? Everyone has a hose, or a bucket, or *something*, and I'm just standing around, watching. I can't even help my own mom."

"Your mom doesn't want help, Ariel."

"Then what is it she wants?"

"She wants her daughter back."

Ariel let out a hollow laugh. "Doesn't seem that way."

"I promise it's true." Gideon put a hand on her leg, causing the hairs on the back of her neck to rise. "And even if she did want help, you can't expect to help anyone if you're on fire yourself."

"You think I'm on fire?"

He smiled. "It's just a metaphor, Ariel. All I'm saying is maybe you should focus on figuring yourself out before you try to figure out everyone else."

She'd forgotten how calming he could be, how she could give him a tangled necklace of thought and feeling and he could hand it back to her, a perfect chain of reason. She could still feel his hand on her leg, the warmth of it.

"I've been thinking," she said, "would you let me pay back the money I borrowed? I don't have enough to pay you all of it, at least not right now. But I'd like to start with something. Maybe a couple hundred a month—more if I can swing it?"

"Ariel, you don't have to do that."

"Like you said, it's not about the money."

"No, I mean you really don't have to. Your mom already did."

"What?"

"After you left, I told her I lent you the money and she freaked out. She paid it all back to me. We're good."

Ariel felt a tug in her body. All this time, it was her mother she owed, her mother's money she'd squandered. It was her mother who had tried, at least partially, to right Ariel's wrong. "Then I'll pay her back," Ariel said.

Gideon nodded slowly, as if considering what this would mean for the both of them. "You know where she lives. You can send your checks to the house." With this, he stood up. As he looked down at her, Ariel could see the minute ways in which he, too, had aged—laugh lines around his eyes, a loosening of skin in his neck. Still, he was the same Gideon she remembered; it broke her heart that she was not the same Ariel to him. "Or you could bring the money by in person," he said. "Maybe once or twice a year—bigger installments. I think she'd like that."

There it was, the same old pull on her heart. "I'll keep that in mind," she said. "Unless, you know, the sanctuary sells."

"Well, we'll just have to cross our fingers and hope we figure something out."

She nodded. "Fingers crossed."

"See you in the morning?"

"Sure," she said, although she knew that by then she would be gone. *Goodbye, Gideon,* she said in her head. *See you when I see you.*

When Gideon stood to leave, Ariel worried Old Crow would follow after, but even as Gideon closed the front door, the dog remained by her side, quietly snoring. Ariel leaned over and smelled one of his paws. She'd always loved the smell of a sleeping dog's paw, a sweet and earthy odor, like a mixture of fresh bread and potting soil. When she was in high school, she had begun each morning by smelling Opal's paw, an act Opal came to interpret as a kind of morning greeting. If Ariel forgot the daily ritual, Opal would stretch her paw toward Ariel's face, to remind her. Not long ago, Ariel had taken Dex's hand in the middle of the night and held his palm to her nose—his skin smelled of salt and beer. A hint of tobacco.

She gave herself another moment with Old Crow, who was still snoring beside her, and then kissed the top of his head. "Goodbye, little guy," she said. "Thanks for taking care of me."

Dex

Dex had knocked on Gideon's camper door, trying not to feel nervous. Gideon answered casually, as if he'd been waiting for Dex to show up. He was drinking an oatmeal stout and had changed into a red hoodie that read, *Middleton High*. "What's up?" he asked, motioning for Dex to come inside.

"That's a good beer," Dex said, pointing to the bottle.

"Want one?"

"Maybe another time." He wanted to get on the road, to get to Buddy. "I was actually wondering if you could give me Ariel's keys—she said you have them?"

Gideon sipped his beer. "You going somewhere?"

"I am."

"Nothing's open this late on a Sunday."

He explained about Buddy, about the deer and the hospital in Salina. "He's kind of an asshole," Dex said. "But he's my best friend—he'd do it for me. And Ariel—she doesn't seem to care at all."

"I take it she's not going with you."

Dex shook his head.

From a drawer in the kitchen, Gideon removed the purple carabiner and keys that Dex had come to associate with Ariel's hips.

"Thanks," Dex said, taking the keys. "And for everything else, too. I know it's been a strange couple of days."

Gideon shrugged. "Last week I watched a shih tzu try to hump a duck, face-side first."

Dex smiled, grateful for the small reprieve of humor.

"You feeling all right about everything?" Gideon asked.

Dex realized how badly he needed to be asked this question—to have a reason to organize his thoughts and feelings into words. "I guess the thing that still bothers me," he said, "is why Ariel didn't tell me about this place. It's such a big secret to keep, and for what? What did she think I'd do—dump her because she grew up on an animal sanctuary? It doesn't make sense."

"It's hurtful, right?"

"Yes," Dex said, realizing he needed that word. "It's hurtful."

"I'm going to tell you something painful," Gideon said, "not because I don't like you but because I do." He put his beer on the counter, sat Dex on the sofa, and explained how, the day before, Ariel had tried to kiss him. "We didn't actually kiss," he said. "You should know that. But she tried to."

Dex nodded, the camper going fuzzy in his periphery. Without warning, an elephant sat on his chest. His heart buckled under the weight. "She has pretty bad balance. Maybe she stumbled into you or something."

"Dex," Gideon said, a knowing look in his eyes. "It was just a burst of emotion thing—a mistake. But I thought you should know."

Dex could only nod.

"You all right?"

"Sure," Dex said. "Or I will be. Eventually."

"Of course you will." Gideon stood, signaling their conversation was over. "Drive safe out there. Keep an eye out for animals."

"Thanks, man." Uncertain what else to do, Dex gave Gideon a hug.

· · ·

As he was walking to Ariel's car, his head feeling lighter and lighter, Hippo bounded over, tail going wild.

"Hey, dude," Dex said, a pinch in his throat. "Looks like it's time to say goodbye." He'd never said goodbye to a dog before and found it equal parts sad and awkward. He tried to smile at Hippo, not wanting his sadness about Ariel to affect their goodbye. Hippo deserved more than that.

Hippo looked up at Dex. *Are you serious right now?* his eyes said. *I thought we were going to be best friends!*

Dex saw that Gideon was standing outside his camper, watching them. "You know, if you wanted to take Bam-Bam with you, I could handle the paperwork."

"The thing is, I don't really *like* dogs."

"Is that so?"

He looked at Hippo. "Don't worry, my man. I wasn't talking about you. You're different."

"He's been here for years," Gideon said. "He could really use a home."

"I wouldn't know how to take care of him."

"Food, water, somewhere to sleep. When he needs to poop or pee, put him outside. Any other questions, there's this thing called the internet. Or Ariel."

Dex looked at Hippo, who had placed a paw on Dex's boot so that his toes spread apart. Normally, Dex would have worried about mud ruining his boot, but he found he no longer cared. He stooped down to face Hippo man-to-man. "What do you think, dude? Want to come live in Lawrence? Be a townie dog? We could get you a little jean jacket, maybe some Vans. All the lady dogs'll go wild."

Hippo pressed his nose to Dex's and stuck his tongue up Dex's nostril. His breath still smelled like ass.

"If for some reason things don't work out," Gideon said, "you can always bring him back."

"What if the sanctuary's sold by then?"

Gideon looked out toward the pasture, as if thinking about the horses. "The truth is, we really hate when people bring them back."

In the car, Hippo sat in the front seat. "Do I buckle you in? Or are you supposed to have a car seat or something?" Hippo looked at him and stuck his tongue out, doing the wide-lipped smiley-face thing that made Dex's chest feel airy.

As they were pulling away, Gideon ran over to the car and tapped on the window. "Almost forgot his favorite toy," he said, handing Hippo a tattered cloth rabbit. He then kissed Hippo on the forehead and said, "Be good for your new pops," causing that thing in Dex's chest to lift up and flutter again. With this, Gideon slapped the hood of Ariel's car and sent Dex and Hippo on their way.

In daylight, Kansas looked the same in every cardinal direction. At night, it looked the same in all 360 degrees: up, down, left, right, behind. Every so often, there appeared a sign for one small town or another. Hoxie. Winona. Angelus. Places he'd never heard of. It had been a long time since Dex had driven alone at night, and the prairie's endlessness made him nervous, as if the dark might swallow him whole.

To drown out his thoughts, Dex cranked the stereo as high as it would go. "Hope you like shitty emo music," he called to Hippo, who looked over at him, tongue flapping, as if to say, *Whatever my dad likes, I like.* And also: *I enjoy farting in new places.* He'd been passing some seriously rancid gas.

Dex knew his ears would ring later, but he didn't care. Later was for later, a time when things would feel better. Later was when Ariel would apologize for kissing Gideon—*It was a mistake*, she would say. *It's you I love—it's always you*. Later was when Buddy would be out of the hospital, his car back from the shop, the deer-shaped dent popped back into place, Aunt Caroline's pantyhose still in the back. Later was when Dex would stand at the barbershop, tying a cape around a client—maybe the old nameless business professor who came in every other month, his breath reeking of alcohol—and ask: *How far are we lowering the ears today?* Later was when he and Ariel would be back in Lawrence, in their bed, Hippo cuddling beside them as they discussed what kind of beer to have at their wedding. Later was an afternoon in April years from now, when they would be eating sliced peaches on the balcony of their new house, Ariel's feet on Dex's lap, and he would ask: *Remember that time at your mom's house? With your ex-boyfriend? And all those animals?* Later was when they would shake their heads, incredulous, licking peach syrup from their wrists.

Each time he felt a wave of dread rising inside him, imagining Ariel leaning in to kiss Gideon, or Buddy's head connecting with the windshield, all he had to do was look at Hippo and the wave would slowly retreat. Dex could imagine Ariel's face when she discovered he'd adopted a dog. She would be so *happy*—a happiness that would certainly undo whatever damage they'd inflicted upon each other over the last few days. With Hippo, they could start fresh. This was his thought as he switched the stereo to FM and reached into the center console to look for another CD. Another minute of Fall Out Boy and his ears might start to bleed.

As he rooted around, his hand connected with something small and hard. He removed the object and discovered he was holding a ring. To be certain, he turned on the overhead light, startling Hippo.

Dex imagined Ariel removing the ring, her heart fluttering with nerves. Kissing Gideon in the heat of the moment was one thing, but removing her ring, as if in preparation for it, was another entirely.

"Stupid me," Dex said to Hippo, his heart sinking. "I didn't even notice she wasn't wearing it."

Hippo cocked his head and then sighed, as if to say, *Women. Can't live with 'em, can't live without 'em.*

Anger coursed through him, causing the tips of his fingers to tingle. Before he could decide not to, he cracked his window and chucked the ring onto the highway.

On the radio, Rupert Holmes was singing, *If you like piña coladas.* From an article he'd read years before, Dex knew the chorus to the song originally went: *If you like Humphrey Bogart.* After the song became a hit, it must have been clear to Rupert Holmes that *Humphrey Bogart* was the wrong lyric. How could it have ever been anything other than *piña coladas?* And to think it might have been *Humphrey Bogart?* There were no two words more clearly incorrect. The rhythm was wrong, the cadence, the sound. Dex wondered if, some day, he would look back on his time with Ariel and think this very thing—that she had so clearly been the wrong fit, down to the very syllables of her name, just as he could see that Miranda had been all wrong for Buddy. Ariel would join the world's pile of Humphrey Bogarts—castoffs, innocent mistakes that had come close to ruining the lives of perfectly good men.

Separating their belongings would be the hardest part. Perhaps he would fill a box with the things he wanted most and let Ariel keep the rest. He didn't need much, really. Only his records, his boots, his plants. She could keep renting the house, with its crystal doorknobs and the overgrown backyard both of them refused to mow. He would find somewhere cheaper, with more character and an even bigger yard for Hippo. A place where he could play his music as loud as he wanted, at any time of day.

Here were sadness and relief, both. There was extreme pain in losing the thing he valued above all else, but how liberating, to finally be free of the fear of losing it. There was happiness in knowing the wrong part of his life was over and done with and that he could, from here forward, do whatever he wanted. He didn't even have to stay in Lawrence. He could start over somewhere new, maybe somewhere warm, like Mexico. He could buy a camper, decorate it however he pleased. He would learn to peel and slice mangos quickly, with a knife, for money.

And yet, deep down, this was not what he wanted. Not really. He wanted Lawrence. He wanted Ariel. He wanted the life he had come to expect—a wedding and a honeymoon and an anniversary every year until he died. Kids named Arnold and Piper. What he wanted was someone who would wander into the cold night air, admiring the stars, rather than wake him for his snoring. He wanted a version of Ariel who loved him as much as he loved her.

Just then, his phone buzzed—a message from Ariel. A hot, dark feeling swelled in his chest. He couldn't bring himself to read it. Whatever it was she had to say, he didn't want to hear it—at least not right now, when he felt comfortable in his anger—and so he put his phone in the center console and closed the lid.

"I am sad," he said to the car that did not belong to him, on his way to see a friend he had hurt. "I am sad, and lonely, and afraid."

In his mind was Buddy's voice: *Welcome to the club, motherfucker.*

Beside him, Hippo sat up, leaned over, and licked the side of Dex's face. Dex reached over to put his arm around the dog.

"Thanks, dude," he said. "I love you, too."

Ariel

After consolidating her most important belongings into one bag, Ariel snuck into the house. She was relieved to hear her mother moving around upstairs, the shower running. In the kitchen, she found a grocery list and began writing a note on the backside. She knew she needed to write quickly—her mother did not take long showers—but tried to focus on what she wanted to say. *Sorry things didn't work out. I'm going to see if Joy will give me a ride. If you ever want to talk, please call me.* She wrote her phone number carefully, in neat print, and signed her name. Then, figuring there was nothing to lose, she added the words: *I love you, Mom. I always have and always will.* She then removed the framed photo from her tote bag and left it on the counter, next to the note. The cat fountain she filled and put beside the sink.

Twenty minutes into her walk, she was surprised to see headlights materialize in the distance, a pair of predatory eyes growing larger. At first, she was afraid—nothing good happened at this time of night in the country—but then, once the lights had settled upon her, she recognized the truck as Joy's.

Joy slowed to a stop and rolled down her window. "Ariel, what the hell are you doing?"

"I was walking to your house."

"Why? What happened?"

"I'm stupid is what happened." She felt the heat from Joy's truck. "And cold. Can I get in?"

"Of course," Joy said, reaching to unlock the passenger door.

"What are *you* doing out so late?" Ariel asked, sealing herself into the truck's warm interior. A band with fiddles played softly on the radio. Her shoulder ached from where the strap of her bag had cut into her skin; it felt good to sit down. "You're not heading to the sanctuary, are you?"

"No, I couldn't sleep, so I was going to camp out at Stubbs Lake and listen to the frogs, do some painting in the morning." She pointed to the sky. "I like to paint the sunrise."

"I didn't know you painted."

"Just watercolors. My dad taught me."

At Ariel's feet was a wooden box with metal latches.

"Why were you walking to my house?"

"I was coming to ask if you could give me a ride to Salina." For some reason, she wasn't nervous asking Joy for the ride, and for some reason Joy didn't hesitate to say yes.

"Maybe that's where I was headed all along," Joy said, not a hint of whimsy in her voice. Perhaps, for her, the world had always been a series of karmic events leading one into the other. Her father's death had led to Gideon had led to the Bright Side, which had led to this very moment, this very expanse of darkness before them. Who knew the topography of tomorrow? There were no maps, no use trying to create them.

"I'm sorry your visit didn't turn out the way you wanted," Joy said, aiming her headlights toward the dim constellation of town, where they would get gas before heading east.

"I think I knew, from the very beginning, that it wouldn't. But that's why I needed to try."

"Do you want to hear something that'll make you happy?"

"Sure," Ariel said, although she could think of nothing at the moment that could make her happy.

"Gideon texted me, told me Dex adopted that pit bull who's been following him around."

"You're serious?"

"That's what he said—told me they left together."

Ariel thought of the time a golden retriever puppy had licked Dex's hand while they were eating outside WheatFields. He'd immediately gone inside and washed his hands. When he came back out he'd said, *Can you believe the things animals get away with? What if I went around licking people in the street?* She knew he'd been partially joking, and yet the joke had bothered her. What kind of person didn't like puppy kisses?

"Dex—he doesn't *like* animals. Especially dogs. It's a big rift in our relationship."

"The thing about people," Joy said, "is that sometimes they surprise you."

Ariel thought about it. What if Joy was right? What if Dex really did love this dog? Growing up on the sanctuary, she'd seen it happen before: a cranky old man would show up with his wife, twice as intent on not getting a dog as his wife was intent on getting one. As Ariel and Mona led the couple through Dog Town, introducing them to dogs, the man would make a string of sarcastic comments—*I'm not trying to start a flea circus, Evelyn*—while Evelyn, or whatever her name happened to be, would coo over each dog—*Look, Milton, he's got two different-colored eyes, isn't that something?*—glancing at Milton for some kind of response despite knowing that nothing she said could ever make him see dogs the way she did. And yet, without fail, Milton would eventually come upon a dog—it was always a surprise, which dog could turn a cold heart warm: a beagle or a German shorthaired pointer or a one-eyed Lhasa apso with kennel cough—and Milton's eyes would visibly brighten. *What's this guy's story?* he'd say, crouching down to scratch the dog behind its ear, or laughing as the dog nosed his crotch, and Mona and Ariel would exchange looks, knowing that Milton was feeling, for the first time, the rush of love and kindness his wife felt each time she saw a dog. Ariel knew that the right dog could win anyone over. So if Hippo really had managed to soften Dex's heart, wasn't that what she'd always wanted? She wondered what it would feel like, to share her love of animals with Dex—a love that encompassed her home, her childhood, her history. She felt something stir inside her: hope.

"That is good news," she said. "I've wanted a dog for a really long time."

"It works out perfectly," Joy said, "because Bam-Bam's been wanting a home."

At the Shell station in town, Ariel filled Joy's tank. "I'll be right back," she told Joy. "I'm going to grab a few things inside."

"Will you get me Twizzlers?" Joy asked. "And a coffee?"

"Got it."

The convenience store was about to close, and judging by the look of him, the cashier was on the tail-end of a long, tiresome shift. When Ariel walked in, he said a quick hello and she waved back before making a beeline for the snack aisle. She quickly found what she was looking for: Joy's Twizzlers, but also a jar of creamy peanut butter, a bag of pretzels, and three packages of trail mix, from which she would remove the chocolate chips.

As she went to the checkout counter, she felt a sudden shift in the room. She recognized the attendant. Years ago, she and Gideon had come in to buy bananas and WD-40. When they'd gone to check out, the man asked to see Gideon's green card. Gideon explained that he was born in Texas—and besides, who needed ID to buy WD-40?—but in the end he'd waited outside while Ariel paid. "You know, my son's about your age," the attendant had said to Ariel. "And he's white as the Lord himself."

"Did you spit in his face?" Mona had asked when Ariel told her what had happened.

"No," Ariel had said, turning down her eyes. "I just paid and left." Her mother had thrown up her hands in disappointment.

"Find everything all right?" the man asked now.

"Yes," she murmured back, her heartbeat in her throat. As he rang up her items, she found herself humming with anger. It was the same anger she'd felt all those years ago, but injected with a new anger—the anger of knowing she had been too scared to stand up for the one person in the world who had always stood up for her, the one person, aside from her mother, who had always loved her completely.

"Do you remember me?" she asked the clerk. *Speak louder,* she told herself. *Stand straight.*

He was older now, the hair on his head reallocated to his eyebrows and the tops of his hands. "Can't say I do," he said, squinting as if to see her better.

"I grew up here," she said. "Just outside of town. On Sanctuary Road."

He smiled at her, his eyes heavy. "Well, welcome home. You want a receipt?"

"The thing is," she said, meeting his eyes, "a long time ago, you wouldn't let my friend buy something here. You asked to see his green card."

The man frowned. She saw that his name tag read: *Ralph.* "I can't say I remember that."

"That doesn't mean it didn't happen."

He handed Ariel her bag. "Well, then. I guess I'm sorry, anyways."

For a moment, she thought about accepting his apology, wishing him a good night. Instead, she heard herself saying, "Fuck you, anyways." And then, "I loved him."

For a moment they could only stare at each other, as if Ariel had spoken in tongues. Before he could say anything, she turned and sped out the door, not bothering to take her change. Outside, her heart was going wild. The wind was cold and strong.

In the truck, she burst out laughing—a nervous, exhilarated laughter.

"What's so funny?" Joy said.

"Nothing," she said, still laughing despite herself. "Nothing's funny."

Joy eyed her. "If you say so, crazy." She reached into the plastic bag for her Twizzlers. "What's with the peanut butter?"

"Dex's friend—the one who's hurt. He likes it."

"Huh," Joy said. And then: "No coffee?"

"Damn it," Ariel said. She looked back toward the store, its lonely rectangle of light. At the counter, Ralph rubbed his eyes, as a baby would, and then turned toward her, perhaps to see if she had gone. He was just a man. A man who probably didn't have much money, who was tired and growing old and had likely worked the same tedious job for most of his life. A man who was sometimes small and mean, but who, at other times, was probably not. She thought about something Sunny once said of Kansas: *It wants so badly to be perfect, but there's always that crack in the corner.*

As they drove, Ariel felt an approaching wave of regret, both for what happened at the station and for what she was doing—running away, for the second time. First it lapped at her toes, just barely a feeling, but then it reached for her ankles, then her knees, until it was at her neck, threatening to draw her under. She couldn't shake the feeling that this was the last time she'd ever make this drive—the last time she'd ever see the Bright Side. Never again would she sit on the porch and watch the Free Dogs chase fireflies. Never again would she feed Ginger a carrot or hold one of the chickens to her chest, feel the tiny motor of its heart, a muscle exactly as determined and complicated as the one inside her own chest. Never again would she find Gideon making breakfast at the stove, the sweet smell of cinnamon apples in the air. Never again would she ride in Old Baby with her mother, feeling the grooves of the air as her mother sang along to a Beatles song. *Little Darling, it's been a long, cold, lonely winter.* One by one, the animals would find new homes. Eventually, so would her mother. And what would her mother become then, without the animals? Without the Bright Side? Just a woman, alone, without any family. A woman who had tried to do something great and had lost everything along the way.

"Pretty quiet over there," Joy said.

"Yeah."

"Want to talk about it?"

Ariel looked out the window. "It's just that, all these years, I was okay not coming home because I knew it would be here. I took that for granted. But now—now I may never come back. This may really be it."

"You never know what could happen."

"Yeah," Ariel said. "But still."

As they crossed the town limits, a sign read: COME BACK AND SEE US SOON!

They went deeper and deeper into the prairie, the sky around them heavy and bright with stars. Ariel thought of the time when she was a little girl and had gone outside on a freezing night in January to look for Peanut Butter and Jelly in the sky, where her mother said they might have gone when they died. She'd been outside for an hour, no feeling in her hands or face, when she saw a figure approaching her in the darkness. She'd started to scream, but then she heard her mother's voice saying, "Hey, it's just me. It's all right." Her mother wrapped her in a quilt, handed her a cup of cocoa, and sat down beside her on the grass. Together, they'd taken turns pointing out shooting stars. "There goes Jelly," her mother had said. "Probably chasing a space-skunk." Where was her dad on that night? When Ariel thought about her childhood—the beginning days on the Bright Side, and all the ones after—it was always her mom around. Her mom and the animals. It was one thing her mom had been right about: she had always been there.

Unable to help herself, Ariel began to cry. She'd come back to find something but was leaving more empty-handed than ever.

"Hey," Joy said. "You okay?"

How could Ariel explain it to Joy when she could hardly explain it to herself? Despite everything that had happened—the years she'd been away, the mess she'd made of her return—she had the acute sensation that she was, for the second time, leaving behind everything she loved. There was also the pit of fear she felt for her mother. What if the sheriff came back? What if, in addition to everything else, her mother ended up in real trouble?

"I just—" Ariel said, garbling her words. "I just— I don't think—" She took a deep breath and forced herself to say what she wanted to say. "Can we turn around?" The words came out with a force that startled her.

"Did you forget something?" Joy asked, pulling onto the side of the road.

"No—it's just—it wasn't right, how I left. I need more time. I want to try again." It was what she'd wanted to say six years before, when she'd sat in Gideon's truck and watched the Bright Side disappear in the rearview mirror.

She understood that to turn around was, in a way, to turn from Dex, but she had to trust the feeling in her body, the sharpness in her gut that intensified the farther east they drove. She knew no matter what happened, Dex would still be there—he loved her. It was the only certainty in her life, wasn't it? He loved her, and she loved him, and how lucky she was, to have someone who would wait for her, whose love she did not question despite all of the times she questioned her love for him. It was something the animals had tried to teach her, this unconditional, unwavering love, a love that did not diminish if Ariel forgot to feed or exercise them, if she accidentally stepped on their paw. A love that required no words or promises, no conditions or qualifications. She wanted to love Dex completely, her love an open field he could explore without feeling lost. A love that would reassure him just as his love reassured her. She wanted to love him the way an animal loved—openly, absolutely, wildly—and she could. She *would*. She knew in her bones she was capable—it was just a matter of trying. She thought about her mother, about Joy and Gideon and the animals. She would practice this love with them, first. This is what she would do with her time at home; rather than ask for forgiveness, or try to fix a situation that was not hers to fix, she would practice showing love.

Joy made quick work of a three-point turn so that the moon now hung before them.

"Thank you," Ariel said, feeling a weight lift from her body.

"Honestly," Joy said, pressing the gas, "I was worried we'd get all the way to Salina before you'd ask."

Mona

Mona found herself, as she had more and more often lately, wishing the animals were gone. The house seemed to breathe around her, the breath of all the animals causing it to billow and collapse, billow and collapse. Over the course of a normal day, she experienced few moments of true solitude. Even in the shower, a cat would inevitably paw at the curtain or clamber all the way inside for a drink. The times she did manage to steal a moment to herself, her mind raced with all that needed to be done: repairs she needed to make, supplies she needed to purchase, animals who required veterinary care. She thought of her annual doctor's appointment in Middleton, where she would sit in the waiting room for fifteen quiet and uneventful minutes, reading an issue of *People* or *Time* or, once, a special edition of *Maxim* that outlined all the ways to please your lover with an ice cube. In moments like these, she would pretend that her life was not her life. Sometimes, she played a game called housewife, in which she imagined she was a buxom redhead living in Orlando, Florida. She had no children, no job, not even a pet goldfish. Her name was Kathy, and all she had to do all day was eat fruit and keep the kitchen tidy. Sometimes she would go shopping, but for the most part she stayed at home, watching television or reading mystery novels. When her husband returned—a man who always looked exactly like Daniel except with bigger muscles—he would scoop her up, twirl her around the kitchen, and tell her to go get dressed—he was taking her to Disney World. But this was not her life. In real life, Disney World sounded like a deep circle of hell. In real life, her daughter had just left for the second time, leaving only a note and a framed picture of what had once been Mona's family, her world. She'd also left a water fountain for the cats, a present Mona appreciated almost as much as the picture. She hated when the cats licked the sink faucet.

She tried to remember that she had spent the past six years in the same condition in which she now found herself—alone, in her home, the animals conducting their nightly activities. Nothing had changed, really, except she no longer had to worry about what had become of Ariel. At least she knew Ariel was healthy and with someone who loved her. Still, she felt that something had been lost. This time, she was the one who asked Ariel to leave. This time, it really was her fault.

What was it, she wondered, that held some families together? Why, for instance, had Joy returned home but not Ariel? According to Coreen, Joy's childhood was a far cry from a cakewalk. Beau was an alcoholic, Coreen was unhappy. Still, they had remained a unit. Maybe that's who she needed to talk to: Coreen.

Like a reflex, she found herself picking up the cordless. The clock read quarter past eleven. After a few rings, Coreen picked up. "Don't tell me somebody died," she said into the phone, breathless. It was clear she had been sleeping.

"Well, somebody probably did," Mona said, "but it's nobody you or I know."

"You can't just call in the middle of the night—you know I worry."

"Everything's fine. I mean, not fine. But nobody's dead. And nothing's on fire."

"Then what's the matter?"

Across the kitchen, a cat named Stripers jumped onto the counter and pawed a roll of paper towels onto the ground. She was an old calico—eleven or twelve—and had been one of Ariel's favorite cats back in the day. During a giggly afternoon, she and Gideon had given her the nickname S. T. Rippers, on account of the cat's penchant for ripping up carpet and blankets. Now, having gained Mona's attention, Stripers swatted a crystal butter dish from the counter, so that it shattered against the floor.

"Would you mind if I came over?" Mona asked Coreen. "I need to get out of this house." She knew Coreen might interpret this as a come-on, but it was a misunderstanding she was willing to risk.

Before she left, she swept up the glass from the butter dish, not wanting any of the animals to cut their feet.

At Coreen's, Mona let herself in. She knew Coreen had spent the last fifteen minutes preparing for her arrival: tidying up, combing her hair, dabbing her wrists with Clinique perfume. As expected, Coreen was at the kitchen table with two cups of tea and a plate of shortbread cookies.

Coreen's house had always been a place of creature comforts—flat-screen TVs, cooked meals, clean carpets—luxuries Mona couldn't help but savor during the brief afternoons or evenings she spent with Coreen. Just coming over for dinner felt like a vacation, one that made Mona wonder what her home, her life, would look like had she not filled them both with animals.

"Been a while since you've been over at night," Coreen said, cupping her mug as if for strength.

"Has it?"

Coreen smiled the melancholic smile that had become her trademark in the weeks after Mona turned her down. She was always sad those days, but tried to feign happiness. "Nobody likes a sad sack," she had once said, turning to wipe a tear.

"You know, the boys were over here earlier. Ariel's fiancé—he's something, huh? I always pictured her with a farm boy, or maybe a nerd. Someone a little less . . . *hip*."

"She seems pretty hip herself now—or something. She's definitely not as shy as she used to be. But it doesn't matter anyhow. She's gone. Left a note saying she was getting a ride from Joy."

"Right. Joy texted me about that. I was going to call you, see how you were holding up, but I'm always so hesitant to call you these days—"

Don't make this about us, Mona wanted to say, but held her tongue. "I guess that's good news—that the girls are getting along. And that she didn't ask Gideon to take her. God knows that's the last thing we need—Ariel trying to squeeze between Gideon and Joy."

"I don't think that's what's happening, Mona. Do you?"

"That's the problem. I have no idea what's happening. It's like I woke up on planet Ariel. All of a sudden up is down and down is up." She did not want to think about what happened at the deli—how the sheriff had stopped by the sanctuary. She did not want to think about anything at all.

"You sure you're all right, Pineapple? I know it's been a rough couple weeks."

Mona put her head in her arms. The last thing she needed was Coreen calling her pet names. Coreen had come up with Pineapple when they first started spending time together. *You might be prickly on the outside, but on the inside you're sweet as anything.* "I'm okay," she said. And then, as if someone had pressed a button on the side of her head, she began to cry. How long had it been since she'd had a good cry? Even when Opal died—a kick to the gut when she was already down—she hadn't cried. She had still felt numb from the fire, from mourning Squid and Aleira.

"Oh, Mona," Coreen said, a trace of giddiness in her voice. She was excited, Mona understood, to witness this sudden aperture of emotion. It was what Coreen had long tried and failed to evoke in Mona; Mona knew she was not about to let the moment pass without some gain on her part. "Come here," she said, putting her arms around Mona. For a moment, Mona allowed herself to be comforted. She breathed into Coreen's body—she smelled like she always did, a combination of Clinique perfume and the country apple hand soap she kept at the kitchen sink.

"She tried to come back, and I pushed her away—I made her leave. I was so *mean*—I practically screamed at her."

"It's all right," Coreen said, stroking her hair. "I'm sure it's nothing you can't fix."

"She tried to help by giving the Trump sign back to Fuller. And I tore her up about it—told her to leave. Why, when she was just trying to help? When all I've wanted was for her to come back into my life?"

"Because you're you. You try to be a hard-ass but really you're soft—you *want* to be soft."

"I'm an idiot is what I am."

"Joy's with her right now," Coreen said. "We can call her. We can tell them to come back."

Coreen's phone was on the table. Mona watched as she tapped the screen, bringing it to life. The background was a photo of her and Joy taken on a trip to Austin, Texas, the year before. They'd invited Mona to come along—Gideon had offered to care for the sanctuary in her absence—but, to nobody's surprise, Mona had declined, saying she needed to be home with the animals. In the picture, Joy and Coreen stood before a wall that was spray-painted with the words I LOVE YOU SO MUCH in looping red cursive. It was something she could never imagine doing with Ariel—posing before a kitschy tourist site, their arms around each other. But why not? Why couldn't they have this if they tried? A thought occurred to her: maybe Ariel had already been to Austin, had stood before this wall and taken a picture with someone else. Dex, maybe. Or any number of people Mona didn't know. There was so much she didn't know about Ariel, and she had not paused to consider that much of it might be good. She had so many questions for her daughter, questions she hadn't asked when Ariel was home because to ask them was to admit a curiosity that could stem only from love—a love she did not want Ariel to see, for she had convinced herself, over the years, that Ariel no longer deserved it.

"What would you have done if Joy hadn't come back from California? Would you have been able to forgive her?"

"The thing you seem to be forgetting," said Coreen, "is that Ariel did come back."

"But it took her six years."

"And it can take you six more to reach out to her, or you can act like a grown-up and call her." She slid the phone toward Mona.

"I really do hate these things. In twenty years, everyone's going to have the same brain tumor." Mona tapped the side of her head.

"Would you just make the damn call already?"

All she had to do was press the green phone icon—one tiny motion and she could reverse the course of the weekend, the course of the last six years. *Stupid cell phones,* she thought. Certain gestures shouldn't be this easy. She should have to ride a horse through the night or send a series of handwritten letters that Ariel would read under the glow of a candle before penning her own response.

She glanced up to find Coreen eagerly eyeing the phone, as if waiting for the finale of a movie. She knew Coreen cared about her and genuinely wanted her and Ariel to make good, but she couldn't shake the feeling that Coreen also wanted to witness this call for her own benefit; perhaps if Mona opened her heart to Ariel, she would, in the heat of the moment, look up and decide there was enough room for Coreen, too.

"I better get going," she said, and slid the phone back to Coreen. She stood and grabbed her keys.

"Really, Mona?"

"Good night," she said. She suspected she'd made a mistake, but it was too late to do anything about it. She went outside to her truck, leaving Coreen at the table with two full cups of tea.

Back at the Bright Side, she microwaved a bowl of green beans and ate them plain, with her fingers. A cat had thrown up something pink and fuzzy on the kitchen floor, but she didn't bother to clean it. She was so tired, and going out with wet hair had chilled her to the bone. She wrapped herself in a dog blanket—a pink Little Mermaid comforter from Ariel's youth—and sat on the living room couch. Katydid, Old Crow, and Daisy jumped up and competed to be nearest to her. Daisy had soiled her diaper, but Mona was too tired to change it right away. She would do it in a moment. For now, she needed to sit.

She thought about the note Ariel had left, her cell number scrawled out in small, exacting print; Ariel put a line through her sevens, just like she did. What she would have given, years ago, to have Ariel's phone number. Now it felt dangerous, a code to a safe that held something more valuable than Mona felt comfortable possessing.

Daisy began to whimper, nudging her nose into Mona's arm. *A little help here?* she was saying.

"All right, all right," Mona said. "Hold your ponies." She scooped Daisy under the shoulders and carried her into the kitchen. After swapping the soiled pink diaper for a khaki one with screen-printed frogs, she set Daisy onto the floor. The old dog simply stood where Mona had put her, her gauzy eyes fixed on the counter where Ariel had left her note. A black cat named Onyx was up there, taunting Daisy, and swiftly batted the scrap of paper onto the floor. Excited by the fluttering paper, Daisy toddled over on her arthritic legs and took the note into her mouth, gumming the paper with all her might, which was not much, but enough to do damage.

Mona saw what was happening and panicked. "Drop it, Daisy," she said, running over to retrieve the paper from the old dog's mouth. Her heart steadied when she saw the numbers were still legible. Daisy looked up at her, remorseful. "It's all right, baby. You didn't do anything wrong."

If she was waiting for a sign, Daisy eating Ariel's number was as close as she was going to get. She took the cordless and sat down at the kitchen table. One by one, she dialed the number, her heart beginning to race. She then placed the phone against her ear and waited. Across the kitchen, Onyx the cat began to lick a cast iron on the stove.

Just as the phone began to ring, Mona heard a noise at the front door. For a second, Mona felt frightened—ever since the fire, she startled easily—but it was Joy who appeared in the kitchen. "Joy?" she said.

"Hey, Mona," Joy said, an excited look on her face. She turned to glance behind her.

And then there was Ariel, her cell phone ringing to "Tiny Dancer." Her face was flushed, her eyes red. Drops of moisture spotted her cheeks; for a ridiculous moment, Mona wondered if it was raining outside.

"Are you calling me?" Ariel asked, looking from her phone to Mona.

Mona set down the cordless. "Tiny Dancer" was one of her favorite songs; it seemed impossible Ariel might like it, too. "I thought you left."

"I did," Ariel said.

"Then what are you doing here?"

"I decided to come back." She glanced at the counter, where Stripers was drinking from the new water fountain. "Hey, it's working," Ariel said, nodding to the fountain, a nervous half smile on her lips. She sniffed and wiped her nose on her sleeve.

"Yeah," Mona said. "I guess it is."

She thought then of the day Peanut Butter died, years ago, shortly after they moved to the Bright Side. He always slept in Ariel's bed, a fact that had made Mona jealous at first—*What, a younger version comes around and you don't want to sleep with me anymore?*—but which meant, ultimately, that Ariel was the first to find Peanut Butter's body the morning after he passed. "Mama, what happened to him?" Ariel had asked, hysterical. "Why won't he wake up? Make him wake up."

"This is what happens when you die," Mona had explained. "Your body stays behind, but the rest of you moves on."

"To where?"

"Nobody can say for sure. It's one of the things people just live without knowing. But some people like to think you go to heaven."

"Is heaven scary?"

"No, not at all. It's beautiful, and safe, and filled with love."

"Like the Bright Side?"

"Yes," Mona had said, her heart filling. "Just like the Bright Side, but with even more animals. And all-you-can-eat nachos." This made Ariel giggle.

Now here was this same little girl—the girl who once stayed up for hours helping Mona pick ticks off the dogs after they got into a nest of dead bunnies, the girl who once wrote a poem about each animal and then went around the Bright Side reciting her work for her muses to enjoy. She was the same girl, Mona told herself, just as she herself was the same girl who once cowered under her bed with Howie, thanking a God she didn't exactly believe in for making a world with animals.

Without saying anything, Mona stood up, closed the space between them, and took Ariel into her arms. For a moment, she was terrified—what was she doing, taking back this person who had so deeply hurt her?—but then Ariel hugged her back, and every atom of terror softened to relief, and then to gratitude. Each day, she held dogs, cats, chickens, rabbits, and ducks. And yet her own daughter— it had been years. The fabric of Ariel's jacket was cold, but beneath this she was warm, sturdy. She smelled of the night air, of animals.

"I'm sorry, Mama," Ariel said. "I didn't mean to mess things up."

"I know," Mona heard herself say. When Ariel tried to speak, Mona held her tighter.

For a moment, the two simply swayed together, as if at sea. Mona had always liked that *daughter* rhymed with *water*. Both of them elemental, necessary, and yet impossible to keep in your hands.

"I know you're fine without me," Ariel said. "But can I stay? For a little longer?"

Mona said, "We were never fine without you," the truth of it like a splinter she'd finally worked from her skin.

She hadn't realized how much it mattered, this act of touching. It was one thing to talk about forgiveness, but it was another to forgive with the body, to forgive with bones and skin and blood. It was something the animals understood instinctively, that the deepest emotions could not be translated into language, for they existed in the body and not the mind. And they were animals, weren't they? Bodies that sought the comfort of other bodies, that needed affection to survive. Bodies that, forced to live in a dark, unreliable world, had only each other to lean on. And here it was, now, in her reach: everything she'd convinced herself she didn't need, because to admit needing it would make continuing on in its absence unbearable. It was the feeling of Ariel in her arms, their hearts an inch apart—the feeling that her daughter had finally come home.

Acknowledgments

It takes a village to write a book, and I am so fortunate to have stumbled into a village of brilliant, patient, and kindhearted readers, writers, teachers, and friends.

Thank you to my agent, Susan Golomb, who believed in this book when it was just a squiggly, messy draft. You are a book genius, and your early vision and feedback were invaluable. Thank you also to Mariah Stovall for the additional feedback, kindness, and patience.

Thank you to my editor, Marysue Rucci, for helping sculpt, shape, and polish this book. I can't say how much I've valued your support and wisdom throughout the revision process—thank you for always having faith. Thank you also to Zack Knoll, who made this process so painless and easy. You are still the lollipop at the doctor's office (again, sorry for the gross metaphor). Additional thanks to everyone at Simon & Schuster, particularly Hana Park, Wendy Sheanin, Tracy Nelson, Kassandra Rhoads, and Heidi Meier.

Thank you to Laura Moriarty, who read the first chapters of this project when I was an undergrad at the University of Kansas, and whose early encouragement inspired me to return to this story over and over again. You are a human gumball machine of insight. You have no idea how much of your advice has followed me over the years. Thank you.

Thank you to Alternative Breaks at the University of Kansas, a program that first introduced me to animal sanctuaries—one of which inspired the first iteration of this story—and which showed college-aged me that the world is much bigger than Kansas. Your commitment to teaching service and encouraging purposeful travel is vital.

Thank you to Pam Houston, who gave me the time and space to write the first draft of this book. The ranch will always feel like a second home, and you will always feel like a second mother. Thank you for sharing your animals, especially Livie Lou and William, whose infinite goodness and sweetness is hopefully felt in these pages.

Thank you to Bernadette Myers, Emma Bogdanoff, and Nicola Pearson, who read drafts of this project along the way. Your collective wisdom helped make these pages stronger.

Thank you to Maggie Pahos, queen of shoulders-to-cry-on, for all your love, guidance, and support throughout this process and for your pivotal feedback at every stage along the way. Whenever there's a writer-doubt thunderstorm in my brain, you always appear with an umbrella (and puppy pictures). You are a tidal wave of goodness.

Thank you to my mom, my biggest cheerleader and the most supportive parent a writer could ask for. You've never doubted my dreams, and I can't thank you enough for that. I returned to this book for you, because you kept asking: Are you ever going to finish that animal book? You taught me to be a woman of my word—so, here you go.

Thank you to Pat Dingle, my Ding, who proved to me there are good, kind men in the world. You stood by me through this book, during all the ups and downs, and for this I am infinitely grateful.

Thank you to all the animals in my life—past, present, and future—but particularly Romeo, Pongo, Bunny, Wooster, Olivia, William, the ranch sheepies, Isaac, Deseo, Roany, the Birchwood chickens, Peach, Luca/Carlos, Onyx, Esme, Pup Howdy, Rey, and Freya. What a sad planet this would be without you and your kind.

About the Author

BECKY MANDELBAUM is the author of *Bad Kansas*, which received the 2016 Flannery O'Connor Award for Short Fiction and the 2018 High Plains Book Award for First Book. Her work has appeared in *One Story*, *The Sun*, *The Missouri Review*, *The Georgia Review*, *Electric Literature*, *McSweeney's Internet Tendency*, and has been featured on *Medium*. She has received fellowships from Writing by Writers, a residency from the Helene Wurlitzer Foundation, and has taught at Seattle's Hugo House. Originally from Kansas, she currently lives in Washington State. This is her first novel.